Phantacea Publications featuring

Jim McPherson's
PHANTACEA MYTHOS

- *PHANTACEA* **One to Six**

(1977-80, a series of comic books with artwork by various artists)

- **Forever & 40 Days – The Genesis of *PHANTACEA***

(1990, a graphic novel with artwork by Ian Fry, background material and a short story featuring the Damnation Brigade, the Death Dodgers & Signal System)

- **Feeling Theocidal**

(2008, Book One of *'The Thrice-Cursed Godly Glories'* trilogy*)

- **The War of the Apocalyptics**

(2009, the first full-length entry in the *'Launch 1980'* story cycle*)

- **The 1000 Days of Disbelief**

(2010-11, Book Two of *'The Thrice Cursed Godly Glories'* trilogy, consisting of three mini-novels: *'The Death's Head Hellion'**, *'Contagion Collectors'** and *'Janna Fangfingers'**)

- **Goddess Gambit**

(2012, Book Three of *'The Thrice Cursed Godly Glories'* trilogy*)

- **Phantacea Revisited 1: The Damnation Brigade**

(2013, graphic novel featuring a complete story sequence primarily excerpted from Phantacea One to Five, various artists*)

- **Nuclear Dragons**

(2013, the second full-length entry in the *'Launch 1980'* story cycle*)

- **Phantacea Revisited 1: Cataclysm Catalyst**

(2014, graphic novel featuring a complete story sequence excerpted from Phantacea One to Seven and Phantacea Phase One #1, various artists*)

- **Helios on the Moon**

(2014, the third and final full-length entry in the *'Launch 1980'* story cycle*)

**E-versions also available*

Phantacea
Publications
proudly presents ... 
Helios on the Moon
Jim McPherson
The third full-length entry in the
'Launch 1980'
Story Cycle

HELIOS ON THE MOON

- Auctorial Preamble -

****

Thus ends Phantacea Phase One.
So I intended to write on the inside front cover of Phantacea Seven in 1981. Except, it never got finished. I next reckoned on writing it about a decade later when Phantacea Phase One #15 came out. Except, this time, that project never got beyond the #1 stage; not in print anyhow.

Phase One #2, along with a number of background stories, were ready for press; as were the scripts and reprint art for a good deal of the rest. While most of these last did make it into one or another of the graphic novels subsequently released by Phantacea Publications, prepublication orders didn't warrant carrying on the Phantacea Mythos at that time and, especially, in that form. (Artists aren't just temperamental, they're costly.)

Let me repeat: '*Thus ends Phantacea Phase One*'. Sounds good, after all these years, but "Helios on the Moon" does much more than that.

It also ends the '*Launch 1980*' story cycle, my personal project to novelize the Phantacea comic book series. Plus, for those who felt the ending of the last trilogy, '*The Thrice-Cursed Godly Glories*', as presented in "Goddess Gambit", was not absolutely clear as to whether anyone survived – or anyone not explicitly done away with already didn't – that'll be sorted starting about nine chapters, or *'moons'*, from now.

Not surprisingly Ninth Moon shares commonality with "The War of the Apocalyptics", the first book in the *Launch* trilogy, in that it continues winding down the stirring saga of the Damnation Brigade and their erstwhile companion in supra-doings, Kid Ringo, nowadays Ringleader.

As for the Family Thanatos and their never-remembered **'guest'**, the fiendish, always smiling fellow who speaks in bold-italics, they show up three moons prior to D-Brig et al. Of course non-devic characters didn't just precede non-devic characters literally, in terms of literature, they preceded them chronologically.

Witness "Feeling Theocidal" and "The 1000 Days of Disbelief", which were set in the Cathonic Dome's Fifth and mid-Sixth Millennium respectively. Or "Forever & 40 Days", which featured a series of graphic story snippets set before there was a Dome, let alone a Genesea necessitating one.

The previous book in this trilogy, "Nuclear Dragons", divided into four parts. *'Indescribable Defiance'* began it with the launching of the Cosmic Express. We saw what happened to one of its cosmicars in War-Pox, and to the cosmicompanions aboard it in Gambit. We're about to begin finding out what becomes of one occupant of the control hub, one of the other cosmicars and the seven cosmicompanions occupying it.

Nuke's first part additionally brought our attention to the highly disconcerting matter of a perceived menace on the Moon, something also alluded to during War-Pox, and what governments and top dog corporations were doing about it. For starters, they set up the United Nations SPACE Council (*'Society for the Prevention of Alien Control of Earth'*) and appointed the by now 80-year old Great Man, Loxus Abraham Ryne, to run it.

He promptly had built, and launched, the United Nations of Earth Spaceship (UNES) Liberty. Not long before Hel-Moon gets (over more so than) underway, it boldly blasted out there in order to deal with said menace, be it alien or otherwise. (Go with the otherwise.)

In terms of the titular pair who provided *'Indescribable Defiance'* with its sectional sub-heading, did you know the Space Shuttle Columbia took off secretly in December 1980, months prior to its official inaugural flight? Returned safely as well. You do now. You're also not too many moons away from finding out whom it was transporting towards the Liberty, which is already in lunar-synchronous orbit.

Nuke's second section, *'The Strife Virus'*, focused our attention on, among others, a pair of (very) long lasting, inveterate nasties, Daemonicus and Strife. Both first appeared, or at least were mentioned, in Feel Theo, the initial book of the *'Glories'* trilogy. To say the least it seems they're extremely difficult to deal with permanently.

Until, that is, in terms of her anyhow … well, that would be telling too much for a preamble. That said, while preambles may be no place for telling all that's to come, I would be remiss if I didn't at least remind you of All, capitalized.

Nuke readers will recall the Phantom Freighter, whence Crystallion and Hell's Horsemen, whence also Sharkczar. And what have they got to do with Incain's She-Sphinx you might ask. Once again I refer you to Feel Theo, as well as "Janna

Fangfingers" and GAMBIT. Ginny the Gynosphinx is no Andy the Androsphinx. She moves. And when she does, be smart. Stay out of her way

Speaking yet again of FEEL THEO, the time-tumbling Dual Entities featured in a number of its story snippets, if perhaps not explicitly so in its underlying narrative, the one-day saga of Thrygragon (Mithramas, Year of the Dome 4376) as told from a number of different viewpoints. As foreshadowed during the course of *'The Strife Virus'*, they do much more than feature in this book; hence its title.

In some respects remarkably, NUKE's final two subsections, *'Supra Survival'* and *'Sinking and Swimming'*, did leave a few tales left to tell. One who won't be telling them is the deviant Legendarian, Jordan *'Q for Quill'* Tethys. (The legendary 30-Year Man, aka 30-Beers, came as close as anyone in the Phantacea Mythos comes to being a protagonist throughout the *'Glories'* trilogy.)

GAMBIT readers may recall that, for a change, Jordy's latest lifetime did not seem to be in jeopardy once the moment of its moderately cliff-dangling dénouement arrived. Indeed, they probably assumed that either he or the improbably enormous, ever-fishifying Fisherwoman had saved everyone worth saving.

That was certainly one of the impressions left. Another was that the subheading for GAMBIT"s final third, *'Endgame-Gambit'*, meant endgame everyone. When it comes to the Phantacea Mythos, it's always dangerous to make assumptions. That's why it's anheroic fantasy (anheroic = without heroes).

I do feel fairly confident in leaving you with one, almost certainly accurate assumption: *Every ending begets a new beginning.*

And a correction to my opening statement.

Thus begins the ending to Phantacea Phase One.

Jim McPherson
Creator/Writer
The *PHANTACEA* Mythos

****

Titular Moons

HELIOS ON THE MOON

— 30 Maruta - 10 Tantalar 5980 —

Jim McPherson

A *PHANTACEA* Mythos Print Publication
James H McPherson, Publisher

ISBN 978-1-92844-01-4
First Published 2014

FIRST MOON: His Stories

========

October 21, 1968

On the third Sunday of October 1968, Loxus Abraham Ryne, the Mesopotamia-born, Dutch-Iraryan patriarch of the Illuminated Faith of Xuthros Hor, was on the Greek Island of Scorpios attending what some billed as the wedding of the decade. The Great Man's then Number One, O'Ryan James Maxwell, approached him with the latest news.

"No sign of the Zerosses, Abe, but Dem's Dim has come through again. Aremar's hot on Heliopolis's heathen ass. How do you want it?"

"Well done, Max. Make that incinerated."

========

Dem's Dim was Dmetri Diomad, who was all of 15 in 1968. Acting on his transmitted intelligence, one of AMERICA's best operatives, James Aremar, himself only twenty-five at the time, tracked Heliopolis – El Draco as Kad had, not-so-jokingly been known as in his childhood – to the Island of Santorini in the Aegean Sea. With five companions, his so-called Spartae or Dragon's Teeth, the Greek revolutionary escaped in a high-speed boat. Aremar was in immediate pursuit.

Hours later, off the shore of Trigon, the usually uninhabited, triple-peaked islet that had been the Zeross family homestead for most of the century, Aremar blew the boat out of the water. Heliopolis and his five Spartae weren't done yet, though. Showing off their remarkable strength and fitness, they swam to shore before Aremar could overtake them.

Fearing what traps the self-proclaimed anarchists may have laid for them on Trigon, Aremar ordered a softening air strike. It was a prudent step. Never take chances with a madman and his whiz-kid-followers on their home turf. This was all especially true of Trigon, which old-timers like his superior, Big Max Maxwell, once tried to convince him had actually, um, gone astray from the surface of the Aegean Sea during the Second World War years of barely a quarter century earlier.

Another twenty-five year old, Mik Starrus, piloted one of the planes that hit Trigon. It was his bomb that struck an outcropping of Gypsium on Mount Telepassa, the islet's third and smallest peak. The whole landform shook visibly then vanished. POOF! Gone – Trigon, Heliopolis, the Spartae! No blaze of glory, no volcanic eruption, marked its passage. It just wasn't there any more.

Trembling in terror, his hair going white almost on the spot, Aremar swore all on his boat, everyone who had seen the impossible happen, to secrecy.

He simply reported mission accomplished to Maxwell.

========

"Jim got him, Abe," Big Max duly told the patriarch later that day on Scorpios. "Heliopolis is history."

In a minor burst of (presumed) prescience, Ryne said he devoutly hoped not.

=========

A few days later, during a particularly painful debriefing – call it a grilling, for that was what it amounted to, over very hot coals – Aremar, Starrus and the rest of those who had seen the incredible event finally told Maxwell and Ryne the truth. There was no longer any point in trying to hide the facts. Anyone with a month old map of the region could see for themselves.

The pistol-packing Great Man tried to put the best possible spin on it. "There were no bodies found on Salvation Island either," he reminded his Number One, referring to the nuclear annihilation of Ryne's nephew, Jesus Mandam, in 1953.

"That's because everyone but Blind Sundown and Raven's Head was obliterated," snarled Maxwell.

"No bodies found on Damnation either, Max, but the Crimefighters are no more back than the Conqueror or The Rache's supras."

"But both Salvation and Damnation are still there, Abe. Trigon isn't. That's the point!"

"Maybe it sank. Island's do that, you know?"

"Most islands don't have Gypsium on them."

=========

The invariably striated, like a human brain, ever-glowing rock was very hard to locate. It sort of appeared and disappeared, as if it had a will of its own. Which of course some believed it did. Not for nothing was the miraculous substance sometimes called Godstuff. Not for nothing was it as often, or perhaps even more often, called Brainrock.

Although pockets of it were found in the environs of Sedona Arizona, the Yucatan Peninsula and, perhaps surprisingly, around the Palestinian Dead Sea, Gypsium was generally dug out of the ground in the vicinity of volcanoes or, more commonly, around meteorite craters and cometary blast sites.

(To the Western World's abiding gall, the largest known deposit of Gyps was in Soviet Siberia, in and around the site of 1908's Tunguska *event*. This fluke of happenstance more so than planetary geology gave the Soviet Union a huge advantage in the Supra Wars of the late Forties, very early Fifties, when Sedon St Synne and the otherwise anonymous Gypsium Genius known as the King Conqueror secretly made their base in the Ukraine.)

It was also found on two other dinky, tri-peaked islets: Easter Island, in the Southern Pacific, far off the west coast of Chile, and much smaller Centauri Island, off the coast of Maui in the Hawaiian Archipelago. Additionally, one of the least advertised discoveries made by Neil Armstrong and his NASA buddies, when they physically went on the Moon the next year, was that Gypsium Godstuff was prevalent there.

That wasn't the reason why the United Nations of Earth Spaceship Liberty, with its multinational crew of well over a hundred men, was orbiting the planetoid today, over a dozen years after Aegean Trigon disappeared, never to be seen again. But it probably had something to do with it.

There were, sure as shit, aliens down there (from the Liberty's perspective). Had to be, if only because someone was bombarding the planet with thought-altering mind beams and who else but aliens could do that sort of thing? Had – and this was only one of all too many theories being bandied about in the corridors of tremendous political and financial power – they come hither to mine it only to subsequently decide to stay and conquer Planet Earth because it was so pretty?

The question needed asking, and answering. Which was why the Liberty would not be shooting first; at least not for a few minutes after arrival over top.

========

Sunday, November 30, 1980

Some one hundred and seventy thousand light years earlier, Weirstar exploded. It wiped out the entire planetary system of Weir, possibly the first and, according to descendants of its survivors, greatest civilization in cosmic history. Its cause was artificial but the nearly insane Entity who instigated the star's destruction had taken care to move the most progressive society in all of Weir's worlds to a planet in a relatively nearby star system.

That planet became what to this day its inhabitants still occasionally call New Weir. There, synchronous with the scheduled launching the Cosmic Express, another astronomer – this one black-skinned, as were all male, self-proclaimed 'Utopians' of Weir – was being called to task in the Courtroom of the Visionary.

Also like every other Utopian, regardless of whether they were black-as-night males or white-as-light females, he didn't have a given name, just a designation.

Completely unimaginatively, his was Mr Astronomer.

========

Throughout the cosmos, courtrooms were much the same as they were on the Earth. The judge sat on a raised dais behind his or her bench, used a gavel (unless he was sitting in England or Wales) and pronounced sentence. Secretarial staff sat in front of the judge's bench. Prosecutors, defenders, appellants, advocates, adversaries, all were arrayed facing the judge.

This being a courtroom of a visionary there was no jury nor any audience, save those invited. Above and behind the judge's dais was another platform, inset into the wall. Traditionally three empty chairs, more so than thrones, were placed upon it. They were for the three deities of New Weir, the Trigregos Sisters: Devaura, Sapiendev, and Demeter. Immortal and ageless, the Sisters rarely appeared, but the empty chairs remained as a symbol of those who truly ruled New Weir.

The judge was the nominal Visionary. Black-skinned and tattooed with the symbols of his office – in his case the letter, or chromosome, 'Y' – he would sit blindfolded as he listened to the person or persons making his or her case or cases. He would take in their arguments with both ears, whereupon he would open both eyes, the horns of the Y, and peer into the future, the shaft of the Y.

As with any prognosticator he would see any number of potential futures. His task wasn't to see *'the future'* as such; that even Utopians acknowledged wasn't possible. Rather, he was expected to *'judge'* the best possible future and thereafter pass sentence on ways appropriate to attain it. His ruling was made public and almost invariably heeded. At least it was until unforeseen circumstances changed such that it must *'needs be'* changed as well, sometimes by the same visionary, sometimes by different ones.

By a vagary of Utopian genetics, other than the pigmentation caused by their gender, all visionaries looked the same – just as all astronomers looked the same, just as all geneticists looked the same, and so on. Privately, every person was unique, with his or her own individual appearance and personality. Publicly, though, one could tell what anyone was bred to be just by looking at them.

Rebel or radical types seldom existed. Under New Weir's system they would have been detected while still in their development tanks and simply discontinued. Once born, though, life was both sacrosanct and very long by human standards. Talk to a Utopian and they would say theirs was the ideal society, which was why they deemed themselves Utopians. Capital punishment for example – indeed punishment in any form – had no place, never had, in either Old Weir or New Weir.

Of course, since New Weir had been around for millennia of millennia, almost no one used such terms as old or new on a regular basis anymore. Weir was just Weir. The Recurring Entity who founded it made one law and one law only: *'There shall be no law!'* As if, given such a solitary commandment, there could be any other way, consensus was how the vast planetary confederation of Weir was governed.

The role of the visionaries therefore was central, albeit not crucial, to the workings of Weir. Events could change and, with them, their visions of the best possible future for Utopian kind. That it had thrived for thousands upon thousands of thousand years – that in all likelihood it would continue to thrive endlessly – was evidence that the most fabulous visionary of all time had been that selfsame Entity.

Illuminaries of Weir knew the Entity had a name, two of them. They and everyone else also knew there were two of them: a her-story and a his-story, as it were. No one paid much attention to Illuminaries any more, though. Very few of them were born and none were deliberately bred. Who cared about the past in a society dedicated to the future?

The present was just nature's way of carrying on.

========

The judge's gavel was a pipe.

========

He screwed off the top of the mallet, inserted a raw fibre called *'haoma'* or *'soma'*, removed the nib at the end of its handle, struck a match, and lit the stuff. He puffed it into smoking cinder and inhaled deeply. Held it for a long while, mentally focusing himself for the task ahead, then exhaled profoundly.

With the courtroom thereby filled with the smell of interesting incense, he adjusted the blindfold covering his two eyes and summoned the appellant. "Step to the bench, Mr Astronomer!"

The judge took another toke off his gavel. Relying on his ears only, he heard the heavy-set scientist shuffle to his allotted place in the courtroom.

"I am here, visionary."

"You have a petition to present."

"I have."

The astronomer was in his caste-mould. Overweight, with his genitals sucked into his physical mass and therefore out of sight, he would have been naked if there was such a thing on Weir. His black-skinned body was tattooed with comets, novas, nebulae, galaxies and other phenomena common to those in his trade. A planetary ring orbited around his head at eye level.

Officially he was just another scientocrat, one whose specialty just happened to be the stars. That he was one of the upper echelon in his field was the only reason he was dignified by the appellation of *'astronomer'*. Otherwise the visionary would have addressed him as scientocrat. Privately he would have his own name or names – but that was his business. Publicly, the astronomer was everybody's business.

"State your case and state it succinctly," the visionary dully yet duly recited his token rote. "Complications and contradictions, I shall perceive. Once you are finished, I shall gaze into the future. As myriad and as many, as many possible *'Ys'*, as I can foresee. I shall then render my decision, which is in no way binding and entirely subject to events yet to happen. Proceed."

The astronomer sized up the visionary, not that there was much to size up. This one looked much like any of his breed: blindfold, Y-tattoos (Y = Wise), steam pouring out of the top of his head like a sputtering volcano. If he had been a woman, the astronomer wouldn't have approached things any differently.

(Female Utopians were white-skinned. As a consequence their tattoos were black or shades thereof. Given that sex, as opposed to sexual category, was a private affair; given also that, next door to forever, the only embryos allowed to develop were those spawned by artificial, masturbatory techniques; gender bias had virtually never featured in the Utopia of New Weir.

"I believe I have discovered a link between our universe and another one."

"These galactic gateways are called wormholes." Visionaries had a tendency to make statements rather than ask questions. They also had a tendency to interrupt, for reasons of clarity.

"A wormhole between our universe and another one," the astronomer corrected himself obligingly. He spoke confidently, sure that the visionary would share in his personal vision.

"There are wormholes and there are wormholes; just as there are universes and there are universes. Ours may be a microverse to another macroverse and vice versa. It is as if the entire cosmos is a series of eggshells, one within the other. You've cracked one shell and found a way to another. This I understand. But you must be more specific, astronomer. I require exhaustive information."

The astronomer let out a foul-smelling fart. This was a typical reaction to a visionary and traditionally considered appropriate. Its odour mingled with that of the visionary's smoke. Those in the invitation-only audience, most of whom were scientocrats or members of the media, inhaled deeply. This would be a good session.

Suddenly there was an audible gasp. Someone pointed to the platform above the visionary. Three indistinct yet obviously female forms appeared in the chairs. The Trigregos Sisters had deigned to manifest themselves. This session wasn't just going to be good; it was about to become unforgettable.

In an ironic sense, the astronomer couldn't have been happier. He respected the ways of Weir but, like many Utopians, wasn't a big fan of the triplet goddesses. *'There shall be no law'*, the Entity had declared. Then why should there be deities to lord or lady over those at least nominally beneath them?

"To be more precise, I have discovered a wormhole to a specific planetary system. It is in the same microverse where, I have also discovered, the remnants of the devic race settled some seven thousand of its years ago." The excitement already filtering through the spectators became voluble. The visionary slammed his mallet on its pad so hard that the soma dislodged. He had to bring the gavel down on the still-burning wad two or three times just to extinguish it.

Silence returned to the courtroom even quicker. As a result the visionary felt no need to lecture the audience on proper decorum. He well-understood what his fellow Utopians were feeling. Already in his mind hundreds of possible Ys were roiling around. This would be the most difficult vision of his career.

"You have my attention, astronomer. Pray continue."

"How do I know this? Very simple. According to ancient documents, devils – Shining Ones, Great Gods, like the three now sitting above you, and their third generational Master Deva offspring – give off a distinctive, easily detectable energy signal: a signature, if you will. According to my readings, the third planet of this system is the only one inhabited."

"Devas like to be worshipped."

"Just so. It has a number of continental land masses separated by two major oceans and a number of lesser ones. The northern part of one of these oceans positively glows with devic radiance. I believe it curtains a hidden continent, a land mass that is largely unknown to those on the rest of the planet."

"I shall do the speculating, astronomer."

"As you please. Very well then. Based on my best evidence I would say that it has been separated from the greater world by devic energy for upwards of five to seven thousand cycles of its solitary sun. Were it less then I would further postulate, as opposed to venture, that the energy would be more widespread."

"Astronomers do not commonly examine ancient literature. You gleaned such arcane notions as devic radiance from consultation with an Illuminary."

"I have access to an Illuminary, that is true. The detecting devices I, um, rediscovered are also exceedingly ancient. "

"This wormhole of which you speak. You say you detected it. You did not make it."

Now it begins, thought the astronomer. These visionaries were insidiously insightful. "It was either there all along or just recently appeared. However, I could not access it without additional devices, these ones of my own invention."

"So," grunted the visionary, relighting his pipe, "It seems I must now refer to you as Mr Astronomer-Inventor."

"The technology pre-existed. I simply adapted it to my needs. Should you wish to address me as Astronomer-Adaptor, I shall not object."

The visionary digested this impertinence without objection. Rudeness was welcome in his courtroom. "Technology which only an Illuminary would recall, no doubt."

"As you say."

"You must not seek to hide details, astronomer-adaptor. I cannot read your mind but I can see through you. Obfuscation has no place in this courtroom."

"I apologize for my lack of clarity."

"Utopians do not apologize. The comparative proximity to devils seems to have clouded your mental acuity – just as the Ys I can already perceive are muddying mine. You have found a cosmic interface with a sun system that radiates devic energy from a specific area of its third planet. You seek my approval to go through it, which you have not done as yet. You have a reason for that."

"It is not exactly open. There is a spatial membrane in place between our universe and theirs. In symbolic terms it is of a consistency similar to cellophane. I have reached into it and, while it stretches, it shows no sign of weakening or breaking. Clearly more experiments are required."

"This still somewhat sealed opening is not large."

"Presently no larger than a small man or big boy."

"It sounds a rather unique phenomena. And you discovered, as opposed to made it, Mr Astronomer-Would-Be-Explorer."

"I was tinkering in my workroom, looked over my shoulder, and there it was."

"You are telling me there is a trans-space tube of some sort in your house."

Although visionaries never made notes, there were those who privately speculated they born with supersized biological storage systems wired into their brains. This might seem an admirable quality but Old Weir had once been ruled by a Mother Machine, a master computer. The Male Entity, who helped create the first devil and therefore, at least indirectly, the three sisters who'd fully manifested themselves only moments earlier, did not believe in masters, machine or otherwise. (When it came right down to it, he was quite old-fashioned.)

It wouldn't be a stretch to suppose the sisters shared their co-creator's feelings in that regard. Indeed, today's Utopians went to extraordinary lengths to ensure its equivalencies of First Weir's Mother Machine ruled no one, except perhaps lesser machines they oversaw and more like regulated than controlled.

"In my basement, yes."

"I see. And this anomaly suddenly just appeared."

"Some weeks ago, yes."

"And you did not notify the Planetary Council immediately because you wished to study it further."

"I needed to stabilize it first. I have done that."

"No doubt with the judicious use of cellophane, a technical term for adhesive plastic. You wish to exploit this phenomenon."

The astronomer judged it time for the speech he had prepared with his mate in anticipation of just such an opening. "You don't have to be an Illuminary to be aware of the sorry history of Old Weir. How our ancestors, blessed with lives longer than even ours are today, were obsessed with becoming immortal. How that obsession led them to create what we call mandroids and into whose artificial beings they funnelled their spirits, or consciousness, just before imminent death claimed their birth bodies.

"We are taught that these manmade monstrosities, as they proved themselves to be, very nearly came to dominate the entire planetary system. We are further taught that, in those distant times, Utopians publicly had individual names, and that the geneticist Cabalarkon was the name of antiquity's greatest hero."

"As well as ultimately, though perhaps through no fault of his own, its greatest villain."

"Ironically rather than ultimately I would say."

"And I would agree, if only in the interests of precision."

"Most generous of you." Buttering up a visionary was considered poor tactics, so the astronomer made sure he sounded sarcastic enough not to offend anyone. "Cabalarkon was leading the rebellion of natural-born Utopians against their artificial oppressors when the Male Entity appeared in Weir System once again.

"The geneticist or biomage, as they referred to his sort then, went to the Entity for advice and got more than he bargained for. The Entity used one of Cabalarkon's own eyes to create a new being — a living weapon, a champion of individuality, a nearly-omnipotent god-thing by the name of Sedon."

"Who named himself Sedon."

"If you prefer. And for reasons unknown I might add."

"Not a matter of might, astronomer. You just did."

"So I did. The might belonged to Sedon, who promptly slew the Entity and shortly afterward adopted Cabalarkon as his father. He thereafter went to extraordinary extremes to guarantee that Cabalarkon survived, potentially anyhow, at least as long he would – and Sedon, like his offspring and theirs, proved immortal, even unkillable, though in many respects appreciably that was never confirmed beyond a shadow of a doubt."

"I will not quibble with the word *promptly* to cover twenty odd years. Nor will I quibble with your assertion that it was the Moloch Sedon, as his descendants acclaimed him, who vanquished the mandroids and their Mother Machine, and not the Recurring Entity. We can't be absolutely certain of that either which way and my engagement is not with the past."

"I haven't said any of that yet."

"Which is why you are an astronomer and I am a visionary. You were also going to say something trite to the effect that the Devil Sedon proved worse than the devils Cabalarkon and his freedom fighting confrères knew as mandroids. I shall spare you the embarrassment of unnecessary wordiness. Continue."

"I'm not sure I should, given you're so very good at anticipating me. However, as the risk of embarrassing myself, it's not at all surprising that Sedon went on to destroy First Weir's Mother Machine; not when you consider Cabalarkon's crusade and the attitude towards authority of who created Sedon in the first place. What is surprising – though not anymore – is that many, many centuries later the apparently ever-undying Entity returned to Weir System."

"Undying I shall quibble with, astronomer. The Entity recurs, that is adjective sufficient for our purposes."

That got the visionary not just an obligatory burp and simultaneous fart from the penitent but an eruption of gas as noisy as it was noisome from most of the invitees. Even though two members of the audience had to be hauled gasping out of the courtroom by their neighbours, this delighted the blindfolded Utopian.

What the three great goddesses, who were more gaseous, as in insubstantial, than solid, as in corporeal, thought went unrecorded; albeit mostly because they had yet to say anything. It was a safe bet they weren't very happy with the male centric tone of the visionary. Plus, they almost certainly knew what the astronomer was coming to next — them!

He didn't disappoint.

"By then Sedon had created the six great gods, the Thrygragos Brothers and the Trigregos Sisters, and they had procreated thousands of spirit beings known as Master Devas. Cabalarkon was still alive, a vampiric being, in some respects – howsoever ironically – a living mandroid; one kept going by absorbing the essences of Utopians suffering from Imminent Death. In other words, the very disease he'd hoped to eliminate with the creation of Sedon, albeit for the benefit of future generations of True Utopians, kept him going ever afterwards at their expense.

"The Entity was merciless. He deliberately destroyed Weirstar, caused it to go supernova. With it went its entire planetary system, what we refer to as Old Weir. But in many respect it was to no avail. Sedon and the Thrygragos Brothers, together with a few hundred – perhaps as many as a few thousand, but no more – Master Devas, somehow managed to escape. How, we don't know but escape they did."

"Radioactively rendered infertile," inserted the visionary.

"So we're to understand."

"Prior to this the Entity had already moved our ancestors to New Weir."

"Alongside Cabalarkon and the esteemed Sisters sitting above you, yes. Yes also, in the interests of brevity, more time passed. The Entity, as is his wont, weakened with age. Sedon eventually found his way to New Weirworld and, as was his wont, preyed on that weakness. He contrived to slay the Entity yet again then, in the Sedonshem, a vessel of his own conjuring, departed Weirworld for parts ever unknown."

"Carrying with him Cabalarkon, the three brothers, and every other still-extant devil but for the Sisters. Who remained behind and became our deities."

"Quite rightly, too. However, while a vastly reduced agglomeration of devils got away cleanly, they were pursued by our very own Warriors of Weir."

"A million of them, the Trinondevs, on generational ships, set out in pursuit of the fleeing devils. Very few Warriors of Weir ever returned to New Weir and, tens of thousands of our years later, not even ancestral Illuminaries know what became of the Devil Sedon, Thrygragos, the rest of their devils or, for that matter, the rest of our Trinondevs and their asteroid-sized starships."

"Allow me to add: Until now."

"Allowed ... provisionally."

The astronomer took that hint, too. "My petition is this: I want to go through the gap in my basement. I want to finish the job the Recurring Entity and our heroic ancestors started. I want to eradicate devils once and for all time. I want to do this for all of us, for everyone who has ever lived and for everyone who will ever live. We brought evil into the cosmos; it needs be falls to us to abolish it."

"Singlehandedly."

"Of course not. I wish permission to access ancient technology. With it, I want to outfit an expeditionary force with the best weaponry we can muster. Suchlike, I assure you, pre-exists. It only awaits rediscovery. Illuminaries and the descendants of Trinondevs, ones either once returned or left behind, will join with me. This we can accomplish."

"You are aware the Entity proscribed weaponry; declared it redundant, its manufacture both pointless and wasteful."

"I beg you – hear me out!"

"There are no beggars in Weir."

"Implore you then."

"Like violence, that too is counter-productive. Weapons have no place in any utopia. It is otherwise, we find we have need for them, then ours is no longer a utopia. Yet it is, a true utopia; has been for multiple thousands of years and so it shall remain. We can, do, and must live in peace and conviviality with each other. Aggression has been bred out of our gene pool. It is a vile contagion."

"Surely only aggression to each other; not to devils."

"Our deities are the mothers of what you so suspiciously referred to as Master Devas."

"Suspiciously? That is the term used in our annals."

"Annals written by Illuminaries. I shall not repeat this again. It is not my task, the task of this court, to focus on the past."

"Yet we cannot dismiss it. Our deities turned on their father, their incestuous, usurious brothers, and their disloyal offspring. They joined the Entity in trying to destroy them. I was going to summon an Illuminary to testify to that fact but now there is no need. Ask the Sisters yourself, if you do not believe me."

"Belief is not at issue. Neither am I, nor this court, ignoring the past and doomed to repeat it. To imply otherwise is absurd. It indicates foolhardiness."

"And there are no fools in Weir either."

"Antagonism is only an offshoot of aggression, astronomer. Invoking higher authority is an intolerable transgression on the dignity of this court. I have no need to rule on your petition. It is denied on impropriety. You shall dismantle your apparatuses forthwith and present yourself to the College of Astronomers. They shall determine whether your genes are worth preserving."

The astronomer panicked, tried to mollify the visionary. "I meant no disrespect. My emotions got the better of me. I appeal to you to reconsider."

"Emotions have no place in this proceeding. You are akin to your petition. You are both dismissed."

The astronomer tried a last strategy. "As you wish, but first I choose to exercise the right to know your rationale."

"Which would be proper had I used my Y-vision and rendered a decision. Which I have not. Your suggestions are out of line. That is the end of this business."

The astronomer stood firm. "It is your responsibility to rule on my petition; not to dismiss it on purely technical grounds. I shall have you impeached."

Murmurs from the courtroom told him he'd struck a responsive chord. He accepted that he had been a fool to challenge the visionary in such a way but the visionary had been a bigger fool in seeking to dodge his duty. Duty, what Utopians called '*dharma*', was the glue that held their age-old society together.

"Much better." The visionary leaned back and, beneath his blindfold, closed his eyes.

Inwardly, he examined a thousand-million possible futures. Most had such infinitesimal differences that simple prophets, low grade precognates, high grade logicians, and potential visionaries still in training would mistake them for the same possible future. To his mind he had done with them easily and quickly but, for those in the courtroom, he remained silent for what seemed like an eternity. For the visionary it was an eternity – a multitude of them.

And there was no doubt about any of them.

"Very well, here is my decision." Was he smirking? "Your petition is denied. You shall dismantle your apparatuses forthwith and present yourself to the College of Astronomers, who will determine whether your genes are worth preserving. Before complying, however, you wish to know why."

Choking back his anger, the astronomer forced himself to respond in a calm voice. "I do."

"As is only proper. In the interests of freedom, this court shall have no secrets. To restate the elementary, we of Weir live in a Utopia. Duty binds us but we exist for the furtherance of knowledge. In all our existence – New Weir and Old Weir – we have learned more than any other sentient race in the multiverse.

"Still and yet, we remain basically ignorant. It is that ignorance that provides us with our primary rationale for continuing our own existence. Were we completely omniscient, we would have no reason for carrying on. A fundamental precept – the fundamental precept – is that we do not interfere in the progress of another world until we know all there is to know about that other world.

"Not paradoxically, however, there is no such thing as knowing everything there is to know about everything. This does not mean that we are stagnant. It does mean we concentrate on furthering our own self-interest; which is, as stated at the outset, the furtherance of knowledge. It is not for us to influence others.

"Sedon and his three sons may be the epitome of evil but his three daughters are our deities. They do not interfere with us; we do not interfere with them. What you are proposing is an aggressive act against a planetary system that has housed Sedon and his devils, by your own estimation, for some seven thousand years.

"It could be that the inhabitants of the planet you identified have formed a symbiotic relationship with devils. I cannot countenance changing that relationship. At the same time, an opportunity has presented itself and we must protect ourselves." He paused as if considering how best to phrase the balance of his judgement.

"Granted, we could use this wormhole and refine your apparatuses such that we could observe what devils are doing these days. Observe, not invade, I say again. I examined that possibility and discounted it out of hand. In devils, at least in the Moloch Sedon and his three sons, we are talking about highly intelligent beings. More — highly powerful ones.

"I have seen that the inhabitants of this third planet, the dominant race thereupon it, are also highly intelligent, albeit primitive, virtually infantile beings. They are riven by senseless tribalism, petty squabbles between organized religions, faiths and creeds. Even the colour of their skin and, to somewhat lesser degrees, their gender and sexual orientation drives them apart, not together.

"I have seen them using Atomics on a daily basis to fuel their homes and industries. I have seen them use Atomics against each other. I looked into the possibility of sending some of us through your wormhole, in order to educate them about Atomics and other suchlike doomsday material. I have seen what they will, more often than not, do after that. Indeed, to repeat myself somewhat, we could provide them with a superfluity of useful knowledge. But they are so volatile, they may corrupt that knowledge to use against us.

"That is one reason your apparatuses must be dismantled. There are many others. For example, there is the strong possibility that this wormhole of yours is not some kind of cosmic accident. I have seen that it may not just be a way for us to go in pursuit of devils. It may be the devils' preliminary way of going in search of us!

"The Sisters do not mate with anyone anymore because they can't possess any of us. They might be able to mate with their father or brothers or even their own offspring. They might even desire it. But after all this time, who can say devils are still infertile? Certainly not you, I, or even them, the three above me. Besides, the Utopia of Weir needs no more devils.

"Comes to that, the entire cosmos needs no more devils. That does not mean we should seek to destroy the few who may be left. We are scientists, not warriors. Just as the Utopia needs no more devils, we no longer need Trinondevs. That breed has been expunged from our genetic makeup. At least, so we thought.

"Look into yourself, astronomer. Ask yourself all the questions you need to ask yourself, and others, but never forget that I do not ask anyone anything. I see what will happen in terms of the minutest of probabilities. What you are proposing is Trinondev-style action, pure and simple. Aggression, intervention – call it what you will – but there is no denying its inappropriateness. At the same time, there is no doubting your genius. Just, sadly, your integrity.

"That is why I leave the matter of your genes being impounded to the College of Astronomers. It will be for them to decide what becomes of your legacy because there is little question you've more than just a trace of Trinondev in you. Somehow it slipped through your development team's fingers or, if it didn't – and that too is a possibility – then you are no more an accident than is this wormhole.

"That about sums everything up. My obligations to you and everyone else are met. As always I will be forwarding a complete recording of these proceedings to the Planetary Council. As always, they will form their own conclusions; as will the media here present. I need not remind them of their duty. I trust that is satisfactory. For there is no more."

"So be it," agreed the astronomer. "Do the Sisters have anything to add?"

"If they do, they shall not do so in this courtroom. You have heard my vision. This court is adjourned."

He rose and strode out of the room. The astronomer looked to the three chairs above the visionary's bench. They were empty.

Had it been a trick of the light or had they actually been there?

========

"Wake up, History. Something's just happened!"

The ouzo had put him to sleep. He came to with a start. "What is it, Mnemosyne?"

"Two LAC Squads have been sent down from the Liberty."

"So deal with them. Do as you've been programmed."

"As I've programmed myself, you mean."

"Same thing. Just follow your instructions."

"When haven't I, Kadmon?"

"Yeah, right! The genie and her three wishes. Lifetime after fucking lifetime. You're stuck in a rut, milady. And it's not purely because you love rutting either."

"That's not fair. I live to serve you."

"Precisely — unlike any other machine, you do live."

"Whatever you say, my love. Yet, despite a hundred deaths, so do you. Who's that down to except me?"

"I'd say Gypsium Godstuff but there's no point. You no more understand it than I do you. Just let's get it right this time, Memory. Okay?"

"Oh, I fully intend to, Hel!"

****

Second Moon: **The Moon: Above, Below, Beyond**

========

Sunday, November 30, 1980

Despite the fact that he was barely thirty-seven, James Aremar was a steel grey, no-nonsense veteran of AMERICA.

========

Squad leader of the task force that was supposed to take out the leadership of the Black Rose in '68, the total disappearance of the tiny but nonetheless substantial Aegean Island of Trigon was the fright of his life — what caused him to go grey in the first place. Thereafter nothing fazed him, which was why he had been Alfredo Sentalli's first choice to become commander of the Cosmic Express.

For some reason, Loxus Ryne argued against it. Instead, he had spent most of the previous decade acting as the Great Man's chief lieutenant, a position OJ Maxwell held from just after the Second World War until the late Sixties. Aremar's reward had been the command of another ship, albeit no mere Vietnam-era torpedo boat this time: the United Nations of Earth Spaceship Liberty.

Construction on the Liberty began in mid-1978, some six months after satellites started to detect beams of some sort incoming from the Moon. It was built in total secrecy; much of it only pieced together in *'Earth-Shadow'*, the region of outer space occulted by planet from planetoid. Like Project Centauri, it was funded by all the nations of the Earth.

Unlike the Cosmic Express, its components were largely manufactured in the USSR. Also unlike the Express, it was a shared-technology venture. Gypsium, at least the technology developed by Professor Romaine Kinesis and his associates, belonged exclusively to New Century Enterprises and did not figure into its design. Neither did Solidium, in many respects its counteragent.

The Liberty was conventional in every way — except it had never been done before. Then again there had never been aliens on the Moon before.

========

Aremar stalked the control deck of the UNES Liberty like a wildcat looking for something to tear apart. He couldn't sit down, seldom stopped pacing. He had been trained for action and action was what he craved.

"Report, all stations. Report, I say."

Sean Smythe, his chief of operations and, at nearly sixty, the eldest man aboard the Liberty, dutifully reported: "Nothing to report, sir. All is in order."

"The hell it is, sir," complained Aremar. "Billowing bazookas, man, it can't be. Double-check. Are we maintaining precise moon-orbit? Are our stabilizers fully functional? Weapons systems ready to fire? Have the Lunar Assault Crafts landed? Have we engaged the enemy?"

"Yes, sir. Yes, sir. Yes, sir. Yes, sir. No, sir."

"You must be the great-grandson of imbecilic baboons, Smythe. What do you mean by 'no, sir'?"

"Yes, sir. I mean no, sir. We have not encountered the enemy, unless he is us."

"We're not up here for our health. We're not going to get terra-tans through our God-cursed spacesuits. Why have we not encountered the enemy?"

"Appears to me, commander," said Smythe, well-used to Aremar's rants, "That there is no enemy to encounter."

"What? Idiot of idiots! We've come all the way from the bleeding Earth to the God-cursed Moon and you're telling me we've targeted the wrong crater. Where did SPACE find you? Tossing paper planes in the middle of first year physics class."

"Give over with the abuse, Jimmy! I'm telling you there's nothing there because our instruments are telling me there's nothing there. Every prior indication we had pointed to this crater as the source of the beams that have been permeating downstairs for the past two, three years. Maybe we're wrong. Maybe our instruments are faulty. If there's an alien stronghold up here, then it should be down there, in that crater, but I don't pick up anything out of the ordinary. End story."

"Blow the fuck out of it anyhow, Sean."

"Hadn't we best contact Earthbase Houston before we go on the offensive?"

"Of course we better. Get the downside jokers on radio. Find out if they see anything more than our instruments are picking up. Oh, and Sean?"

"Jim?"

"Don't call me Jimmy. Not in front of the men."

========

Two Lunar Assault Crews shuttled to the surface.

========

One, to a man, was Soviet Red Army. Not surprisingly a Russian, Leonid Kulagin, commanded it. Ned Johnson led the other; American Marines, bar none. Each LAC craft disgorged two dozen men supplied with the lunar equivalent of two- or three-man tanks and one-man harrier sky-sleds, the former of Japanese design, the latter British.

They deployed their men dutifully around the crater which, as Johnson put it, seemed to be nothing more than a big old hole full of moon dust. He radioed as much to Sean Smythe and James Aremar, who were still aboard the Liberty along with two more LAC squads – one Chinese, one Indian Commonwealth – and another dozen engineers and medical support staff.

"Any radioactivity?" queried Smythe.

"None to speak of," responded Kulagin. "Caught a whiff of Gypsium when we first probed the place but that isn't surprising. American moon-walkers have reported that before. Haven't picked up anything else out of the ordinary."

Aremar took over communications from Smythe. "Houston suspects, and our instruments apparently confirm, that there are no bug-eyed Martians on the Moon after all. Instead, there's likely a transmitter of some sort; maybe a few of them.

They may turn out to be terrestrial. That probably means WORLD's work. Are you reading me?"

Kulagin and Johnson exchanged knowing glances. Neither were old enough to remember WORLD in any great detail. The so-called Worldwide Order had its heyday in the Sixties. After a rather public debut – a kidnapping-double-murder in April 1960 – it went underground.

Reliably reportedly, it thereupon spent a couple of years beefing up its war chest by leasing out its expertise and providing communication links to criminal associations such as the Triads and Yakuza of South-East Asia, and the Mafia of Italy and the Americas. Its tentacles were soon everywhere and its ambitions became grandiose.

A blanket organization dedicated to extortion, terrorism, and, ultimately, conquest, at its heart proved to be a bunch of unrepentant Nazis, Japanese supremacists, and trans-global megalomaniacs. The patriarch's Alliance of Man set up AMERICA largely to deal with WORLD; thought it eradicated by 1970. Rumours of its continuance persisted, however.

Clearly Loxus Ryne and his chief lieutenant, James Aremar, were quick to ascribe what was going on up here to the devil they knew. Neither Kulagin nor Johnson necessarily shared that notion. "We read and are awaiting your orders."

"LAC One – that's you, Johnson," Aremar's voice crackled over the radio. "Advance slowly and deliberately into the crater. Beware booby-traps. At the slightest show of resistance, retreat. We shall concentrate fire on the crater from the Liberty. If you locate the transmitter, locate anything of interest, dismantle and preserve it. We shall wish to examine everything you bring back. Good luck, Ned."

"Luck has nothing to do with anything, Jim. Let's go."

Ned Johnson waved his squad into the crater.

========

A few minutes later, Kulagin radioed the Liberty. His voice was shaking; he sounded spooked, if not out and out terrified.

"They just disintegrated."

========

At Earthbase Houston, Loxus Abraham Ryne read the dispatch from the Liberty dispassionately. A communication technician requested further directions. Ryne flipped back a couple of pages. He circled the word, *'Gypsium'*, and ordered a plane readied to take him to Centauri Island.

"Anything else?"

"Something's coming in now, sir." It was a picture. "Apparently it appeared near the Liberty almost concurrently with the disappearance of LAC One." Ryne took a glance. Although few would recognize it, the Great Man knew exactly what it was: a cosmicar, one of the Cosmic Express's six. He spoke to Aremar directly.

"Maintain a holding pattern, Jim. Do nothing until you hear from me again. That'll probably be in about twenty-four hours. I'm shifting my personal HQ from Earthbase Houston to Centauri Island. If the Liberty or the LAC squad left on the Moon come under attack, you are to retreat. Do you recall Trigon 1968?"

"How couldn't I? I've never seen nor heard of anything like what happened there before nor since."

"I believe you just have. Ryne out!"

========

"LAC One secured, Kadmon."
"And the bits of the Cosmic Express? Analysis!"
"One cosmicar, seven humans, all alive, and all possessed – by Master Devas!"

========

"Damnation! Which ones?"

"Haven't had time to figure that out yet. Wait until you hear the rest. The other bit's what's left of the control hub. There were supposed to be a dozen or so men and women on it according to the probes you had me run on the thing last week. All that's left is a star-sled, an ejection pod, with only one man aboard it. He's the Silver Signaller Solar, the one who went by the name Avatar Sol on Centauri's island. You know who that is."

He nodded.

"You want me to rescue him?"

"Who's possessing him?" She told him it was one of the Atomic Triplets: not Equinoctial Autumn nor Equinoctial Spring, Cautes or Cautopates. No, it was Solstitial Summer, Novadev, the one who didn't make it to the time of the Death's Head Hellion, circa 800 AD Outer Earth Time. (Not that Master Morgan Abyss lived let alone, probably, ever visited out there.)

He shook his head sadly. Despite the passing of thirty-five hundred years and, what, forty or so lifetimes it seemed like almost yesterday that the idiot devil got so drunk he blew the heart of Strongyne, the Island of Strong Women (nowadays Santorini or Thira, in the Aegean Sea), into the sky and promptly got cathonitized for his troubles.

Which beat getting annihilated, like so many of Strongyne's inhabitants, those on comparatively nearby Crete and throughout most the Eastern Mediterranean. (To this day wonder-struck New Age speculators, and even a few scholars who should know better, argued about whether Santorini's eruption led to the Ten Biblical Plagues of Egypt. Then again they also argued about whether Santorini was Plato's Atlantis.)

"Goodbye, old friend, old enemy. I'd hoped we'd be friends again. We part a final time. For the Good of All and the Greater Glory of Humanity."

========

"Mik! Get with it, Mik. We're alive."

========

Thirty-seven year old Mikelangelo Starrus, captain of Cosmicar Two, could hear his wife yelling at him through the circuitry of his space helmet. He tried to respond but the pain was too great. The worst migraine he'd ever experienced hadn't been this bad. And he'd had some royal doozies, especially after he dropped that bomb on Aegean Trigon and, moments later, it wasn't there anymore.

"Captain Starrus, Cosmicaptain Starrus, it's Sol. Help me!"

Starrus fought back the pain and opened his eyes. He was rooted to his seat but all systems seemed functional. He voice-activated the screen built into the visor of his helmet. At his command, it ran a quick diagnostic on the cosmicar's innards. His fellow cosmicompanions – wife Nidaba, her sister Inanna (Enan), Enan's husband

Anon Sasarian, Viraf and Ahura Mazda, and the solitary bachelor among the crew Xerxes Alchaemid – were secure in their places.

The car's structural integrity was intact; its hull undamaged. Satisfied, he ordered a scan of the exterior; all A-OK there as well. So he extended its external cameras' focus. With some difficulty, he finally pinpointed Colonel Avatar Sol. That they were in outer space didn't surprise him; that Sol was in a pod some small distance from the car, with no sign of the rest of the control hub or its occupants, did.

"For God's sake, Cosmicar Two, if there's anyone in there, come and get me. This is Sol, your commander. Answer me!"

"Mik, are you there?"

"I'm here, Nidaba. Opinions?"

"Don't have enough data," offered Anon. "There was this black space then all these little stars then a big one, like an eye. The Express blew apart. Now we're out here. We're together but we're alone. If that's Sol, then where are the rest of his hubmates, not to mention the hub itself?"

Xerxes Alchaemid broke in: "We're near the moon. The other spaceship out there's the Liberty. We've been briefed on it before. Its mission supposedly has nothing to do with us but I always wondered if that was true. I say we activate the Gypsium fuel and hightail it back to Earth."

"Negative," insisted Starrus. "No Gypsium. It's only meant for travel in space. Xerxes, assess our standard fuel capacity. We'll go back to Earth the way we would into any atmosphere. Ahura, is that Sol?"

"It's his personal pod, Mik. It's just like ours but his seems to have been shorn of its star-sled capability – its self-propulsive components – and its manual override controls. He's a lame duck. His life-support can't last long."

"What of our pods, Viraf?"

"All intact."

"That means mine is the best-equipped to rescue Sol. All right, I'm going. Depressurize the cabin, Enan. Wish me luck, Nidaba." Pointedly, she didn't.

The pod that was his seat sealed itself. A hatch opened and he dropped into space. Free-falling until he was safely away from away from the cosmicar, he ignited his short range thrusters and went after Avatar Sol.

========

"The Trigon Terminator is going for the Tooth, Kadmon. It's too late to prevent Tiecher from going critical but I might be able to hold it off long enough for him to take them both out at the same time."

"Vengeance is beneath us, Mnemosyne. You know my precepts."

"I have just determined that Mikelangelo Starrus is possessed by Lord Order."

"Do it then. And hurry!"

========

Colonel Sol went critical just before Cosmicaptain Starrus reached him. In what was more of an implosion than an explosion, Sol seemingly sucked in on himself; simply blinked out of existence. Something happened to Mik Starrus. Suddenly a being absorbed the entirety of the cosmicaptain and his pod as well.

For a brief second, Thunder and Lightning Lord Yajur appeared in space. Five hundred years had passed since he was cathonitized, made a star in the night's sky above his homeland, thus bringing an end to the 1000 Days of Disbelief. He looked as he commonly let himself look. His hair was bolts of electricity, his brown body Apollo-perfect, muscular and dressed in a blazing chlamys. All three of his eyes were wide open. He raised his lightning blade and pointed it at the moon.

"I know you're there, entity. Wait for me. Shan't be long!"

Yajur resolved into Starrus and his pod. The cosmicaptain propelled himself back to the cosmicar. Once he was aboard and all systems were restored, he shucked his pod and removed his helmet. Nidaba helped her husband out of the rest of his space-suit. He helped her out of hers.

They looked at each other. She gasped incredulously: "Mik, your forehead!"

A third eye glared out of it!

========

"Where does the old man get off telling me to maintain a holding pattern?" grumbled James Aremar.

========

"And what the hell's he so bloody worried about a tracing of Gypsium? We just lost two dozen of my best men downside and two dozen more are waiting like targets in a shooting gallery. Holding pattern, my butt-end! We either go into that crater with all we've got or we skedaddle out of here, tails where our dicks should be. I tell you, Smythe, Ryne's hamstringing us."

"I've been with Loxus even longer than you have, Jim," noted Smythe calmly. "He's not infallible, that's for certain, but he's usually proved right in the long run. Ask me, Gypsium's a damn good reason for holding off. You know what Professor Kinesis says about the stuff: To touch Gypsium is not so much to touch the unknown as it is to touch the unknowable. Take a break, captain. I'll keep you posted."

"Any contact with the cosmicar?"

"Nothing yet. I told you, I'll let you know the moment we have something."

========

"I'm sorry, Kadmon. I think Novadev destroyed himself — and Ti Tiecher, Avatar Sol, with him — but Starrus-Yajur escaped. Where are you going?"

"To get my sword."

========

"Your sword's from the future, at least one possible one in terms of when we are now. It may not be needed here. We're still not much more than ten years after your initial lifetime. The ninety-nine you've experienced between then and now could be irrelevant, as in inoperable. I have secured the SAG Gap, anchored it in near-space. We anticipated devils might become involved in our designs. We have prepared for it. Kindly let us carry on with the plan.

"To do otherwise, to do what we have so often done during your previous lifetimes, to improvise, to make things up as we go, that's the recipe for continuing failure. Do you really want another hundred lifetimes when we're so close to your first? What did you say to me less than an hour ago?"

"Let's get it right this time!"

"Exactly!"

"You're right, milady. We can handle this ourselves."

========

Reluctantly, Aremar retired to his ready room off the bridge. Two seconds later he screamed at the top of his lungs: "Smythe, get the fuck in here!" With a half dozen security officers behind him, Sean Smythe raced into the cabin. Aremar was pointing at a bouquet of flowers in the centre of the conference table.

"What is that?"

"Roses?"

"Exactly. Black Roses!"

****

Third Moon: **The Ubiquitous Uncle Universe**

========

Sunday, November 30, 1980

The Ubiquitous Uncle Universe, his own name for himself, returned home. Atom-aunt, his private wife, a physicist and an hereditary Illuminary, was waiting for him.

Like all females in the Utopia, she was white-skinned. Her black or greyish tattoos were trigonometric functions, sine curves and such like. Like him, she was still in work mode: clothes-free and apparently sexless. Not that it mattered one way or the other.

They were mates and, rebels that they secretly were, only they knew she was pregnant. At least so they believed.

========

"How did it go?"

"As I feared," responded the astronomer-inventor-explorer discouragingly. "The visionary dismissed my case. His rationale was cogent and compelling but nothing I hadn't thought of beforehand. How did they discover what I was doing in the first place? Could the kids have blubbered something in school?"

"What, that you spend hours in the basement and won't them down there to play anymore? I told you, Ubi. Your superiors must have realized you were working on renegade projects when your performance on assigned duties fell off. I know how the system operates.

"In any case, the visionary probably did you a favour. You better destroy the link and hope to Trigregos the Astronomy College or the Planetary Council doesn't find out just how far you've gone or how much it wasn't an accident the link appeared in our basement. They could impound your genes."

"And find out I've already disseminated them into you. They could force you to abort. Worse, they could annul us."

"Don't you mean execute?"

"If we're deemed non-beings, it isn't a matter of execution. You know that!" He paused to re-rein in his emotions. Utopians didn't – couldn't – suffer from stress but today hadn't exactly been a featherbed full of rose petals. Actually, come to think of it, it sort of had. But it was also full of rose stems barbed with thorns.

"I'll dismantle the plank tomorrow. Don't see how that's going go to get rid of the wormhole, though. Where are the children?"

Utopians didn't have children per se. They had assignments, ones that were born in Development Tanks and raised by usually 2-person Development Teams. "Son-shine's playing soccer and Star-baby's on the debating team at programming school. She's a natural Illuminary. I hate to see her fake her heritage. Hope the Sisters' will protect her as well as they protected us when we were growing up."

"Guard your thoughts, wife. I'm convinced the Planetary Council's employing telepaths."

"Since when haven't they?"

========

Mik passed out.

========

It was an odd sight, given the weightless conditions inside the cosmicar. His third eye subsided the moment he lost consciousness but his magnetic boots held him fast to the floor. Thinking fast, Nidaba Starrus grabbed her husband's shirt and picked up his helmet. She yelled for help. Viraf Mazda and Anon Sasarian shucked their pods, as did Enan (Anon's wife and Nidaba's sister).

Together, the four of them removed his boots and strapped him to a cot in one of the seven cubbyholes that served as private space for cosmicompanions. Xerxes Alchaemid – with the exception of Starrus all those aboard the cosmicar were Iranian; Iraryan, if you listened to Loxus Ryne, who considered Iran his ancestral homeland – left his pod and took over Mik's, which had the captain's controls. Ahura Mazda, Viraf's wife, took over Alchaemid's role as second-in-command.

"Status report, Ahura," demanded Alchaemid.

As with everyone on the six cosmicars, each was trained to perform the other's duties. She reported everything still A-OK, so Xerxes established artificial gravity. Thereby freed from weightlessness, the Sasarians and Viraf Mazda began a visual inspection of the interior of the car. Nidaba stayed with Mik who was already showing signs of fever, if no longer even a tracing of a third eye.

"The Liberty is seeking to contact us," reported Ahura.

"Request help," yelled Nidaba.

"Negative," insisted Xerxes. "Think sensibly, Nidaba. Until we know Mik's status, we have to presume contamination. It might be gone now but we all saw what was shining out of his forehead. Nothing I've ever heard of could account for the development of a third eye in a human being."

(Pre-Muslim Iranian adherents to Magian Fire Faiths or Zoroastrianism, called Parsees in modern day India, did know about Devas, capitalized. However, they considered them vastly inferior demons to their gods, who numbered three in Zoroastrianism, the same as the Catholic Church's Holy Trinity. Be that as it may, some of these gods or demigods {called Asuras, usually also capitalized, in their language} were/are depicted with three eyes.)

"We must presume we're on a plague ship, but we can't tell anyone that. Not unless you want to get us blown into noughts and crosses. Retain radio silence."

========

That was Sunday night.

========

Monday, December 1, 1980

A rap on the door. "It's open," said Loxus Ryne, who'd arrived on Centauri Island late that afternoon, Hawaiian time. Professor Romaine Kinesis and O'Ryan James Maxwell entered the oversized suite Ryne usually commandeered for use as his office-cum-control room whenever he was on the island.

"Sit down," the patriarch told them. "Pour yourselves a drink. Forgive me if I don't get up. Had a long day." Max spilt a concoction of vodka and orange into a large glass. Rom, who rarely drank anything except bottled water, sipped just that.

"Now then, gentlemen. What are we going to do about Helios on the Moon?"

========

That was Monday night.

========

Tuesday, December 2, 1980

The little witch — call her Hush; almost everyone did, at least to her face — awoke from her drug-induced sleep shortly before dawn. She wasn't alone.

"Hello, baby."

"Hello, daddy homunculus."

"Where are Max and the professor?" demanded Hiyati Samarand.

"On their way to the Moon?" guessed the enchanted child.

========

That was Tuesday morning.

========

James Aremar stepped onto the bridge of the UNES Liberty in a state, not all that unusual for him, of angry intensity. "Bloody wonderful, isn't it, Mr Smythe? SPACE put enough money and technology into this bucket to bankrupt more than a few countries and still feed their starving citizens. Yet here we are, less than an hour from the Moon by shuttle, and as good — or as bad — as sucking our thumbs."

"Better than sticking them up our butts."

"I gather you've still nothing to report."

"Not from the Moon nor the cosmicar. From the Earth, more than a fair bit."

Sean Smythe pointed to the pile of printouts the Liberty had received in the past twelve or so hours since he, Aremar and the primary crew were on relief.

"It seems Mr Ryne has been a busy man on Centauri Island. On his instructions, we have been preparing to launch one of our two remaining shuttle crafts. We're to rendezvous in earth orbit with the Space Shuttle Columbia and take on two passengers. All things being equal, by week's end we shall have the pleasure of entertaining Professor Romaine Kinesis and our mutual friend and former boss, O'Ryan James Maxwell."

"Kinesis, eh. The old man must have figured there was something to the Gypsium and black roses after all. Sending us a pro, pun intended. Okay, I guess I can see that, though Kinesis is well over forty and not in the best of shape. Don't understand Maxwell, though. He must be older than you."

"Not by much. And in a hell of a lot better shape, I'll wager. Neither of them make much sense to me. Why do they have to be up here? Anything they might be able to contribute they could from Earth-side. Unless ..."

"Unless Ryne wants Maxwell to take over my command."

"That isn't what I was thinking but, then again, what I was thinking is even less likely."

"Would you care to elaborate on that?"

"Maybe Abe's figured out what's going on up here. Kinesis knows more about Gypsium than any man alive and Maxwell's much like you. He's always been action-oriented. Maybe Kinesis built a weapon and Maxwell's going to use it."

"And maybe pigs can fly. Which they can, if Pink Floyd's to be believed. Week's end? Bafflegab and beeswax, what're we supposed to do in the meantime. Hold our dicks and retain a stationary position. Or is that statuary position?"

"Not quite, Jim. Centauri's people have been in constant contact with us. Ryne's authorized a move to retrieve the cosmicar. I've made all the preliminary calculations. It'll fit into the docking bay for Johnson's shuttle and, since Johnson isn't likely to need it again, the area's there. It'll be a tricky manoeuvre but, with the proper pilot in the fourth shuttle, we should be able to pull it off. Have any recommendations as to who the proper pilot would be?"

"Meaning me. Very clever, Sean. All right, bring everything you have on the cosmicar into my ready room. Put the shuttle's operational crew on notice."

"Shall do. BTW …"

"BTW?"

"By the way, who're Pink Floyd."

"You're joking. What the hell do you think they were playing in the mess damn near everyday we were training for this?"

"That I was … joking. I gather they did more than *'Dark Side of the Moon'*."

"Damn right they did. Album's called *Animals*; song's called *'Pigs on the Wing'*. Do we know if they're still alive in there?"

"Depends how high they flew, the pigs I mean. You know what happened to Icarus."

"Yeah, yeah; ha, ha."

"As of Sunday, yes. As you know, or should know, our techs managed to pick up an anomalous blip on our sensing devices shortly after we detected the cosmicar. There were no visuals and we're still analyzing the data. Near as we can make out something blew up external to the cosmicar. What it was, we have no idea. However, they cut off radio contact with Centauri Island immediately thereafter.

"That may mean nothing. May mean they're dead, though I doubt it. No way to tell without getting inside."

Suddenly alarms blared throughout the Liberty. Red lights flashed. "Battle Stations! Battle Stations!" came the automatically-triggered computer voice in a dozen languages. Aremar stood stark still; glared at Smythe silently: more dumbfounded than, for once, accusingly. Projected on the big screen was an amazing sight.

There appeared to be a grey hole in the blackness of space. A huge shape was straining against what might have passed for a membranous seal from the other side of it. Were it not for its proportionate immensity, it looked like a young, humanoid boy. Two pudgy hands seemed to be struggling to break through the membrane that was holding it back. The cosmicar was comparatively a child's toy between the enormous hands.

On a secondary screen, the stunned deck crew of the Liberty saw a beam of light come out of the cosmicar. It sliced through space, straight into the hole and the godchild. Light, boy, and hole siphoned in on themselves and, like water going down a drain, soon vanished. Minutes passed then the cosmicar too was gone.

A faint tracing of energy led towards the Moon; to the very crater where Ned Johnson and his LAC Squad had disappeared on Sunday. The alarms silenced as abruptly as they'd gone off. James Aremar was still rooted to the bridge. It was he who, typically tactfully, broke the deadening quiet.

"Fucking Hell!"

========

This was still Tuesday!

========

The transparent shape that was thirty-five years dead Mnemosyne D'Angelo Heli-opolis's lookalike stepped out of the wall into their living quarters on the uppermost level of one of the three towers that made up the Lunar Citadel. Helios dissolved the hologram creature he was playing chess with and turned to his mate.

"Well, milady, do we have more guests?"

========

Almost immediately full-bodied Miracle Memory (also Machine-Memory) nodded confirmation. "Any we know?" asked her perennial companion.

"Too early to tell. I placed them under stasis beams so their mental patterns have been temporarily nullified. The only one we knew about for sure, Mik Starrus – the Trigon Terminator, as you so aptly called him – was possessed by Thunder and Lightning Lord Yajur. We'll not be having the pleasure of his company, I'm afraid."

"Too bad. There is much I would like to know about my first death. Much of it Mik Starrus could probably tell me."

"James Aremar's on the Liberty. He was the one who ordered the bombing strike that Starrus led. Shall I bring him over?"

"Not just yet, milady. In due course. I intend to have some fun with Genial Jimmy first. Anything else?"

"I know how much you love surprises. It gets your blood going. But I can't surprise you if I tell you everything all at once."

"Gamesmen relish challenges, that much is true. Successful gamesmen relish advance knowledge even more. I intend to be successful this time."

"Then you should know that, if all goes well, come Saturday or Sunday Rom Kinesis and OJ Maxwell will be on the Liberty."

"Intriguing. What's Ryne up to, I wonder, sending those two? I shall review their files after I finish the game. Keep me posted. How's supper coming?"

"Would you like to hear the menu?"

"Nothing extraterrestrial, I trust."

"Hardly. Going Greek all the way: lamb, butchered this morning, our own calamari, salad, dolmades, hummus, pita; usual fare. When you're cooking for a couple of dozen American Moon Marines, it's best to keep things simple. No steaks, burgers or deep-fried chicken, as per your request."

"Good. Wouldn't do to make them feel too much at home. You may go." He returned his attention to the chess board.

"Uh, Kadmon?" Unbidden, his foe reformed itself into the shape of Miracle Memory. "This is a partnership, you know."

"Of course it is, milady. I just thought you had better things to do with your synapses than to try to beat me at chess. What with everything going on, you don't need more distractions."

"You made a mistake three moves ago."

"I was not playing you three moves ago."

"You are now."

========

Bathed and in his pyjamas, the little boy had gone downstairs to the living room to say good night to his uncle, the father-half of his and Star-baby's development team. Although at home and sound asleep, Universe – or Ubi as his wife, Atomaunt, referred to him in their private moments – was still in his astronomer persona: tall, puffed up and overbearing, with the white tattoos of his profession glinting out of his otherwise night-black skin.

His halo, what looked like the rings of a Saturn-like planet, had slipped over his face and was bobbing weirdly as he snored.

========

Ordinarily, Son-shine knew him in his at-home persona: still a bit bulbous, due to a non-Utopian predilection for overeating, but with an unexaggerated physiognomy, stubble beard, crew-cut, and wearing clothes (commonly draw-string pants, slippers or sandals, and a loose sweatshirt). However, his uncle had been enduring a lot of stress the last couple of days: doing overtime at work to try to catch up with his assigned duties, then coming home and going down the basement to do who knows what.

While Tom, as his uncle called Atomaunt, the child's developmental mother, was upstairs tending to Star in the bath, the little boy thought to take advantage of Ubi's exhaustion. He crept to the head of the stairs and, much to his surprise, found the door unlocked. Chancing it, he slipped down the stairs and flipped on the light.

He had only been down here a few times since it ceased being a big playroom, but it was vastly different from the last time he'd been here. Then it had been one large room thoroughly cluttered with work benches covered with books, note pads, gadgets, gewgaws, scientific instruments whose function he could only guess at, and computer terminals hooked up to Weir's thoroughly automated but purely functional, as in subservient, Mother Machine or one of its offshoots.

Son-shine knew a little of the first Mother Machine. Almost two hundred millennia earlier, it had occupied an entire planet, the nerve-centre of the ancient planetary system of Old Weir. It stored every bit of information Utopians managed to collect and was accessible to every Utopian who wanted to consult it.

However, sometime before the destruction of Old Weir, it became at least semi-sentient and an actual mother. Mandroids were its offspring. Dull automatons at first, they eventually became the receptacles for the intelligence, the consciousness, the compos mentis spirit, of dying Utopians.

Then came the Solitary Entity and, with the collaboration of the be-named hero Cabalarkon, a geneticist, he co-created the Devil Sedon, the first devazur. This Sedon killed the Entity, apparently not for the first nor the last time. He thereupon broke the stranglehold the Mother Machine had been exerting on Weir System. His actions plunged Old Weir into what its annals still referred to as its Darkest Ages.

In time, the Entity returned but she/it/he – unless there were already two, a definite male and a definite female, by then – was manifestly insane. It or she or he or all three caused Weirstar to go supernova. In that apocalyptic moment the entirety of Weir System was wiped out. And that included the Mother Machine's planet, her with it, and, albeit only by design, Sedon and all the other devils he, the Devil, capitalized, created between appearances of the Entity.

That selfsame Entity had a glimmering of mercy left in his being. By some technological miracle, so the story went, he transferred one the outermost planets of Old Weir to a nearby, uninhabited galaxy. That planet became New Weir and that galaxy, over the course of multi-millennia, became New Weir System. Perhaps ten thousand planets, lit by at least two thousand stars, now comprised Galactic Weir.

Each one had a Mother Machine of it own, with satellite systems that shared information with other Mother Machines and their satellites. Having learned their lesson from the first one, multiple generations of subsequent Utopians resolutely kept them unintelligent. Mandroids, too, were kept things of the past and the Entity, though he'd returned a few times over the millennia, perhaps to survey all he'd wrought, never again repeated the process that resulted in the creation of Sedon.

There were those – young and foolish schoolyard braggarts for the most part – who claimed this was First Planet, the original New Weir; the one founded by old King Kad, as the Entity came to be called. Ubi and Tom had educated Son-shine and Star-baby in a more accurate, and more tolerant, assessment of their place in Weir System.

Virtually all ten thousand planets could claim First Planet status because all of Weir was first in the minds of its inhabitants. There was no first planet per se, there was only Galactic Weir. One could go from one planet to another, one star system to another, and feel completely at home. There were even, his developmental parents further claimed, with no hint of teasing, those among the Ancient Alive who had actually been to all ten thousand worlds.

Come the tenth anniversary of his release from his birth tank, only a year from now, Son-shine would embark upon the traditional Journey of Weir. It would take perhaps a dozen years, touch upon forty to fifty planets, but, by the time he reached manhood and was allowed to begin contributing his genes to the universal pool, he would learn the veracity of their teachings.

So they promised; so was promised every Utopian. And so it would be.

Right now, given the curiosity of children everywhere, he was bound and determined to learn what his uncle was doing in their basement.

The back-half was now panelled off. Numerous holes had been bored in the walls. Devices of some sort or another had once gone through them but nothing did now. His uncle had obviously disconnected everything that went into the new room but, as he'd overheard Ubi exclaim to Tom and their visitors last night: "It just won't go away!"

What wouldn't go away Son-shine was about to find out.

He entered the back room; very nearly lost his bearings dizzyingly immediately. There was a wooden gangplank, easy to see. Where it went, to a greyish, somehow-sealed hole at the far end, was equally easy to see. What was above, below, and to either side of the plank was impossible to believe. Outer space? Couldn't be.

A decorator's trick? Son-shine went onto his stomach and hugged the plank. He pulled his comb out of the shirt pocket of his pyjamas and let it drop. If the floor was where it should have been, it would have fallen maybe two inches. Instead it just fell and fell and fell before it got caught up in the tail of a passing comet and went shooting forth.

Barely off his belly, he crawled down the gangplank to the porthole at the end of it. Tentatively reaching out, he touched its plastic membranous covering. It was translucent – he could see through it into more outer space. He poked at it, at first hesitantly, then more and more forcefully. It stretched but wouldn't break.

With confidence in his own invulnerability – another universal trait of children – he got on his knees, tried to punch through the stuff. No go. He rubbed his nose against it, peered through to the other side. There was a funny-looking car there. Didn't have wheels; was streamlined; had exhaust pipes, front, back, underneath and over it.

He stuck his arms into the membrane; reached out, tried to grab it like his kid-sister would a toy. Something blasted out of the thing, burned his hands, knocked him ass-backwards onto just that, his bum. He looked up. A big, brown-skinned man stood on the plank between him and the porthole.

He was wearing a short, white tunic. Had bare legs with sandals strapped up his calf. His hair was a thundercloud. Son-shine spotted lightning flashes going off inside it. Scarily, he had a third eye. Even more scarily, he carried a long, glowing, fractal-edged sword that looked like one of those lightning bolts with a hilt.

The boy scrambled to his feet. Ignoring the abyss to either side of him, he fled down the gangplank. Slamming the door to the back room behind him, he raced through the basement then up the stairs to the main floor. That door he not only slammed but had enough sense to click the padlock shut. Still not content, he stumbled up the stairs to the top floor and dove, fully bed-clothed, into the bathtub with Star-baby.

"Ubi," shrieked Atomaunt. "What's going on? If you've frightened the boy with one of your stupid stories, I'll ..."

========

For the first time since Sunday Mikelangelo Starrus opened all three of his eyes. Nidaba reacted in fright.

========

Dominated by voices within his head – his own, Lord Yajur's, and one other's – he suddenly realized what he could do. He became akin to a five-pointed star: head, one point; arms, one point each; legs, the other two points. He apprehended the peril of the Godchild, cut himself through the cosmicar's hull, fused it shut with his next, virtually simultaneous move, and blazed towards the hole.

He didn't bother wrestling with the boy from the macroverse, simply sliced the membrane between the two universes, and went through it. It didn't just seal behind him; it collapsed upon itself. It wasn't Mik Starrus who stood on the plank on the other side of the membrane. It was Thunder and Lightning Lord Yajur, the Unity of Order.

Macroverse, microverse, the relative size of beings from one to another, none of that mattered. He, one of Thrygragos Lazareme three next-door-to-simultaneous firstborn, was that powerful. Or, put another way, the Universal Substance was that fulfilling. He was also in a state of confusion.

Recently decathonitized, after nearly five hundred years as a (very bright) star in the Sedon Sphere, he couldn't wait to commence righting the universe. Yet, could it be? Was the universe actively helping him out? Had to be. Lord Yajur somehow sensed where he was; what he had just become: A one-man – make that one-devil – invasion force into what had become the Utopians of Weir's homeworld.

Bordering on impossibly long ago, when Grandfather Sedon formed the Sedonshem, him in it, and thereafter took off to conquer everywhere they went except here, the Mighty Moloch (now mostly a huge, otherwise incorporeal eye-mouth in the sky above his own Hidden Headworld) left his mothers on this very planet. Not only that, Yajur somehow also sensed, they were still here.

Almost as remarkably, he additionally gleaned – possibly from the air itself he further fancied – that his mothers remained as inimical to their own children as they had been by the time Grandfather abandoned them, his sole, second generational daughters, to their fates.

In the Name of Order, Yajur promised himself, he'd soon sort that out. And them, you, if they were listening to his thoughts, which they probably were. It was a two way street, though; had to be. Otherwise how could he have learned so much about this place, and the devic race's stunningly enduring female progenitors, so seemingly instantly?

(Even though born singularly, in litters or broods of three, devils were never certain which of the Trigregos Sisters was his or hers conceptive, let alone birth-mother. They did know who their fathers were: Yajur's was Little Star Lazareme, aka Thrygragos Everyman, an oft-times whimsical Great God if ever there was one.

(A little star only in comparison to his father, Dark Son Sedon, Lazareme used to delight in taking on the likeness of the Male Entity, albeit with three eyes, when-ever he deigned to appear before his firstborn. Rather, whenever they forced them-selves to see him as he wanted them to see him, not as they themselves did naturally.

(Which was their idea of Godhood; in Yajur's case as an idealized version of he himself, his individual self.)

He and the Sisters would have a reckoning. They would resolve their differ-ences or, if they proved irreconcilable, he would destroy them before they could destroy him. Also, in the Name of Order!

========

At barely eight centuries old, Ubi Universe was still relatively young by the Utopian standards of New Weir.

========

It was almost unheard of that one of his comparative youth should be granted the status of a named-position, a specific profession, especially that of *'Astronomer'.* His, though, was a particular brilliance. Ones with polymath potential as high and as rawly broad-ranging as his usually burned out, quite literally, before they attained their millennium — when their deserved accolades began to dignifiedly accrue.

That he'd attained – more like been granted – a named-position so young bespoke of the Planetary Council's hope that he would finally start to focus, if not precisely hone, his evident-to-everyone talents. Yet, of the ten thousand planets, he'd been too preoccupied doodling around with a rash of his own pet projects to visit even half; of the two thousand stars, he had thus far missed seven hundred.

Considered therefore uncultured, untraveled, it was equally evident to some of his professional elders and, especially, many of his (jealous?) contemporaries that he lacked the proper temperament to ever reward such accelerated treatment.

Nonetheless, he and his mate, the physicist, who was at least twice his age and, presumably, exerted a settling influence on his wilder side, had been accorded the privilege of becoming a developmental team before their second millennium of existence. Theirs was a unique example but the Planetary Council of this particular world had a long history of being at the forefront of change within Galactic Weir.

This was, after all, where dwelled the Trigregos Sisters.

========

The self-named Ubiquitous Uncle Universe awoke with a start. He could hear his wife-mate screeching from upstairs. Something about frightening the boy. Of late he had been so tired that he hadn't been paying much attention to Atomaunt. He groaned to his feet and limped towards the door leading to the basement. It blew out in his face.

Staggering backwards, he regained his balance as a creature burst through the door. It was something from his, and the Visionary's, worst nightmares.

It had a third eye. That made it a devil.

"You are?" he fumble-mouthed bravely.

"Yajur, Lord of the Sparking Azuras."

"That means nothing to me."

"Nor should it. I am beyond your ken."

So this is what a Master Deva looked like given flesh: brown-skinned; dark hair that sparkled with an electricity that effectively formed a cloudily glowing turban on the top of its head; some kind of simple garment: a short-skirted toga, Universe supposed; bare feet; muscles where he had only fat. This son of Trigregos and one of their Thrygragos Brothers seemed to be about his size, but perhaps he could be any size he wanted to be now that he had flesh.

(Master Devas were possessive beings, yes, but certainly at first they weren't fleshy beings. Only their parents had what passed for physical coherence – a co-agulation, as it were, of what some said was actually Master Deva essence – and the Sisters, as often as not, not much of it.

(By contrast, according to Illuminary annals transferred insubstantially, as if by osmosis, generation after generation, Master Devas amounted to nothing more than unformed energy somehow differentiated by his or her sense of self, of individual-ized intelligence. They were Spirit Beings, plain though never simple.)

Heavy in the jaw; three eyes set deep in the skull; somehow translucent: this Yajur shone with might as much as light. The great long sword in his right hand looked like a bolt of pure lightning. Power, entirely powerful, entirely fear-worthy, that's what devils were given flesh. Ah, but did their very physicality betray weak-ness? Could they be killed like any other hard-body, man, woman or whatever?

Universe was torn between attacking and bowing down in obeisance. The for-mer was what the innate, if frowned upon – and, apparently, personally poorly suppressed – Trinondev part of him wanted to do. After multiple millennia of honouring (instead of just tolerating) the Trigregos Sisters, the indoctrinated, thoroughly modern Utopian part of him urged the latter reaction.

He chose to do neither of the above. He stood fast. "What are doing here?"

"You talk in questions and expect answers in return. I am as stated, and shall not repeat, the Unity of Order. Where are my mothers, the three Great Goddesses?"

"Ah, as to that, you could have just asked nicely. You're already carrying a big stick so there's no need to thump your chest and put on a show. Follow me."

Puffing himself up as best he could, given his complete lack of practise when it came to posturing, he carefully guided Yajur – who probably spent hours, on a daily basis, posing in front of a mirror – out of his house. Seeing them leave from an upper floor vantage, Atomaunt said a silent *'thank you'* to her heroic life-mate and hurriedly wrapped towels around Son-shine and Star-baby.

"Come along my dears, seems we're going to have to start your Journeys of Weir a wee bit prematurely – by a few hundred years."

Connections having already been made, albeit not confirmed for their children, Tom guided Son-shine and Star-baby through the pristine expanse skirting what might be called First Weir City if it had a name other than home. By dawn, the three of them would be on their way to a destination beyond Weir System; beyond Galactic Weir; in some respects, beyond even its otherwise all-encompassing macroverse.

For Atomaunt, it was a dream come true. For Son-shine and Star-baby, it was an adventure starting. Too bad about Uncle Ubi.

He would have to find his own way to salvation … to the Celestial Sphere.

========

"Are you sure this is wise, Yajur?"

"Wisdom has little to do with order, Utopian. Order is beyond wisdom. Order is the natural state of the cosmos. It is so far over and above immutable laws that what ignoramuses such you and your fellow scientocrats identify as its laws are nothing of the sort. They are just the way the things are. But, thanks to the pernicious influence of my breed brother, Order is also what we must now seek to re-achieve.

"In my absence unchecked by anyone, Chaos has been running rampant for five hundred years. In that time he has severely, yet not irreparably, damaged the fundament. Fortunately for everyone, I'm back. I embody Order. It, through me, can and will re-impose itself. Thereafter, and this time not just through me, through you and yours as well, it must rigidly enforced.

"Only then shall we thwart he whom your Earthly cousins named Unholy Abaddon not even two thousand years ago. Only then can the cosmos return to its natural lawlessness." He paused, must have realized he'd been pontificating – more like ranting – and smirked slightly, almost like a Utopian would. Or a human, for that matter.

"You were taking me to my mothers, I believe."

"I know where they were last seen. I'll be happy to take you there; perhaps show you a bit of our Utopia in the process."

"I've no objections to a quick peek. But we'll do it my way."

Lord Order, as he preferred to Yajur, the name Illuminaries of yore gave him, grabbed Universe by the arm. (Antique Illuminaries could have called him Vishnu, but it was already taken.) He elevated the two of them effortlessly into the sky; proceeded to frog-walk Ubi, on the very air itself, towards metropolitan spires he could easily make out many miles away.

The astronomer, as he quickly appreciated, lived in a small neighbourhood; a kind of woodland township amidst vast stretches of greenery. Beyond a forest teeming with wild life and huge, ancient trees rose another kind of forest — blocks of tall buildings linked by walkways, some with moving sidewalks. The only vehicles he could see besides those pedalled by people with their feet were self-contained carts that emitted no exhaust.

"I admire much of what I see here, Universe, but Thrygragos Lazareme, my father, would be appalled. He's also called Thrygragos Everyman for a reason. He likes his places messy, full of people, dirt streets, crude dwellings, tiny farms, smoke billowing, the smells of defecation, butchery, and decomposition. This world, as near as I can make out, is highly structured, pristine, and very efficiently run. Your king must be very wise and very strict."

Universe had to laugh at that; a highly disconcerting act in and of itself.

Shouldn't have thought *'highly'*, he instantly chastised himself mentally. Refocused straight ahead, on where this Yajur was marching him, rather than any other place. To do anything else, especially to look down, only caused the devil to tighten his grip. And that hurt enough already.

He'd already apprehended, with a fingernail-driven pinch and resultantly dreadful certainty, that he wasn't dreaming any of this. His feet didn't feel like they were touching anything at all while they headed toward the metropolis at, it had to be admitted, a remarkable speed. That, he'd additionally self-determined, was due entirely to the fact they weren't flying per se. How the devil was pulling it off – he wasn't just levitating, either; his legs were moving, were therefore doing their propelling – was beyond him.

Further to his present circumstances: laughing, let alone talking of anything while walking on nothing, was a decided shock to the system. It couldn't be anything else. And it was no easy trick to master. (Fortunately he hadn't been chewing gum when he encountered the devil; had he been, continuing to do so might have proved too much multitasking even for a named astronomer.)

Yet he couldn't allow himself to quake, howsoever inadvertently; couldn't show Yajur any sign of weakness. He could – he must – talk as he walked. And he did.

"Kings and governors, though we know of them, are like their laws and enforcers. They're not the Utopian way. Only wild animals mate and bear their own young. Ours is a dictatorship of commonsense and mutual self-interest. We survive so well partially because we have no natural enemies, not even ourselves.

"We have no need of a large number of people because we Utopians live healthily; sometimes into our fifth millennium, sometimes longer. Our elders continue to work until they die. Sickness occurs, rarely; as do accidents and natural disasters but, on the whole, our need for a steady replenishment-stock of young people is not great.

"Our administrators, such as those who currently sit on the Planetary Council, are drawn by lot from the population at large. We rule, if I dare use the word, by consensus. Those who cannot abide our ways are simply not born; their genes are extirpated in our breeding pools. All things considered, I think you will find our existence very orderly."

"Superficially, perhaps. I agree that in a truly orderly world rulers and their rules, as well as bully boys, and girls, to ensure their compliance, are counterproductive to prosperity, let alone any measure of worship-inducing serenity. I nevertheless hold that, for now and the immediate short term future, they will serve an indispensable role. They will act as a means to an end: the return of Order after so long in the throes of Chaos.

"What worries me about this Utopia of yours is how, in such a stale environment, anyone can challenge anyone else, let alone his or her self. Have you outlawed progress, the drive for adventure, individual entrepreneurship, personal betterment, fulfillment?"

"We have outlawed poverty, plague, famine, overpopulation, slavery, warfare, even aggression towards one another. We are not complacent. We have our dreams. There is always something else to learn. All of Weir's worlds are neither as homogeneous, nor as successful as this one, but most are. There are flaws in any system but you have to look very deeply to find any in our Utopia."

"A society that has not found a way to conquer death cannot be considered perfect. We devils are deathless. Are you?"

Without waiting for an answer, he released his hold on the astronomer. Ubi plummeted pell-mell, screaming all the way, arms and legs, head and neck, flailing wildly, towards the ground. Just before impact, Yajur appeared out of the air itself and caught him. The dark-grey matter between-space, of Samsara, mundane reality, was as universal a substance on Weir as it was on the Whole Earth.

"I thought not."

========

Other than size, there was very little hush-hush about Hush Mannering. That was especially true when it came to her mouth. It could motor.

"Nice ring you got there, Daddy Dolph."

"Why thanks, Miss, um, Dodgson, wasn't it?"

"Was, indeed. Mommy Barb Black had one, too. Make that had one, seven."

========

"That's nice."

So was the day, Dolph Dulles thought distractedly. It was certainly true; another glorious day in the paradisiacal hothouse that was this (albeit only acting) Chief of Security's life on Centauri Island. It was equally true that, as acting chief, he had a lot to do, so he didn't bother to ask where she'd suddenly come from.

Had she been waiting for him outside and around the corner from the cafeteria he just come out of? And, if so, why? Was he that charming?

Then something she did say finally registered: "Wait a minute. My mother's maiden name was Barb Black."

"Was it really? Isn't that funny. Mine wasn't."

"Then why did you call her mommy?"

"Same reason I call you Daddy. It's one of my cutesy little quirks."

"Hold on. Didn't you give me this ring?"

"Did I?"

"Maybe not. Listen, little girl …"

"Hush."

"Hush."

"No, hush – as in I'm not finished talking yet."

"Say what?" he gasped, stunned at her presumptuousness.

Dolph Dulles couldn't believe her insolence. (Septuplewoman Barb Black kept her married name after her husband, Andrew *'Droid'* Dulles's death.) Surely there was a limit to what even little charmers like the Fatman's, um, niece (wasn't she?) could get away with. On second thought, not having kids of his own …

"Glad you asked. About her ring, she had six brothers and sisters, right."

"Um, well, sort of. She was real close to a few of her best buds. Got me to call them aunt or uncle. But for some reason they called themselves Quadrupleman, unless it was Quintupleman. Look, I'm kind of busy right now and …"

"I want you to start thinking about them. Not your mom, you need a clear head and that might make you sad and ruin everything. Just the two still alive."

"My Doubleman uncles?"

"That's them. Thanks. Talk soon. Bye."

No, he wasn't charming — but she was a charmer. And he was the one charmed.

========

Lord Yajur, too, had been having second thoughts.

========

Only his were about having had Ubi seek to take him anywhere. Just wasn't on anymore. Couldn't be, not even in an extreme situation such as this. He wasn't above the Head anymore; wasn't anywhere near the same cosmic backyard; and, besides, he couldn't have got out of the night's sky in order to go down to Hadd or New Valhalla, where the Dead walked, even if he'd wanted to. (Which he often did.) He wasn't sure even Sparking Azuras could reanimate Utopians.

Then Universe gasped; something dead men didn't do.

On third thought, he now felt safe surmising, the catch hadn't come too late. The fall hadn't killed Ubi, just left him breathless, though presumably still not death-less. It knocked him out, not killed him. Breathing his own howsoever unwarranted sigh of relief – even decathonitized devils stranded in some other world shouldn't kill lesser beings for fear of losing potential worshippers – he cut them both back between-space to whence they'd come.

Evidently feeling only remotely remorseful at having discomfited the fellow so unnecessarily, he unceremoniously dumped his unconscious cargo on the pavement in front of his house. The day was clement enough, so why bother bringing him inside? It wasn't as if he cared about the astronomer. Besides, he had no intention of apologizing to anyone anyhow.

Opening his third eye as wide as he could without detaching it – which he could have easily done, were he in the mood for parlour games – he scanned the skies. He was looking for tracings of devic energy; found hints of just that over the city's centre. Wielding his lightning blade to slice through the Weird, as devils generally referred to between-space, he cut himself to its vicinity.

He enjoyed making a spectacle of himself so he strode the rest of the way on the air itself; did so in full view of the multitude already gathering in the towers and outdoor walkways.

"Quail, mortals," he bellowed. "The gods have returned!"

========

Suddenly he found himself in a dark space much like the Cathonic Dome — the night's sky above the Hidden Continent of Sedon's Head; ditto the day's sky consequently also called the Sedon Sphere. His lightning blade was sheathed. Defiant of his will, it remained so despite his efforts to draw it.

Three indistinct, yet clearly female figures appeared in front of him.

========

"Wrong, child," they spoke in unison. "The gods have never left. And we are all the gods Utopians will ever need."

"Mothers!" Yajur inclined his head in slight deference to their antiquity. "We thought you dead."

"Wrong again, child. You wished us dead."

"That is unfair. We wished you back with us."

"So that your demon fathers could force us to bend low and bear more of you. That would be unsatisfactory. As well as unappealing and probably impossible, since the Entities rendered you and your fathers sterile when the Female caused Weirstar to go supernova at the Male's command. Or has that changed? Are they fertile again? Are you?"

Master Devas such as his brood-down sister, Metisophia (Titanic Metis, Wisdom of Lazareme), and his younger brother the Librarian (Biblio Drek), ones more inclined to speculation than he was, not to mention learning, claimed the Sisters fused when they made love and split apart again to bear their children, albeit at the same time.

Somewhat similarly, it seemed to Yajur, they sometimes spoke individually, in different voices within the same stream of verbiage; that they vocalized, as it were, different sentences within the same paragraph; that the nevertheless harmonious sounds he heard only seemed to be coming from the three simultaneously.

For that reason he was slightly unsure as to whether he should address them either one at a time or collectively. He chose to stand where he was – on whatever he was standing on in this grey non-space – and speak past them, on the additional assumption they were only projecting what he was perceiving.

"It may be we, and they, never haven't been," he advised the nothingness where they may or may not actually be. "It may be our offspring always were – and invariably still are – as we were when last you saw any of us, your third generational children in particular: namely, Spirit Beings."

"In other words, if you or they ever were fertile you didn't notice."

"We noticed if our shells had offspring, always assuming we hung around that long before moving on." He reckoned that wherever he directed his response, they'd hear him. "As for offspring we could definitely call our own, and no one else's, those we didn't start noticing until we acquired daemonic bodies.

"They're nowhere near as mindful as we were millennia before they started coming along; indeed, they're so useless about the only shells they can dominate are the meanest animals, simpletons and Dead Things. Sill they are ours and, once they have hold of someone, do seem to foster them worshipping whoever their parents were. So I guess that makes them not completely useless."

"Daemons, eh? Do other planets have these daemons?"

"If they did, we didn't realize they might be useful once we debrained them."

"Not the most observant of species are we. But daemons, necessarily debrained, are how you gained physicality. We were wondering."

"Then be grateful I have illuminated you."

"Show gratitude? Now there's a novel request. We habitually decline to be grateful to anyone, if only because Weir System's Utopians, equally habitually, decline to be grateful to us, for our manifest beneficence."

"But not your magnificence," he placated. "You survive without worship."

"We survive on whatever is available: fart fumes, if needs be. Stellar energy, more likely. As you can see, sentient inhabitants hereabouts have done very well by us. If anything they would be grateful to you — for your absence. Tell us, son, who are you and of which tribe?"

He told them. "Better than the other two, we suppose," they considered. "But only moderately. Thrygragos Lazareme at least had some small degree of passion; not to mention the occasional inclination to apply it appreciably. The other two might as well have been impregnating one of these Utopians' development tanks for all they cared about pleasing us."

That the Sisters held Lazareme in higher regard than Great Byron and Varuna Mithras – not to mention their Father Sedon himself, whom they'd left out of the equation apparently intentionally – didn't surprise Yajur. Multiple millennia ago they'd had a thing for the Male Entity, humanized his distaff half, the miraculous Mnemosyne Machine; spent many an hour sharing the same bed.

Perhaps they had more recently as well, whilst he was an impotent star. The Entities, along with Trans-Time Trigon, randomly tumbled throughout space as well as time whenever and wherever he died. And of course Lazareme looked like Helios not just by design. Sedon fashioned him, his firstborn, out of Helios just as the latter formed him out of Cabalarkon (Sed's Daddy Cabby) and Sedon thereafter did for Thrygragos Byron out of himself.

(As for Thrygragos Varuna Mithras, he'd heard of the VAM Entity so maybe Mithras wasn't a Great God so much as an amalgam of Master Devas. Indeed, maybe that's what the 'A' in the middle stood for, '*Amalgam*', not this Ahriman or Aryanman the likes of Metis and the Librarian used to prattle on about.)

"No longer. He spends most of his time asleep and the rest guzzling beer with his best buddies, some of whom aren't even devils, let alone his own children."

"How very little else has changed over the intervening multi-millennia."

A pause, a snigger … or two … or three. Familiar names bandied, more like snorted, derisively. He sensed smarminess. Little wonder Sedon abandoned them here all those selfsame multi-millennia ago. They must have been as unlikeable as they were, by then, useless for anything except annoyance.

From his hosts, who might also be ghosts, there came an audible emission, a final grunt, a grumble, or burp, of resignation and, at last, a welcome return to the business at howsoever many hands at once: "Sparking azuras are unknown to us but, regardless of that, we acknowledge no lords nor any masters. In this we are very Utopian; very Dual Entities as well.

"We are also Trigregos. You may address us individually, by our given names or our attributes. Demeter is the Body, Sapiendev the Mind, Devaura the Spirit. You may also chose to speak to us jointly. We shall address you as Ambassador Yajur. Are you representing just Thrygragos Lazareme or the other two as well?"

"The mind-fucker or the peashooter," Order queried unpleasantly, if irresistibly, echoing their overheard characterizations of, respectively, Thrygragos Byron and Thrygragos Mithras. No immediate response; no discernible change in expressions either. Risible they weren't — as in they wouldn't rise to his bait, no matter how humourously he reckoned he'd couched its delivery.

He shrugged, as yet only vaguely sensing he'd just missed something important in the question. "I believed either perverse happenstance or fantastical fortune brought me to you," he declared. "I now suspect it has to be Grandfather Sedon's doing, albeit for reasons untold. I will, however, accept the appellation '*Ambassador*' …" He nodded more so than half-bowed again; did so more reverently than the first time.

"For the nonce," he qualified, obstreperously. Pressed onwards: "We must speak frankly, mothers. Are you indeed individuals, as we have always been taught? Or are you a collective being which, seeing the way you talk as one yet appear to be three, would make more sense?

"Why do you speak of Lazareme and his two brothers so disrespectfully? Why are you so hateful of your own children? Have you lost the capacity for maternal affection after so many millennia away from us? There is much we do not know about each other. Much we can, even need, to learn from each other. We have so much common ground to explore.

"Dissolve whatever this place is. Take me to your palace; let us sit and drink soma or Cathy, if you have any. Let us be reunited, reacquainted, long lost mothers and long lost solitary son."

(In some respects not surprisingly, Cathy was Cathonic Fluid. It was made of distilled Brainrock, the same miraculous Godstuff his power focus was in its molten then hardened form, not its distilled or liquefied form.)

"You speak eloquently, ambassador, and perhaps we do suffer from a hormonal, maybe even oxytocin deficiency of some sort. But that is neither here nor there. Your actions betray you for what you are: callous, egocentric, monomaniacal, ignorant, and unrepentant.

"We have seen enough. Return to whence you came. Inform *Brother* Sedon that we are on our way back to him … and Lazareme … and Byron.

"But not to lay with them. To slay them!"

Yajur inclined his head yet again, seemingly in sadness. "Seems I was wrong. Grandfather Sedon did not send me hither to be his ambassador."

The remorse was a feint. He came up full of vehemence. "I am his assassin!"

He went for the hilt of his lightning blade, determined to get it out this time. It was coming but before he could withdraw it entirely, he got caught in a sturdy bubble of sheer energy. Rocketed out of wherever he was between-space, blazed into and blasted apart Universe's house. Went through the already reformed SAG Gap, streaked past the Moon and the UNES Liberty, and only regained his senses in another, all-too-familiar dark space on the planet below.

It was neither molten nor liquefied. Was alive!

========

Captain James Aremar demanded and was put into direct contact with Loxus Abraham Ryne on Centauri Island. They exchanged a few choice words.

Doubleman Sean Smythe winced to hear them. Except in the case of direct family, the patriarch was not known as a forgiving man. Considering where they were, in outer space, if he chose to punish Aremar for his effrontery, many others — Smythe likely the most amongst them — would suffer from the blowback.

"What are playing us for?" Aremar was venting so loudly he no doubt expected the Great Man could hear him on the planet below. "Complete idiots? Hey, I can tie my shoelaces, dress myself, cook my own breakfast, shit in the right pot. I'm thoroughly trained, Loxus. Isn't it about time you let us in on what's going on?"

Crackled back the always effective voice of the Great Man: "You will continue to keep me informed, Jim. Ryne, out!"

========

"We are sorry about your family's absence, astronomer," said Trigregos.

"We are also sorry about your home. Given we caused the latter, the former was for us serendipitous. We needed to maintain this wormhole of yours until we knew for certain what our three brothers and children had become. Now that we do, it was just as necessary to destroy it."

Uncle Universe nodded stoically. "Houses can be rebuilt. With your inter-session my wife and children are well on their way out of Weir System. I shall join them presently."

It was time to ask them the question that had recently been bothering not just him. He and Atomaunt had talked about it without resolution. The Visionary had alluded to it, too. "When we were in our development tanks, you tampered with our genes, Tom's, mine, probably even our assigned young ones, Shine and Star?"

It was a fair query; one that, to their credit, they treated respectfully. "For many thousands of years we have felt a kind of tugging on our own genes," explained the sisters, perceptibly speaking as one. "It is very hard to describe but, in time, we came to realize that our brother-creator, Sedon, or someone equally malevolent, was seeking to remake us.

"His-their reasons became manifest once we began hearing from the Female Entity that our devic children were being killed, presumably by her male equivalent — he having become entirely insane once again. What Dark Sedon — let's say it is him – wants is more breeding stock; us or our reincarnations. We had to find a way to discover if that was what we truly wanted as well. Seeing this so-called Unity, this 'Lord Order', has steeled our resolve."

The voices diverged but still seemed as if all three were talking at once: "Our own offspring are now solid beings, have been for some four thousand years we're to gather. That means they've long no longer needed to fuse with each other in order to become variations of Demogorgon, the Conglomerate Deva, whom the Female Entity sometimes still refers to as the Unnameable."

Although she sounded only subtly different, another one carried on their soliloquy: "We knew a later version of the Conglomerate Deva as Thrygragos Varuna Mithras. He wasn't a bad sort, as devils go: Friendly, if a bit too full of himself for our taste; sometimes so much so he'd crack into two or three distinct individuals. But Memory says Mithras died – got himself obliterated, as she put it – perhaps only as long ago as your Atomaunt has been alive.

"If Yajur's any example, the ones left are as intransigently narcissistic, and hence as intrinsically evil, as Sedon and his two actual brothers always were. Yajur's protestations to the contrary, they care nothing for freedom, for individual self-determination. They wish only exaltation — to be worshipped not necessarily wholeheartedly but endlessly."

Were the sisters taking turns yammering on? Had to be; though, howsoever admirably, the three streams of consciousness remained locked onto a solitary topic: namely, how intolerable their loveless offspring remained. "And proper worship – what doesn't so much keep them going as allows them to thrive – necessitates adoration from, and the consequential subjugation of, those who would forsooth worship them."

It seemed to him it had just become Number Two's turn: "All that said, the Dual Entities, in the days when both of them were reliable, taught us too well to allow us to resubmit to our brothers' dubious affections.

"We believe the hole in the wall of your basement was an effort by the Entities to further educate us. We have learned. We have destroyed the hole. That does not mean Sedon and/or his lackeys will stop trying to have us reincarnated. Eventually, we will have to face him. Eventually, we shall have to defeat him."

The third sister now spoke: "We manipulated your genes, yes, but we do not expect your coming child to become our lone champion, our sole paladin. Many more millennia will have to pass before you and yours can develop into new Trinondevs. We shall have a reckoning: us with the Great Gods and their children; with our selfsame children.

"Yours and Tom's children shall be but the progenitors of our army. They cannot be allowed to develop within Galactic Weir, however. That would go in the face of all the Entities have urged on us and we have urged on you Utopians. So that is why we sent them away; facilitated their leaving, put better. The new Warriors of Weir shall be bred beyond Weir."

Once again, they seemed to speak simultaneously: "We three are used to deal in terms of thousands of years. You Utopians are used to living them, though nowhere as long, as interminably, as us. Who knows? Perhaps you will still be around to lead our forces against that of Sedon and his devils. You and yours will be leaders, not simply more pegs in the cooperative jigsaw that is this society."

"I like this society."

"As do we. Necessity will be served, astronomer."

"Necessity has always been served in the Utopia of Weir. Consensus addresses necessity. Give me time, perhaps only a few days. A chance is all I ask. I can come up with a way to rid the cosmos of your brothers and your children – and convince the Planetary Council of its efficacy. I can be very persuasive."

"So we bred you to be."

Unsaid but understood was the fact that the Trigregos Sisters were also devils. And Ubi Universe intended to play no favourites.

========

A huge eye, a star with a mouth, approached him.

"BACK SO SOON, GRANDSON?"

"Not grandson, though you are the grandfather of all liars. I have been to Weir, real Weir. I have met the Three Sisters. Your sisters, not your daughters!"

"BACK SO SOON, NEPHEW?"

****

Fourth Moon: **Starrus On The Liberty**

========

Thursday, December 4, 1980

Daybreak was now Twilight, the land thereof, aka Sedon's Outer Nose. The Mighty Eye-Mouth in the Sky did not have an outer nose. Sooth said, neither did the Moloch Sedon when he walked the Hidden Headworld himself. Which he could do; while simultaneously remaining the brightest star in the Sedon Sphere.

There wasn't much he couldn't do on the Inner Earth. Including, one might suppose, growing an outer nose.

========

Demetray evening, the second day of Tantalar, the tenth month of the Sedonic Year and the second month of the Mithradic Ternary was, in its own way, as exciting as Sedonda Night for Headworld stargazers. When darkness fell on Sedonda, more than sixty stars were missing from the Cathonic Dome. Amateur and professional astronomers alike pulled out their dusty star maps and tried to determine which Master Devas no longer shone in the Sedon Sphere.

That debate was continuing when, two nights later, one star apparently returned. It was in the eastern sky, the area generally thought to be populated by the catasterized sons and daughters of Thrygragos Lazareme. It was the brightest star there, which probably meant it was Lord Yajur, the Unity of Order. Bigger than anyone remembered, it had a distinctly reddish tinge to it. If there was such a thing as an angry star, this was it.

It was still there the next night, Birhym the third of Tantalar, bigger and redder than the night before. Star Sedon – which ordinarily was the lone, Inner Earth star in the northern sky but had a known, albeit chaotic history of wandering – had joined it in the east and actually seemed smaller, less luminescent, than Star Yajur.

During the early evening, the heavens were almost as bright as during daylight. The brilliance was coming from the two stars, seemingly at war with one another. Towards middle midnight, what would have been midnight over Hadd and northern spots along the same meridian, Star Yajur flared out of the Cathonic Dome.

By dawn, Sapienda, Thursday on the Outer Earth, Star Sedon was back in the northern sky. Stargazers throughout the Hidden Headworld assumed he'd won. And maybe he did; though, for devils, cathonitization was punishment, not reward. So maybe it was the other way around. Or maybe it was a win-win situation.

Star Yajur got away, again, but Star Sedon was still there. Which, for denizens of the Whole Earth on both sides of the Dome, was probably for the best – because it meant that it, the Dome, was still there, too. After all, no one in their right mind could possibly want a second Great Flood.

Ah, but what about those in their wrong mind?

========

Alarms went off throughout the Liberty.

========

"Battle stations, battle stations!" came the automatically triggered voice in a dozen languages. Stark naked, James Aremar raced out of his quarters onto the bridge. He was brandishing his prized, early post Civil War era Colt '45; took one look at the scene presented before him, a dozen of his men pointing their weapons at a human form lying prone on the floor, and silently glared at Doubleman.

Sean Smythe bent over, placed his pistol against the newcomer's temple, felt for the carotid artery, nodded. Someone shut off the alarms, no one relaxed.

"We know him, Jim. It's Mikelangelo Starrus, the guy Big Max wanted to take your place as Cosmicommander-Designate but ended up as only a Cosmicaptain. Cosmicar Two was his baby, until it disappeared a couple of days back. He's still alive but … here, have a closer look."

He turned Starrus onto his back. With the muzzle of his gun he indicated a bulge in the man's forehead, just above where his eyebrows met.

"What is it?"

Smythe nudged the bulge. It was a flap. Underneath it was an eyeball. "An eyelid. Mik's got a third eye."

"Fucking Hell!" cursed Aremar, rather predictably. Sometimes he simply wasn't in the mood to cuss creatively. "Three of you pick him up and bring him to my ready room. The rest of you keep them company. I don't want him killed but, if he makes one false move, I want him pinned. He makes a threatening gesture, I want him pin-cushioned. Where're my clothes?"

"Where you left them, I guess."

========

"Nothing yet, Smythe?" demanded Aremar much later that day.

"Dick-Fifty! Something might have happened to Abe Ryne, Jim. Protocol says we defer to his son, Erech."

"That little twerp? Perdition with protocol. He's a God-cursed idiot! Shit, Sean, you know what he's like. He does nothing without the old man's say so."

"There's a reason for that."

Aremar took a few seconds to figure out what Doubleman was implying. When realization hit, it was akin to an epiphany. "Autosuggestion – Ryne's fabled *voice*?"

"Knowing the patriarch," agreed Smythe, "Erech would already have his instructions."

"Get hold of him then. Where is he?"

"Already have. In Paris. On his way back from Budapest where he arranged for his mother to be taken to the States. It seems the killer countess is dying. A bit more than twenty years too late, if you ask me." Erech's mother Ramona nee Avar really was a countess. Rather, she became one when her father Zygion (the Axis supra codenamed Count Viper) died in the midst of two wars: the worldwide conflagration and the Secret War of Supranormals.

Not too many years after WWII ended, long by then Countess Avar almost certainly assumed the identity of the Queen Conqueror. That being the case, it could only have been a short term nom de guerre since it eventually turned out her supra-side was none other than Faceless Strife. Except, during those selfsame Supra Wars, which began in 1938 but didn't end until late 1955, no one realized it. And, if she could be believed, that included Ramona herself.

(On April 30, 1960, Ramona-Strife had killed – or been responsible for ordering the death of – Trebleman Joan Smith, the last of the four female Psychic Siblings. Their surnames indicated they weren't related by birth but the shock of her murder, of suddenly becoming a Doubleman and not a Trebleman, had traumatized both Smythe and Johann Schmidt for years afterwards.)

"And …"

"He says go with the flow."

"Whoopee! What's that supposed to mean?"

"Adapt, adopt, and improve. Whatever presents itself."

"And what's presented itself is Mik Starrus."

"Must be time to talk with him then."

========

Although the Cosmic Express was more impressive, not to mention far more ambitious, the UNES Liberty beggared anything humanity had managed to construct, launch, and keep in space to date. Its construction may have been supervised by personnel seconded from New Century Enterprises, a US-based company, but for all that it was primarily a joint effort between the Soviet Union and the United States.

The States may have provided most of the ready cash needed to compensate NCE and its workers, but much of the advanced technology that went into it benefitted from discoveries made by the onetime anonymous Conqueror (later on the King Conqueror to Ramona's at the time equally anonymous Queen Conqueror). Albeit by then as the self-designated Conquering Christ, the lone truly verifiable *'supranormal'* genius of the Twentieth Century revealed himself to be Jesus Mandam in 1951.

Jesse spent most of the last ten years of his short life in the USSR. (He died on his 33rd birthday, ostensibly in an unscheduled explosion of a hydrogen bomb that he no doubt helped the Soviets build.) Indeed, until the eccentric, perpetually-helmeted Silver Signaller who called himself Shelter brought aspects of it to the UN's Space Council – and thence to New Century Enterprises – most of Mandam's notes were the exclusive property of the Soviet Union.

Since supras were a well guarded secret; since as well they had hardly been a factor since 1955; very few today were aware of their existence. Of those, almost all were backroom men – along with, much more rarely, backroom women – who operated furtively from within the Vatican, the Pentagon, the Kremlin, the United Nations, and certain very large, very pervasive, multinational corporations.

About the only public personage was Loxus Ryne, head of the philanthropic Alliance of Man and the patriarch of the obscure, so called Illuminated Faith of Xuthros Hor. Despite being nearly eighty, the United Nations appointed him chief of SPACE (the Society for the Prevention of Alien Control of Earth; which, like AMERICA, the Alliance of Man for the Extermination of Resisting International

Criminal Agencies, was his own acronym). Ryne was given the right to choose his team leaders.

As a consequence, lunar coordination was in the hands of veterans from AMERICA, notably the cripple Dr Immanuel Dark. In a number of respects this made sense. Ryne's mission was to preserve the status quo. He ate and drank secrecy. Secrecy, and results, were his mandate. Naturally he preferred to deal with his own people – which was why James Aremar, the prematurely grey protégé of the Great Man, was made overall commander of the Liberty.

OJ Maxwell had always been Operations Chief of AMERICA. However, towards the latter part of the Sixties, in deference to Max's advancing age – the man who, on Centauri Island the previous Sunday, became Mr No Name was between forty and fifty during AMERICA's heyday – and the fact that Ryne preferred to keep him close to his side, a young but bold and highly effective Aremar became Field Commander for most of AMERICA's strike forces, including the notorious bombing of Trigon in 1968.

Although barely thirty-five when Ryne approached him ten years later, Aremar had no qualms about taking on the Liberty. He was a child prodigy, with a knack for all things mechanical, who had come to the attention of Loxus Ryne and the Alliance of Man at an early age. A natural engineer, the Alliance insisted he take his baccalaureate at the University of Houston in General Humanities. While with AMERICA he completed, by correspondence, a masters degree in Strategic Affairs through the nearby Academy of Man.

As academically accomplished as he became, his gift wouldn't be denied. He taught himself to fly, even designed the ultralight in which he trained on the weekends. Once AMERICA was disbanded shortly after crushing WORLD in '70, Ryne and his advisers, predominantly Immanuel Dark and Virginia Mannering, relented and allowed Aremar to join the aerospace division of New Century Enterprises.

Conditioned by his years in AMERICA, Aremar was an adrenaline addicted action junkie. He insisted on test piloting NCE's most experimental planes, especially ones he'd helped design. On weekends, he graduated from target shooting and hunting to thrill-seeking, survivalist sponsored, wilderness jaunts. Once he was lowered naked by helicopter high up in Yellowstone National Park and reached a town, three days later, still naked but wearing the pelt of a cougar.

For a time he dated Jane Ryne but it didn't work out. Eight years younger than he was, the patriarch's daughter by Barbara Plantagenet wasn't nicknamed Tempest for fun. He'd never forget the night she wanted him to share their bed with the other Jade Tempest, another James as well, her twin brother.

'You're a regular rock,' she backhand-complimented him: *'Unfortunately I prefer my men vegetables. At least they breathe.'*

In fact, his mind was almost as rigid as his body was supple. Deeply conservative, he believed strongly in the survival of the fittest. If he worked for the WORLD instead of the AMERICA, he'd have been just as fanatical. For him winning was everything. He didn't mind stepping on toes but preferred crunching heads.

Even though he cultivated the gruffness of a marine, his quasi-military experience was limited to AMERICA. Despite its name, that organization operated under the banner of the United Nations. It was only sent against criminal agencies that had little or no political clout. Like the Czarist Glomen (whom Russian communists despised), the Worldwide Order (who were mostly extortionists), or the Greek Black Rose of Anarchy (who, by definition, anyone in any kind of authority thought worse than the pneumonic plague), AMERICA never targeted the Mafia or, much to the consternation of some of its financial backers, trade unions.

Like Abe Ryne (who was revered by old timers, on both sides of the Iron Curtain, as the man who once convinced Adolf Hitler to shave off his moustache), Aremar was considered apolitical. The only cold war baggage the patriarch carried was his UN passport. Aremar's was from the States but, given his other, most spy-worthy knack – his uncanny ability to speak dozens of languages without a trace of an accent – customs agents generally assumed he was a native and rarely bothered to ask for it. Thus, besides his credentials and reputation as someone who ruthlessly got the job done, he was an ideal choice to command the Liberty.

James Aremar was a deviant – though he knew it not, the son of Emperor Energy, the long gone leader of the wartime Society of Saints, and the supranormal called Headmistress. However, as Ryne often remarked to his few confidantes, the ones whose memories had not been wiped by amnaesthetics or redacted by Anthean witch glamours, Aremar was the kind of supra all men should be.

He was man for the future, when the Tower of Babel ceased being a homonym for babble and a single language, universally understood, became the norm.

(*'He's an able man,'* the patriarch would say. To which the now nearly sixty year old Anthean teacher, Virginia Mannering, another often called Headmistress, would invariably respond: *'More like a Cain!'*)

Over a hundred and fifty men – at Aremar's insistence, no women were allowed aboard – were shuttled to the UNES Liberty less than a week earlier. Of these, almost a quarter were from the Soviet Union, another quarter from the United States, and the remaining eighty or so from just about every civilization on the Known Earth. Aremar knew them by name; knew most of their languages as well.

He wasn't a people person. Highly opinionated, he was brief to the point of snappy; could be quite demeaning. Well-versed in tactics, his experience was respected. To a degree, so was he. However, he had already gained a justifiable reputation amongst the crew for being a stern, oft-times unreasonable disciplinarian. When he was in charge, it usually wasn't a case of shape up or ship out; it was a matter of you're good or you're not here.

He believed in second chances about as much as he believed in an afterlife – which was, as he put it, zilch multiplied by nada then divided by zero.

========

Cosmicaptain Mikelangelo Starrus spent the balance of the day in sickbay (the infirmary), under heavy guard,.

========

Another eminently able man, he busied most of that time sleeping. As he rested something almost as remarkable as it being there in the first place occurred. The bulge in his forehead – eyelid, lashes, and all – subsided. Now it was little more than a pimple. When he woke up, only his two human eyes opened.

He was allowed a supervised shower and given back his cosmicompanion uniform, which had been thoroughly examined then cleaned. He ate heartily but hardly said a word to his keepers. Seemly confused, he occupied an inordinate amount of time nervously rubbing his forehead. It wasn't so much that it was itchy. It was more like he was trying to massage his memory and, with it, his mind back together again.

Starrus was a test pilot, something in which his somewhat similar looking *'host'*, James Aremar, had also dabbled. Also like Aremar, Starrus was thirty-seven. Unlike his host, he had seen more than his share of combat. Bracketed by his years in AMERICA were two stints in Vietnam, first as a non-national volunteer until '65, then flying for Air America, a CIA run operation in South East Asia during the early Seventies.

Thereafter he'd gone on to Project Centauri, what New Century Enterprises (NCE) advertised as a privately sponsored astronaut program. He would have been Cosmicommander had not Avatar Sol showed up and won over Alfredo Sentalli, the main money man behind the Express. (Abe Ryne, whose father Charan founded NCE at the turn of the century, retired in 1955.)

'These things happen,' his mentor, OJ Maxwell, consoled him. *'So does shit. But you don't roll yourself in either feeling sorry for yourself.'*

His mother had been a Swede who moved to Toronto Canada, where Starrus was brought up, after giving birth to him in Northern Italy. Therefore, on Sean Smythe's recommendation, Aremar assigned another Italian Canadian, Luke Domenis, a member of the multinational Lunar Assault Crew Four, to be with the Cosmicaptain. Domenis was barely twenty-five, the same age Starrus had been when he dropped the bomb on Aegean Trigon and saw the entire island vanish.

About the only thing they had in common was their heritage and the fact they spoke English and Italian equally well. Domenis was no psychologist; his background was police work. As per his instructions, he tried to befriend Starrus but they hadn't clicked in either language. When he told him that Aremar and Smythe wanted to see him, Mik mumbled something in a language he took to be Swedish.

"I know Swedish as well," grinned Aremar, just before he and Smythe entered the infirmary.

"If it comes right down to it," said Smythe, "I know Italian better than both of you."

He didn't add why that was the case. (Only Ryne and a very few of his closest advisers knew the true origin of the Psychic Siblings.)

<<"How do you feel, Mik?">> asked Aremar in Swedish.

<<"Remember us?">> queried Smythe in Italian.

"Speak bloody English!" demanded Starrus.

"Hey, cool down, bud," cautioned Smythe. "Unless you haven't figured it out yet, we've a bit of a situation here. You have any idea where you are?"

"Seeing you two, it has to be the Liberty. What day is it?"

"Thursday, Houston and Centauri Island time."

"Five days since the launch. What's happened to me?"

"We were hoping you'd be able to tell us, Mik," soothed Smythe. "We spotted your cosmicar and something else out here on Sunday night. You guys were transmitting all sorts of gibberish between each other then there was some kind of blip on our screens. A flash of light, an explosion, blanked us for a few minutes. The cosmicar was still out there but you'd stopped transmitting.

"Two days of silence later, Tuesday, downstairs finally gave us the okay to bring the car on board. We were working out how to do just that when we picked up another beam of light coming out of the car. It headed straight into something massive that had appeared in near space. The beam and it collided, sort of melded: cauterized the fabric of time and space, if you will; healed it over, if you won't.

"At almost the same time, the cosmicar itself vanished. Hours later one more bolt of light came out of where the object had been and headed straight for Earth — straight for the northern Pacific Ocean. Whereupon it vanished, as if extinguished either in the atmosphere or in the ocean itself. That was the situation until you popped onto the bridge first thing this morning.

"That about size it up, Jim?"

"Except for a couple of three-letter words like why and how."

"I can answer a third one, I think," offered Starrus, who looked and sounded noticeably more comfortable now that he was with people he knew fairly well. "Who? The something else out there on Sunday was Colonel Avatar Sol, the commander of the Cosmic Express. The flash of light you saw was me or, rather, what had happened to me. The Tuesday lightshow was also me."

"You don't look like a bolt of light to me, Mik," observed Aremar sardonically. "Got any theories?"

Starrus indicated the little lump in the centre of his forehead, just above where his eyebrows met. "Checked this out?"

"Spotted it instantly," deadpanned Smythe. He hesitated, then decided to bare all: "Damn near forty years ago I had one of those things myself. Ever heard of the devil-ray?"

"What are you on about, Smythe?" demanded Aremar.

"You might as well know the truth as well. Forty years ago there was no Sean Smythe, no Johann Schmidt, no Joan Smith, no Barb Black. No Double, Treble, Quadruple, Quintupleman. We weren't septuplets, weren't Psychic Siblings.

"We were a regular teenager by the name of Leandro D'Angelo. We had regular parents, Raphael and Sophia; regular brothers and sisters, too: Anita, Peter, Claudia and Gabriel, to name the eldest besides myself. I was the fourth, born in '26, a year before Gabriel. More came later.

"You wouldn't know Gloriella or the twins, Aires and Thalassa, whom my parents adopted in 1933, the same year Glory was born. They were already twelve or so: waifs wandering the streets of Mussolini's Roma. Even if you've heard of us, you probably don't know about Marcello, '*El Nino*', who was born in '35 and died, was killed in fact, in '39.

"You told me you'd read about Belificent, Jim. She was WORLD's second victim, murdered after her wedding to Aristotle Zeross. The Worldwide Order's first was Trebleman Joan Smith, also once me. You've met my two surviving sisters, Tereza and Anna Maria, and my brother, John Paul. Yes, I'm one of those D'Angelos."

========

Sean Smythe explained that, in 1943, he, Anita (Nita), Pietro (Peter), Claudia (Cloud) and Gabriel (Gabe) had been exposed to the devil-ray, a device made by their maternal grandfather, Sedon then Satan St Synne. He skipped his always classified activities during the war entirely; noting only that whatever he'd been able to do, he could no longer. His powers, if that was the word to use, had atrophied.

He was a Norman Normalman again. Only there were seven of him instead of one. He claimed Loxus Ryne and a few others, notably his long time confederates, the Maxwells and Headmistress Virginia Mannering, knew that Doubleman – back then, a year after the end of the war, Septupleman – was all that was left of the once feared supra *'Syndicaliste'* (a French word, with an *'e'*) called Amoebaman.

Smythe's real parents, Raphael D'Angelo and Sophia nee St Synne, were deliberately kept in the dark. They thought Leandro dead, like Nita, Peter, and Raphael's sister, Mnemosyne eventually Heliopolis, another devil-rayed victim of Sedon St Synne. For thirty five years, as one self after another was killed or died, he had never told anyone what was now only Doubleman's secret.

As he listened to Smythe speak, Aremar slumped into a chair; contemplated how crazy this whole mission was — always had been! Beset by doubts, he opted for bravado. "Any idiot could have figured out you had an unnatural bond with the other Doubleman, Johann Schmidt, but who could have guessed you were once the same person?"

"Not you obviously. If you'd known more about supras, maybe you'd have suspected it. Especially had you seen us together very often. For the last two decades the patriarch has deliberately assigned us different tasks. Right now Schmidt is attending to Ryne's business in another matter — tracking down Harry Zeross, Ringleader, the so-called Last of the Supranormals, as it happens.

"Truth be known, other than the strangeness on Centauri Island in '65 and, to a minor degree, the Hong Kong business in '70, Johann and I only worked together once since Belificent's murder. Much as I might like to, were circumstances different, I won't bother teasing you when that was." His eyeballs glinted anyhow.

"Like the Great Man, OJ Maxwell, you, Jim, you, Mik, and Dmetri Diomad – captain of the only other cosmicar located thus far – both of us, both Doublemen, were involved in the 1968 bombing of Trigon. If Ryne's coded messages from Centauri and the bouquet of black roses that suddenly appeared in your ready room Sunday night are any indication, our past isn't just coming back to haunt us.

"Our past is back, with a vengeance."

========

"I want you to think carefully," requested Smythe of Starrus. "Have you had any contact with Sedon St Synne?"

"Not as such. A year or so ago I was approached by his granddaughter, Tereza, whom I gather is sort of your sister, and her husband, Simon Lancz. They were trying to recruit me for Signal System. I was already committed to the Cosmic Express, so I turned them down. But before I made up my mind, I went to Stanford for the interview and St Synne's on the life-support there. Does that count?"

"Perhaps, perhaps not. When you were with AMERICA did you have any close encounters with Strife, other than the final assault on WORLD's stronghold in Hong Kong?"

"You know bloody well I did. I was an agent of AMERICA. On three separate missions I came face to face – or is that face to non-face? – with this Strife. Once, as Schmidt would remember if he was here, we had her figured as the girlfriend of one of the Black Roses; Echion Sangati was his name. Until Kong, she slipped through our fingers. Damned elusive that one. Never figured out how she got away Scot free every time."

"Fortunately we did. Eh, Jim?"

"I don't tell stories out of class, Sean, and I don't see what you're getting at."

"Trying to find out how Mik got a third eye. Only way that can happen is if he was exposed to either St Synne's devil-ray or Strife's miracle key. Problem is, I haven't heard of either doodad since the Forties. Mind you, once St Synne showed up again in '52, there was all sorts of talk of the Soviets having the ray at least. It was never verified, however."

"Sorry, I don't buy it," disclaimed Aremar. "I shouldn't have to remind you how cooperative the Soviet Union's been on this mission. We wouldn't be up here without them. And WORLD's Strife was no closet supra; not even an honorary member of the Soviet Supra Supreme for all her misdeeds on their behalf.

"She was an Anthean or some other sort of witch gone rogue. If they're trained in what Headmistress called the Forbidden Way – forbidden since '65 or so, that is – they could do things most people find incredible but clearly weren't, um, how shall I put this?" He searched his remarkable vocabularies. "Unnatural? Impossible?"

Neither Starrus or Smythe were prepared to say. They let him sort it out himself. He was the multilinguist after all.

"Anyhow," compromised Aremar, "To the best of my knowledge, you can't train to become a supranormal. You either are or you aren't. The training part comes later. If the Strife of ten years ago had a Miracle Key, surely she would have used it. Your notion of a devil-ray may have something to it, Sean. I mean, what are thought beams if not another kind of ray."

"Put that together with your theory that the Moon could be the Antheans' Big Shelter," grasped Smythe, amazed yet again at Jimmy Aremar's insightfulness. "And that they might be using their beams to send Panharmonium Propaganda downstairs, it isn't that much more of a leap to say they hit the Express with a devil-ray."

"Precisely. And if we further assume that the devil-ray, for whatever reason, only works downstairs, they then triggered the Gypsium in the Express to bring all their newly made three-eyed wonders up here. Is it or is it not true that all those aboard the Express were the children or relatives of documented supras from the war until roughly '55?"

"In other words they were potential supras," Sean Smythe understood.

Before he moved to SPACE, Smythe worked with Maxwell on Centauri Island for most of the Seventies. They had often wondered why Al Sentalli, undoubtedly at the urging of Loxus Ryne, had selected such a comparatively young crew – no one was over forty – and, more especially, ones with such a dubious background. If Aremar was right, Antheans had a lot to do with it.

"The ray," concluded Starrus, who had been listening intently, "Awakened that dormant potential – made latency patency!"

"But the Ants fucked up," added Aremar. "Their ray fractured the Express. At least one of the cosmicars ended up downstairs." He was referring to Diomad's, the one they'd heard earlier in the week that had turned up in the Aleutians. "And yours popped out a little short of its mark; that is until Tuesday, when whoever is down there retrieved it. The rest are probably inside the Moon already, along with maybe even this Avatar Sol character. Maybe you better tell us what you could do when you were a supra, Sean."

"Maybe I better clarify that a little. The only thing myself or any of the others could do after roughly mid '46 was communicate with each other mentally over distances great or short. That's why we were called the Psychic Siblings. However, what Leandro did was manufacture bodies.

"Not necessarily duplicates of himself, though he could do that too, but other functioning, generally short-lived adults. These constructs, for want of a better word, were amoeba men. Leandro was Amoeba Prime. We Amoebamen could do that, too – albeit with even shorter lifespans for ours. But, like I said, not for long after Prime died on Sakhalin in '46."

"Yet, for some reason, seven of you survived Leandro."

"That we did," Smythe said to Aremar and Starrus. "Guess we'd become true individuals by then. Let me tell you, while we had it, it was an awesome ability. Done entirely by concentration, as near as we could figure. However, where the bodies came from or where they went, we never learned – though the D'Angelo children's Aunt Dolores, Superior Sorrow, occasionally talked about some place called Shadowland. She said we were shadow warriors given substance out of the Grey. According to her, this Grey was universal. She also called it Samsara, the stuff that binds."

"Well, whatever it is," observed Aremar, "These extra bodies of yours had to come from somewhere. That's a certainty. We could speculate endlessly but I think St Synne's device was well-named. Call it black magic if you like, but I reckon his ray caused people to become possessed, quite literally, by devils; turned them into supranormals. Somehow those devils are still around and, devil-ray, Miracle Key, or whatever, Mik is possessed by one – just like Leandro D'Angelo back in the Forties. Know any good exorcisms?"

"Death?" cracked Sean. "As I said, Leandro's devil, if that's what gave him his abilities, didn't transfer to me or any of my so called Psychic Siblings. Not for long anyhow." Smythe saw Starrus go pale and hastened to reassure him. "Mind you, when Nita and Peter were killed, their devils went back into the typing pool, as it were, only to be pulled out later on – either by the devil-ray, in the case of Memory of the Angels, or the Miracle Key, in the case of the monstrosity, Demon Land."

That wasn't what Mik wanted to hear, either. "Then again," the Liberty's Doubleman hastened to qualify, "There are dozens of examples of powers wearing off after a few years."

"Years!" gasped Starrus, unable to suppress his anxieties any longer. "I don't want to die, but I sure as fuck don't want to be possessed by Lord Yajur for years, not even minutes."

"Who's Yajur? The devil?"

"I guess. The name just came to me. I've been so confused these last few days. Hell, Tuesday and Wednesday night I thought I was a fucking star fighting another fucking star over territorial shining rights. Somehow I got away and came looking for Nidaba, that's my wife, and Cosmicar Two. It wasn't there so I sliced my way into the Liberty.

"Don't worry about the hull's integrity. Seems my back draft acts like a welder's torch. Any gash I might have made would have sealed instantaneously."

"Sounds more like teleportation," remarked Smythe. "You probably came through interspace, this Grey we were just talking about. Ants do the same thing via their agates."

"Gypsium!" croaked Aremar.

It didn't matter if Kadmon Heliopolis was on the Moon; if Rom Kinesis was on his way here; if Harry Zeross was reputedly married to a slow-to-age Anthean higher-up named Melina nee Sarpedon (former Witch Superior Morgianna's husband's oppositely coloured twin sister); or if Ringleader's late brother's wife, Hiliarti, was now the Sisterhood's acknowledged Superior.

It didn't matter if the so called Gypsium Triumvirate – Kinesis, Heliopolis or Zeross, who was the same age as both he and Starrus – were responsible for what was up here. Mere mention of the ineffable Godstuff was enough to acidify his stomach and make what was left of his hair go from grey to white then start falling out in figurative clumps.

"You know what they say," shrugged Smythe needlessly.

Starrus swallowed his own aversion to the dreaded word Gypsium (which Rom Kinesis supposedly coined in 1948), and all it brought back to him, then persevered: "I figured we could help each other. We're veterans of AMERICA, after all, and I didn't like the look of that citadel. It reminded me of Trigon."

"Wait a minute!" Aremar leapt to his feet. "What citadel?"

Mik Starrus suddenly began to glow. Domenis went for his gun. Aremar didn't have time to yell anything at anyone before a flash of energy atomized the bathrobe he was wearing and Starrus was on his feet. Domenis cowered backwards, gun forgotten. Everyone did.

The cosmicaptain was all light, just not yet blindingly so. Manufactured a skin-tight, black and gold suit of clothing; spread his arms and legs, became akin to a five pointed star; his third eye a beacon shining out of his forehead. A beam of radiance sliced through the hull. It hit the supposedly empty crater on the moon's surface.

On screens throughout the Liberty, via transmission to Earthbase Houston and thence to Centauri Island, appeared a magnificent structure. It had the look of a domed pagoda surrounded by three stylized, pointy-tipped, more like pinnacles than minarets. Could have indeed passed for a metallic island. And not just any island, either.

As Starrus had just said, at least superficially it did resemble the Aegean island of Trigon that sank or otherwise disappeared a dozen years earlier. Besides being made of metal there was one major difference between the Lunar Citadel and the triple-peaked, natural landform, however.

Magnification showed a stylized black rose imprinted atop the dome.

=========

Just then they all heard it – the twang of an unearthly electric guitar.

HELIOS WAS ON THE LIBERTY!

****

Fifth Moon: Yajur On The Moon

========

Thursday, December 4, 1980

No alarm sounded this time; no automatically-triggered computerized voice chimed "Battle Stations!" in a half-dozen languages.

There was instead just the insistent twang of what could have been Jimi-Hendrix-style feedback tipping the opening notes of an overture being played by a Celestial Orchestra. Men put down what they were doing, tried closing their ears to the resonance, resist its hypnotic pulsations.

To no avail. Not even a deaf man, had their been any aboard the Liberty, could have withstood it.

One by one, the self-styled Liberators of the Moon became transfixed.

========

An energy bubble formed in the centre of the flight command deck. Through it stepped a being apparelled as if a Walt Disney wizard, complete with floor-length gown and conical cap. He had long, dirty brown hair that stretched to his waist and an equally long, well-combed beard that hung almost as far. The man was Caucasian; had the look of an ancient seer without appearing to be very old at all.

He was left-handed, like Hendrix, but his was an electronic lute rather than a Stratocaster guitar. Neither was it a right-hander turned upside-down. Sure, it was a custom-made job, but no one there would ever likely find out who built it — assuming the wannabe magician didn't build it himself, in his spare time — because, in some respects, it hadn't been built yet.

Twiddling buttons and plucking strings, the therefore more like technomage altered the twang slightly. The floor between the flight deck and the infirmary below became immaterial. He floated down through it to the room where Starrus, Aremar, and Smythe were meeting. Jimi Hendrix had been dead for ten years; the man who made such an impressive entrance in front of them had predeceased Hendrix by a couple more.

Suppressed within Mik Starrus, the battered spirit being that was Lord Yajur thought the figure Anti-Patriarch Cain gone young again. The beard was much the same; maybe the man was, too: the very man — make that Entity, in his first lifetime — who destroyed himself, and so much more, six hundred and sixty-one years before 'Uncle Sedon' raised the Cathonic Dome nearly six thousand years ago now.

He was (probably) mistaken, though. This wasn't Abel's brother; his slayer, dot-ditto. This was Cain's father, Alorus Ptah, the First Patriarch of Golden Age Humanity and the man who had made, not made himself, the Male and Female

Sphinxes that very nearly devoured the entirety of the devic expeditionary party as led by Yajur's father, Thrygragos Lazareme.

The sphinxes actually had names, the devil recalled: Ginny the Gynosphinx and Andy the Androsphinx. They still existed as well: the former, who nowadays called herself All the Invincible, on the Prison Beach of Incain, at the southernmost extremity of the Head's Cattail Peninsula; the latter, long moribund, on the Outer Earth's Giza Plateau in Egypt. Among those who escaped such an ignoble fate, Yajur could count himself, his father and his two immediate siblings, the eventual Unities of Chaos and Harmony (Balance) as well as Panharmonium.

Once, when he created the Moloch Sedon, the first devil or Devil, capitalized, Utopian scientocrats of the time considered him the Solitary Entity. At other times, he was so seriously insane he was almost universally referred to as the Mad God. Long no longer alone, he called his female equivalent Miracle Memory; the others had her as the Mnemosyne Machine, though she was all-but-impossibly much more that. Machine-Memory often called him History or, sometimes, just to maintain perspective, *'His Story'*. To that he'd reciprocate with *'Her Story'*.

Not so very long ago (Wednesday, starting near the Outer Earth's Centauri Island, to be precise), while in her evidently mobile, personal Shelter between-space wherever, she further claimed he was cured. At that time Ramona Avar (Lady Guillotine) wondered if he was cured in mercury.

He wasn't. If he was cured, which was by no means a certainty, it was in Gypsium-Godstuff. Whatever else he once was, or would be again, since he tumbled through time like happy children did hula hoops, (he asserted) he was Kadmon Heliopolis in his one hundredth lifetime.

Which meant he was back in action a mere dozen years after his first death.

========

"Greetings, old friends, old enemies," said the Merlin, capitalized, as in wizardly — not merlin, lower case, as in falconiform. "I am Helios, Light of the World, called Sophos the Wise. I bring Brilliance, Enlightenment and Freedom to the Whole Earth."

He strummed some power-chords. The room became sparkly, shimmering with colour, like the Northern Lights; like, as well, much the same thing Yajur's brood sister self-generated so often before Chaos as good as killed her, thus instigating the 1000 Days of Disbelief, a mite less than 500 years earlier on the Inner Earth.

"I am the original technomage, the precursor of Old and New Weir's scientocrats. I am the Wizard of Wit and Wisdom, of Warped Waves and Wondrous Ways, the Lightray Lunatic. But my lunacy is that of love and peace, mutual understanding, mutual respect and, above all, happiness. I am the Holograph Houdini. My *'Holocaster'* plays the most mesmeric of melodies. Monitor now, as it manifests the most miraculous of motion pictures."

He began to tease the strings, creating a backbeat and lead simultaneously. The room resolved into a cloud. Far below lay a Mediterranean Island, relatively tiny and immediately recognizable, especially to the three most chosen of his Liberty-wide audience. With its three distinctive and impressive rock spires surrounding its hump-like crown, Mikelangelo Starrus, James Aremar, and Sean Smythe knew it at once as Trigon.

As if unseen angels they zoomed in for a closer look. Three boys were climbing one of the rock spires. The youngest was around five, the middle one about eight, the third perhaps twelve or thirteen. Smythe remembered Aristotle Zeross, Kadmon Heliopolis and Romaine Kinesis. He knew he was seeing either a re-enactment or, somehow, actual footage from the renowned – at least among certain supras – events of the summer of 1948.

The middle one, by far the most adventurous of the three, helped his cousins climb to the peak of the first tower, Mt Telepassa. There they discovered a strangely glowing outcropping of stone. It looked like nothing less than the oversized remains of a petrified human brain complete with cellular layers — a SCUBA diver, Aremar had seen similar, though non-glowing, coral-covered rocks off the Caribbean Coast of the Yucatan Peninsula and Costa Rica.

This was Kadmon Heliopolis, the son of Greek-born Freedom Fighters (to some). Anarchists the pair of them (though the mother was twenty years younger than the father), they died or were killed during the War. He touched the rock; immediately vanished, only to appear on one of Trigon's other peaks. As it happened – and perhaps neither ironically, nor even strangely – it was the one named after his namesake, Phoenician-born Cadmus Agenorid, the not altogether legendary founder of Grecian (as opposed to Egyptian) Thebes.

The eldest, Rom Kinesis – whose father was gypsy born, whose mother was Kadmon's paternal aunt, and who were both supranormals, the same as Kadmon's father, the first Olympian – was next to touch the brain-like stone. He too disappeared, only to pop up on the island's third peak a second later. As Yajur, though probably not Starrus (who currently seemed to be dominating their joint being), would have been acutely aware, it was named after his sister Unity.

(In a unprecedented ceremony attended by all the gods, devils that they were, Harmony married the real King Cadmus of Thebes. Standard mythology, though, has her as Harmonia, the by-blow of an illicit affair between Aphrodite and Ares; as, therefore, the product a union between Love and War. A thousand to fifteen hundred years after the reality that became the myth, itinerant Illuminaries of Weir added Datong to Harmonia, but devils always addressed her as Harmony.

(That selfsame mythology has as her power focus, her Tvasitar Talisman, the Necklace of Harmonia. While this was fair enough – Harmony's was a Brainrock necklace – according to accompanying legends, it brought nothing but misfortune to its wearers or owners. Primarily these were female descendants of the legendary versions of the homonymous pair: queens and princesses of the ill-fated House of Thebes. Clearly mythologists should have called it the Necklace of Disharmony.)

Thinking this great sport, the holographic threesome hailed each other across the chasms, from peak to peak. Their amplified voices echoed throughout the Liberty. The baby of the band, Harry (whose parents, relatives on one side or the other, had adopted both Kad and Rom, among a host of others, during the war), was the last to touch the rock. Instead of disappearing, however, the youngster somehow summoned the other two back to the tip of the first spiralling, earthen tower.

The electro-lutanist sent his music into the ozone. (Hendrix would have been delighted if he lifted audience spirits as much as the Holocaster Houdini did that of those on the Liberty.) The echo of triumph resounded as the three kids repeated their experiments: one went to one peak, another to a different one. Then they, and the Merlin, got really going ...

Scenes flashed by, an adult Kadmon featuring in most of them. A cataclysmic flood washed over an Island Kingdom ... Atlantis? ... Strongyne? ... Trigon? ... over a continent, Africa? A star ignited then went supernova. Three-eyed creatures – many, but by no means all, humanoid – attacked other three-eyed creatures. There were three-eyed monstrosities as well.

Cadmus Agenorid, Phoenician-born, eventual King of Thebes, brother of abducted Europa (their mother was named Telepassa), beloved of non-Datong Harmonia (daughter of mythological Venus and Mars), crushed the skull of a huge, serpentine atrocity; hacked out its teeth, hundreds of them, and threw them over his shoulders.

They rose into men, fought until only five were left ... the Trigon Spartae? ... Shelter and the other four (Sharpshooter, Sasquatch, Styx and Solar), without their helmets? ... Avatar Sol as Chthlonius Tiecher ... Solar again? Had to be. There were spaceships and, conversely, struggles between Stone Age Neanderthals and Cro-Magnon Man. Images of alien beings, ones that even the most accomplished fantasist couldn't have described, let alone drawn, came and went just as quickly.

Faces kept recurring: not only of Kadmon and the five Spartae; not only of Mnemosyne D'Angelo-Heliopolis, whom Smythe had known better than he ever cared to admit; nor her only (acknowledged) child, Kadmon's half-sister, Europa, whom all three of them had at least met. There were often variations of Loxus Ryne, his – but for Aranyani – always twin offspring, four wives, and their relations.

Visions changed blindingly fast then the three children were back on the first of Trigon's peaks. The middle one, Kadmon, pulled out a knife and chipped off three chunks from the rock. The three held hands. Single rings materialized on their left ring fingers. They were slight things, with thin bands and tiny, glowing gemstones. The wizard was wearing one as he continued to play his Holocaster.

Smythe, the only one who had known Heliopolis, Zeross and Kinesis in their childhood, realized all three had similar circlets. Then again, the last time he'd seen Harry, he had rings on every finger, usually more than one, as well as bracelets, anklets, and earrings. Which, of course, was why he was called Ringleader.

The lunatic took his pyrotechnic display of visions and sound to a crescendo then, abruptly, cut to silence: "Romaine named the brainy rock Gypsium. After his heritage."

He adjusted a few buttons and moved into a more melancholy mode. The scenes changed with the music. Time passed. Images went by quietly. Some were highly suggestive. Rom, apparently the same age as he had been in the first sequence, experimented with homosexuality. Was that Alastor Molorchus? Became celibate four or five years later, after an encounter with a woman with two-toned hair ... had to be Aranyani (born Ryne become Maxwell but always Nightingale), who currently lived and worked in Houston Texas.

Helios, resolutely heterosexual, providential in his women after starting at a surprisingly early age ... Was that Aran again? Was that Strife in a dark alleyway? No, even more horrifically it was his sister Europa, a Mother Mnemosyne lookalike. On the other hand – though the then young and remarkably attractive Crystal St

Synne was often in the background – Harry Zeross only seemed to have eyes for a truly beautiful girl with stark white hair. Just as he was mostly a teenager struggling hard to become a man, Belificent D'Angelo was a woman striving to remain a teen.

Smythe recognized some of the imagery from days he had lived through himself. Sometimes he even appeared, though more often than not it was one of his psychic siblings; Joan Smith, Johann Schmidt, the deaths of Barb Black and Bill White. Septupleman was also four-sevenths Septuplewoman. Septuplets becoming Sex, Quintuple then Quad, until there were only three left.

The wizardly, self-proclaimed technomage flourished anew. Heavy beat, heavy-action, paying absolutely no attention to the linear passage of time. December 25th, 1955, an Alliance gathering to celebrate what the Illuminated Brotherhood of Xuthros Hor always called Xmas Day; a designation that was almost as common as Christmas Day nowadays. The destruction of the ten members of the King Crime-fighters by the Magnificent Psycho (Saul Ryne), with Harry as a red-faced cherub sitting at the feet of a horned Loxus Ryne.

Quiet times again. Kinesis in a hut working on postulates that would eventually become the Cosmic Express or, more likely, its Gypsium fuel. Heliopolis along with his Five Dragon's Teeth climbing mountains. Zeross falling out of the sky onto a feast table surrounded by night-black men and daylight-white women ... the Sarpedon Summoning Children, black-as-midnight Demios and white-as-daylight Melina, who looked to be in their early twenties but, to judge from teenage Harry's appearance, were probably more like forty or thereabouts?

More power chords. They were back to April-May 1960. Faceless Strife. Murder most foul – Trebleman Joan Smith, Bel barely Zeross. The lute went from symphonious to cacophonous. Months flashed into years. Here the Himalayas. Hear the Himalayas! There's that continent again. Continent? A demon's facial silhouette geologically sculpted!

The Merlin sang 1968. Since the lyrics were in Greek likely only Aremar understood them, but Mik Starrus knew when his featured bit came. It was accompanied by more feedback, the kind of sound effects more akin to the undisciplined raunchiness of a Neil Young than the sublime Hendrix of *'A Third Stone from the Sun'*.

Starrus was flying the plane. Dropped the bomb that hit the top of one of Trigon's three peaks. The whole island shook; then it was no longer there.

POOF!

========

And, with that, silence returned; a shimmering silence made all the more eerie because, though they could hear nothing, an echo still resounded in their heads.

The Houdini put down his lute and fiddled with the buttons one last time. "That should do for now," he said. "The Liberty is a magnificent construct; proof of what the people of the world can do when acting in unison. Proof of what I will do; without further interference from you, yours, anyone or anything else, thank you very much, Lord Ordure."

(Even if, as suppressed Yajur believed, the Male Entity had begun life as Cain, Slayer of Abel, and not as Kadmon Heliopolis, this Lightray Lunatic shared his assumed namesake's extreme distaste of Enforced Order.)

"What you are now experiencing is an intensified dose of what people throughout the Whole Earth have been experiencing since I came to the Moon two years ago. Do not think of it as compulsion. It is not mind control. Consider it mind cleansing. Not brainwashing, brain-freeing. No priest in any religion anywhere in the world has ever done what I am doing — saving Whole Earthlings from devazur-kind and their puppet abominations.

"For thousands of years humanity has been suppressed; the masses manipulated by the powerful elite, the ruling classes – nowadays the corporate giants of the status quo – the very folks who employ you. They care nothing for empowerment. They care only for enslavement. You will soon realize you are not Liberators. You are Debilitators. When you awake, it will seem you have been asleep all your lives.

"When you awake, it will be as if you have awakened for the first time. You will be truly illuminated. I look forward to seeing you then."

========

Leaving the crew of the Liberty in thrall, he went back, by the grace of Gypsium and via the Universal Substance, to the Moon.

========

Helios materialized in the guest wing, as he thought of it – the third tower of his lunar citadel. In another part of the same tower, the two dozen members of Ned Johnson's LAC One were undergoing a similar induction into the wondrous ways of absolutely independent-thinking as their fellows were on the Liberty.

The technique was much more effective on a captive audience – a term which made Helios cringe – than on an entire planet milling with intelligent men and women. But time was short and he had already determined that those of the Liberty were more misguided than antagonistic to his ends. The comparatively gentle persuasion he was *forcing* on humanity wouldn't work with these ones. Here, in the part of the tower where he chose to appear, were his real enemies: devils and devazur-possessed mortals.

Milady Mnemosyne – Her Story, the Memory Entity; (probably) not the Titan, the mother, by Zeus, of the Muses – was solid and waiting for him. She was his one true love; his constant, though sometimes unwelcome companion during most of his hundred lifetimes. She was a trinary being: part computer, part human, part devil. Even though, like him, she shared a hatred for devils, in the single greatest irony of their seemingly interminable existences, she could only become truly flesh and blood when she possessed one of those selfsame Sedon-spawn.

Tonight – hard not to think of it being anything but night on the Moon – his devil-touched, Melanochroid lady was dressed in a black, loose-fitting top, matching silken pants, and had a greyish kerchief covering her dark hair and forehead. She stood on a ramp overlooking a series of pallets upon which lay the six men and women she had taken from Cosmicar Two on Tuesday (Demetray on the Hidden Headworld, named after Trigregos Demeter).

Beams of light penetrated their foreheads, keeping the devils within them in an uneasy stasis. It was unlikely either the devils or their human shells were conscious; they certainly wouldn't be in pain and probably weren't even dreaming. Were it not for their lifesigns, their hearts beating, their chests rising, their inhaling and exhaling, he might have mistaken them for inanimate corpses.

"What is troubling you, milady?" The Merlin hugged her from behind. "Have you finally determined which devils are possessing which humans? Or is there something else?"

"I think," she intoned softly, "We made a mistake not inhibiting the development of the Cosmic Express. We were blinded by your first lifetime's friendship with Rom Kinesis. His goals, those of Alpha Centauri, whom he only knows as Alfredo Sentalli, and the Anthean Sisterhood, were laudable. We know from previous lives in what passes as those below's future that the Express launched Humanity on its conquest of the Stars; a conquest that was inevitable and highly advantageous in many respects. But..."

"But, you feel, we have inadvertently created another timeline by our return to the century of our births?"

"Sometimes I feel we create our own story, that the timeline only exists as we know it. You were born, Kadmon. I wasn't. Not as such! I never had a chance to grow up and experience life the way you have. You made me, after the image and likeness of your stepmother, Memory of the Angels. Made me out of her genetic remains, so you say, but based on Old Weir's Mother Machine intermingled with essence of Datong Harmonia, the devic love of your second lifetime, that of King Cadmus of Thebes.

"I am not Mnemosyne D'Angelo Heliopolis, the sister of Raphael, Dolores, and Celestine, the Celestial Superior; not your sister Europa's mother. The human Mnemosyne is dead, only a memory. This one was never truly alive, hardly even a reminder of that Memory. I am only an approximation of life."

"You have been my lover, my companion, my nemesis at times, true, but my guiding spirit always. I share your doubts about letting the Express go now. I had not anticipated the involvement of devazurs opposed to Great Byron's plan to escape the planet. For, if your analysis is accurate, that seems to be what's happened.

"I further discount the likelihood of a single cosmicar being thrust deliberately against us. The Unity of Order is one thing, but these other ones seem hardly a threat. They were in that cosmicar purely by happenstance. I also don't hold with your notion that there can be alternate timelines. We are part of the one line; we just skip and jump about it.

"I point to devazurs as proof. We keep coming up against them, in lifetime after lifetime, but they are not static creatures, at least not as static as us. They are evolving beings: never aging so long as they don't want to, sure; undying until someone figures out how to kill them, appearances are not deceiving; immortals, consequently maybe not quite so much so; but different, somehow, yes, each and every time we encounter them.

"Yajur is a perfect example. Future Yajurs, Vajras, have never talked about Mik Starrus as one of his former host shells. That's because Future Vajras are Yajurs from our past, even if they seem to exist in a universe thousands of years ahead of this stream. I hold that the timeline is dependent on us. We are the Dual Entities, you and I: Adam Kadmon and the Cosmic Woman. What might be these peoples' future is either in our past or our current present. What is the true future, milady, are days we have yet to live."

"We are not God," argued Mnemosyne. "Though I sometimes think we are God's playthings."

"You also believe that God is Gypsium."

"What's left of the primordial Godhead; what's left of the mass from whence came the Big Bang, yes. As far as that goes."

"Speculation is useless, milady. For all I know, from Trigon exploding until I awoke on Sedon's Head in '75, I could have spent seven years stuck in some kind of tub in the Soviet Supracity dreaming up my hundred lifetimes. To my mind, I was a normal man with certain gifts, one of which was to survive despite the odds. Even if that's entirely fanciful, I firmly believe we can end the threat of devazurs to the Whole Earth."

"Your descendant, Xuthros Hor, the Biblical Noah, thought the same thing. That's why he caused the Great Flood five thousand, nine hundred and eighty odd years ago."

"Odd? I thought it was exactly?"

"I meant odd in terms of months. Ironic, isn't it, twenty years from now humans throughout the Outer Earth will be celebrating the start of a new millennium. They'll think it marks two thousand years after the birth of Christ, which we both know it won't be, but what they really should be celebrating is the start of the seventh millennium after the Genesea and Dark Sedon raising the Cathonic Dome."

"Given Humanity's current lack of patience with just about everything going on around them these days, they'll probably celebrate it a year earlier – nineteen years from now."

"Split the difference and they'd be closer to the truth."

"How so?"

"Because, in early May, Year 2000, the same conditions that allowed Hor to unleash the Flood will repeat for the first time since he pulled it off. It's called the Grand Alignment, which is to say the planets Mercury, Venus, Mars, Jupiter, and Saturn, as well as the Sun, Moon, and Earth, will all be roughly in the same celestial configuration. No telling what will happen then."

"All very interesting, I'm sure, but it won't be anywhere near as exciting as what we'll have accomplished long before then, milady. Once the Dome is sealed and humans are no longer susceptible to devic possession, we can concentrate on the Head. Concentrate on reuniting it with the Whole Earth — albeit minus devazurs. Our future begins today, but that of the devils could end very soon. Now tell me what you're finding so disturbing?"

"Her!" she indicated Nidaba Starrus, lying immobile on a table. "And them." She motioned to her five fellow cosmicompanions. "They've something to do with us, her in particular."

"What do you mean something? Access your data banks. You're supposed to know everything that has happened to us in all of our previous lifetimes. Hell's Teeth, lady, you won't even let me wake up after another death before draining memories of my last life into your storage tanks."

"Memory cells, of which I have a limitless amount."

"Like I said ..."

"Maybe I'm malfunctioning, but I think those within them are our children from nearly ninety lifetimes ago. That woman, the wife of Mikelangelo Starrus, is possessed by the same devil I thought I was possessing; just as you, my husband, not hers, should be possessed by Lord Vajra. They were man and wife, the Lord of Light and the Dame of Darkness, in their future, our past.

"These two relatively early epitomes of Light and Night can't know anything about the ones we suppress inside ourselves. But what if they find out?"

"A pickle of a conundrum," granted Helios. "But a rutabaga of a catastrophe? I doubt it. I was just with Starrus. Nothing untoward happened. You must've been staring at Nidaba for hours now. Nothing's happened here, either. Recall the reason I took over and kept Vajra was not entirely to forestall what he was doing in our last life.

"We, you, had this theory that if I held onto the devil I would become as immortal, as unkillable, as him. Except, I died again. Which probably means one of two things: either Vajra died at the same time or he escaped me just before I was killed. Quite conceivably Vajra is no longer inside me, not that I'm about to call him out to prove it."

"Yet I can still become flesh and blood, which means I still possess Erebe. From that I conclude you've Vajra. The devils are beneath their shells, us and them — and we better keep them there. What if we lose control of their future selves? What if the primitive Yajur and Ereba actually meet Vajra and Erebe face to three-eyed face?"

"When past and future come together, can there be a present? Or will reality collapse and we go back to square one, the Godhead, and wait for the next Big Bang? Didn't Einstein have something to say about that?"

"Old Albert changed his mind a lot," said Memory, with a trace of whimsy. "About me too, if my recollections of Human Memory are at all reliable."

The real Mnemosyne D'Angelo had been an Afrite, an offshoot branch of the Superior Sisterhood of Flowery Anthea dedicated to Aphrodite, whence (for antique Illuminaries of Weir on Earth) APM, Aphropsyche Morningstar, and the fine art of lovemaking. In the Classical Age she might have been a temple prostitute into whom men poured their devotion to the Great Goddess.

Afrites were sexually skilled and by no means monogamous, though they generally had very good taste when it came to choosing their partners. To his mind, Einstein was only marginally better than Sedon St Synne, another of the real Mnemosyne's amorous adventures. Miracle Memory was clearly more frightened about the prospect of a time paradox than he was.

"If there is a God, man," she shuddered, "What has He wrought?"

"He, milady? What about She? Or It? She-he-it? Say it fast: Shee-it! What about shit? God is shit, excrement. And, as important as shit is, we are what matters: we and humanity. Trouble yourself no further. We have prepared for every eventuality, you and I. If I am Helios on the Moon then you are Shelios on the Same. Through us, humanity wins!"

"Only if we do, too, Kad."

========

Mikelangelo to Starrus to three-eyed devil to Yajur to Order.

The Lord of Sparking Azuras was a big, electric-haired, brown-skinned humanoid wearing a simple tunic and wielding a sword that appeared to be nothing less than a hand-held bolt of lightning. He manifested himself out of the substratum of Mik Starrus, examined the electronic lute, and promptly smashed it apart.

He turned to James Aremar and Sean Smythe, regarded them curiously, mentally dismissed them as inconsequential. The Man on the Moon was anything but that.

========

Yajur slashed through between-space.

He, the Warped Wizard's Lord Ordure, emerged where Helios, the Warped Wizard himself, now was — in the second wing, the second tower of the Lunar Citadel. It was an exercise room, a dojo, with mats and padded walls. The Male Entity was drenched in sweat and, but for a headband, stripped to his shorts. Gone was the Mickey Mouse costume, conical cap and gown; gone was the waist-length hair and beard.

Instead, Heliosophos appeared an ordinary man: maybe thirty, Mediterranean with a slightly receding hairline, thin, albeit still with longish sun-blond hair, and a decent set of biceps. He was short and slender compared to Yajur, held an unopened oblong box, and seemed to be waiting for the Unity. The two faced each other: one, Helios calmly unlatching the box; the other, Yajur, in a rage, lightning blade ready to slice and dice.

"Face me, Entity!" challenged the Unity of Order. "Or are you too cowardly?"

"It is you have who drawn a weapon, devil," noted the prohibitive Cosmic Man on the Moon quietly. "Must be you, the coward!"

For a brief second, Yajur hesitated; whereupon, despite his best instincts, sheathed his lightning blade. "You dare taunt me, human? No matter. I don't need a weapon to destroy your ilk."

Helios laid the box on the floor without opening it, stepped into the centre of the mat. "About time we had some fun."

In his first lifetime – so long, yet so comparatively few years ago now – at the 1960 Olympic Games in Rome, Kadmon Heliopolis was expected to win the Gold in Greco-Roman wrestling. He was also expected to be a medallist in fencing, certain track and field events, and various swimming competitions as well as captain the Greek Water Polo Team.

All of which, the sheer abundance of events he might win, convinced his guardians, (Harry's actual parents) Angelo and Megaera Zeross, his primary teacher and mentor, Headmistress Virginia Mannering, and his biggest backer, Loxus Abraham Ryne, not to allow him to compete in any of them. Heliopolis did so many things so well he was clearly a (howsoever otherwise ordinary) supranormal.

And Order was clearly a devil.

========

Lord Yajur raced forward, lunged. Helios flopped onto his back, caught the Unity with his feet in the midsection and, using the devil's own momentum, tossed him over his shoulders. He hit the nearest wall, which shocked from contact. Thunder and Lightning leapt to his feet, not oblivious to pain so much as betrayed by his own stupidity.

"Should have known you would cheat, human." He touched the hilt of his lightning blade, readying it to slash them both elsewhere between-space – to outer space, where he didn't need to breathe to live but Helios did and wouldn't. "This is your environment. You set the boundaries. Why don't we go outside and see who is really the master?"

Helios squared himself. "Love to. Later. Mnemosyne, do it!"

The wall fired. Yajur vanished. Helios went for a shower. Mnemosyne joined him: "He was right. You cheated."

"Milady Memory, there is no such thing as cheating a devil!"

"I've been thinking. I could jettison Erebe the same way."

"Not just yet."

========

Yajur, cathonitized by the Unity of Chaos nearly five hundred years earlier and only freed, for a second time, a few hours ago, found himself being sucked, inexorably … **INTO** *A BLACK HOLE!*

****

SIXTH MOON: **The Family Thanatos**

========

Devauray, Tantalar 6, 5980

As the streets erupted throughout the Outer Earth, as well as some of the more civilized centres of Sedon's Head, all was serene on the Frozen Isle of Lathakra. Even though it lay across the Sea of Clouds, off the coast of The Argent, site of some of the worst rioting on the Hidden Headworld, Helios's beams had no effect on the volcanic, formerly horn-shaped island.

Old King Cold and his onetime Empress, the Scarlet Sorceress, weren't simply the rulers of Lathakra. Its two races, the Intuits and the Fikings, worshipped them as gods. Rightfully so! They were the first born of Thrygragos Varuna Mithras. Along with Rudra and Umashakti Silvercloud of Byron's initial litter, they were the eldest and, excluding the suicide, Unholy Abaddon – the now two-eyed Unity of Chaos and Thrygragos Lazareme's last surviving firstborn – most powerful Master Devas left on the Head but for one.

One whom no one remembered unless he was physically in front of them.

========

All week, via the fumes of her thousand-plus years' appropriated cauldron, Methandra and Tantal Thanatos had been following events on the Outer Earth with singular intensity. Sedonda, Sunday on the outside, had seen the definite decathonitization of their son, Antaeor or Earth, as well as the possible reconstitution of their eldest devic daughter, Castella or Day, and the second pair of Elemental Twins, Aires and Thalassa, Air and Water.

Those two last were now separated. Sea Goddess had stayed on the Outer Earth while Airealist and the one they no longer regarded as Day, Gloriella nee D'Angelo Dark, had been on the Head since early this morning. They had been preceded by Antaeor, whom the outworlders called Demon Land. All three were now in Temporis, the subterranean protectorate of Dand Tariqartha.

Known variously as the Time-Space Displacer and/or the Chronocollector, among other nicknames, Thrygragos Lazareme's fourth-born Persian or Earth Magician specialized in replicating, mostly for his own amusement, half-life mantels out of the same tellurian ooze whence chthonic critters such as daemons (with or without the '*a*') and feeorin faerie farts came.

Also in the Thousand Caverns that Devauray-Saturday were Mithras's Eighth, the Primary Apocalyptics: Carcinogen the Leper (Plague, Disease), Mars Bellona (War), Nakba Ramazar (Catastrophe, Disaster). With them besides the fourth generational Thanatoid – the real Demon Land, not Peter (Pietro) D'Angelo, nor any of the other devaray victims who thereby gained his abilities howsoever short-termed

– were the Vultyrie, the Headless Apocalyptic of Sudden Destruction's two-headed, yet nearly mindless mount.

Far, far more importantly, OMP (Old Man Power, to give him his supra-codename; Obadiah Melvin Power, to give him his entirely spurious cover name) sent a sixth Master Deva (seventh devil) through the Dome during the course of the preceding week. This was Mater Matare, Mother Murder, the self-appointed Apocalyptic of Death.

She had been pregnant; was that no longer.

Antaeor Thanatos was now in a small part of Temporis known as the Faerie Garden. It was unique in the Thousand Caverns in that its feeorin inhabitants were not only alive, they had never been replicates. Much to their dismay, if not quite absolute disgust, the earthborn wights on their way next door, in order to disrupt its celebration of the Dand's 4,000th anniversary of becoming an independently solid individual, had just realized that they were no longer its most exceptional feature.

The fourth generational Earth Elemental had taken up a position designed to block an entry cave that led, along a long tunnel, to the selfsame cavern wherein Matare had just given birth. Datong Harmonia – the Unity of Balance as well as the Lazaremists' realized, not idealized, version of Panharmonium – had just torn out of the Weird not far from where the Thanatoid was waiting to repel whichever members of the Damnation Brigade the Dand chose to send against him.

Tariqartha could not replicate devils per se – he could handle their most common appearances easily enough but he couldn't imbue any of his duplicate with their abilities – so it had to be the real Harmony. Until then they had thought her wiped out by her brother Unity, that of Chaos, nearly five hundred years ago. For one who was reputedly incomparably beautiful, she looked, it had to be said, gods-awful. That wasn't what immediately caught the fays' collective eye, though.

Nor was it was who she was tangling with: two members of the band of deviants the Dand warned were on their way. One was the Dand's own half-son, Kronokronos Akbarartha, while the other was an natural-born Anthean adept a couple of them actually remembered as Wilderwitch, no other name.

Nor was it the body of an anaemic, three-quarters naked scarecrow of a man lying on the ground close by. It was what lay near him, a curved sword, and what was strapped to his left arm, a circular mirror. Both were made of Brainrock. And, around her neck, the Witch was wearing a similarly glowing scarlet tiara.

Harmony was fighting them for possession of the Trigregos Talismans.

========

All sorts of stuff happened.

One of the least interesting was her declaration that she wasn't going by Datong Harmonia anymore. Given what Chaos did to her five hundred years ago – given what she'd gone through since, which was mostly decomposing whilst being pinned to a rock of steadily depleting Gypsium that nevertheless kept her semi-sort-of alive, if unconscious – that was understandable.

She hadn't become the Unity of Disharmony. She'd become Freespirit Nihila.

========

Nihila won. She also knitted herself almost entirely back together by draining some of the life essence of both Kronokronos Akbar and the Witch; some, but nowhere near all. Wilderwitch took her one-night-stand lover, the father of her consequential only child, by his arm and tossed an agate at their feet.

With the Crimson Corona no longer around her neck, it activated this time. They were gone and the Unity was left staring after them. A Gypsium hoop appeared beneath her feet. Before she realized what was happening, Nowadays-Nihila had fallen through it; was halfway across the continent.

Nevair Neverknight, Unmoving Byron's most violent offspring, was charging at her. The ebon-armored, long ago decathonitized paladin – at one time the never-mythological centaurs' devil-god – was crazed with bloodlust. She barely reacted in time.

"Harmonious landings, Balance," laughed Aristotle Zeross, Ringleader, the second so codenamed. "Wherever you land!" He was still in the Faerie Garden. So were the Trigregos Talismans. He wanted them, too. That's why he was here. Bent to pick up the discarded Crimson Corona.

Vetala's soldier wasn't dead. Or, if he was, it didn't matter. His mistress, Nergal Vetala, was the Blood Queen of Hadd, once Iraxas, where Dead Things walked. Did more than just walk, sooth said. Had tea and scones with their (usually) Irache descendants. When Vetala was around, they bowed before her. So did her soldier, who also bled for her.

He now had hold of all three Sacred Objects. Was the Trigregos Titan.

========

Plenty more stuff ensued. On both sides of the Dome. Couldn't help it. That's what stuff did ... ensued. When it wasn't just happening, that is.

========

On the Frozen Isle of Lathakra, now 8-inch-tiny Tantal and now 10-foot-enormous Methandra breathed simultaneous sighs of relief. They didn't know how, let alone who to thank, but Ringleader was still alive and that's all that mattered. They had also already forgotten their now-departed guest of a few minutes earlier.

Even though he would have loved to accept Hot Stuff's thanks, preferably in bed, he wouldn't have minded. What he would have minded was if they remembered he existed when he wasn't there.

"That was too close," yelled King Cold at the top of his lungs.

"We're going to have take charge, husband," whispered his Crimson Queen, also his immediate sister, at the bottom of hers. "No one can help us but ourselves!"

"All right. I'll take care of the children we've found and guarantee the cooperation of Dr Zeross. Just make sure you don't lose sight of him."

As he cut himself elsewhere, she took a chance. There was one child he couldn't take care of, a child beyond the Dome. She had to get her home and knew how. She contacted All of Incain, who still believed she couldn't eat her even though Methandra hadn't been humanizing Her Story, the Mnemosyne 3-Thing, for a number of decades. (All never did attain much more than the merest modicum of intelligence its template, First Weir's Mother Machine, achieved many multiple millennia long ago and faraway.)

"The portal stays open, machine. Until we say otherwise. Go against us and we will shut you down once and for all time!"

========

Iron Lord Abdullah Ziderite, (arguably) born in the fourth litter of Thrygragos Varuna Mithras, was the devic Master of Magnetism.

In the second millennia of the Dome, Father Mithras spent much of his time beyond the Dome as Kronos-Saturn to Divine Coueranna's Great Goddess Rhea or, according to some traditions, Erda. Seizing on his thought-father's absence some forty-five hundred years ago, Magnetism allied himself with a few other Master Devas, the indigent Lemurians of the by then fifteen hundred years Hidden Continent, and their tellurian, mantel, or mandroid servants. These last included the Master Mother Machine, All of Incain (now over six thousand years formerly Ginny the Gynosphinx).

They raised a revolt against the Three Great Gods; even managed to trap them within All for a comparatively brief period. (Brief, at least in terms of thus far seemingly endless, devic lifetimes.) Led by the two Thanatoids of Mithras, the two Silver-clouds of Byron, and the three Unities of Lazareme, a majority of the eldest Master Devas rallied to their fathers' defence, and eventually defeated the Iron Lord.

Faced with extermination – mandroids weren't considered beings by Devil as well as Demon King Sedon, let alone lesser ones – All exchanged the Thrygragos Brothers for survival. Lemurians fled into the seas, seldom to emerge over the next few thousand years. Those mandroids that weren't obliterated were driven beneath the surface of the Head where, eventually, many of them were subjugated by subterranean Master Devas such as Dand Tariqartha and Mithras's fifth born, Lords and Lady of the Underworld (Yama Nergal, Gibran Nimiki, and Shal Ereshkigal).

In stark contrast to the likes of Domdaniel-Pride, a sixth born, and Novadev (Mithras's embodiment of Summer Heat), of the Eleventh, who were cathonitized for their firsthand involvement in the killing of lesser beings, Ziderite accepted indefinite imprisonment within Incain.

In a way it was almost a reward. Until Nevair Neverknight was inappropriately cathonitized during the Crimson Conspiracy, Grandfather Sedon never voluntarily decathonitized any devil. Still hadn't — voluntarily!

Centuries after Ziderite's failed revolt, in the Year of the Dome 4376, came Thrygragon. Mithras was killed thanks in large measure due to Demogorgon, called the Unnameable, the Conglomerate Deva or Devil-Eater amongst devazurkind. It too (unless it was a she, Lamia of the 12th) was now within Incain — as were Novadev's litter brothers, Tammuz (also Cautes, Equinoctial Spring) and Osiraq (also Cautopates, Equinoctial Autumn), who were put there in 4825 YD.

Because All was beholding to the Dual Entities, either Tantal – who had hold of the Male Entity at the same time his sister-wife had hold of the Female Entity – or Methandra herself could release Magnetism, the Idiot Twins, or the Unnameable, Mithradites all. They did that, they'd deprive All of most of its (her) energy.

And they would. All knew it, too.

========

Sea Goddess had not stayed with her twin and the rest of the Damnation Brigade.

========

Not that she was afraid of the Apocalyptics. Or anyone else for that matter. (She'd been the one primarily responsible for defeating Mater Matare and the others in their first encounter on Damnation Island last Sunday.) No, she'd left them for the simple reason that she wanted to be away, by herself, for a few days. She had too many things to sort out.

For one, unlike Airealist, she was sure the devil called Antaeor Thanatos, Demon Land, was their blood brother. For another, she figured it followed that, even though she had no third eye, nor any more eyes that the human two, she was at least part-devil herself. She was hardly the only one in that regard. Indeed, two of those who did figured they were her parents from the days they were possessing the Dual Entities in the Teens and Twenties.

She'd flown to Los Angeles the night previously. Extracting herself from the unwanted attentions of Erech Avar-Ryne, the patriarch's son, she took to the ocean.

On land, she had never come across anyone who could run as fast as Wildman Dervish Furie. Sure as well, Rainbow and Raven's Head could fly at tremendous speed, as could her twin brother, albeit nowhere near as rapidly – or for anywhere near as long – as the other two. But when she was in the water, her natural element, she could swim quicker than any of them.

Her intent was to go all the way around the Baja Peninsula then, at Cabo San Lucas, head into the Gulf of California where her undersea palace probably still stood. She was past Ensenada when she heard her brother calling to her. Surfacing, she beheld the ghost of Airealist hovering in the sky.

"Help me, Thalassa. I'm trapped!"

"Aires! Where? Show me!"

He led her eastward, toward Hawaii and Centauri Island.

========

Well-satisfied, the Scarlet Sorceress refocused the visionary vapours of her long ago confiscated cauldron on the Faerie Garden.

To her astonishment Harry Zeross was no longer there.

========

Desperately she flashed forth her enhanced far-sight, searching throughout the Thousand Caverns for any sign of him.

It was a futile task; as always in Subcranial Temporis there was too much going on to single out a living man. Then she looked above Temporis, into Sisert, the Silent Sands of Cathune Bubastis (the cat-faced Apocalyptic of Drought, another Mithradite whose heyday occurred on the Outer Earth during the half-millennium-long Mediterranean Goddess Culture.)

There hovered the reviled Byronic Nucleus.

Made up of Great Byron and his second-born (but primary) Nucleoids, it took the form of an enormous, bodiless, three-eyed head. It could and, in the last five hundred years, too often did cathonitize Master Devas who, to Byron's mind, got out of hand. In hateful fact, forty-seven years earlier on Sedon's Peak, it sent seven of her children (Ereba, Castella, Antaeor, Acheron, Auraura, Orinth, and Constantin) to the Sedon Sphere.

An eighth, whom she'd named Veronas, their epitome of the Summer Season, had betrayed his parents and siblings to Thrygragos Byron and his spawn. For his troubles Tantal had executed, not cathonitized, him. Still not satisfied, he thereupon banished his attribute, the season itself, from the Frozen Isle forevermore. Two others, their Thalassa and their Aires, the second born of the two pairs of Elemental

Twins, Methandra saved by accessing the Wandering SAG Gap and, she thought, sending them to the Outer Earth.

If it turned out the adopted D'Angelos weren't fourth generation devils, their Air and their Water, they had to be their shells. How else would they have acquired their power foci? Unless they'd somehow killed them. And if they'd done that, well, the Scarlet Sorceress would have no compunctions about avenging them.

It wouldn't be the first time either she or Tantal had disregarded Father Sedon's dictates against sanctioning the killing of lesser beings. It certainly wouldn't be the first time they'd allowed their adherents to kill anyone, period. One doesn't very nearly conquer an entire continent without one's armed forces counting copious coup, as Hadd's still alive and talking Iraches might put it.

(So might its dead, but still walking, Iraches, Except for the most part they were Haddazur-animated zombies and, as such, preferred eating to yapping.)

Although, that being the case, the temptation would be to kill the D'Angelo Elementals herself.

========

"Wait," yelled Aires, interrupting Blind Sundown's attempt to tell him what to do if they did come across their flying foes. "Something's happening. I hear birds. Thousands of them. There!"

'Damn fools', thought Sundown for his Beauty's benefit. 'The devils must truly know nothing of your full powers. All the better for us, eh, Lady?'

Suddenly Raven's Head jerked sharply. Sundown instantly knew why. Airealist had leapt into the air.

========

Airealist was his codename. An aerialist's costume, complete with a cloud-printed sky-blue cape, was his outfit. Under a variety of glamours cast by Wilderwitch and/or one of her fellows sisters – Fisherwoman sometimes, prior to her falling out with Sea Goddess over Atlantean; Sorciere more often; Superior Sarpedon most often; once in a while even her little mother, Hush Mannering – being an aerialist was also his profession.

(Aires D'Angelo was the only one of the ten re-embodied supras to wear what passed for a uniform. He wasn't the only one to either hold down a regular job or have to wear glamour, however. Yehudi Cohen, the Untouchable Diver did, too. In his case, though, it was because he could never take off his wetsuit. In Aires' case, it was because he, like his twin sister, barely aged after turning twenty-one.)

Despite Sea-she's warning at YVR, he'd stuck with the rest of the Damnation Brigade. Not much more than an hour after Thalassa's plane took off for LAX (Los Angeles International Airport), they'd allowed the Byronic Nucleus to bring them inside, all the way up to the top of Sedon's Head. Together with John Sundown and Raven's Head, he was now in the Pre-Columbian Cavern of Temporis.

They were hunting Apocalyptics, specifically Nakba Ramazar, the Headless Apocalyptic of Sudden Destruction, and his double-feather-headed, two-feather-bodied mount, the Vultyrie. (Amongst devils it almost went without saying that Catastrophe, as they commonly called Ramazar, with no head, had far more brains than the Vultyrie did with two.)

"Get back in the saddle, you idiot. This is no time to get separated," shouted Sundown. "Beauty's commanding the birds to scatter."

Sundown knew Airhead before he became Airealist. (They were both Summoning Children – reputedly the Elemental Twins were the eldest by a few days, even a week.) Deep down he knew wouldn't heed him. Only Aires's twin, Thalassa, and, to a far lesser degree, her latter-day boyfriend Cerebrus, had ever been able to moderate his impetuous nature.

As Aires neared the birds, he slowed his flight. Clipping his Aerod – his omega-shaped *'portable trapeze'* – into the very air itself, he hung a few hundred feet above the grasslands and conjured a series of very loud thunderclaps. The noise seemed to panic the animals, disrupt their senses, confuse them. It was a warning. If they kept coming, Aires would have no other choice except to incinerate them with lightning bolts, buffet them with sleet, or drench them in a torrential downpour.

Whether the birds realized what he was preparing to do to them, whether it was Raven ordering them to disperse, or whether it was the between-space gash in the air itself – what had suddenly slashed open behind Aires – that frightened them off, the effect was the same. The birds scattered.

"See, Johnny?" Aires hollered. "I'm as good as ever."

Blind Sundown reined Raven's Head towards the sound of Airealist's voice in time to see (through her) Aires sucked into a slice in the air and disappear. He couldn't believe Raven's eyes. Spurred his extraordinary mount towards where Aires had vanished. Raven flew right on as if there was nothing there except air. Which, by then, was all there was.

"More devil's work," Sundown muttered aloud. Raven wasn't the only one who heard him. Despite how faraway they were, so did Catastrophe and the Vultyrie.

As pitiful as they were by the standards of almost every other sentient being, the latter's birdbrains were nevertheless powerful enough to boss about birds, hence the opening attack. Blood would soon be flowing; as per usual with devils, virtually none of it theirs.

That's what worshippers did: Died for those they worshipped.

========

Suddenly the very ground in front of them reared up. A massive brick wall, grinning and with three eyes, blocked their pathway.

"There are no greater menaces to humankind than Apocalyptics and their allies. Myself included!"

"Did he really say that?" groaned the Witch, sounding far more horrified at what he'd just said than horror-struck at the threat he presented.

========

"About time you showed up," Kronokronos Akbarartha fairly shook with rage. The Goliath grotesquery had seized his being on Damnation Island. Consequently he desired not only vengeance but vindication. "Listen, Witch. Do as I say and don't argue. Vault him. Get to the next cavern. Help the others. Nihila said you were more powerful than you realized. Prove it. This one's mine. I'll be along shortly."

"Not a chance," protested Wilderwitch. "We'll take him down together. It'll be quicker that way."

With speed belying his size, Akbar picked her up bodily; almost effortlessly tossed her over top the earthen monstrosity. She must have covered fifty yards before crashing into a lily pond. She did not drown in Des's pond, as the Diver once cracked. Far from it. Emerging soaking wet, she was so angry she could have steamed herself dry.

(Or, if she still had Harmony's necklace, gleamed herself thus.)

For a brief moment she thought to return to Akbar's side. Once she helped him vanquish the fourth generational Thanatoid, she'd teach the big, cocky oaf a lesson he'd never forget. She'd put him through the torments of the damned without sending him to Hell. How dare he treat her like an American football? She'd cut him down to size.

The cavern exit was only a hundred or so yards away. A primal urge drew her towards it. "To hell with you, OMP," she muttered to no one in particular, not even the toad-riding faeries once again hopping from lily pad to lily pad that she'd so disturbed making her unscheduled entrance then exit. "You don't deserve my help."

Gazelle-like she sprinted out of the Faerie Garden. The farther she ran into the cave-tunnel between it and the adjacent cavern, the closer she came to Mater Matare and the fourth generational horrors she'd given birth to not so very long ago. Wilderwitch now understood why the Kronokronos Supreme had been so insistent on taking on Demon Land by himself.

She felt the same way about the Death Goddess.

========

The Scions Thanatos had three other children, two of which were also fourth generation devils: Sedunihas and Motan. The thirteenth and last, Klannit, had also been the first one born. She was an azura spirit being, the only one they ever had – the only one Methandra ever had, make that. Arguably only his father, Varuna Mithras, had more azuras than Tantal.

Klannit wasn't just the Thanatoids' only azura. She was the first azura ever born and that pre-Dome. Was proud of it as well. Tantal hated her.

But not just because of her insufferable hubris.

========

Although they tried, the Byronic Nucleus hadn't enough power left to cathonitize Tantal or Methandra in Antheal (April) 5933.

Instead, just after red-skinned, fiery-haired Methandra accessed the SAG Gap to send away their second set of Elemental Twins, Air and Water (Fire and Earth were their first born set), Smoky Sedona cast upon them the Spell of Disproportionment. Ever since that day, when one was tiny, six to eight inches tall, the other was gigantic, ten or twelve feet high.

For the majority of the recent year, blue-skinned, icicle-bearded Tantal had been the giant, Methandra the gnat. The change could come at any moment, though. Either that or the condition could linger for many more months. That first time, Methandra had been the giant. She was also pregnant. Fearing for her unborn, Tantal forged an ice statue for Klannit to occupy. He then managed to transplant the foetuses to her womb.

The thereby solidified azura carried them, never truly developing, in what was in effect an internal cryonics chamber, for twenty-two years. Finally, in 5955, they were transferred back to Methandra. It was a calculated gamble. Methandra had just become gigantic again, would likely remain so long enough to give birth. Shortly after she went into labour, she reverted to six inches.

Sedunihas was now twenty-five but looked to be about five. He was also deaf. Even though he learned manual sign language, the only individuals he could communicate with mentally were his mother, who bore him, and Klannit, who carried him for so long. Which was one reason Tantal hated her. Another reason was that Motan was born not deaf but dead.

Rather than bury him, Klannit pressed his body, a tiny mote of dead flesh, into amber. Bizarrely her still frozen, but always mobile, self often wore it around her neck in an amulet. Then again Janna Fangfingers, the vampiric de facto ruler of Hadd for so long, wore a Crystal Skull around her neck.

In it, she boasted, she kept the spirit or soul self of her twin brother, Sraddha Somata. Which would have ordinarily been a very odd assertion, perhaps bespeaking mental illness, if the Somata twins hadn't been so exceptionally gifted in life. After all, mortals, not even long-lived hybrid Utopians, were supposed to be able to dominate, let alone take possession of devils.

(Other than in the usual, howsoever hypothetical sense of an immortal soul, Utopians were no more likely than anyone else to have Spirit or Soul Selves. Still, he and Janna were deviants. Their devic half-parents were Thrygragos Lazareme, whom mortals saw as their idea of God, and his firstborn daughter, the incomparable Harmony, who even Tantal couldn't help but admit was the most beautiful female he'd ever laid eyes on save, if she was nearby, Methandra herself.)

Although her mirrors were the conduit through which the Thanatoids redirected the worship of their Intuit and Fiking adherents to power All the Invincible in the absence of the Idiot Osiraq, when it came right down to it Klannit wasn't too popular with Methandra either. Sedunihas, though, all but worshipped her.

========

Yellow-skinned Sedunihas and Klannit, whose icicle-like body was polished mirror-smooth, greeted Airealist. "Our parents will be with you presently, Air."

"Parents busy," signed the deaf-mute artist. "Want see statues?"

"He is very good," said and simultaneously signed Klannit.

"Yeah, um, right!"

Airealist promptly passed out.

========

Akbarartha, the acknowledged Kronokronos Supreme, did not trumpet his triumph. Quite rightly. Antaeor Thanatos did not lose so much as fall asleep. Whereupon the nearly gigantic faerie buried him alive; as if that was any way to deal with a devil who arrogantly embraced the cognomen of Demon Land.

He briefly dreamed of his father. Old King Cold appeared in his mind and spoke directions. He began to soil-swim towards the Frozen Isle of Lathakra.

========

"How's it going, wife?" inquired tiny Tantal upon his return to her presence.

"You've held your end up well, husband," gigantic Methandra whispered. Not wanting to deafen him, she tried to keep her voice well below boom-box volume. (Sedunihas's inability to hear – worse, his inability to make himself other than deaf

– still sickened her.) He nevertheless clutched his ears reflexively, if perhaps a tad overdramatically.

Partly as a reward, but mostly as an apology, she considerately poured him a thimbleful of beer.

"Air is here," she thought to him this time. "Artist is taking care of him."

"I'll not embrace him in this condition. I've some pride left. I decided Earth should make his own way. Stars Dream and Sleep aren't in the Sedon Sphere anymore and, if you can't resist howsoever multipurpose faeriedust, you won't be much good if they find their way back to the Head. Besides, why should I reward a comparative failure with a free ride home? Still and all, he shouldn't be too long."

Dream was Phantast, their immediate brother in Varuna Mithras's firstborn litter of three. Sleep was Mordira surnamed Faeriedust, a comparatively lowborn Mithradite, but one Phantast Thanatos had always found favour in – not that he needed her to cast dreams. Both were cathonitized during the failed debacle of the Crimson Conspiracy most of two thousand years past. Presumably they were possessing cosmicompanions on one cosmicar or another – possibly, even dangerously, the same one – either on the Head or beyond the Cathonic Dome.

Tantal had no fear of the two remaining Great Gods, Byron or Lazareme. He got on as well with their eldest extant offspring as he did with Methandra. (These included the firstborn Silverclouds of Byron, though the Great God her father hadn't released Umashakti-Gravity until earlier in the week. Her crime? Assisting the Thanatoids in their efforts to gain power foci for their fourth generational children in 5933 YD.)

But, if Phantast did return, he and his sister-wife would no longer be undisputed leaders of the Mithras Spawn. And, given what he almost pulled off with the Crimson Conspiracy – a reassertion of the devils' former position as the Outer Earth's foremost deities with himself, not Grandfather Sedon nor any of the Thrygragos Brothers, as their top dog top god – Phantast might be able to attract more adherents than both of them combined.

"I've been busy, too," the Scarlet Empress told him. "I made contact with Water, though she thinks it was her twin. She's incredibly fast but doesn't realize the extent of her abilities and can't access the Weird. That leaves her with half an ocean to cross before she even reaches the Head's entrance. Nonetheless, by Mithrada or Demetray at the latest, she'll be in position to go through the Nag Gap. After that either of us can cut her here."

"So long as All, the Frog Queen, and the rest of their ill-met ilk continue to cooperate, that sounds excellent," he congratulated her as magnanimously as a dinky devil dared do.

"I served notice on them as well," she imparted. "There's no question they're pursuing their own agenda but All's convinced we can shut her down – and not just because we once controlled her creators, the Dual Entities. After all, the Machine Master Moulder is dependent on the likes of Magnetism and the Idiot Twins to energize her.

"We're the eldest Mithradites left. If anyone short of Grandfather can get to them, have them withdraw their sustenance, it's us."

"Recall when we began this five years ago?" Cold criticized his wife just as thoughtfully, as in telepathically. "We believed Sedon dead since '53. Back then it seemed inevitable that control of the Head would fall to the victor of a contest between Queen Amphitrite, her amphibians and witchy allies, All, their tellurian followers, and we devils. It was to be a no holds barred, but honourable, final fight for the Head and thence the rest of the Earth. But it was only to begin after we get our children back."

"Only in your imagination. And only after we defanged the Byronics and their nowadays far more technologically advanced humans."

"Isolated them to Aka Godbad, like we did before." (He was referring to the time, circa 4800 YD, that, but for the subcontinent Byronics called home, they almost conquered the Head.)

"Your point being?"

(If they could avoid it, neither of them ever mentioned the Death's Head Hellion, her peculiar but pivotal link to All of Incain, and how they ended up asleep for 1100 years. That Master Morgan Abyss, to give the Hellion her full name and title, was a Melusine Piscine, not a Lemurian per se – though they were cousin races, products of Old Eden's discredited science – therefore went without saying, or thinking, explicitly.)

"Not that it's all in my imagination, that's for sure. That Sedon survived the treachery of Wiccan Warlock – that the duplicitous bastard's Hydrogen Bomb didn't kill him, only knocked him out for a quarter century – makes no never mind. It remains them against us. Our first strike shall be to shut All down regardless.

"That hasn't changed. They know it; we know it; everyone does. But even if Lemurians have as much sense of honour as their machines, which is to say none, we shall fight them fairly, not violate our oaths and destroy them expeditiously, using our attributes. Your threat was premature and entirely inappropriate, woman."

"And your enthusiasm for an Armageddon-like battle to the brink of extinction strikes me as just more of your patriarchal fanaticism. Just because you were identified with the Northern European Hanging God of Antiquity is no reason for trying to live up to that image of despondency. However, I'm willing to go along with your Phantast Follies so long as we get our children back first. Unlike you, I've still hope for the next generation."

Tiny Tantal well knew of his wife's Anthean tendencies. Among the eldest still extant Lazaremists they got along with were Flowery Anthea's surviving second-born sisters, the Life Goddesses: Krepusyl Evenstar and Titanic Metis (Metisophia, often called Wisdom of Lazareme).

The former, currently the Grey Lady of Twilight (Crepuscule, Sedon's Outer Nose), was once Mariamne Dawnstar, whose effective protectorate, the Land of Daybreak, Sedon moved across the Hidden Headworld (some said) because she jilted him, scorned his affections, the same as Methandra had throughout the centuries she steadfastly remained Mithras's Virgin.

Their enduring friendship with Metis was all the more remarkable when you considered that Methandra confiscated her Tvasitar talisman 1200 years earlier, during the early stages of the expansion of their eventually massive empire.

The two highborn Lazaremists were among the main movers behind the witch sisterhoods' efforts to rebirth, if that was a verb, or otherwise bring back the three Great Goddesses their mothers. Even though it, their version of Panharmonium, struck him as a dystopia, as an unrealistic world without glory, and wanted no part of it, he wouldn't abandon his sister-wife, not after so long; would indulge her.

Victory was what mattered to him. So long as his family triumphed in the end, he'd happily die in the fight. (Which wasn't very likely, he'd acknowledge if pressed. After all neither of them died when the Atomic Twins blew themselves up at the Gates of Cabalarkon in 4825 – thus causing the radioactive wasteland now known as the Ghostlands – just fallen asleep for a very long time.)

"I'll take care of the distasteful Zeross business, wife. You didn't answer my question by the way. How're you doing?"

Something of a showman herself, Methandra broke her Brainrock walking cane, her firebrand power focus, into tiny pieces. These she tossed underneath the cauldron, causing the flames to heighten. Her cane, which was more of a matchstick than a walking stick, reformed itself. She used it to stir the scarlet waters of her broiling cauldron. Its fumes formed an image in the air.

(The cauldron once belonged to Wisdom of Lazareme, whose power base was once not far from Lathakra on the Cattail mainland. Even though Titanic Metis probably could have reclaimed it any time she wanted during their Thousand Year Sleep – more like 1100 years – and thereby regain her solidity, she preferred to remain a spirit being. Titanic, as it applied to Metisophia, referred to her rebellious tendencies.)

"Better than the Apocalyptics. See for yourself."

"No time."

========

Somewhat later Judge Druj, as the myrionymous highborn was sometimes called in ancient Persia, reappeared in the central chamber of the glacial palace.

"Things have heated up in your absence, Smiler," squeaked Tantal, who was sipping beer through a straw from a tiny thimble. "I had to take some executive action."

========

The palace was indeed carved out of a glacier high up in the Labrys Mountains, the volcanic backbone that effectively divided the Frozen Isle into two distinct realms: that of the Fire Kings on the west, Sea of Clouds side, and that of the Intuits on the east, Ocean of Psychron side.

The treacherous, due to poor visibility, but not impassable – if you were a master mariner – Sea of Clouds separated Lathakra from the Cattail Peninsula, Sedon's Ponytail. The Cattail itself was a forbidding, if not so much so volcanic, mountainous region, particularly on its eastern extremities.

Sedon's Peak sat centrally on the peninsula. Molten Brainrock filled its caldera, forming a lava lake. Tvasitar Smithmonger, Anvil to his fellow devils, not only dwelled there but continued to forge devic power foci as required. Peculiarly, given their pedigrees, the highborn Lazaremist was Klannit's beloved from the days when both were stuck inside daemonic lovers.

(Azuras were so dishwater dull they mostly lacked even a rudimentary sense of self-awareness. Few warranted a name of their own. The redoubtable Klannit had much more going for her than just a strong personality and an affinity for mirrors. To his credit, once he discovered how to gain individual solidity only to find out Klannit couldn't – not in the same way – Tvasitar never fell out of love with her.)

Fire Kings were King Cold's large-framed, fractious, as in hot-blooded, mostly blond and blue-eyed, battle-craving subjects from the days when Lathakra was Sedon's Horn. Intuits were big-headed, mutant telepaths bred, then forsaken as ugly undesirables, by Old Eden's heartless scientists long before Humanity's Golden Age even began. Howsoever ironically given who they chose to worship, they were generally small and robust, with reddish or brownish skin.

Fire Kings reminded Outer Earth outsiders of Scandinavian Viking types. Intuits were akin to the Inuit of northern Canada, Danish Greenland and Soviet Siberia. Contrarily to many, they were mostly followers of Tantal's Crimson Queen (and onetime Scarlet Empress) from when she, by herself, ruled Mythland, the Jewel in Sedon's Crown (the Mystic Mountains, sometimes also Sedon's Headband) and the then, effectively, seat or foot of Sedon's Horn.

Tiny Tantal and ten foot tall Methandra were used to his comings and goings by now. They needed only a couple of seconds to remember who he was and thereafter recall all they had been doing together for the past five years.

For his part, the Judge (Druj = Lie) was happy to see Tantal the mouse he always figured he was once again. He still cherished the hope that in one of her periods of hugeness Methandra would simply crush her drunkard husband out of existence. It hadn't happened yet. But that didn't mean it never would.

Did that make him Sedon, down from the sky? Probably not.

=========

Of all the females he had known in the millennia of his daemonic, as opposed to his vastly longer devic, existence – and there had been many, hardly all of them Mithradites – only his natural wife, Primeval Lilith, Earthborn Princess of the Whole Earth, her mother (their mother, in some respects), and one other was Methandra's equal in his mind.

Night-shrouded Lilith had been irretrievably lost to his daemonic aspect within Ginny the Gynosphinx, unless it was Andy the Androsphinx, long before the Great Flood or Genesea. That one other wasn't Pyrame Silverstar, for a very long time Queen Gomorrah to his by now fused daemonic and devic King Sodom (not Sedon, he insisted).

As he'd just ascertained atop Dustmound, at Hadd's dead centre (Vetala's joke, not his), that one other had only recently revivified after almost precisely 500 years of physical and mental Death. She had, as a result, become so irrationally crazed she'd returned the very antithesis of her formerly incomparable self.

(Ah, but was she so far gone she'd become beyond retrieval? He'd find out; it was on his to-do-later list.)

True, if he was brutally frank with himself, his never-rewarded fascination with the ever-manipulative Mistress of Mythland mostly had to do with her unwavering resolve to remain Mithras's Virgin until she got what she wanted. Which wasn't him. Nonetheless, as Outer Earth rudely as it sounded, Methandra's wasn't called Hot Stuff just because her attribute was Heat.

Like most devils, Miss Myth hadn't become independently solid until roughly two thousand years after the Genesea receded and the Moloch Sedon transformed the already Hidden Headworld into a unified landmass. In the succeeding centuries, he had admired her from afar. So had Sedon and her nominal father, Thrygragos Varuna Mithras, particularly after Fitna Marutia (Strife) proved herself such a discordant bitch as the Zodiacal Age of Aries wound down.

Indeed, so had many other Master Devas and at least one other Great God, Thrygragos Lazareme, who was as rambunctious as he was dissolute. But she only had eyes for her biggest and baddest brood brother. Which of course explained why the consistently cantankerous King Cold pursued, and successfully bagged, so many other female devils.

He had no fear of getting burned. He wouldn't; not with his chilly disposition. He did it as if to spite – more like punish – her for wanting him all to herself.

(Miss Myth was no misnomer. Her protectorate was Mythland, the Jewel of Sedon's Crown; not Lathakra, which belonged to Tantal. As for her becoming Klannit's mother – Tantal was Klannit's father – that didn't count against her remaining Mithras's Virgin. At least it didn't in her mind. Both her and Tantal been eaten by daemonic lovers when she, they, in the usual fashion, conceived the universe's first identified azura.)

When this was all over, there'd be a reckoning between the cretin Cold and himself. Willingly or otherwise, Heat would be the prize. And he would win her.

Of that the Smiling Fiend had no doubt.

"Such as?"

========

Raven's Head blanked out. Exhausted. Plummeted earthward. Radiant Rider arced out of the cave-tunnel from the cathedral dungeon into the Calvary Cavern.

The Quadrang Nucleoids formed together as one incredibly powerful unit. Above Sisert, the Byronic Nucleus did ditto. An Apocalyptic Nucleus blew the top off of the cavern. Rose up. A rainbow caught Sundown and Raven. Deposited them beside a severely injured Wilderwitch atop Calvary Hill.

Gathered Dervish Furie and the Untouchable Diver in its iridescence. Flew up, through the hole in the roof and into the Silent Sands of Cathune Bubastis, once the Apocalyptic of Drought. If she was still upstairs in the Sedon Sphere looking down on them, Cat might have been licking parched lips in anticipation of company.

It had been lonely in the night's sky since Sedonda-Sunday.

========

Centurium was the now *'living'* central cavern of Temporis. Replicated during the French Revolution, its main feature was a precise reproduction of the chateau and grounds of Versailles. Within the great palace, Dand Tariqartha listened as his half-daughter explained what had happened to the Kronokronos Supreme.

(Queen Amphitrite, one of Shenon's two Aortics and, as such, one of Witch Isle's Quarter Queens, had been devil-possessed when she conceived her only child. The Dand her Dad rendered Lakshmi's consequential half-father – a mantel he'd replicated to look like the Greco-Roman god Neptune-Poseidon – wholly alive, and therefore safe to possess, mostly because he'd never made love to a Lemurian before.)

"I don't know why he did it, father." Lakshmi – a Kronokronos in her own right, even if the Dand's daughters were generally referred to as Kronakronas – was crying. "He had Cerebrus, was coming back to me, then he saw Bellona. Must have figured to finish him. I saw Carcinogen coming out of the air and yelled at the top of my lungs. Akbar just pitched forward and his sceptre blew them both apart."

"Except the Mithradites survived," said the Dand calmly.

"The Mithradites survived," agreed the still amphibious, but only half Lemurian, nevertheless effective princess. "The Leper grabbed Bellona and vanished." (Tariqartha had been occupying a self-replicated, water-breathing version of the Greek-Roman God of the Sea, Poseidon-Neptune, when she was conceived. Amphitrite, after all, was the name of the mythological god's truelove.)

"Well done, son."

Kronokronos Akbarartha came from behind the screen of some curtains into his father's antechamber. Lakshmi controlled her emotions; didn't rush to embrace the near-giant. He and Tariqartha clapped their similar looking clubs together then turned to the young woman whose eighteenth birthday was celebrated only yesterday. Akbar opened his arms but her pride was damaged. She held her ground, ignoring him; spoke directly to the Dand.

"You let me spew on and on. Why didn't you tell me he was alive?"

"We are battling for the survival of Temporis, girl. My son and this Damnation Brigade of his are the best hope we have to beat the Apocalyptics. Cerebrus was their leader. It made sense to try to rescue him. You handled that part very well, by the way. War was on his last legs so it also made sense for my son to try to take him out. Plague was a surprise factor.

"I mentally commanded Akbar to take that dive; he had no idea his sceptre had teleportive qualities here in Temporis. Frankly, neither did I. But mine does and it worked. Will work again. You shall be rewarded for your efforts on our behalf. Here, as a token of both my gratitude and my trust, this is yours."

Tariqartha reached out his power focus. Stunned, yet as coyly as ever, she hesitated. Looked first to the Dand then to the Supreme. "Why me? He's your first surviving born and you're a devil. Without it, won't you cathonitize?"

"I'm cathonitizing as we speak. It's the perfidious Corona. It almost wiped me out thirty-five years ago; it's finished the job today. I have passed my power sceptre to my son. On his behalf I give you his." He proffered it again. This time, perhaps only feigning reluctance, she took it.

"The defence of the realm is now in your hands," he said to ex-OMP. "Prove worthy of your birthright, your sheer awesomeness. Rule it well."

Tariqartha faded from sight. Sadly, Akbar watched him go. Quick as a flash, Lakshmi brought her club against his. It felt as if he'd been hit by a runaway train. He fell to his knees.

"Lakshmi?" he gaped, stunned by the blow. "What have you done?"

"You heard the Dand. The defence of the realm is in my hands. I need no outsiders to help me. Be gone!"

She slammed the sceptre onto the ground. He vanished. She went to the palace infirmary and did the same to Cerebrus. Then she went back up to the Hall of Mirrors. After ascertaining that the Apocalyptics no longer were in Temporis, she gave the long distance boot to Wilderwitch, Blind Sundown and Raven's Head.

While there was no sign of Airealist, they were the three that had stayed behind in the Cavalry Cavern lying injured – the Witch severely – or powerless, when Gloriel rainbow-rushed herself, Furie and the Diver upstairs in pursuit of the Apocalyptic Nucleus. These last she couldn't see from the Hall of Mirrors but she could see the hole in the roof of the Calvary Cavern. This she contrived to collapse and thereafter seal.

No one would ever venture inside that ill-charmed hollow again.

(The Calvary Cavern was where, in the next to last act of the War of the Apocalyptics, supras battled Mater Matare and her fourth generational offspring to a mutually near-ruinous standoff; this after the newly born devils had slaughtered so many hundreds of Temporites, fays included, in order to mature so rapidly and so strongly. As its name gave away, it was recreated moments after one of the most arguably important, but certainly controversial, events in human history — the Crucifixion of the non-Mandam Conquering Christ.)

Finally satisfied with all her good works of the last few minutes, she used her sceptre to contact Quarter Queen Amphitrite, who wasn't physically faraway. "Dand Tariqartha is gone, mother, cathonitized. But his talisman and all his powers are mine. So is Temporis and its replicated mantels. Mine to command. Have Crystallion destroy Centauri Island. We've all we need."

"Soon, youngster," came back the amphibious Aortic. "Soon!"

========

Never had human eyes beheld such a sight. Two titanic entities of pure power: a tetrahedron with the face of Medusa on each of its four sides; the Byronhead with its three eyes and three Nucleoids inside. Both were indescribably immense. They glowed with the intensity of the core of a nuclear reactor.

Two nuclei circled above Sisert. Sized each other up then struck out. Gloriel instantly realized this was no place for mortals.

Or angels!

========

In Frozen Lathakra, the mutual destruction of the Byronhead and the Apocalyptic Nucleus was felt immediately. Smoky Sedona's Spell of Disproportionment, which Spellbinder had enforced on Tantal and Methandra Thanatos since Black Lazam 5933 snapped. Tantal was once again seven feet tall; Methandra around six.

The two embraced joyfully. The Smiling Fiend backed into the shadows, burning with jealousy – that most ignoble of all ignoble emotions. Where was his reward? To what purpose were his efforts if Methandra was still enraptured by such a monstrously stupid, beer-guzzling buffoon as Old King Cold?

Despair, cousin of despond, was short-lasting. Mirth returned in a matter of seconds. Perhaps, they'd make more babies, more fourth generational devils. Devils that ultimately he'd command. He was their real father; the father of the now lost, but presumably just as retrievable Apocalyptic Nucleoids.

He was the conceptive catalyst as much – no, more; much more – as the Thanatoids taking possession of the Dual Entities that fateful day in Azky (June) 5908, the last month in the Lazaremist Ternary of the Sedonic Year. Or the Primary

Apocalyptics taking over Archon Oberon at the same time as Matare took over Cabala Erda back in 5850. His was, not to put any blunt point on it, the insertive thrust in each and every one of those occasions.

Master Devas couldn't possess other Master Devas. But his daemonic half could and did. Daemons just did it externally, not internally.

Methandra and Tantal broke their embrace. "What's so humorous, Smiler?" demanded the King of Lathakra.

"Existence!" he exulted.

========

He'd done it!

The first and most difficult aspect of his grand scheme was complete — and with a bonus. Great Byron was already gone. Sedon's Head was finally his for the taking.

The rest of the Whole Earth would be next. And thence, again and at last, the stars!

****

Seventh Moon: **Anarchism Forever**

========

Devauray, Tantalar 6, 5980

It happened so quickly.

One minute they were out on the deck of their seaside retreat basking in the surprising heat of a Tantalar Devauray in the Weirdom of Cabalarkon; the next they were in the heart of a frozen hell. One thing Melina nowadays Zeross, white-as-daylight twin sister of black-as-midnight Demios Sarpedon, was sure about: those were ambulatory snowmen come to haul her and her mixed-blood daughters elsewhere.

And she was helpless to do anything to stop them.

========

A purebred, hence absolutely alabastrine Utopian woman, her Outer Earth supra-codename had been Illuminatus. But that had been over a quarter century earlier. She was now the High Illuminary of Weir; had been, actually, since even earlier. All things being equal, then Master Kyprian Somata, who trained her, wanted Melina to succeed her as Master of the Weirdom of Cabalarkon.

It didn't happen. Something else that didn't happen was her marrying Master Kyprian's eventual successor (in 5950), Saladin born Nauroz, Kyprian's grandson. What did happen was her training in all things devazur — the Weirdom's ancestral enemies. It stuck. It didn't need to in order to realize where she was.

Ambulatory snowmen – called Yeti or Almasty, Sasquatch or Shurale, even Woodwose (Wood Goblin) and Bigfoot, when they slipped through dimensional fabrics between-space and ended up on the Outer Earth – were native to one place and, at least in its early centuries, only one place on Sedon's Head. The same was true of icemen; except, in their case, they were more akin to tellurian mantels than snowmen, who were at least mammalian.

That place was no longer called Sedon's Horn.

========

Saturday, December 6, 1980

"Hear me, rulers. My all-pervasive thought beams are permeating the Whole Earth. Changing the coherence of sentient beings everywhere. Converting your serfs to my way – the way! The way of totally self-determined freedom.

"Hear me, fascists. Helios is on the Moon. Destroying you!"

========

The United Nations of Earth Spaceship Liberty had been orbiting the Moon for ten days now. Sunday, two platoons, Lunar Assault Crews, shuttled from the UNES Liberty to the Moon's surface. They secured the perimeter around a large crater. One LAC Squad, two dozen men led by the American, Ned Johnson, ventured into it. Johnson, all his crew and all their equipment, had been instantaneously disintegrated.

Almost a full week had passed since then. The Russian, Leonid Kulagin, leader of LAC Two, together with his twenty-four men and all their equipment, was still on the Moon; still overlooking the apparently empty, *'big old hole full of moondust'*, as Johnson had originally described the crater.

The Soviets had meditated upon the hole while they waited on further orders from the Liberty. Sometimes it was just a big old hole. Sometimes they could see within it a huge, tri-towered, metallic citadel apparently with the capacity of holding a few hundred people. An alien-made island of life in the midst of desolation. Sometimes nothing, sometimes everything.

Usually by Sean Smythe – who, at fifty-plus, was probably not physically fit enough to be in space in the first place, let alone the Liberty's Number Two – Kulagin was kept apprised of everything that was going on upstairs. That the citadel actually existed had been revealed Thursday by a supranormally powerful human on the Liberty. His name was Mikelangelo Starrus. Supposedly the supra had gone across to it but hadn't been seen since.

As yet there had been no explanation for what had happened to him. Doubtless no explanation would be forthcoming. The crater was domed by a radiation field made out of Gypsium. LAC Two were well aware of what that meant. *'Whomsoever touches Gypsium touches both the unknown and the unknowable'.* Kulagin was as brave as the rest of his men. They feared not so much the unknown as the unknowable.

They feared Gypsium.

Kulagin had been told that, other than Jesus Mandam, twenty-seven years dead now, only three men knew enough about Gypsium to use it. One, Aristotle Zeross, hadn't been seen in three years – although there had been rumours aplenty on the Liberty that he might be behind what was happening up here.

Another was Romaine Kinesis. He had been consulted when the Liberty was being constructed and was the brains behind the non-traditional, Gypsium-propulsive, secondary fuel of the Cosmic Express, the mother craft of the cosmicar that had appeared in near-space, also last Sunday, but had disappeared on Tuesday. The third member of this Gypsium Triumvirate was reportedly as dead as Mandam, though not for quite as long. That was Kadmon Heliopolis and, as such, thought not to be a factor today.

They were related, these last three. Heliopolis's mother was Argiope Zeross, the sister of Angelo, Aristotle's father. Kinesis's mother was Roxanne Heliopolis, the sister of Agenor, Kadmon's father. As boys in 1948, they had not so much discovered as named Gypsium on the Aegean Island of Trigon. Twenty years later, in October 1968, Heliopolis was killed when the island itself sank, never to rise again.

Once the citadel on the Moon had been revealed, it was shown to have three towers just as Aegean Trigon had three peaks. Earlier today, the speech of someone called Helios on the Moon had been broadcast through their transmitters. Dead or not, it now appeared that Kadmon Heliopolis was very much a factor.

There were those on the Liberty today who would have far preferred aliens.

========

The first, ultra-secret and never-to-be-revealed launch of the Columbia from the Kennedy Space Centre took place Thursday afternoon, December 4, 1980. Once in orbit, 40-something Professor Romaine Kinesis and (no-longer-thought) 60-something O'Ryan James Maxwell were transferred flawlessly to the Liberty's multi-purpose Lunar Assault Craft Three. Thereafter they were transported directly to the Mother Ship in moon orbit.

Eleven years earlier Apollo XI made much the same journey in approximately three days. LAC III did it in under two.

Then again, Apollo XI didn't have the assistance of Gypsium or a Gypsium Man.

=========

Saturday, around noon, satellites orbiting the Outer Earth detected a brief burst in the sky above the ship-shunned North Pacific.

The Soviets accused the Yanks of conducting an illegal, open air nuclear test. The Americans were of the opinion that a Russian atomic submarine had blown up in the middle of the ocean. Scientists throughout the world speculated endlessly about undersea volcanoes or meteorites colliding with the atmosphere.

Doomsters swore it was a spacecraft bearing the Anti-Christ. Mystics nodded knowingly, referred to the prophecies of Nostradamus, and smugly awaited a rose to bloom in France and bloodshed at the Vatican. The Chinese denied everything. They never said they wanted Hong Kong. Not really.

Later that night, while preparing for Lunar Assault Craft Three to arrive at the UNES Liberty after its near-Earth rendezvous with the Space Shuttle Columbia, Sean Smythe collapsed at his post. He was taken to sickbay in the deck below the bridge and placed under round-the-clock medical surveillance. Thus he was unavailable to greet the new arrivals when they finally made it there early Sunday morning.

That wasn't as remarkable as, at least in the view of the medical attendants, the fact that he was still alive. It was as if he was waiting for someone.

Some ones!

=========

"Johann Schmidt! Johann, This Is Sean. Amoebaman's Alive! He's A Three-Eyed Devil. No, A Six, Nine, Twelve-Eyed Fucking Hydra!
"He's Got Four Bloody Heads On Four Bloody Necks!"

=========

Sunday, December 7, 1980

Doubleman Smythe had been dying since what passed for Saturday night on the UNES Liberty.

Not just withering away quietly of old age – by his most negative reckoning, he was only fifty-four – Sean was actually losing substance. Sunday afternoon, after Kinesis and Maxwell were well-rested from their Gypsium-accelerated trip to the Liberty, its commander, James Aremar, informed them of Smythe's condition.

Even though they both knew him quite well, Maxwell was especially disturbed to hear the news. "Run that by me again?" Big Max demanded. Aremar did.

"And those were his last words?"

"Last scream, more like," said Aremar. "So it's true, what he said about him being this Leandro D'Angelo and having a mental link with Johann?"

"The last bit anyhow," granted Max. "There was a real Sean Smythe just like there was a real Johann, Bill White, Mary Schwarz, Ann Bianco, Barb Black, and

Joan Smith." He named the seven Septupleman (men and/or women). "I knew them all during the war and they did have an amazing, long-distance rapport. I'm not sure I'd go so far as to say they were amoebas made by Leandro, though. Supras never officially existed, you know," he added cagily.

"And Starrus didn't officially have three eyes," noted Aremar. "Except he did."

"Hadn't we better go see Sean, Max?" wondered Kinesis.

"We should have seen him as soon as we arrived, pro," said Max pointedly. James Aremar wasn't one to take even an oblique criticism lightly.

"And have two more God-cursed dead men on my ship?" he spouted. "Billowing bazookas, in case you didn't realize it, you two blowhards were out on your feet when you got off the LAC craft. Don't look much better now, as a matter of fucking fact. Want a mirror?"

Unsaid, but understood by Rom and Max, was that Aremar didn't particularly want them on the Liberty. Then again, they weren't just the two middle-aged men – late middle-aged in Max's case – Aremar thought they were. What they were was as yet unrevealed and Max at least wanted to keep them that way as long as possible.

"He's right," acknowledged Kinesis. "We needed our sleep."

The Psychic Sibling Barbara Black, one-time wife of Andrew *'Android'* Dulles – the supra code-named Mr Automatic – had been romantically entangled with Max's adoptive father, Colonel Jock Maxwell. They first got together at the conclave called by Jesus Mandam in September 1952 and stayed together long enough to have a child a year later. Not wishing to hurt his adoptive mother, Bonita nee O'Ryan Galvin, Big Max as much as accepted paternity for Dolph and took it upon himself to support the lad.

Perhaps ironically, after Barb's death a couple of years later, and as Max's duties with the Alliance of Man increasingly kept him away from Ottawa, it fell to the elder Maxwells to raise the boy. Thus Dolph was brought up by his real father. That youngster's situation was somewhat analogous to that of Simon Lancz and Bruce Dre'Ath a decade earlier.

In Simon's case, it was the obverse. OJ as BJ (Baron Justice) had assassinated the newborn's father, Donar Lancz, the Teutonic Templar or Terror as the Allies called him, in 1943. Except – according Simon's mother, the beguiling, golden-haired, but doomed Valfreja *'Freya'* Lancz – Big Max was Simon's actual father. Like Bruce, Bunnie's grand nephew, he was raised by the elder Maxwells first in Scotland then in Canada after they moved there in the late Forties.

Jock and Bunnie were still at the child-rearing game – helping to bring up Timothy James, Big Max's leg-crippled son by Aranyani Nightingale, in Vancouver. Now seventeen, TJ was more their child than Max or Aran's. (Aran, in fact, was not even allowed to see the boy. Understandably. She was the one who ruined his legs because, she claimed, the Devil did not take kindly to cripples. That she never faced criminal charges for her actions had a lot do with her father, Loxus Abraham Ryne.)

Max's involvement with the once seven-strong Psychic Siblings was more than just accepting some responsibility for Dolph. Much like father, like son, up until her in effect execution in April 1960, he had been romantically attached to the last of the four female members of Septupleman, Joan Smith, for nearly a decade.

Although conspiracy theories as to the party actually guilty of her murder varied widely at the time, Max eventually determined the ultimate blame lay with the Gynosphinx – a woman who looked a lot like a young and healthy Corona Power, but turned out not to be. (As for who was really behind WORLD, well, it was an acronym and, um, so was AMERICA and SPACE. Guess who coined them?)

In June '65, immediately after Doubleman Johann Schmidt strangled Horatio Kephren (the self-codenamed Anthrosphinx and son of the original Second World War Sphinx, Seth Kephren), Max personally plastered the female sphinx all over the walls of a unfinished room in the underside of Centauri Island with the bazooka part of his hand-made three-in-one rifle. He didn't think another version of her could be responsible for Smythe's current condition, but there were disturbing parallels.

For one, the Gynosphinx had clearly mind-manipulated Joan in '60 and, for another, five years later she overrode the better instincts of the two remaining siblings, Smythe and Schmidt. She in fact got her roost beneath Centauri Island first by controlling Johann then, through him, Sean, who was in charge of island security in those days. More importantly to his mind, when Joan was killed, Johann and Sean almost died as well.

Thus, if the offshoots of the devil-ray victim-cum-supranormal called Amoebaman Prime, Leandro D'Angelo by birth – he knew that Smythe had been telling the truth but hadn't seen any reason to confirm it to either Aremar or the professor – were so close, if Smythe was dying because of something on the Moon, what was happening to Johann Schmidt?

Aremar accompanied them to the infirmary, explaining everything that had happened since Cosmicar Two appeared in near-space, as if out of nowhere, last Sunday. If Kinesis hadn't encountered the Whirling Deva a week earlier, if Maxwell hadn't discovered he was some sort of No Name thing, or at least had access to one, they might have been tempted to laugh in his face. Knowing what they now knew, having experienced the insanity that had come of their lives and the world around them firsthand, the two were almost stoical in their reaction to Aremar's news.

"Nothing surprises me any more, Jim," pronounced Maxwell. But I know something that would surprise you, he thought to himself.

Probably only seven or eight people left alive – himself, his adoptive parents (Jock and Bunnie), Abe Ryne, Headmistress Virginia Mannering, the Antheans' former Superior Dolores D'Angelo, the little trickster and, possibly, though unlikely, Hiliarti Schroff-Zeross, the Ants' latest Superior – knew Aremar and Starrus were twin brothers, the sons of two of the most powerful supras ever known.

They'd been kept apart as much they could, given they both worked for AMERICA in the late Sixties, mostly because Superior Sorrow feared proximity to each other would trigger latent supranormal abilities inherited from their never-identified (other than by codenames) parents. That was clearly Mik's case. Had the same thing happened to Aremar? There was no evidence so far, but how could he be sure?

Far more disturbing was Aremar's assertion that Starrus went to the Moon Thursday and hadn't been heard from since. Max well-remembered Abe's declaration that if Emp En or that time's supra Headmistress had been on the same side as either Hitler or the King Conqueror, the Allies wouldn't have won the war. Helios on the Moon was already a daunting prospect but if Starrus – who sounded like he had come into Energy's abilities, or something similar – had joined him, what chance did any of them have?

"When it comes right down to it," added Kinesis, "Kadmon being still alive and on the Moon almost makes sense."

"How so?" wondered Aremar.

"Gypsium, Jim. During the late Fifties and early Sixties, when I was doing most of my schooling and early research work, it was a given that the largest deposit of the stuff was in Siberia, beneath where what might have been a comet collided with the atmosphere in 1908. Nowadays there's a lot of talk of a larger deposit in the Yucatan Peninsula – its delivery system, whatever it was, killed the dinosaurs, some say – but it's even more spread out than the one in the Tunguska Region.

"We also know of good-sized concentrations in Arizona, Northern Quebec, Easter Island, and in the vicinity of a growing list other ancient and not so ancient impact zones. Furthermore, it's a fact Gypsium generates inside the Earth and comes out in volcanic lava flows, which accounts for our discoveries on Centauri Island and, before that, on Trigon. And you know what happened to Trigon."

"Rom's always wanted to bomb Easter Island," said Max. "Just to see if it would vanish like Trigon did." He wasn't joking and neither Aremar or Kinesis laughed.

"When I had the opportunity to examine the rocks brought from the Moon a decade ago," continued the professor, "It became clear it, here, down there, held a veritable mother lode of Gypsium. So, like I said, it makes sense. The Moon's pocked with craters. Nothing we can do about that. Question is what we're going to do about him; them, if Starrus is still down there?"

"Stop him, them, of course."

"You sound like Abe," grinned Max. His was a chilling smile, thought Aremar. Almost like he had too much face.

"Ryne conscripted you," James Aremar reminded Maxwell – not that Loxus Ryne had not conscripted Aremar, too. "He had NASA then SPACE shuttle you up here, so he must have had his reasons. Can you send Helios back to whatever hell spawned him?"

"I wonder if that's where the word came from?" the professor muttered absently. (He wasn't an archetypal absent-minded professor, just sometimes talked to himself without realizing it. The Great Man, Abe Ryne, did that too, though Max was pretty sure he did it deliberately. Kept a miniature tape recorder in his pocket as well, presumably just in case he said anything worthy of posterity.)

"Hell, from Helios, the Sun. Both places are supposedly damn hot. We know the sun is for sure."

"Guess we're about to find out, pro," said Max.

"Actually," said the Liberty's captain, "I'm pretty sure it came from Hel or Hela, the Norse Goddess of the dead not killed in battle. She was Loki's daughter, doubled as their queen of the underworld." (In addition to an unnatural gift for languages, Aremar had an almost Godling-like fascination with ancient myths and religions, not that he saw much difference between the two.)

"I like my idea better," said Kinesis.

Aremar opened the infirmary door. Smythe was lying on the bed. Quite literally he was a shell of his former self; almost transparent, virtually vanishing before their eyes. Instinctively – maybe he had learned something from Hush in the short time they spent together Sunday and Monday – Max placed his hands on Smythe's fragile-looking forehead. Universal substance flowed out of its fount between-space, what old-timers like his Godling foster parents sometimes called Samsara, and into the stricken man.

Although his skin colour went a ghastly grey, he was suddenly entirely solid again. And with it. "Jesus Christ! That you, Max?"

"It's me, Sean. Not Christ. Or Jesus anyone else. Something's happening to you. We're amongst friends here. Tell us about it while you still can."

"Thanks for the encouragement. Guess I'm not here for the long term. Shit slapped on the smacker, Max. I'm wallowing in the crap of nearly forty years past."

"Afraid we all are, Leandro," Maxwell said consolingly.

Aremar gave him a withering glance but held his peace. Oh well, thought Max, given their situation, trying to keep supra-secrets just that, secret, was probably a pointless, perhaps even dangerous waste of time. He blurted out something he shouldn't have, maybe Hush or some other witch, Morgianna Sarpedon perhaps, could redact it later, to use witch-lingo. (Always assuming top-drawer witches weren't up here on the moon with Helios pulling his strings, that is. Also always assuming they lived through whatever they'd have to do.)

"So you do remember. Thought as much. Amnaesthetics never affected you," grinned Smythe hollowly.

"I was never hit with amnaesthetics. Abe Ryne liked me just the way I was. I lost my supranormal abilities shortly after the war ended. Much the same as you."

"Except, when Leandro D'Angelo died in '46, I wasn't just him anymore. I was Septupleman: seven distinct individuals. Only two of us are left now and I'm on my way out."

"Don't ask me how but I've somehow found powers again myself, Sean. A lot more than Justice ever had. I can hold you together."

"For how long?"

"Give me a chance," pleaded Max. "I haven't been a supra for thirty-five years, man. Have next to the vaguest idea of what I can do yet. Tell me what's happening to you."

"Amoebaman, the real Amoebaman, Amoeba Prime from before our Prime was ever devil-rayed, is on the Moon," said Smythe, reiterating his thought-shout to Johann Schmidt, the one Adolph Dulles picked up the night before on Centauri Island. "His name is Constantin Thanatos, though he's possessing – his words – a guy called Anon Sasarian, just like the Yajur-being was possessing Mikelangelo Starrus."

Which means, Max again thought to himself, proximity to Aremar didn't trigger any abilities Mik might have inherited from their parents. Perhaps desperately, he took that as being good news. "How do you know this?"

"We've been having a kind of mental communion, him and I. Tells me he's a fourth-generation devil, a grade down from Master Deva, whatever that is – something to do with Hinduism, I think. Word means Shining One but it's where the Greeks got Zeus and the Romans *'deus'*, for god.

"Seems being fourth generational is a situation unique to him and his siblings. There's ten of them, though there could be a dozen, maybe more, by now. Other than five of the others are on the Moon with him, he doesn't know how many of them there are for sure. Or even if suchlike are exclusive to his family anymore.

"Until they came along end-Teens, early-Twenties, these devils only had three generations: Father, Sons and Holy fucking Ghosts, only there's nothing holy about them. Claims they were quite literally stars for ten years. Then part of him, his powers and a little of his mind, was sucked out of the night's sky and filtered into me, Leandro, by Satan St Synne's devil-ray."

"Satan St Synne was Sedon St Synne, Leandro D'Angelo's maternal grandfather," Aremar provided for Kinesis's benefit. The professor grunted quietly; perhaps in acknowledgement, more like in awareness. Max shushed them both. Smythe kept talking.

"He says I'm part of him, not a real human being at all. Says my nearness is the only reason he's conscious while the others are still out of it. Says sacks of shit more," Smythe quavered visibly and grit his teeth in an effort to stifle the agony. "He's devouring me. In the name of Christ, let me go!"

Maxwell did just that. Sean Smythe completely faded from sight; didn't leave a corpse: just wasn't there any longer.

"We're too late for him," he stated the obvious, though he further realized it might not be quite as obvious as all that. "But I've a sense Sean's somehow still around. Might even be able get him back eventually, but I'm not going to try it right now. Don't want this Helios being the only one full of surprises."

What one wants, one rarely gets.

========

Alarms went off throughout the Liberty.

"Battle stations, battle station" *came the automatically-triggered computer voice in a dozen languages. Aremar raced out of the infirmary and ran up to the bridge. He unholstered his prized Colt; was in no mood for trifling. About time bullets flew, he was thinking. Kinesis — but not Maxwell, for some reason — chased after him.*

"Report!" demanded Aremar. "What's going on now?"

"It's Kulagin, sir. He says they're coming out."

Aremar had almost forgotten LAC II, under the command of the veteran Soviet cosmonaut Leonid Kulagin, was on the Moon. Had been since the previous Sunday.

"God curse you, man. Who? On screen!"

========

Two dozen men in SPACE's uniforms-cum-survival suits, now coated in a silvery substance, were marching out of the Lunar Citadel that Mik Starrus had supranormally revealed on Thursday. Unmistakably they were Ned Johnson and Lunar Assault Crew One (LAC I). Waving banners emblazoned with a Black Rose in the airless space of the Moon, they were shouting over their transmitters.

Their words were piped through the Liberty without anyone flipping a switch.

VIVA LA LUNA

VIVA EL SOL

LONG LIVE HELIOS

ANARCHISM FOREVER!

"Attack!" came Aremar's order from the Liberty. Like the rest of his men, Kulagin hesitated. Johnson did likewise. At his signal, the latter's lunar attack crew dropped their weapons and flung open their arms. Spontaneously the Soviets did likewise. The two LAC squadrons embraced each other.

"Come along, Leo," said Johnson. "Let me show you paradise."

Fifty men walked towards the citadel and went inside it.

========

"Right, you sons of bitches," swore Aremar on the bridge of the Liberty. "If you won't attack, I'll do it for you. Ready a barrage. Target tower one. On my command."

"No use, sir," said one of his technicians. "Weapon arrays won't power up."

========

"That's the problem with 'puters, Jim-jab," said a newcomer speaking with a phony-sounding Scottish brogue. "There's always one smarter. Mine's been running this ship since I got rid of the malodorous Sparky Fuckhead three days ago." (Sparky was a nickname used by Yajur's less than adoring public 500 to a 1,000 years earlier, during the Hidden Headworld's halcyon centuries of the Harmony Unity's version of Panharmonium, the one wherein she acted as a one-woman Trigregos Sisters.)

"Hello, Rom. Long time no see. Lot longer time for me than you."

"You're not Kadmon!" challenged Kinesis.

"Nay, laddie. I be the Laird of Lethal Letters."

In a kilt, sporran, tweed jacket, knee-length socks tied with garters, and brogues (oxford shoes) much more genuine than his brogue, he was certainly dressed for the part. With a full beard and no moustache, his hair was dirty blond with a hint of grey. He had a tartan tam-o'-shanter on his head and a matching sash pinned to his right shoulder by a brooch. Both the tam and the brooch featured a Black Rose, an anarchist symbol from way, way back – to the time of the Etocretans, the True Cretans, if not to Atlantis, Lost Eden – festooned on it.

Slung across his back were antique bagpipes. In a black, metal-reinforced leather sheathe to his right side – Kinesis remembered Kadmon was ambidextrous but tended to use his left hand slightly more than his right – was a long, thick-bladed, basket-hilted claymore. In his right hand, he held a strangely glowing stick shaped like the letter 'Y'.

"Bullshit. You're God-cursed Helios come for tea!"

Aremar pointed his revolver at the newcomer but before he could pull the trigger – in a spacecraft, no less, though not one then currently experiencing weightlessness – the Laird waved his stick. The Colt flew out of his hand and across the bridge. Suddenly Aremar was on his knees, sweating in terror. The Laird released him.

The rest of his men and Rom Kinesis had watched the brief encounter without making a move to help. None of them even offered him a hand to get up so, shaking visibly, more in anger than because of any injury, Aremar hauled himself to his feet. He glared at his fellows on the bridge, particularly Kinesis, but refrained from any further threatening gestures.

The Y-Stick was obviously similar to Rom's arm rods, which were hidden beneath his long sleeves. Nonetheless, Kinesis thought to himself, it was a pretty elementary use of Gypsium. He figured he could do better, but wasn't ready to tip his hand and become the Gypsium Man quite yet.

There was also no sign of either Maxwell or Mr No Name to back any play Doc Defiance might chance. Big Max had said this Helios, whoever he was, wasn't the only one with surprises up his sleeve. Kinesis just wished Max had shared whatever strategy he'd developed.

"All right," braved Aremar. "Call yourself whatever you want. What are you doing here?"

"Curiosity, laddie. Those were your men down there, yet you were willing to kill them? How come? That's a Y-question. Answer it carefully."

"Were is right; meaning wrong is why. Except you're who's wrong, all wrong. Somehow you've managed to turn my SPACE men against us; the same as you're trying to turn the whole world upside-down. It won't work on me. I know my loyalties. Either I'm going to find a way to destroy you or you're going to have kill me; kill us all."

"Am I indeed, Jimbo?" the Laird said. "Druther not, sooth said. Had enough of killing myself. So has the world. That's what I'm doing. Making it a safe place for everyone – man, beast and bog. To prove my good intentions, I'm inviting you to supper. Tomorrow, that'd be Monday night. No need to drive. Spirits will be free and plentiful, so I'll provide the transportation as well. Don't thank me. RSVPs unnecessary. C.U. then. Ta-ta."

He put mouth to pipe, let loose a brain-splitting squeal and was gone.

Reflexively angrily, Aremar whirled on the professor. "What's the matter with you, Kinesis? That was him. No matter what he calls himself. Why didn't you challenge him?"

"And end up like you, humbled and on your knees? I'm a scientist, Jim, not a fighter. What's happened to me this week is almost beyond belief. Besides, in case you haven't noticed, we're in a spaceship. In outer space, for Christ's sake. I'm like Max. Still not sure of what I can do. We start going at each other with Gypsium in the Liberty, God alone knows what'll happen."

"You're telling me you're God-cursed supras?"

"Why'd you think Ryne sent us up here?" the usually mild-mannered professor verbally blasted Aremar. Frustration, and a complete lack of confidence in the abilities of Doc Defiance, overwhelmed his better senses. "To hold your bloody hand?"

"Fucking Hell!"

Regaining at least partial control of himself, Rom reverted to reason, his scientific stock-in-trade. "Besides, if that was my cousin, I owe it to whatever's left of our mutual family – which, I grant you, isn't much, and all of it on the Zeross side – to try to help him overcome whatever madness has possessed him. Not to challenge him, as you say; not to take him on, with no chance for compromise and only limited opportunity for success."

(Although Rom's mother was a Heliopolis, Roxanne, his father's sister, Megaera, married a Zeross, Angelo.)

"Hell, in a fair fight, Kadmon would probably box your ears and I'm a wimp. No, supper sounds good to me. Besides, it's the only way I can think of whereby I could get into that citadel without trying to teleport there myself. Don't know if I could pull that off, to be frank. Not up here. And like I said …"

"You're a waste of time. So is Maxwell. Where is he?"

"Oh, I'm sure he's around someplace."

========

The Laird stepped out of the teleport chamber and into the third tower of the Lunar Citadel. Mnemosyne was waiting for him.
Suddenly he was caught in a stasis beam.

========

"Hey! What's going on? I can't move."

"Because you're not the same Helios who left here."

"Have ye gone mad, woman? I'm the Laird of Lethal Letters. Of course I'm the same Helios." He managed to raise the bagpipes' tooter to his lips. "I warn you, computer. I will not tolerate treachery."

She released him, though not only because that's what he wanted. "You were milligrams heavier. Now you're back to normal. What was it?"

"Interesting," said Helios removing his laird makeup and false beard. "Something must have attached itself to me on the Liberty, tried to follow me back here between-space. Luckily it was clumsy, not really aware of what it can do. You spotted it and it fled. Unless it's somewhere in here now."

"Impossible. I'd have detected it."

"How can you be sure? You've had viruses before. I want you to check out your systems, all of them — here, Trans-Time Trigon, Rep-Trigon in Temporis, and even in the remnant of the King Conqueror's attempt at recreating it, and you, in the Ukraine. We have to be wary of more than just devils, Milady Memory. The Liberty may be disarmed but I want the Gypsium Curtain raised again and I want backup shields in place."

"They already are. I'm in tune with Samsara, mundane reality. I can handle anything that comes out of it. What are you so concerned about?"

"Just that: Samsarites, Bodhisattvas. Program yourself to repulse Multivoids."

"Boddhis, in this era? Of course! That's what Maxwell's become." She paused, as if to access her memory circuit but actually more out of human habit. No matter what form the three-thing was in – human, devil or just built-in-place machine – her memory circuits were always instantly accessible.

"Bad Boddhis," she considered, "Not the ones Buddhists believe in, the ones we came across in previous lifetimes, started out as glorified mandroids, Utopian half-lifes, roughly the equivalent of Tariqartha's mantels, in one way, or Callion-clones, in another. Big Max Maxwell was reputedly one of the first two or three of those last. But they shouldn't have evolved into Samsarites, into effectively new life forms, until centuries from now. Only it isn't centuries from now anymore. It's now."

"That sort started now, yes, but developed already? I can't see it. Not unless you're right and we've happened into an alternative timeline. There must be another explanation."

"That he is akin to the ones Buddhists believe in? They do exist and not always in today's future. Devils encountered them a few times while the Sedonshem crisscrossed the cosmos."

"So you've gleaned from all the devils you've used to humanize yourself over the ages."

"Who can't lie."

"Maybe not, but where did he come from all of sudden? I'll never buy into any of that alternative timeline nonsense. That's our Rom Kinesis, our James Aremar."

"But not your Lord Vajra; not my Erebe, Dame Darkness?"

"Of course not. Contrary to what you may believe, time paradoxes don't drive me nuts, milady; they're impossible. We time-tumble; no one else does. He must be an anomaly; one either we, or someone else, will eradicate shortly, before he has a chance to multiply. We have to assume he is a premature Void and act accordingly. You remember how to handle them?"

"You don't call me Memory for nothing, my love."

"They can come at you from anywhere and everywhere at once," he recited to himself. "Got to bombard them with Gypsium. They'll reflexively make themselves composed of Solidium. That's when you hit them like mandroids. Fracture, fragment them, then teleport them helter-skelter, into a multitude of voids. By the time they pull themselves back together it'll be the end of the universe. Or as good as!"

"I did invent the process," she protested.

"You also invented Voids as I recall," he challenged her.

"Not any time soon!" she snapped. "All right, I'll do it. But that doesn't mean I'll like it. Ask me it's time, past time, to dump Maxwell and the Liberty, along with the six cosmicompanions left and their cosmicar into the Black Hole after Starrus-Yajur. Let whoever's on the other side, if anyone, deal with them."

"I told those over there I was tired of killing. And so I am. But that doesn't mean I won't reconsider. Let's give it another day, milady. I might still be able to conscript Rom and Max, maybe even Aremar."

"Besides Demonites' bastard, Dmetri Diomad, and Mikelangelo Starrus, Maxwell and Aremar are the two main ones who did you in in the first place," she reminded him unnecessarily.

(Himself a bastard in that his parents weren't married when they had him, Demonites was the first born of Angelo and Megaera born Kinesis, who didn't become a Zeross until some time after Dem's birth in 1931. Dem's Dim, as they sometimes thought of him when they were younger, was born in 1953. He was only most likely Demonites' son because his parents pretty much raised him, on Trigon, while Dem himself was away on Crete or elsewhere, on AMERICA's business.

(If he was, then Dmetri's likely mother was Roxanne nee Heliopolis, Kadmon's aunt, if she wasn't his much older sister by his own father, her brother. Which wasn't as farfetched as it might seem. All sorts of strange, mostly never-remembered 'stuff' happened during the Godling Guild's Summoning of 1920.

(Even though she was around 40 when she died having Roxanne over that Christmas-New Years period, photos from the era showed Kadmon's grandmother, Aerobe nee Catreus, was a stunner. Reportedly she was also a Lovely Lady Afrite, the same as Roxanne became once she fell under the influence of none other than Mnemosyne D'Angelo, herself eventually Heliopolis, Moon Memory's template.)

"Don't let any false sense of fraternal affection for Rom Kinesis misguide you," the Mnemosyne 3-Thing added. "They're our enemies."

"Just because we hadn't thought of them as they seemingly are, doesn't mean we can't handle them."

"I know that tone. You're spoiling for a fight. Don't lose it now that we're so close to getting it right."

"I wasn't joking, Memory. And, if I am spoiling for a fight, which I am, you're the only one who'd give me a good go-round."

Still defiant, Mnemosyne goaded him. "And what good would that do? A word from you and I cease functioning. That's how you programmed me, But don't forget where we are. I cease functioning and what happens to your life support systems. You die, we'll only get together again in your hundredth and first lifetime. I've said it before, do you really want another life when we're so close to your first?"

"You're not much fun this lifetime, milady," noted Helios without giving her the satisfaction of telling her she was right.

Moderately chastened, the trinary, ternary or tripartite being that was the Female Entity offered a compromise. "At least let me jettison the cosmicompanions, especially Nidaba."

He still wasn't going for it. "As for them, they might be able to subsume the devils inside them; to become supras in their own right, like my father before me and Human Memory before you. If they don't there's always eyeorbs. The Black Hole remains a last resort only. Like I just said, I've given up killing."

"You're too much the carnivore for that," she as good as scoffed. "All that's really changed about you is that you've started to confuse yourself with God again."

"God, milady?" Helios sounded hurt. "I thought I'd cured myself of that pretension lifetimes ago."

"This is getting us nowhere."

"You're right," he placated her. "Be vigilant. It's time I got some sleep."

Showing her humanity, the Mnemosyne Machine in human form had to laugh, albeit in a pleasant, not a scoffing way. "It never ceases to amaze me how you, Heliosophos, self-proclaimed Wisdom Incarnate, still has to sleep. Mind if I join you?"

"You don't sleep."

"I wasn't about to."

"That's what I hoped you say."

"Hoped or telepathically programmed me to say?"

"Hoped. Don't you program yourself these days?"

"Not as well as I thought."

========

"Where've you been?"

Maxwell was still in sickbay. He looked haggard, was even talking to himself, when Kinesis entered. "Nowhere, Rom," he lied. "Just sitting here thinking out loud."

It wasn't true. 'Bad Boddhis bite,' he thought, but this time made sure he didn't audibly mutter.

========

Kinesis sat on the cot where Sean Smythe had vanished. "That something else you picked up from all those years with the Great Man?"

"Must be, I guess. What was that all about?"

Kinesis told him about Kulagin and his men entering the Lunar Citadel; then about the visit of the Laird of the Lethal Letters, whom he now believed was indeed his cousin, Kadmon Heliopolis. Even as a kid Kad, he'd enjoyed dressing up; was good with languages, too, albeit not anywhere near Aremar level.

Was as skilled at picking up accents from radio broadcasts as he was at suppressing his own Grecian one while speaking a different tongue in the tourist centers of Iraklion (Heraklion), Crete, and Athens, on the Mainland. Was a child prodigy in so many ways the Zerosses, who raised them all, both during and after the war, feared he might be targeted by embittered enemies of the Black Rose for his precociousness alone. No wonder their tutor on Trigon during the war years, Headmistress Virginia Mannering, called him El Draco.

"He's different – Kadmon, I mean. But so are we. I don't see the point of trying to turn back the clock. He's invited us for supper tomorrow night. All of us. Everyone on the Liberty. Aremar doesn't want us to go, thinks Helios will mind-control us. Ask me, why'd he bother, given what he can do?"

"Whatever that is."

"Whatever indeed," Kinesis shrugged, appreciating that by that Max meant Helios wasn't God. Couldn't be. Otherwise He, capitalized, would just wave subtle matter, filigreed fingers and do just that: whatever He heavenly well wanted to do. Except, of course, what religious types – which neither he nor Max were – actually wanted Him to do.

"Anyhow, Aremar's trying to get hold of Loxus right now. The Great Man will probably overrule him. It's just the *'in'* he wants for us to get close enough to Helios to use whatever we've got, our supranormal shit, on him. Regardless of that, Aremar and the rest of his men will go armed to the teeth. Likely so will you. Which means we'll all get our bums busted.

"I'm sorry, Max, but I have to wonder if it's worth the struggle. Why don't we just join Helios? You know he's right about what we've done to the planet, and ourselves. Maybe his way is the way. Men and women are born knowing the difference between right and wrong. It's what beaten into us afterwards that so fucked up."

Maxwell chose to ignore that. A fighter all his life, he wasn't about to give up so easily. Nevertheless, he controlled himself by not calling the professor what he was: a mush-minded, idealistic coward who never recovered from the nonsense his born-rich, philosopher foster father, Angelo Zeross, was forever spouting.

Not that there was anything wrong with cowards, he supposed, succumbing to Helios-inspired thinking. They just shouldn't be in a battle zone.

"I can't believe he'd have me or Jimmy. We might not be the fascist pigs he was railing against in that rant he broadcast, but I'm sure we'd qualify as their lickspittle. We did help kill him, or wanted to, remember? The Heliopolis I knew never had much in the way of a forgiving nature and, if Starrus's absence is any indication, this Heliosophos fellow doesn't either."

"You don't think he is Headmistress's El Draco, do you?"

"Don't really care who, or what, he is, pro."

Kinesis tried a different tact. "Still think Smythe is around?"

"Same thing. Wish I could be sure. Way back in the Big Bloody, even when Amoeba Prime wasn't on our side but the Psychic Siblings were, the Society of Saints had a ploy we used a number of times. One of our agents would take out the real thing and substitute either an amoeba or someone like me who was good at impersonations. Sometimes the old gambits are the best."

"You spoke German like a native."

"Victor Richter was a native. And Baron Justice had a very, shall we say, Plasticine-like body in those days."

Kinesis had observed, especially during previous conversations re the *'Big Bloody'* and Max's role in it, that his difficult friend had a disturbing tendency to talk about himself in the third person. It was almost as if he wasn't named Richter for the first two decades of his life.

As for SOS – The Society of Saints, they had plenty of disagreements, politely put, with the Black Rose of Anarchy, Agenor Heliopolis's band of mostly Greek freedom fighters. Among them, Rom couldn't help but include a few supras, his parents most notably.

"Same as No Name does today."

"No Name's way beyond anything Justice ever was, pro, but he could probably pull the same stunt. What I'm getting at is that the so-called Psychic Siblings were bodybuilders, and I don't mean weightlifters, for a time. As well, just in case you don't know, Amoebamen numbered way more than the seven who survived the war as Septupleman."

Kinesis wasn't aware of that but it made as much sense as anything to do with supras did. He also wasn't about to interrupt Maxwell.

"Amoeba Prime, Leandro D'Angelo, was much more powerful – getting tired of that word – than that. Sometimes he acted as both the person who did the taking out as well as the one who replaced them. He could take people into himself and hold onto them, for awhile, just as well as he could manufacture substitutes."

"Wow!"

The exclamation came out inadvertently. Sometimes, especially when it came to supranormals, Kinesis couldn't suppress his amazement. And, to think, now he was one of them. How cool was that? More to the immediate point, how dangerous was that? Very, he answered himself silently. Max was still prattling.

"This devil, Constantin Thanatos, whom I assume is every bit as powerful as Prime – there's that word again – seems to have sucked Sean back into himself. Conceivably, he could do something similar to these five siblings of his. Suck them in, then eject them outside of whatever prison Helios and his buddies, assuming he isn't a one man show, is keeping them in.

"They'd have abilities probably similar to those imparted to the D'Angelos by their grandfather's devil-ray getting close to forty odd years ago."

Kinesis, who was born in late 1936 but hardly ever left Trigon during the war years, gave him a quizzical look.

"By that I mean," Max picked up, though he might still be talking mostly to himself, "Helios could be entertaining a Winterlady, a Madame Midnight, a Klarion, a Demon Land or, I expect, potentially any number of other, unrelated devils like your Devil Wind. If they got out, they'd cause him a lot of trouble. Hopefully that'd distract him long enough for us to take him down ... What?"

"You're not just talking to me, are you?"

"Nope. I've been sitting here trying to get Sean to understand everything I've been saying and thereby plant a plan of action into this Thanatos's mind."

"So you do think Smythe's still around."

"Figured it was worth a poke."

"All the same, I wouldn't make a habit of it. People might think you're even weirder than you already are." Feeling a bit spooked, Kinesis switched from the cot to another chair. "All right, say you did get through to him and he, or rather this devil of his, does what you want. How are we going to get to the Moon?"

Maxwell looked at him poignantly. There was no denying his intent. "Me, eh?"

"Gypsium, pro. Ringleader teleports, obviously so does Helios. Have I ever told you about your mother?"

"Not convincingly." What little he knew — now recollected, more like — came from the little trickster, Hush Mannering, who'd closeted herself with Max and him after they demonstrated supra talents on Sunday the Thirtieth. Max, though, had never been redacted by Hush or her witchy cronies so he was worth listening to on the subject.

Maxwell confined himself to Roxanne nee Heliopolis's time as the supra codenamed Slipper from the Forties until amnaesthetics facilitated the rewiring of her memory in the early Fifties, at which point she allegedly lost her Slip-skills. He didn't feel it necessary to talk about the events of '65. Let Rom continue to think her dead in '60, not killed on Centauri Island five years later, mostly because he, Max, had been too slow to stop the Gynosphinx in time.

After he was finished, Rom shook his head. "So she was a self-teleporter, could take others with her if she was holding onto them, could hide in Samsara, like some of these witches you were just mentioning, and was a dirty fighter along the lines of this fellow Airealist — who was an adopted D'Angelo but, you reckon, had his powers before he was hit with St Synne's devil-ray."

Clearly it was Rom's turn to think out loud. "I know I travelled through the Universal Substance on my way to close to Damnation Isle and that Devil Wind sent me back to Centauri the same way. That doesn't mean I can do the same thing to you; doesn't mean I can hide in Samsara; and certainly doesn't mean I can fight, dirty or otherwise."

"You said the Laird's Y-stick was a lot like your rods."

"I also said it struck me as a bit simplistic compared to what I know I can already do with Gypsium. But that's no guarantee he can't do a lot more. He might have been teasing me. Point being, your assertion that whatever Helios, Harry or my mother could do with Gyps I can as well strikes me as either optimistic or, more likely, fallacious. We can or could do only what Gyps lets us."

"You've no confidence in yourself."

"What about you and this No Name character? He still around by the way? Didn't see you on the bridge."

"But he was — not on it, but part of it! By the other way, mine, I now believe he and I are the same thing. As near as I can make out we're, I'm, not like the dichotomous beings Mr Brilliant and Dr Dark were. Call it I then." He paused, not really sure he was making sense, even to himself. "Anyhow, I tried to hitch a ride to the Moon in the Laird's sporran. Got detected then rejected, though not by him I don't think. Made it back here, however. Through Samsara."

"Through outer space?" Kinesis was extremely impressed.

Although the how continued to elude him, Maxwell was almost as pleased. "All by myself, too. Which makes me think you can do the same thing. However, whereas I was rejected, possibly by Gypsium, which you figure is somehow sentient, possibly by some other agency, one that neither you nor I know anything about, you might make it."

"With you along for the ride."

"Gypsium might be more, shall we say, sympathetic to a Gypsium Man willingly carrying a hitchhiker than a Gypsium Man unwittingly carrying one."

"Might be," granted Kinesis contemplatively. "Look, as I told James Aremar awhile ago, I'm a scientist. We left Centauri Island before we could be properly trained — assuming properly can be by a little witch you call a trickster. I suppose I don't need to define the scientific method to you but, what I'm saying is, we should take the opportunity, this hiatus before supper tomorrow night, to train ourselves."

"In order to give a decent showing of ourselves, you mean?" As it happened Max was thinking somewhat the same thing. "To make a decent fight of it. To acquit ourselves well. And if Helios stomps us, well, at least we earned his respect. Maybe he won't kill us; maybe he'll adopt us instead."

"Don't be so cynical, Max. I want to even the odds, that's all. The Scientific Method?"

"Observe, hypothesize, test, analyze, retest," listed Maxwell, not really remembering what it was. "I'd like to get to the Lunar Citadel before the turn of the century, pro. Preferably before supper tomorrow in fact."

"Can't say it's impossible," granted Kinesis. "Not after all we've been through already this week. Right then! We'll begin in this room. Once we've an idea of what we can do we'll start going around the Liberty then – God forbid!, God help us! – have Aremar launch a LAC craft and see if we can get there. First of all, we better formally reintroduce ourselves."

If someone had just walked into the infirmary expecting to see Professor Romaine Kinesis and O'Ryan James Maxwell he wouldn't have thought he was in the wrong place. He would have thought he was on the wrong planet. Wrong planetoid? Wrong ship? They transformed into their supra-selves: big, darkly Mediterranean tanned and glowing; plump, ghastly white and prissily primped as kneaded dough.

That, at least, they could still do.

========

"I'm Doc Defiance, the Gypsium Man. And you, friend, must be the otherwise Indescribable Mr No Name."

"Call me Max."

****

EIGHTH MOON: **Repast With The Past**

========

Monday, December 8, 5980

Monday evening Moon-time, the Liberty was an empty husk of technological wonderment, unmanned and in the complete control of a three-thing — a human, devil, mandroid-cum-computer amalgam called Mnemosyne (meaning Memory). Its personnel, even its reluctant captain, were beneath the central dome of the outwardly tri-towered Lunar Citadel.

Thinking himself the perfect host, Heliosophos had made Intergalactic the featured theme of the menu. In deference to Memory's Anthean sentiments, Earth-style vegetarian dishes were also an option. Many of the Liberty's crew were highly-trained technicians or veterans from some of the bloodiest battlefields of the previous twenty years. The vast majority of these hard, almost religiously carnivorous men were opting for vegetarianism.

About the only omnivores were at head table.

========

"Try one of these, Rom," offered Helios, "Soft-shelled crustaceans from the fifth planet in the Alpha Centauri planetary system. Their slug-like interiors amount to the most exquisite of custard filling. They're steamed in their own slime."

With his wont for theatrics, Helios appeared not just bald but hairless. In the tradition of Curetes (or Corybantes) from Crete and elsewhere during Minoan times and later, he had powdered his skin white with gypsum. He wore a cloak of quetzal feathers, like a Guatemalan Mayan chief, and, to incongruously top off his outfit, a tall, muffin-shaped chef's hat.

Adding to his previously announced identities as *'His Story'*, the *'Lightray Lunatic'*, the *'Wizard of Warped Waves and Wondrous Ways'*, the *'Laird of Lethal Letters'*, and *'Heliosophos'* or *'Helios called Sophos the Wise'*, he introduced himself as the *'Quetzalcoatl of Cosmic Cuisine'*, a *'Chef Seriously Sane and Superior'*.

Not for the first time James Aremar wondered what he'd done to get caught up with a madman who wasn't just living his own fantasy but seemingly had the ability to force others to do so as well. What was far more galling was that Helios apparently had no fear of being shot deader than dinner. Anyone who wanted could remain armed.

"Don't mind if I do," snatched Professor Kinesis. "Those starred Betelgeuse bugbears were splendid by the way. Glazed in the beetle's own juice, were they?"

"Actually, yes."

========

"You're not eating, Memory," noted OJ Maxwell, somewhat familiarly given the only woman he ever knew by that name had been dead for thirty-five years.

Then again, this Memory might well have passed for Mnemosyne D'Angelo, ultimately Heliopolis, albeit a Memory of the Angels in her late twenties, some years before her onetime lover, Sedon by then Satan St Synne, hit her with his devil-ray in Vichy, France, in 1943.

"Maybe you should ditch the fright mask."

Like her sometime-husband, sometime-enemy, and oft-times-lover of nearly a hundred lifetimes, the humanized as well as humourously declared Shelios on the Moon had dressed for the occasion. Whereas he was a white god, she was a dark goddess. He had shaved his head — rather, the latest image of himself had a shaved head. Her hair was filled with snakes like a Medusa.

Her face was also one with the Grim Gorgons of Mediterranean myth: scowling, glaring eyes, tongue protruding through bared, sharpened fangs, and a crooked nose that would not have looked out of place on an eagle. With the addition of a Shadow Cloak to offset Helios's *'Quetzal Coat'*, she was, as the followers of Orphism might put it, the face of the Moon contrasted to Helios's face of the Sun.

A Gorgon's face and head was meant to scare off nosey people so Max's characterization of her look was bang-on. It also tended to put folks off their food, which she perhaps hadn't considered when she put it on.

Upon rapid reconsideration she obligingly, as well as instantly, face-danced such that she appeared in her youthful image of a Mediterranean Melanochroid, one with their typically dark, crinkly hair and an oval, blemish-free, but extremely pale face.

"Much better," he told her, albeit without much overt enthusiasm. "Although you don't look any happier. What's bothering you?"

"Not feeling entirely myself," she admitted. "I guess you aren't either."

"It hasn't affected my appetite. I suppose you remember us."

"Of course I do. Kad doesn't call me Milady Memory for nothing. You were codenamed Baron Justice whereas I began my supra-career as Circean. It was a very long time ago."

"Barely forty years," protested Maxwell. "Just before Olympian stole your affections. I admit I was a randy young buck and you were a more – what shall I say? – mature woman. But we were dynamite together. You initiated me."

"And Brother Raphael was horrified. Good Catholic girl like me an Afrite. Disgraceful, he said at the time. Not for the first time either. Mind you, for him sex was just an excuse for getting Sophia pregnant again."

"They're still alive you know."

"And I'm not. At least not entirely. Funny how things turn out isn't it."

"As near as I can make out, no pun intended, there's very little funny about you. How you'd end up like this, Memory? A veritable Shelios on the Moon, as you ever so cleverly put it, together with another dead person, here in a citadel that is apparently way, way beyond the technology of even Jesus Mandam. Not to mention everyone else on the planet below."

"That's a very long story."

"So is mine, only I still don't know all the beginning bits."

"Not as long as mine. Maybe we should trade. Stories, I mean. Don't fancy Lesser Magellan toe-brains myself."

"Rather like them myself, but you're right: *'Chacun a son gout'*, each to his own taste. Not particularly fond of your cholesterol-free silicon chips either." Max laughed at his own joke. He knew Memory was part machine. Memory didn't laugh, probably for the same reason. "So what have you been up to these last thirty-five years? Since Strife supposedly killed you on Sakhalin Island, I mean."

"Nothing much. Another ninety-nine lifetimes is about all. In some respects, it started with Eden, not the Garden, though that's where it was – Atlantis."

========

Edenites, she told him, Atlanteans if you prefer, knew the ice was melting. Had been for centuries. They tried to buttress their continent – which was in the environs of what was nowadays' Sargasso Sea – against it. But, by the time Trans-Time Trigon came back to Earth for the start of Heliosophos's sixty-first lifetime in approximately 5600 BC, it was a hopeless cause.

Remarkably, most had already taken to the stars to escape. This suggested Edenites were descended from the so-called *'itinerant angels'* of the not necessarily heavenly Celestial Sphere, a star-spanning race of humanoid beings whose home lies in the heart of the Milky Way. Equally so – which is really to say, who can say – they might have begun as shipwrecked Utopians from the much farther off Planetary System of either New or Old Weir.

What wasn't very likely was the notion they were native Earthlings; their technology was simply too advanced for that to be a creditable postulate.

Those that didn't fly off back to the stars, whence their ancestors came, abandoned the sinking continent years, if not decades, before it gurgled its last glug. These journeyed to the neighbouring continents of Africa, Europe, South and North America as well as Asia, Australia, Antarctica and the eighth continent, what was actually a massive archipelago – call it Mu or Lemuria, if you want, though its actual name was Pacifica, the Places of Peace – in what you now see as the North Pacific.

Regardless of where they came from, in its prime Atlantis was the seat of civilization on the Whole Earth; its people the self-evident Masters of the World. The rest of the planet was largely undeveloped. These refugees were the progenitors of the so-called Golden Age of Humanity. It lasted from about the time Trigon came to Earth until the Great Flood, a period of about sixteen hundred years.

It was called the Golden Age not because it sounds romantic, though it does. Atlanteans actually had golden skin, though some were more yellow or white and others more brown or black. The reason for this is they fed on golden apples. Yes, the very stuff of legend. They didn't grant immortality, though they did bequeath very long, health-filled lives — those ages given to the Biblical patriarchs in Genesis were representative. Neither were they just fruit from the Tree of Life in the Garden of Eden.

Like the American legend of Johnny Appleseed, the refugees planted the fast-growing trees wherever they went. And, as I said, their influence extended throughout the globe. Interestingly, understandably given the Genesea, they left only one monument on what I will call the Outer Earth: namely, the apparently male Sphinx in Egypt.

I say apparently because it – let's call it Andy, for Androsphinx – it doesn't have any wings; this in contrast to the females, who were always depicted with wings.

At any rate, albeit long immobile, Andy, the Egyptian Sphinx, survived the Great Flood that brought about the end of the Golden Age. It doesn't take much of an eye to see it still bears the scars, in the form of water markings, to show for it as well.

Much of its face, often reconstructed in Pharaonic times, has been eroded. You may have heard that it represents the Pharaoh Khafre. In fact, it was Helios.

========

"Alorus Ptah didn't start out as the Biblical Adam," Mnemosyne continued. "Make that the second Adam since, as any Biblical scholar worth his salt will tell you, there were two Adams in the Bible. He began as Kadmon Heliopolis, a Twentieth Century man who had already been killed sixty plus times.

"Our Eden wasn't just a garden. It was a landform that followed him, from lifetime to lifetime and throughout time and space. You were familiar with it, Aegean Trigon, the home of the Family Zeross and all those they helped raise right up until 1968. And I didn't start out as his Eve.

"As you well know I began existence as Mnemosyne D'Angelo, Codename Circe: a supranormal born in 1909, a Twentieth Century woman. I was thirty-one when he was born in 1940; his mother, Argiope nee Zeross, dying in the process. The next year I married his father Agenor, Olympian I, and gave birth to Europa, his only sibling."

"Who most people think was lost in 1960, along with Rom's parents," Maxwell finally contributed. "I'm one of the few people who know she actually killed herself in 1965, after her three daughters were slaughtered by a clone supposedly possessed of the spirit of Donar Lancz, the Teutonic Terror."

"So I understand," regretted Memory. "But I do not blame the clone. Caliban Kopf, the Headsman, couldn't help it that the second Moses Callion fashioned him out of Lancz, whom we also knew as Baphomet during the early years of the war. Nor is it exactly accurate to say he was possessed of Lancz's spirit.

"In effect he was as much Lancz as Moe Two was Moe One or Steltsar was the old Baron, Tyrtod von Alptraum. What he was possessed of was an undying planetary demon named, appropriately enough, Daemonicus. But we were talking about my love."

So they were. And so they continued, though it more a matter of Max listening in on Miracle Memory's monologue.

========

He was barely four when I was killed, but he never forgot me. He had a lock of my hair cut off at my wedding to his father and kept it in a locket all his life; all his lives. It was the same locket into which he later put a sliver of the Gypsium rock they – he, Rom and young Harry – discovered in 1948. It went with him every time he died, just like Trans-Time Trigon, just like Gypsium itself. Which, as I'm sure you've heard Rom Kinesis describe it, is the remains of the primordial Godhead.

First life, your Heliopolis. Second life, the not-so-mythological Cadmus, his namesake, when and where he met and married my other antecedent, the first and therefore highest born Master Deva ever. Harmony was her name, past tense now; Datong Harmonia, to give her another name; the Unity of Balance as well as Panharmonium, to give her a title, two of them.

His third life was his first time in Old Weir. That's where he learned about mandroids, had them hollow out Trigon and build my computer-self inside it; all this after destroying its progenitor, Old Weir's Mother Machine, and, not so coincidentally, helping to bring my Harmony aspect into existence. As you might have figured out from that, we're time tumblers, not time-travellers; especially not controlled time-travellers. Like Kadmon, I reckon controllable time-travel impossible. We follow our own timeline.

I won't bore you with the details but mandroids were, and are, machine men and women that could, and did, absorb the consciousness of living Utopians facing Imminent Death. In this way Utopians thought they could beat endless death and thereby achieve endless life. Of course, it didn't quite work out that way. It never does, though in some respects we're testament that immortality, or something approximating it, can be achieved through the grace of Gypsium-Godstuff. Or whatever it is that keeps us going.

Helios has had ninety-six lifetimes since his third. I am entrusted with collecting his memories after each one so I could list them all, but it'd serve no purpose. However, among the memories I gleaned during Number Three were how to make mandroids, clones and variations thereof, including what might be considered homunculi. Albeit fully grown ones, not the miniature – make that microscopic – human beings early on biologists theorized were present in sperm or eggs.

You see, I was desperate for life, physicality. We experimented with the first two, clones and homos, if you will, or homun beings, if you prefer. Had some success as well, including when it came to consciousness transference. But they're fleshy things, all too fragile for my purposes. So I convinced him to construct a mandroid using the lock of his stepmother's hair as a building block.

Thus I became a solid being. I still wasn't wholly human, though. Sooth said it's too much of a risk to transfer all of my consciousness out of Trans-Time Trigon into any kind of construct. Fleshy things die, all too easily as I'm sure you'd agree. But artificial beings can be destroyed, usually not so easily, true, but with the same effect. And then where would I be? Nowhere, answers that.

At any rate, two lifetimes later we tumbled back to Old Weir. Helios, as I've called him since the Third, therein helped set a biogeneticist by the name of Cabalarkon on the road to becoming the Utopians' to this day revered, greatest hero; their to this day just as much so reviled, greatest villain.

Given what we'd already accomplished in his third lifetime, namely – among other things – destroying their Mother Machine and her mandroids, albeit this time via proxies leftover from our later lives, it had to be done. Was inevitable, you might say; predestined, in a manner of speaking. (Helios and I are so much the cosmic wild cards, we don't believe in destiny either.)

What I'm saying is that without his Fifth, he couldn't have had his Third. Nor any other lifetime, before or after, as far as that goes. Inevitability aside, it was unquestionably the worst mistake he has ever made; one he's been trying to correct ever since. You see, in order to assist ancient Utopians in the attainment of their ancestral goal of individual immortality he used Cabalarkon's left eye as the basis to create, not a new breed of Utopian per se, but an entirely new life form.

This was the first devil. (Capitalize it as you please.) His name was, is, Sedon – which, nearly a hundred and seventy thousand light years later, gave rise to the Hebrew word *'Satan'*, meaning the antagonist or enemy; albeit (a third time) in their reckoning God's, not ours. One of the Moloch Sedon's first acts was to kill my love for the fifth time.

Lifetimes come and go. But only two after our Fifth, which is to say our Seventh, we're down below again — Earth, like the two Weir Worlds and devils in general, keep drawing us back. It is the time of Sodom and Gomorrah. It's roughly 2000 BC; some two thousand years BCE, Before the Common Era, or as you might prefer, circa 3980 BP, Before the Present.

The Moloch Sedon – Moloch meant king, yes, but originally its meaning was much more specific, the King of Devils – had long been Demon King Sedon as well. Long, long before that, by the time of our third lifetime, if you haven't been keeping score, he'd somehow managed to propagate six other devils, the Trigregos Sisters and the Thrygragos Brothers.

Then, starting in that very lifetime, and no doubt with Sedon joining in the general merriment, they begin procreating thousands of other devils – Master Devas, as the third generation call themselves. Vastly fewer of these Master Devas, together with Sedon and the three Brothers, the only independently solid ones at that time, settled on the Whole Earth and even less – barely 500 in fact, and that's according to their own tabulation – made it to the Hidden Continent of Sedon's Head.

Recall what I said a few seconds earlier. I can by now become a mandroid, a solid being, but not a human. Irony of ironing boards, I discover I can possess these spirit beings. Even more stunningly, when I do so I become not only fully human, but still functionally connected to my computer self.

Note I said *'possess'*, not *'be possessed'*. For some reason devils cannot possess mandroids but Helios and I can, to keep things simple, possess them, the devils. Just to clarify that, as we found out in our eleventh life, possessing doesn't necessarily mean controlling them; quite the opposite, sadly. During the forty-two years of that lifetime, Helios and I were more often than not controlled by devils.

So, to recap Our Story, Helios is killed in '68, thanks in large measure to you, Max, the patriarch, Loxus Ryne, James Aremar and Mik Starrus. He's thereby infused with Gypsium-Godstuff, what's also called Brainrock, and becomes a time-tumbler. He next comes conscious in Phoenicia circa 1500 BC.

First lifetime I've predeceased him by more than two decades. Second lifetime is when he comes across my Harmony aspect, who's a highborn Lazaremist, the highest born, by a matter of milliseconds, over her two immediate brother Unities, Chaos and Order.

Third lifetime we find ourselves on Old Weir for the first time. There he turns me into a mean mother of a machine inside Trigon, which had also followed him through the time-space continuum to Lifetime Two and continues to do so every lifetime thereafter. There also, having only lost her a lifetime earlier our time, he helps engender my Harmony aspect; the first offspring of the Trigregos Sisters and Thrygragos Lazareme, the Great God made in his likeness.

Next time I become a mandroid for the first time. Time after that, he creates Sedon. Two times later I learn I can become human by taking over devils. Four times after that devils learn they can control us. Can do more that; can make me pregnant, so long as he's possessed, too. Hence, I might as well tell you, the dozen fourth generational members of the Family Thanatos.

Now let us pass forward; way, way forward. Let's get back to where I started His Story — our sixty-first lifetime. We are on the Earth yet again, this time some sixteen hundred years before the Great Flood or forty-six hundred years prior to our seventh life. Atlantis is overwhelmed by ice accumulated over vast ages finally melting, thus in some respects ushering in the planet below's modern era.

Alorus Ptah, Helios, transfers Trigon from the sinking continent to an island within the Western Ocean of Pacifica. Which is was what we call the entire archipelago you might think of as Mu or Lemuria. This he names New Eden – though today it is called Apple Isle or, less correctly, Corona, which is actually a gulf, Sedon's Human Eye.

Things are swell for us. There's no sign of Sedon and his offspring so, perhaps, we're in an alternate timeline. Helios disputes this, though. He's always believed he's a time tumbler; that his actions do not change the future. That makes no logical sense to me but I've come to accept his perspective. I mean, we have been in the future, long from then and long from now, too. But he's entitled to his own opinions. As am I, howsoever illogically.

So there I am, let's call it 5550 BC, in the Garden of New Eden. We've been there quite a while. Did I mention we don't age very fast? Well, I don't age at all, not so long as I ensure I maintain myself properly. But Ptah-Helios doesn't age much either, not since he started eating golden apples. Doesn't matter, we didn't. Only, without any devils around to possess, I'm a glorified mandroid, remember.

These golden apples serve a second function. The eldritch earthborn – daemons, faeries and suchlike base planetary natives – positively hate them. Which is why they stay away from humanity's rainbow class, Golden Agers like Ptah-Helios's become, preferring to plague the mundane rest of humanity. They're as rude as ever for much the same reason. They're allergic to golden apples.

Dark Sedon, the All-Father of Devakind, is out there somewhere; has to be. We've been ahead of this era many times and in damn near every one of them, he and his are too. But he isn't around now and I still hate being a mandroid, yearn to be human again. Helios isn't overly happy about my artificiality either. He's wandering eyes and one particular dark-haired beauty catches them, and him.

Meanwhile, I have discovered that compositionally these daemon types are very similar to machine men; albeit without being machines, let alone artificial. They've co-evolved naturally, organically, alongside both types of humanity, those who are and who aren't allergic to golden apples. That means, at least in theory, I could use them as I use mandroids, in order to humanize myself. Whereupon happy happenstance provides me with an astonishing opportunity.

The dark-haired temptress Helios has fallen for, she's a demon – the Queen of Demons, no less. And, like I forewarned you she would, she can't stand him; can't stand anyone who eats golden apples. Which is how I figure out what she is underneath all that dark beauty of hers.

Ptah-Helios is going bonkers in frustration but he's too besotted to realize what I already have. Then one night she comes to him. You can imagine what's occurred. Or, if you can't, I'll happily tell you. I did. I've taken her over; transferred my consciousness to hers. Done more than that. I've overcome her aversion to golden apples, at leas temporarily, and in due course she, I, we, become Ptah-Helios-Adam's first wife, Lilith.

Big trouble this. The demon's too mindful. She corrupts me; unless I've corrupted her with my all-too-human desires. In other words, Primeval Lilith is not a nice person, a veritable serpent in paradise. Indeed, she's at least figuratively so much like the one depicted in front of Paris's Notre Dame cathedral, it shouldn't surprise you who commissioned it, albeit a few lifetimes after his 61st.

At any rate, she's controlling me and together we're twisting him around her, our, little finger. So much so that we prevail upon him to move Trans-Time Trigon off Apple Isle to the vicinity of the Gregarian Fields, hundreds of miles, and many islands, east of what's now the Gulf of Corona.

The big ape still hasn't twigged that Lovely Lily wants us off-isle because she still can't stand the sight, let alone the smell or taste of golden apples. As if to show how happy she is about relocating, within a couple of years she rewards him by getting pregnant, We reward him by getting pregnant, that is to say.

What also has to be said is he's never lost his appetite for golden apples. Call it for what it is — his need for, his addiction to, the things. He often returns to Ap Isle in order to satisfy his craving. We don't really care. It's not because we're so engrossed being pregnant either.

We aren't going to age, not appreciably anyhow. Demons aren't built that way. Neither are machines, no matter what you might have heard about planned obsolescence. But Alorus Ptah will, and is; only thanks to the apples it's tolerably slowly. Consequently we don't even notice that Ptah-Helios's eyes have wandered again.

Seems a golden-skinned, hence golden apple eating, Apple Islander has captured them this time. This would be Trishtar Thrae, the Biblical Eve, the second such to his second Adam. And if you knew what Harmony likes to look like – her, his one truelove from his second lifetime and whom we helped whelp in his third – you'd realize what the attraction is, and was, for the next eight hundred-odd years.

Once we find out about her I, Lilith, don't just hate her. We immediately plot to eliminate her. And maybe she, Thrae, realizes it. Or he does. As it turns out, only one thing saves her. She's pregnant, too. Here's where the Bible comes into play. Her jealousy is such that Adam-Ptah finally recognizes the inherent evil of Lilith. So what does he do but eat of the Tree of Knowledge, which now grows on Apple Isle as well as, presumably, the original Garden.

This gives him the skill necessary to concoct the sphinxes, Andy the Androsphinx in his image and Ginny the Gynosphinx in mine, pre-Lilith. Except, and this the awkward part, he might know how to make them, but he hasn't the wherewithal to do so, not even one. So he naturally comes to me, my machine side.

I can't disobey him; can't, dare not, kill him. But I can argue on our behalf. So he holds off activating him — at this point he's only had me make the He-Sphinx, Andy the Androsphinx, the one with his face. He even promises to hold off after we've given birth to his son. Let's call him Cain. And even after he's born he continues to hold off. Call that tit for tat. Because …

Well, you see, he's still visiting Ap Isle regularly. Staying for longer and longer as well. Eventually we start to wonder why. That's when we discover Trishtar Thrae and her son, their son. Let's call him Abel; everyone else does. (Unless it *'Hevel'*, meaning herdsman, to Cain's *'Qayin'*, meaning metalsmith.) Hence the tit for tat splat. I won't harm her if he won't harm me, Lascivious Lily.

Pass not all that much forward in time, same lifetime. Neither Lily nor Thrae have had any more children but there are plenty of other children around, rainbow class minority and the mundane majority. Adults, too; ergo the children. The numbers are quite staggering but now's hardly the time to get into that.

By their twenty-first birthdays Cain and Abel have not only become aware of each other, they're both living in the vicinity of Trigon; Cain in the city Ptah-Helios has been building: call it Kanin, after Cain; Abel in the countryside: call it the Gregarian Fields. They quarrel. But not over the merits of their avocations as patriarchal scholars often burble in their blithering, vacuum-headed denial of all things feminine. No, they quarrel over, of all things, a girl. I mean, how dare they!

Call her whatever you want but I tend to go with Hecate, as I reckon, due to what she does to our firstborn – what Lily did to their father – she's the world's first real witch. Her name doesn't matter because she doesn't hang around once Cain kills Abel. Ptah-Helios banishes him – to the opposite side of the Earth, as it happens – but he punishes Lily by finally activating the Male Sphinx.

Andy has her for lunch one day and I'm back to being a mandroid. To make matters worse, Ptah invites Thrae to move in with him; to move into Trigon, which in effect means she's now living inside of me. Plus, he's charged me never to harm her; more, to look after her as I do him. I let her die, he'll die too, of a broken heart no less. Oh, the melodrama.

The next year, call it 5526 BC, Thrae finally has another son, Pseth Ra, the Biblical Seth. He's the first Golden Ager not born with golden skin. His is, believe it, blue. And not because he's stillborn. So is his sister's, Awan, and she's just as lively; maybe even livelier. She in time marries Cain, who's already eating golden apples if only so he's a shot at living long enough to revenge himself on his father for banishing him and taking out the lovely Lily.

Cain has by now settled in the so-called Land of Nod, East of Eden; both of them, the original and Apple Isle. Which is about west as you can go on the Whole Earth before it becomes east. Nod's in Arabia, in it's own way just about as far away from Pacifica as one can go without getting west of Eden.

That's where he brings Awan once they marry. Time continues to pass, bugger that it is. Thrae has more children. Cain and Awan start a family as well. He still hates his father, goes so far as to declare himself the Anti-Patriarch, to Ptah-Helios's Patriarch, and eventually builds Enoch City.

It isn't there anymore. Rather, what's left of it is under the Arabian desert at a likely unreachable depth. But the city we've moved to still stands; still stood one could say, as in withstood, because that's what it did. It withstood all the upheavals caused by Xuthros Hor instigating the Genesea much more than a millennium later. Like I said it's in the Great Plains of Marutia, not far from the Gregarian Fields.

As an aside, not wanting to get too far ahead of myself, after the Flood, the Cathonic Dome hence in place, by then still only relatively recently arrived Utopians of Weir remake it into the Weirdom of Kanin City. It's one of a dozen or so Weirdoms they set up, although only that of Cabalarkon is still populated by purebloods.

Let's go back to where I was and move on. In the year 5226, on the anniversary of Pseth Ra's three hundredth birthday, Ptah-Helios decides to retire as patriarch and turns over his responsibilities, the leadership of humanity, to Ra. To ease Ra's succession he even has me move Trans-Time Trigon far from Kanin City to the southernmost island in Pacifica, what's now Incain, Sedon's End.

In some respects it's a pointless gesture since Ra has already set up his residence at what we call Power Point Sumeria, comparatively not far from where his sister Awan lives with the Anti-Patriarch in Enoch City. Comparatively not that far from the supposed Gates of Eden, the original Garden, as well. It does establish a precedent, though. For the next twelve hundred years each patriarch resigns on behalf of his eldest surviving son on the occasion of their 300th birthday.

Recall what I said about Sedon having to be out there somewhere. As it turns out, by the time of the Seventh Patriarchy, that of Droch Nor, he's right here on the Moon and he isn't alone. As he has on countless other worlds since leaving New Weir, he sends an expeditionary force down to the planet itself; wants to see if it's ripe for conquest.

The year, if you're counting, is around 4730 BC. It's hard to be absolutely certain since devils, unless I'm possessing one, don't keep records. Ptah-Helios is still around but he's getting up there. Golden apples or no golden apples, nine hundred and twenty-five qualifies as getting up there.

He hasn't been idle. Besides having oodles more children, always by Thrae, he's had me activate the She-Sphinx. We go into them ourselves, our spirits do, just for fun. Much like he is, Thrae is wearing down. I don't know what I can do to forestall the inevitable in either case. Then one day, while romping around with Andy-Ptah I, as Ginny-Memory, discover devils have made it to the planet at long last.

Potentially this is great news for Thrae, since devic possession is notoriously healthy for the one possessed, at least physically. There is one itty-bitty problem, though. Golden apple eating members of the rainbow class can't be possessed. There's a nasty workaround, however; one akin to inducing a coma in modern medicine down below. Ptah-Helios hates it when I tell him but you know what they say about undying love? *'Till death does it stop'*, in case you don't.

What I do is make her sicker and sicker. Finally she's so far gone she can be taken over by a devil; one I've known for a very long time by then but one who's never come across me before. Illuminaries eventually name her Pyrame Silverstar. She's the first Master Deva, third generational devil, to gain a name. But that's another story. I've used her to humanize myself many times subsequently. Which is to say I've used her in many lifetimes subsequently for her.

Which would make that a whole bunch of other stories; none of which, you'll be glad to know, I propose to get into right now.

For Trishtar Thrae, however, hers is a comparatively short-lived reprieve. There's a male demon king out and about again, call him Daemonicus, and he really wants his Queen, Primeval Lilith, back with him. They succeed, too – by contriving to have her eat Pyrame and thus take over Thrae herself.

Stuff continues to happen. Stuff does that sort of, um, stuff. Helios-Ptah manages to stick Pyrame-Lilith back into the female Sphinx, the one with my face. Then he stamps Daemonicus out of existence, at least he hopes he does. Thrae doesn't die, though; not immediately. That's because he, meaning me, has found another devil to possess her; one that suits both of us to a tee, as in tailor-made. It's none other than my still insubstantial other template, the nevertheless splendid Harmony.

One thing relentlessly leads to another. Another leads to a third then a fourth. Thrae dies anyhow; unless she's assassinated. He does, too; one way or another. And when Helios dies, he takes with him Trans-Time Trigon. Where Trigon goes, so too go I. The year is 4726 BC. As the Bible says, my Adam – Adam Kadmon, Alorus Ptah, Ptah-Helios – had been alive for nine hundred and thirty years.

Just for the record, some fifty-seven years later, the Sedonshem landed in Kanin City, thereby instigating the devils' full-scale invasion of the planet. Landed directly atop Droch Nor, as it happened, killing him in the process. A mere babe he was too, barely 365 years old.

The Great Flood occurs in 4000 BC. To stave it off, at least in terms of Pacifica, the Moloch Sedon – the king of both skyborn devils and earthborn demons by then – raises the Cathonic Zone or Dome out of his own essence. It's no big deal for him. He's been doing the same with the Sedonshem – the Devil's Ark, as it were – for much of the previous many multiple millennia.

He thus separates Pacifica, Mu, Lemuria, from the rest of the planet. Which in turn answers where most of the water comes from on account of Pacifica isn't an archipelago anymore. It's a hidden continent. He thereby consequently saves, according to them, something like a final five hundred of his devic descendants from annihilation; what I'd have called devastation had it happened to all of them.

Despite the Dome, which is almost as impermeable as it is permanent, their All-Father has never ceased influencing events negatively throughout the Earth.

And that's the short version of Our Story.

========

"So," said Maxwell, providing his own, much more succinct, summing up: "Big Shelter isn't up here on the Moon like James Aremar figured it was. It's exactly where Kinesis told me he thought it was more than a week ago now. It's in what amounts to another dimension in the middle of the North Pacific."

Memory nodded. "Those on, above, or below it – and you'd be surprised how many do live on or below it, hundreds of thousands – plus those who know of it, but who dwell beyond the Dome, generally refer to it as either the Inner Earth or the Hidden Headworld. Which, the Devil as well as Demon King's head, is what it would resemble from outer space were satellites able to see through Cathonia.

"Not a demon's head full on, I should qualify, but one from its left side perspective. That means only one human eye, the Gulf of Corona, with Apple Isle is pupil; half of a devic one, the Weirdom of Cabalarkon, which of course includes Cabalarkon City, where sleeps Cabalarkon himself, and only one horn, though that's now most of the way south and east of where you'd think it should be. And don't ask me why that is. Not unless you really want to be here until next century."

"All right. How about I ask you instead: How does all this tie in with where we are now?"

"I was just getting to that. Five years ago, when we started this, our hundredth lifetime together, we learned of the Cosmic Express. As you more than likely did not learn before you left the island, Project Centauri would never have got off the ground without the aid of Thrygragos Byron and his now nearly four thousand years' solid offspring.

"For them, its main function was to get the cosmicompanions and their teleportive cosmicars – teleportive because they're at least partially powered by Gypsium-Godstuff – out here such that they could start scouting other planets suitable for them. You see, Byronics regard the Hidden Headworld as an enormous prison; nowhere near as confining as All or the other Sphinx, which had been rendered inactive long before the Flood, but one they nevertheless want to leave."

"But the Express barely got off the ground and certainly never made it to space, not the way it was supposed to anyway. Are you saying this Dark Sedon fellow was responsible for destroying it?"

Memory suddenly grew coy. "Listen, Max. My Man on the Moon is fed up with time-tumbling. To put it another way, he's sick to death of dying and coming back some other where, some other when. He wants done with the Moloch and his devils, yes, but he was perfectly happy to let them flee back into the heavens; to pollute, for that is the word, some other innocent world, assuming there are any left. Devils have been around for a very long time, very little of which they've spent down below on the Earth Itself.

"Even with Gyps, it would take years, probably decades, before those on the Express found a suitable planet. More years before the Byronics actually left. And there are two other tribes of devils, that of Mithras and that of Lazareme, Helios's lookalike. No telling how many of them would go with the Byronics. No telling if Sedon would either.

"Furthermore, Helios's goal is to liberate the planet not just from devils but from enforced and, to not just his mind, very much unnecessary authority. The way he figures to do that is by empowering humanity to think for itself, like the Golden Agers did. The purpose of our thought beams is thus twofold. Make it so devils can't possess men and women anymore and make it so we can't be exploited by our own kind, either."

"You don't buy either of them, do you? Mostly you just want rid of devils altogether."

"Not all of them. As I told you, I love being human."

"And you need them to keep you that way."

"Need one. Helios needs one, too. Devas are immortal, the next best thing to it anyhow. There are those who say the souls of most upper level sentient beings are as well. And I believe that. For individual sentient beings, though, individualized sentience, self-consciousness, if you can appreciate the distinction, does not automatically follow.

"I love Helios; his soul, yes, but also his mind, his principles, his body – and not necessarily in that order. Idunn's golden apples slow down a developed person's aging process tenfold but, unless they want to, devils do not age at all. That might be true for the eldritch earthborn as well, but we can't say that for sure. However, as my love and I both know from howsoever many previous lifetimes, when Helios is in control of a highborn devil, neither does he. At least not very much."

"Does that apply to any human?"

"That I've experienced, no; only to those Brainrock-blessed, like my human sister's Terrible Twins, Air and Sea."

"Which sister – Celestine or Dolores?" asked Max, hoping he was about to get an answer to a question that had plagued not just him for decades. "The Elemental Twins, Aires and Thalassa, always looked like D'Angelos but Papa Rafe adopted them not long after Mama Sofa had Gloriella, Radiant Rider."

"Not long after he found them, put better. Which to be absolutely accurate, was on the same day Sophia had Gloriel: Good Friday 1933."

"Got an answer?"

"Superior Sorrow," Memory told him, sounding surprised he had not realized it by now. "And before you ask, no, she didn't realize they were hers. They were taken from her at birth and raised elsewhere. That happened to a lot of babies born as a result of the Summoning. Call it witch-work, for that was what it was."

"Why doesn't that surprise me," he muttered, thinking of Aranyani and what she did to TJ, their son. "A lot of folks speculated her Summoning Child was Morgianna Sarpedon?"

"A lot of folks speculated wrongly then, Max. Sorrow's made it to her late seventies thinking her post-Summoning pregnancy ended in stillbirths. As for Virginia Mannering, the girl Dolores and Diego did raise, mostly in Mexico, she was the Celestial Superior's grey baby, though I never found out who by. Not for sure."

"She looked, looks, so much like a Ryne everyone figured her father was the patriarch or his father, Charan Ryne. Which was why Ginny never had Abe's kids."

"Be that as it may, it could as easily have been by her brother, Raphael. He and Sophia St Synne had some pretty special kids of their own."

She was referring to Anita (Nita), Peter (Pietro), Leandro (Lee), Claudia (Cloud), Gloriella (Gloriel) and Gabriel (Gabe), all of whom became supranormals after exposure to Satan St Synne's devil-ray in 1943. So did her template, Mnemosyne by then Heliopolis, and Papa Rafe himself, though not Mama Sofa, St Synne's daughter, for some reason. (She did exhibit an amazingly effective, so-called *prayer power*, however.)

"Maybe so, but the ones who didn't die during the Supra Wars aged normally."

That didn't include Marcello and Belificent, neither of whom lived as long as Air and Sea did before they apparently stopped physically aging, but did include the other three: Tereza, Anna Marie and John Paul. All three were in their late thirties or early forties by now and looked it; the eldest, Teri, especially. Of course she married Simon Lancz and had Sapphire, both of whom might account for her premature haggardness.

"Besides, if both her parents were D'Angelos, how come Ginny looked so much like Abe and his father? Or his twin sister, Mary Magdalene, for that matter. I never met her, but she had twins as a result of the Summoning, and from the pictures I've seen the girl, whatever her name was, didn't look at all like that prick Jesse, the Conquering fucking Christ."

"Barsine was her name. I knew her well, knew them all well, but you're right. She didn't look like Jesse whereas Ginny did. But Barsine did look like Athena Ryne, the Magdalene's mom, so that explains that."

"And witch work explains why none of these moms knew whose child they had or even if they had the child they were left to raise."

"It certainly explains most of it. Look, in all of our lives together, we have come across many an incarnation of someone we met before. They're almost never clear, if you get my meaning; have no clear notion of who they were before. Even Helios cannot retain many of his memories from one lifetime to another. The human brain just isn't capable of storing so much experience, not even in dribs and drabs.

"Sometimes he time-tumbles and has no idea he's done it. There have been more than a few times I've deliberately kept him ignorant about what he did before he ended up killed yet again; especially the times he seriously deserved it. He can get quite insane, you know; at times he's been as purely evil as Dark Sedon himself. Worse, in fact."

"Worse than the Devil Himself?"

"Basically Father Sedon and his ilk aren't all that different from Celestial God. Not for nothing is the Moloch Demon-Devil King confused with Satan and the rest of his descendants, fathers and third generational offspring, for fallen angels. They want worship, to be adored; what the Church calls love and devotion, but only results in a glorified form of servitude.

"Helios is a true anarchist; an agent of Chaos, if you wish, though I'd prefer Liberty. And not just because Abe Chaos, the Unity thereof, killed my Harmony aspect – the Unity thereof, as well as Panharmonium, the one he first came across circa 1500 BC – almost half a millennium past now. He would rather destroy than dominate anyone."

"Father Sedon?" snapped Max, smacking himself in the forehead for not picking up on it earlier. "You're fully human now, aren't you? You're possessing a devil. Which one?"

"Aquarian artichokes are very nice. You have to know how to prepare them properly, though. Even then, you've got to eat all its leaves first. Otherwise its heart devours yours."

"If that's a metaphor for love or some such, you've lost me."

"It's a fact."

"Then let me propose another one. You're the one who's ultimately behind what happened to the Express, I can see that now. WORLD, or whatever it was, just provided the means. One way or the other, you don't want Helios so much alive and with you forever as you want this Demon Sedon dead and extinct forevermore."

"Wouldn't you want to avenge your mother's murder?"

Max had a pretty good idea she was not referring to the long-gone and mostly forgotten Leonine Superior, Leonora D'Angelo, who was one of many old-time Godlings who hadn't survived the Guild's Summoning of 1920. Then again, would even a machine call an earlier version of herself mom? Given the same situation he might say prototype.

Of course, when it came right down to it, the woman he occasionally still called mom, Bonita Galvin, wasn't his mother. Hell, she'd never even married the man he used to call dad. "As I understand it," he told her. "My effective mother's a seven year old. Has been for nearly sixty years."

"That'd be Hush, Young Life, Pandora Mannering," she told him. "Celeste Mannering was her mother. We've already discussed her father and his devil-ray, as well as her Summoning Child, who wasn't Ginny. Morg's Hush's Summoning Child, though she had a kid a year earlier, a boy, man now, Saladin Devason. He's a real bastard; in all senses of the word."

"Born out of wedlock as well as an asshole."

"No, she was married – but both her and her husband were possessed when they conceived him. Got the asshole part right, though. That's for sure."

"So, if I'm reading you right, Hush is your Celestial Superior's other baby, the non-grey one."

"You are, reading-wise. Born in '03 or '04, as in 5903 or 5904, when Celestine was what? Fifteen or thereabouts. Father was Judge Warlock, Sedon St Synne."

"Got that, too. Bastard got around, didn't he?"

"Was in-demon-seed, too. Of course he was occupying Daemonicus at the time. He's what's become of Lily's Demon King from our 61st in case you were paying attention. Which is why Celeste was always a bit pixilated. The eldritch earthborn have that kind of effect on most everyone."

"You're calling your own sister a fucking faerie?"

"Better than calling my own mother me!"

========

Elsewhere in the Lunar Citadel, cosmicompanions stirred.

First was Anon Sasarian, possessed as he was by the devilish Amoeba Prime, Constantin Thanatos. Next was Nidaba Starrus, she possessed of Night, Ereba, the very devil – albeit a later, evolved, as in from-the-future, version of her – Memory professed to possess right this very minute.

"They're on the Moon," exulted Klannit Thanatos on the Frozen Isle of Lathakra. No one was around to hear her.

Sedunihas was deaf.

****

Ninth Moon: **Gambit Postlude**

========

Mithrada, Tantalar 8, 5980

Pandora is also both a marine bivalve mollusc and a kind of fish; specifically a red sea bream caught for food in the Mediterranean. When they were together, Fisherwoman (Fish, Scylla Nereid, deposed queen of Greater Godbad, Hadd's invasive neighbour, thereafter simply Lady Achigan) loved turning the tables on the little trickster and fishifying piscine deviations of her given name.

For example, a dorado being a dolphin, Fish enjoyed advising her: 'You're a real pan in the dorado, Hush.'

========

When she was a pretty (if never altogether pretty normal) teenager, Pandora Mannering had two children by Augustus Nauroz: Saladin and Morgianna. Both were still alive. At least they were first thing Mithrada-Monday morning, a week and a day after the launching of the Cosmic Express on the other side of the Nag Gap beyond the Dome. So too, in a manner of speaking, was Augustus.

The just as long ago cursed, female trickster tended to call him Aug the Dog. By contrast, others had him as Gush to her Hush; also as Young Death to her Young Life, especially on the Inner Earth of Sedon's Head. He wasn't on Diminished Dustmound any more than Hush or Saladin Devason were, though the latter had been not so very long ago, briefly and almost fatally.

By now Sal was safely back in the Weirdom of Cabalarkon, which he ruled as its Master. Young Death was much closer, on the top level of the Sraddhite Monastery, a remarkably ancient, cyclopean edifice built on an offshore island in Lake Sedona (Sedon's Teardrop). Not to put too fine a point on it but the Gush was as in *'gushing blood'*. Except, to kill Young Death was akin to buying him an airline ticket, only he got where he was going next to instantly.

For her part, Morgianna was in the thick of the battle for more than just Dustmound. Although alive, in some respects she could care less who proved victorious: the breathing, hearts-beating Living or the Ambulatory Dead and their mostly demonic cronies. All she wanted was to the win the Trigregos Gambit; to win the thrice-cursed Godly Glories.

(Of course, perhaps even when it came to seemingly immortal devazurs, the non-capitalized death – as opposed to any of the Hidden Headworld's various Death Gods, firstborn Thanatoids amongst them – invariably claimed victory in the end. Like most folks, Morg, her preferred nickname, so no pun intended, reckoned she was too good to die anytime soon.)

Once she had them again, and this time got away clear – and still alive, it went without saying – only then would her Antediluvian Sisterhood, the daemon-loving, devil-despising Hecate Hellions, and her father's people, the just-as-much-so Utopians of Weir on Earth, finally stand a chance of ridding the Whole Earth, if not the entire cosmos, of Dark Sedon and his abominable descendants, the devazur race.

(On the far-off Utopian planet of, arguably, New Weirworld, the Trigregos Sisters might have been cheering her on. If they knew about the battle for not just Dustmound, that is. Which they probably didn't.)

She materialized a Crystal Skull in her unhurt hand; cracked it against the deadhead of a mostly shredded dead guy: one Alastor Molorchus, by the name his possibly not quite as long dead parents gave him. As a Sangazur repossessed him, reactivated him, she made her move.

She wore a psycho-overcoat (a psychopomp or teleportive daemon, one of a variety suchlike); had the now Stopstone-crusted Amateramirror (the Soul of Devaura) attached to her bad arm, raised it painfully but protectively; thought herself to the Crimson Corona (the Mind of Sapiendev) and the Susasword (the Body of Demeter).

Got close. Got a blast of enflaming stellar energy courtesy of Blind Sundown and his Solar Spear for her troubles. Should have, and maybe did, count herself fortunate that was all she got. A North American Indian belonging to the Dog Cheyenne tribe, Sundown was a Supra Wars' infamous, self-professed principled killer. She feared him more than any other member of the Damnation Brigade.

He'd deliberately targeted the mirror, not her; was giving her a chance to live. Worked, too; so far. She was fleetingly on fire. Neither her psycho-overcoat nor her pantsuit-demon had any Lava Lout to them, let alone any red fairy Salamander. But the mirror had taken the brunt of the burst and the rain truly was torrential.

So, no, she wasn't on fire for long. However, her broken wrist was now throbbing excruciatingly; all but overpoweringly so. She chanced a glance. Compositionally her psycho-overcoat was scorched unto flaky charcoal; was effectively history. Vetala's Brainrock power focus wasn't; was still sickle-sticking out of her wrist. She grabbed hold of it with her good hand, yanked it out.

Screamed, almost passed out in riveting agony. Screamed the more at her vomited-up Indescribables: "Kill them. Kill them all!"

As if they needed the encouragement. D-Brig didn't either. Although none of them were psychic in the normal sense, none of them trusted Morgianna Sarpedon. She'd had, as the Untouchable Diver might put it, quite the her-story of untrustworthiness pre-Limbo. Clearly nothing had changed post-Limbo.

Wildman Dervish Furie voted to run. He did, right at her; knocked her over, pinned her to the ground. The Diver hadn't voted to do anything. He dove anyways, right at her. OMP-Akbar was in front of Sundown atop Raven's Head, the oversized unicorn-horned, talaria-winged ravendeer. He bent low; slammed the Dand-head of his Homeworld Sceptre onto the Crimson Corona and Susasword.

They were lying on the ground where the Diver and Sundown had cleverly, as well as not precisely, discarded them. They exploded on contact; weren't there anymore. Furie shook Vetala's moon-sickle out of Morg's failing grip and hurled it as far away from her as he could, which was a decent distance.

The Diver tried a different tactic. He rendered her arm intangible, leaving the Amateramirror solid. It fell off her. He grabbed it, rolled away with it, came up, yelled "Catch!", flung it like one of those Outer Earth toys (Frisbees) he'd first seen last week (while in Vancouver) in the direction of Raven, Sundown and OMP-Akbar, who still sat astride the maybe magical, oddly sentient beast.

The old man – in terms of time alive, not physical decrepitude – must have heard *'Splat!'* because that's what he did: Swung his sceptre and, once its head made contact with the mirror, made it go splat. Unlike its Dand-head, what OMP-Akbar exploded with his Homeworld Sceptre rarely came back together again.

That made all three godly glories, better known as the Trigregos Talismans, gone. (Or, at least conceivably, gone into OMP-Akbar's Homeworld Sceptre.)

That meant there was no reason to fight anymore. Theoretically anyhow.

========

Minutes earlier Nergal Vetala lost her final opportunity to win the Goddess Gambit. Lost more than that; might have lost her very hold on continuance forevermore.

Nobody mourned, especially not on Diminished Dustmound, where moaning was the norm and mourning a luxury. The Living few were fighting to stay that way whereas the Dead multitude, if they were moving at all, were acting evangelical; still striving to convert them to their way, the Dead Way.

It was D-Day on Dustmound. The 'D' didn't stand for 'Disharmony'. Not initially it didn't.

========

"Well, well in the well, here we are the gar. That's a fish, by the wavy way."

"So where the fuck are they?"

"Who in the loo – Hadd's toothy Blood Queen or her slaphappy Soldier?"

"Neither, both, the Sedon-cursed Sisters' talismans. I want to see them melted out of existence eternally."

"Yesterday you wanted them for yourself and your firstborn cousins two. Got the marvellous marlin's sword, too. Through your chest and into Fecundity's throne, three."

"Ambition's mutable, lessons learned, goals change."

"You're the groper-goddess, you've the extra eye, you tilapia-tell me."

"You do realize you're talking to yourself."

"Who the seashell else are we suppose to be talking to, the mucky Nowhere Man? Fish-bed-sides, no one else's here; no one can sieve us."

"Have to see about that then."

========

"You turned on us!" Furie yelled at Morgianna from his non-fishy perch above her. "You're no life-loving Anthean. What are you?"

========

"To preserve life, I ally myself with the Dead," acknowledged the disgraced, former Superior of the Outer Earth's auxiliary stem of the Anthean Sisterhood, shouting right back at him. "There are massive differences between Valhallans and Haddit zombies. But I can't expect an ignorant baboon like you to appreciate that."

Bones broken, bashed, battered and bruised as she was, the astonishing woman had somehow managed to suppress what must have been bordering on unspeakable pain from her Vetala-shattered wrist. (Possibly, if unlikely, a few of the Indescribables she'd vomited up moments earlier, ones that now caked her externally, had anaesthetic qualities.) Howsoever she did it, she marshalled the strength to reach up and clasp Furie by both his bordering on goatish, pointed ears.

"I will have the Trigregos Talismans no matter what!" she spat up at him.

Even considering what she had already puked out of her innards – as many or more of the earthborn Indescribables than her one-armed man had been bringing in until the Godstuff imbuing him ceased circulating due to shredding – desperation had driven her to irrational extremes. To clutch him like that was exceedingly risky.

The Wildman could feel her working her wonders on him. They were having an effect, if perhaps not the one she desired. He was still in Dervish mode, as he thought of his supra-self, but he chafed visibly at the racial slur. Found it all the more galling coming from a white-as-daylight witch married for at least three decades to a man even more midnight black than he was.

She should have known better. Anger only made him stronger. Her wiles to the contrary, he was becoming so agitated fighting them off he could feel the Furie clawing to their mutual surface. Not just his father Joshua and his aunt Marea – the old-time Anthean who had helped raise him after his mother Victoria, her sister, died having him – feared that, if the full Furie ever really got going, chances were nothing could stop him.

He'd just get crazier and crazier; become a berserk juggernaut of sheer, raw might. Much more of this and he would not be able to tell who was friend or foe, let alone give a damn. So he feared it, too. That didn't prevent her redoubling whatever she was doing to him. It was almost as if she was deliberately goading him; then siphoning his resistance into herself in order to quicken her own recovery.

(Althean Healers such as Pusan Wanderlust and Codename Illuminatus had that gift. So why shouldn't Hellions? No reason. Besides, Morg was thoroughly well-versed in the secrets of a wide variety of proper Inner Earth Sisterhoods. Not that Wildman Dervish Furie had any way of knowing that. To the best of his knowledge he'd only consciously been on the Hidden Continent of Sedon's Head for two days.)

'We'll just have to see about that', he promised himself silently. "OMP and the Diver just destroyed them," he literally snarled at her, coming closer and closer to losing it, his essential humanity. He hadn't beaten her back yet, not quite, but neither had she in any way backed down.

"There's only one way to destroy those things. Your friends aren't it. Neither am I. Especially not your friend; not anymore!"

Slightly uphill behind them something huge hit Raven's Head. It must have been massive because, protected as she was by her cosmic aura, it bowled her over; sent both Sundown and OMP-Akbar sprawling off her. It wasn't a bowling ball. It was something similar; was more akin to a cannonball. It was huge, though; a huge, ball-like skull. Wasn't crystalline; was blazing.

That was all the encouragement Morg and, before her, Alastor Molorchus's Indescribables needed. They launched themselves en masse at the fallen threesome. Piled on, splaying out, splattering over top them; began to coalesce and congeal the chthonic crud that made them up, made up all suchlike abominations. The were seeking to smother the life out of them. Were doing the same to the Diver, who'd made the mistake of staying solid too long.

Just before they were all over him, all over them, literally, OMP-Akbar shouted at the top of his lungs. What he shouted was: "Bellona!"

========

The sky was growing even darker as it filled with hundreds, perhaps thousands of gigantic vultures, each of which carried at least one Dead Thing. The Cloud of Hadd had returned. Only this time the Dead Things they carried weren't possessed by Vetalazurs (many of whom were Nergalazurs but not all whom were Haddazurs). Couldn't be. They were raining arrows down on them from above. And bullets!

Vetalazurs (Former Fecundity's at least five hundreds of years' ageless azuras) couldn't animate Haddit zombies in a rainstorm. Indeed, their Vetalazurs being unable to hold onto them any longer, Haddit zombies were rotting away instantaneously, dissolving everywhere anyone could look down below.

Those that were not were rapidly trying to dig themselves underground; not that it would forestall their fate for long. Water ran as well through tunnels as it did surface culverts. Besides, Haddit zombies weren't coordinated enough to either flight arrows or shoot guns while flying. Not if they wanted to stay aloft. They'd as likely hit the vultures carrying them.

The Dead had to be animated by Sangazurs, Mars Bellona's sometimes less than a couple of hundred years' ageless azuras (by a number of different female Master Devas, self-evidently none of whom were Vetala-Fecundity). Had Morgianna arranged her own cavalry? No. The majority of Dead Things the vultures were carrying were Japanese Temporites, the sort Cerebrus and Furie encountered in the Pre-Tokugawa Cavern Devauray-Saturday.

At their head rode former Kronokronos Mikoto; formerly alive Kronokronos Mikoto dot-ditto. The risen warlord now knew who'd killed him. Not once, with bullets, but twice; the second time with the Susasword. Valhallan seamstresses had worked their witchery-stitchery, as not just Twilight's fay folk might put it. He was virtually whole again; as wholly full of hatred as ever, ditto that dot.

Sangazur-possession was about the only way in the world, either side of it, to make possible at least the opportunity for firsthand payback postmortem. For him this was personal. Was more than that really. This was war, the Dead against the Dead if necessary.

The prize, other than the satisfaction of revenge, would be the same: the Trigregos Talismans. But, with Vetala vapourizing, they'd only be hors d'oeuvres. With her gone it would now be for control of Hadd, sometimes called Sedon's Mutton Chop, sometimes also called the Penile Peninsula, and not just by wannabe comedians.

Due to the machinations of (mostly) Thrygragos Byron — since heaven-sent, presumably irrevocably — what passed for the Sangazurs' homeland (Sedon's Inner Nose, the Bloodlands, for over a thousand years New Valhalla) was being trundled under by a massive invasion force of (again for the most part) altogether alive men and women from the East (Crepuscule, the Land of Twilight, Sedon's long ago repositioned and thereafter renamed Outer Nose).

A war of conquest was commencing; the objective being a new homeland for Bellona's Sangs and their hangers-on, human and azura. Plus one other ...

Guardian Angel Tyrtod, albeit as Guardian Angel Mikoto, no longer animated the former Kronokronos. He'd preceded them, brought someone special with him; someone who wasn't at all funny. He also didn't have to ride anything in order to go anywhere; his imbecilic host-shell was a self-teleporter of the Master Deva variety.

Devils couldn't possess other devils but symbiotic Sangs could dominate simpletons. Guardian Angel Tyrtod had virtually always been able to think for himself. Was now, not so unusually, doing the thinking for two. One of them was not the dead Warlord. He wasn't Guardian Angel Mikoto anymore – a different Sang had that honour, if it wasn't a pleasure. Nor was he just Guardian Angel Tyrtod.

Tyrtod meant War-Death. He was Guardian Angel Mars Bellona, inside an eighth born Mithradite; the devic Apocalyptic of War.

A bonehead with two eyeholes, a nose hole, glistening teeth (though not fang-like, nor otherwise inhuman), and a goatee; spikes crested his skull, like a Mohawk hairstyle, from where his third eye should be all the way to its occipital backside. He had an incongruously muscular body, wore camouflage pants, combat boots, with bident-spiked toes, and a multi-spiked bandoleer over an otherwise bare chest.

Likely the bandoleer was his power focus. It glowed. All sorts of deadly things emitted from its spikes. His forearms were alterable. As on Damnation Island a week and a day ago, one was a rotating Gatling gun whilst the other was a wide-bored cannon barrel. His ammunition was ordinarily blazing skulls, the same as his fellow Apocalyptic, Catastrophe (Headless Disaster, Nakba Ramazar), whose Tva-sitar Talisman had most recently (as in pre-recathonitization, due to Blind Sundown and Raven's Head) taken the form of a flintlock shotgun.

Bellona's cannon-arm shot the blazing cannonball-skull that bowled Raven over such that Morg's concreting Indescribables could pounce. His arm-Gatling fired Crystal Skulls like the one Morgianna shattered over Alastor Molorchus to in effect reactivate the one-armed man. They cracked open all about Diminished Dustmound and beyond, on the plain below it.

Haddit zombies, those that weren't too decomposed to do so, began to rise anew. They weren't possessed of Vetalazurs; could function in the rain.

They were possessed of Bellona's excess progeny.

=========

Despite, save for their size, being relatively ordinary, Vetala's vulturous Cloud of Hadd would only carry Dead Things and daemons (who, being all body, little mind and no soul, barely qualified as a life form). Give or take a few hundred freelancers, what was left of Mikoto's Two Thousand qualified amongst the former. Amongst the latter – albeit atop the even more enormous Vultyrie – count their usual riders: Rakshas Gatherers of the Dead.

Once – mere days ago, in fact – Rakshashas professed loyalty to Second Fangs (Janna born Somata Fangfingers). Indeed, Warlord Mikoto and his Two Thousand Dead owed their persistence to the demons' relations to her. For over thirty-five years Janna Fangfingers kept tabs on their marauding passage across the Head from her seat atop Vetala's Brainrock throne.

It was she who dispatched the Rakshas Gatherers, via Crystal Skull-sets, to collect them as they fell. She thereupon had them transferred to New Valhalla, Sedon's Inner Nose, where they waited and trained specifically for this day, when Hadd was at its greatest peril and in desperate need of reinforcements.

Now, though, this time thanks to Vetala and her soldier, Mikoto's two-time killer, that Fangs was well and truly dusted. (Seems the reborn, but only recently returned Nergalid never really forgave her for ruling Hadd so wisely in her absence. Never really forgave her for being born a devil-despising Utopian, either.)

(The original Fangs – the Lazaremist lowborn antique Illuminaries named Vladuca Fangfingers, but many of his fellow devils called the Fop – was among the sixty-plus Master Devas who decathonitized the previous Sedonda-Sunday. He, call him First Fangs, regained his power focus, the fang-fingered glove that Janna had been wearing for centuries, only to be taken out, as in taken-in, by an until then empty eyeorb the day before, right here, as Dustmound diminished.)

Consequently, both the Rakshashas and Mikoto's crew lost their paymaster. It was worse for the Rakshas demons. Their devic god, Carcinogen the Leper, after rescuing Bellona from Temporis on Devauray, didn't last the day; was recathonitized, a star once again shining out of the night's sky above the Hidden Headworld.

That couldn't happen to Sangazurs any more than it could to any other species of azura. They lost their shells, they lost their integrity; became akin to absolutely unaware air sprites until an occupiable possibility unwittingly passed their way again and they regained purchase.

Although they could be externally possessive, as often as not invisibly, demons weren't even partially Spirit Beings. Assuming they could be considered life forms at all, they expired – most commonly via incineration – their remains, ashen or otherwise, re-melded with the Earth their mother, as often as not never to re-form.

They could reproduce. So could their faerie cousins, the fays of Temporis, the feeorin of Twilight, or even Outer Earth stragglers sometime known as the Sidhe out there (pronounced *shee*). Even though the planet, their real mother, was notoriously nurturing, the eldritch earthborn themselves weren't family sorts; were only interested in survival at any cost.

Right now howsoever celestial gamblers looking down, or in, probably weren't placing any bets on that last, these ones' chances for much longer persistence. Primarily, as well as noisily, that would be because, paymaster or no paymaster, their attack on Dustmound had as much to do with flight as it did anything else.

The Cloud of Hadd, their Vultyrie relations and their riders were being pursued. The rain may have been torrential but it wasn't thunderously so. The thunder was the distant sound of airplanes high above the actual clouds, that and the drone of helicopter gunships, stroboscopic spotlights flashing, coming in from all directions below them.

Witch-stones suddenly activated all about Diminished Dustmound and the storms and ice-balls' devastated plain surrounding it. Off them came Young Death's cavalry (not his daughter's): Thartarre Sraddha Holgatson, Golgotha '*Black Skull-Face*' Nauroz, the High Priest's brown-robed, shaven-headed Sraddhites, male and female, and the eighty year old Utopian clone's all-male Trinondevs.

There was a goodly, if not godly, number of these last; virtually all that was left of them. Each carried eye-staves topped with empty eyeorbs; held in pouches plenty of spares to reload with once those filled. There were also Godbadian soldiers and Zebranid volunteers. Most were heavily armed with so-called splatter packs: incendiary and/or designed-for-dismembering weaponry like daisy cutters brought in from the Outer Earth by Ringleader, Aristotle Zeross, the week previous.

Every one of those who came through were holding hands with as many and more Athenan War Witches, as led by a different, very much non-vampiric Janna.

(This Janna was Yataghan born Sentalli's wife; the mother, dot-ditto, of his only child, the Fatman's lone known grandchild, whose common name was Gudrun and who usually lived with her parents in Aka Godbad City. The St Peche-Montressor surname was a combination of her maiden name and her married name. Yataghan hadn't been brought up as a Sentalli or even as a Centauri. He'd been brought up by surrogate parents whose last name was just that, Montressor.

(Her given name did come from Janna born Somata Fangfingers, Nergal Vetala's now equally gone, but almost as long vampiric, surrogate queen of Hadd since the 1000 Days of Disbelief. Every female Brown-Robe took that Janna's first name as their middle name. Her twin brother was the Sraddha after whom most of Thartarre's male Brown Robes gained their middle names. He, also born Somata, didn't last anywhere near as long his sister, not bodily anyhow.

(As for Morgianna, as might be expected given her father's last name, she was born Nauroz. A legitimate Somata, Kyprian, the then Master of Weir, gave it to her and Sal upon adoption; an adoption made necessary once their parents were *'devolved'* by the demon-child Tralalorn moments after Mama Pandora bore her in late Tantalar 5920.)

Noticeable by their absence were Centauri's man, Governor Ferdinand Niarchos, he of New Iraxas and the usual host of Petrogod (of Petrograd); the Legendarian (Quill Tethys), a recurring deviant similar to OMP-Akbar in that he had at least one devic half-parent, and the two other Sarpedons, husband Demios and daughter Andaemyn; all of whom remained behind on Sraddha Isle.

(The latter shared the same birth date as Janna St Peche, Star Dark, the late but still lively Garcia Dis L'Orca and a number of other girls whose, for the most part, supranormal or formerly supranormal mothers became impregnated on the Autumnal Equinox of 1952 in Vancouver BC. Exceptionally curiously, not to mention tragically, boy babies given *'birth'* over the same or adjacent days by the same moms-thought-soon-to-be were — save one, Solace's immediately abducted boy — invariably stillborn.)

The Sarpedons were incapacitated. Which in large measure explained why the Trinondevs were so lavishly equipped. Before coming here Golgotha gave Demios his own personal eye-stave for purposes of protection. He'd kept Dem's — reputedly the oldest, pre-Earth stave left on the planet — for purposes of multiplication.

Demios was with his daughter, in their Curia-assigned quarters. The majority of the Sarpedons' Zebranids were still on Sraddha Isle guarding them just in case any of the left-behind Trinondevs got brave and, as per their absent Master's inviolable commands, tried to apprehend them.

Despite their still life-threatening injuries, they might yet prove the lucky ones.

========

Hush and Gush hated each other. Their offspring, Sal and Morg, didn't. Sal did hate her husband, however; mostly because he was far more popular in the Weirdom of Cabalarkon than he, its consensus Master. Consequently, as soon as he could he exiled him. Much to his shock, Morg left with her beloved, never to return.

Many Utopians followed the Sarpedons out of Cabalarkon at the time, in 5950, or soon thereafter. Zebranids were their offspring. They actually were visibly striped, hence their designation. That didn't make them lesser Utopians. Indeed, many were purebloods. However, since they were born outside the Weirdom, they never ate the longevity-sustaining, but foul-tasting slop churned out by Cabalarkon's Mother Machine.

And that left them black and white rather than, dependent on their sex, either black or white.

========

Fisherwoman wasn't there either. Not yet. Then she was, in a way.

========

She was bigger than life; much bigger than Diminished Dustmound, even more extraordinarily. She didn't quote Bob Dylan, whom she'd more than just met on the Outer Earth, howsoever many years ago now. She didn't cry out: *'A Hard Rain's A-Gonna Fall'*, though she perhaps should have. Because that was what started to fall, in addition to wet rain, bullets and arrows.

Neither did she cry out: *'Incoming!'* Which would have been both accurate and appropriate; not to mention seriously non-fishifying. She did look good in a glowingly golden, chain-mail hauberk cut to leave her midriff typically bare in order to show off her bellybutton bauble; no question of that. And there was nothing better against incoming missiles, no matter what they were tipped with, than teleportive Brainrock chains. So everyone there and aware instantly started hoping anyhow.

Fish proved her twisted sisterhood; cried out: "In-Swimming. No condoms!"

========

Separated from Raven's Head, both now struggling beneath the as yet incomplete encrustation of eldritch earthborn, Sundown was blind again. His Solar Spear flared reflexively but didn't totally ignite. He wouldn't let it. Despite Molorchus G-stringing them in from either neighbouring Tal or faraway Satanwyck (Sedon's Temple, Hell on Earth — Morg had brought hers in from the same place, albeit digestively), daemons, with or without the *'a'*, were disgracefully flammable.

Sundown wouldn't have known that; with the possible exception of OMP-Akbar (so long as he banged his own head with his Homeworld Sceptre) probably none of D-Brig-5 would have. He would have known that, minus his regalia, the rightful Kronokronos Supreme was just as much so; hence the restraint. He didn't have OMP's level of strength, either. Raven did; being far more beastly than humanoid, let alone feeorin; maybe even more so.

Decidedly a sticky situation, no doubt about that. It nevertheless didn't take them long to wrest themselves individually free of the too-slow-to-harden, daemonic crud. Sundown leapt to his feet athletically, spear at long last blazing. Raven rolled onto her equivalent, all four, talaria-winged of them; reared forwards, head down like a unicorn-horned, bucking bronco, back hooves flashing smashingly.

OMP-Akbar came up swinging devastatingly; his Homeworld Sceptre exploding upon contact with anything that ventured too close to him. "Over there!" he shouted anew. "That's the devil that did for Davy." (Davy = David Ryne, Cyborg Cerebrus, D-Brig's erstwhile leader.)

Bellona heard him this time. Rather, Guardian Angel Tyrtod heard him. Never an idiot, this despite being inside one, he was equally mindful of the menace to Master Devas and Sangazurs alike that Golgotha (a clone of Ubris, Young Death's father) and his Trinondevs presented, they with their eye-staves and empty eyeorbs. Needs be they died; although whether full-blooded Utopians could be azura-possessed, that he didn't know. (Master Devas couldn't possess purebloods, so probably not all of them.)

Bellona, even with a Guardian Angel internally attached, was a self-teleporter; took himself/themselves to the cratered plains below Dustmound. He/they reckoned that by doing so they'd rendered himself/themselves safely out of range of the Trinondevs. Probably did, too, though it was just as likely the Utopians hadn't noticed Tyrtod-Bellona yet anyhow.

(Cratered, pocked, blasted, during yesterday's day long battle for the Trigregos Talismans between Vetala, her soldier and, at first, the three remaining firstborn females: Methandra Thanatos, Umashakti Silvercloud and Freespirit Nihila. These three fancied themselves stand-ins for the Trigregos Sisters here on Earth.

(Too bad for them Vetala's soldier already had their talismans. He kindly offered to hand them over, albeit only terminally — for them. If it weren't for the belated intervention of the first two's brother-husbands, Tantal and Rufous Rudra, Miss Myth and Uma-Gravity might be stars glaring down on Dustmound from the Sedon Sphere today.)

He, the conglomerate Apocalyptic, wasn't done with interspatial surprises. He opened his cannon-bore forearm wider, ever wider, almost impossibly wide. Out of it grumbled nothing less than the yet mobile remnants of a panzer tank division that first fought together as part of Field Marshal Rommel's Afrika Korps during the Outer Earth's Second World War.

Then as now it was led by another Tyrtod, Tyrtod von Blut (meaning *'Blood'*), a German – make that Prussian – familiar to Dervish Furie and particularly the Diver from before the war; familiar to John Sundown, too, from before he traded his precious eyesight for Raven's reins and the right to wield his Solar Spear. OMP and Raven's Head would have come across him as well, albeit from the two times pre-Limbo when he and his legion served the then-thought alien supra known as Kinsecto beyond the Dome.

Other than from his sparkling clean and pressed uniform – Valhallan seamstresses could handle cloth almost as well as they could skin and bones – War-Death-Blood was hardly recognizable. Thick, unmistakable needlecraft kept his two halves held together. Eerily, from head to crotch they sort of leaked of the visibly glowing Spirit Being that reunited him; this after Devauray-Saturday's, for him unavoidable encounter with the buzz-sawing, pendulum-blade-end of Plague's power focus in Sanguerre, New Valhalla's capital city.

There was little uncertainty as to his identity. Or that of his similarly Sangazur-animated Lost Legion; a few of whom, alive and dead, had been with von Blut since the beginning nearly forty years past. Amazingly, they still had boxes packed with shells for their World War Two era guns and, more importantly, their panzers' cannons.

Tanks were invented for use in Europe. Even though, until today, it hadn't rained here for hundreds of years, Hadd's terrain was akin to the North American prairies; its underground waterways keeping its aboveground vegetation remarkably green, even wooded in areas. Therefore, notwithstanding their otherwise very much battle-scarred, even ghostly, condition, they'd could become very effective hereabouts.

(That their war-worn tanks and armoured vehicles still moved, let alone had mounted guns and ammunition that still fired, was testament to the Sangazurs' inbred dedication to the art, and technology, of warfare throughout the ages. Needless also to say, even though it bordered on the vast, time-quake-plagued Plains of Marutia, Sedon's Cheek, New Valhalla possessed a near-Godbadian level of Outer Earth modern, industrial capacity.)

Their immediate targets were the Godbadian copters above the plains. Many of Vetala's peculiarly-intelligent vultures had turned against them, too. For the most part they weren't the ones who paid the price for their Kamikaze-like strikes. Once above the Godbadians' mechanical birds, the Dead Things riding them leapt off the genuine birds onto the twirling blades of the helicopter gunships.

Sangazurs, the insubstantial offspring of Mars Bellona and a variety of female Master Devas (most productively Mater Matare, the once-again cathonitized Apocalyptic of Death), as well as any other type of non-Vetalazurs that came in alongside them, did not care if their shells were consequently ruined irretrievably.

Sraddhites, Zebranids, Godbadians, even a few careless war witches were dying down there. Spirit Beings would simply possess a new corpse, rise up and fight on.

=========

Warlord Mikoto was still too much in control of his now joint being to sacrifice himself, body and mind, so ingloriously. He scoured the raging war zone below for any sign of his two-time killer. Zip, zilch, nary a blip on his perhaps Sangazur-ameliorated internal radar. Then he got a sense of the Trigregos Talismans and, with them, a glimpse of someone he hated perhaps even more than he did Vetala's vanquished champion.

Was the Crimson Corona calling to him?

=========

Arrows only hurt when they hit; for the most part couldn't kill unless they did that first. Each member of D-Brig 5 has his or her ways of avoiding fatal attractions. In the case of both Raven's Head and Blind Sundown, when in contact with each other they had their cosmic auras. Furie had his unnaturally hard hide, which only got harder, more steel plate-like, the angrier he became. The Untouchable Diver wasn't codenamed such because he couldn't become untouchable at will.

John Sundown, the blind Cheyenne warrior who, like Furie and the Diver, would be weeks' shy of sixty – the same age as Morgianna – had they not lost a quarter century in what they thought of as Limbo but was, in reality, the Cathonic Dome, hopped back onto Raven's Head. Although bodily equine, with a crow-like head and unicorn horn, she was no dumb animal. Was more his partner than his mount, truth told.

She was also the last true ravendeer; at least she was when on the Outer Earth. A maybe magical species that went back to pre-Flood days, ravendeer – perhaps Raven's Head herself, Sundown used to joke – were mentioned briefly in the Bible: Genesis 8:7, to be precise; albeit without the *'Head'* attached to it.

(Noah, the Tenth Patriarch of Golden Age Humankind, reputedly turned a couple of Raven's ancestors loose to determine if the Great Flood had ended and, if so, where he could find the nearest dry land. And, yes, it probably was at the top of Mt Ararat because it was in its vicinity that archaeologists – such as the Diver was in his long abandoned civilian life – determined viniculture began most of six thousand years earlier.

(As Helios called Sophos the Wise could testify, because he drank with him prior to the Flood, Xuthros Hor, to give Noah his correct name, did enjoy his wine.)

Sundown kept the full range of his supranormal attributes a carefully guarded secret. He could not fly, though he could hover and had been seen walking on the air. His skin was hardly impervious and he was nowhere near as swift as Dervish Furie. Nor was he as physically strong as the Wildman or OMP-Akbar especially, though he came close.

Another of his supra-aspects allowed him to see through Raven's eyes and, indeed, anyone else's; so long as he was in physical contact with him or her, it should go without stipulating. His lack of eyes further granted him extraordinary perceptions. His uncanny ability to anticipate and avoid attacks was therefore more concomitant than nowhere-near-inexplicable.

Raven – his beauty, as he often called her – could fly and even on the ground was far faster than Furie ever was. She could even access Samsara, the universal substance between space, the same as the Diver and most witches could, via their agates (a generic term for stepping stones, first coined by the Anthean Sisterhood thousands of years earlier).

As she proved in Temporis, when she overrode the devic Vultyrie's attack-commands, Raven also had a supra-special mental affinity for all sorts of bird-life. Couldn't control birds, not as such, but could often strongly influence their behaviour by sheer force of will exuded. Too bad the vultures composing the Cloud of Hadd seemed beyond her limits in that regard.

Together or individually, she and Sundown emitted a protective nimbus, their externalized cosmic aura or, more specifically to the Cheyenne, exclusion zone. While its exact nature was poorly understood, should they wish it this aura of theirs allowed them to hide within a kind of cloud – an undeniably useful ability outside the Dome, where ravendeer were unknown even in mythology.

They did not wish it now. Besides, here on the Inner Earth of Sedon's Head there was little need to mask their comings and goings. By its standards Raven's Head really wasn't all that over-the-top weird. After all vultures the size of most of those making up the Cloud of Hadd were unheard of out there and the Vultyrie were as big as pterodactyls populating the Floodlands (Sedon's Eyebrow and western Sweat Glands) along with parts of the Mystic Mountains (Sedon's Crown), where they roosted.

Still feeling tentative after her as draining as it was revealing ordeal in Temporis two days ago – not to mention her imprisonment within the Soul of Devaura from yesterday until earlier today – she lacked the confidence, if not the strength, to fly. Not that it made much difference. Her eyesight was acute, eagle sharp. She spotted what was going on over on the plains; recognized von Blut and his Lost Legion and transmitted as much to Blind Sundown in her inimitable caw-whinny manner.

Back on her, their intrinsic, virtually impenetrable aura thus restored, they charged pell-mell downhill; perhaps, just as unthinkingly, leaving their fellow D-Brig members in their wake. All they seemingly cared about were the Lost Legion's tanks and, just as importantly, Tyrtod von Blut himself.

In some respects it was Vengeance Quest time all over again. One of von Blut's identically-aged nieces (by marriage), Brunhilde (*'Burning Hell'*) born von Alptraum, was among those Sundown blamed for the murder of his wife, Solace (*'Sorciere'*), and the kidnapping of their newly born son not quite two years ago as he still counted time post-Limbo.

He may or may not have been wrong about her but, as events on Salvation Island in December 1953 showed, he was certainly right about The Rache's involvement. And Tyrtod von Blut was about the only member of the recidivist Nazis' supranormal revenge squad who got away that brutal Christmas in the South Seas.

As for how he managed it, well, perhaps how he got here explained that.

========

Once Alastor Molorchus was Professor Romaine Kinesis's closest friend and collaborator on what eventually became the Cosmic Express's teleportive fuel. He'd become a teleporter after being thoroughly bombarded with Gypsium – after presumably dying, just as much so – during an experiment conducted by Romaine Kinesis on the Outer Earth's Centauri Island in 1968 its time.

He was also the one largely responsible for bringing the first batch of Indescribables through the Grey earlier today. Would have brought many more in had not, a bare few minutes earlier, Vetala's Trigregos Titan, in one of his final acts, used the Susasword to eject blade after blade at him.

Only slightly less so than a thresher did a field of wheat, they slashed him nigh unto fleshy ribbons held together, tenuously, by strands of muscle, fat, sinew and, yes, a few lengths of scratched but not-quite-severed bone. He couldn't still be alive. And he wasn't. (Probably hadn't been since the standard, ever-so-mysterious *'accident'* on Centauri Island in 1968, the one that brought him to the Hidden Continent of Sedon's Head, leaving only his severed arm behind.)

The ruination that was Morg's Gypsium-gifted, one-armed man nonetheless clambered to his feet. He hadn't needed any of Bellona's Sangazurs to reanimate; Morg's one had been enough. That he could bodily clamber anywhere, let alone to his feet, was therefore only a minor miracle. Given time and the right seamstresses he'd eventually be right as the rain more like pouring down than falling over Hadd right this minute.

(His appearance mattered nary an jot to Molorchus. He was already dead; had been for years. It did – would have – to the ordinarily never-remembered Smiling Fiend animating him up until those selfsame few minutes ago. The astonishing, even unique, multiply-named, demon-devil amalgam was left shell-free.

(Absolutely unshielded, too slow to react, he reflexively glared at the face in the Amateramirror. That face was his own. For once, perhaps for the first time ever, he ceased smiling. Understandably. He was immediately inside it, looking out. When it shattered, he was gone; endgame him.)

Sangazurs not only animated the Dead, they did so without deadening their intelligence, their individuality. Mistress Morg, the Hellion's Morrigan, had stuck one inside of Molorchus yet again; hence the renewed ability to clamber to his feet howsoever shakily. The rotator cuff of his missing arm was doing its G-string thing; was rotating. Entirely unexpectedly there was no more G-thing to do.

Someone had exhausted his supply of the G that let him do his G-thing; to teleport in and, as needed, teleport away anything he wanted, saving himself (for that he needed to bounce Gypsium off a mirror back at himself). For all he knew the Diver made it his own just prior to going into Vetala's Soldier a final time.

(The German Jew – in all likelihood Brunhilde von Alptraum's half-brother – had only learned he could ingest the miraculous Godstuff sometime after they'd tangled yesterday, right here on not yet diminished Dustmound. In truth, it was probably the one-armed man's Gypsium that taught him that invaluable lesson.)

Molorchus had a Hellstone embedded in his chest. Out of it came a War Witch: Dead Dis L'Orca; first name Garcia. By then there was no more Sangazur inside him; was one inside of Garcia. Presumably it was the same one. (Sangs were no more discriminating than bullets or arrows.) Molorchus didn't collapse anew. They'd only traded animating beings. What did happen was he lost said intelligence, said individuality. Was therefore perhaps irretrievably dead at long last.

On the Outer Earth during the Secret War(s) of Supranormals, the bizarre wight now occupying him, body, soul and mind, was known as Auguste Moirnoir, the Black Death. He was a trickster, like his fellow forever seven year old ex. The cigar-puffing Voodoo Child actually had powers, for want of a better word.

And a job — as the Chief Revenant on Sraddha Isle. His duties weren't so much to raise the Dead since, in Hadd, many were already risen, as command them. Which he was good at (especially internally), albeit only two or three at a time, enough for a work crew.

There still wasn't any Gypsium to do his G-string thing. Young Death, as he was best known below the larger Dome, didn't blame the Diver. He reckoned – probably correctly – that Freespirit Nihila, whom he still regarded as Fisherwoman, must be taking it all into herself; her Borealis brolly, put better.

She was up there all right. Was certainly no denying she was facially Fish, albeit with an extra eye and sporting more glitter in her wardrobe than even during the years she spent as Greater Godbad's controversial queen (by marriage, not heredity). She'd somehow grown unheard of huge, bordering on ridiculously so. Those were definitely her feet to either side of Dustmound, though. Webbed toes gave that away. So the legs and all the rest of her towering above them had to be hers as well.

Right this second she wasn't doing much more than regarding the carnage below as if a disinterested spectator. Taking in the sights; that and all the Brain-rock-Gypsium. So much for Plan A: get hold of Molorchus, use his talents to rescue Morgianna; teleport her – his, in most respects, undeserving daughter – away from all this mayhem, too much of which she'd caused.

He looked around for more. Where had Vetala's Brainrock throne gone? Had Fish snagged that, too? No matter. Something glowed over there, quite a distance away — Vetala's moon-sickle. It'd do. Provided he got there before Fish spotted and thereupon robbed him of it. Next question was: Did Molorchus's corpse have enough physical integrity left to make it that far?

He tried, wobbled precariously, pelted forward, face down, ate dirt. Tasted like shit; more like what shit likely tasted like since even a disgusting, to-Hush-despicable, dog like Young Death could not recall actually ever eating shit. Was therefore probably more Dead Thing Rotten than anything else.

Could he crawl? No. How about drag himself forward? Yes. It was still raining; raining arrows as well. Arrows hurt even Dead Things Squirming.

========

Below the larger Dome? Borealis brolly?

========

Fish hadn't been altogether derelict in her duty to support the Living; at least, despite her *'in-swimming'* announcement, to what might be termed a prophylactic degree. One of the first things she'd done to mark her astonishing arrival, besides apparently muttering to herself like a schizophrenic, was spread her fishnet out even higher above gargantuan her.

It was one of her three, howsoever acquired, devic power foci. (The others were a Vesica Piscis, her bellybutton bauble as even she thought of it, and her Fishhook, as she called her Brainrock gaffe.) Then it was as if it was chain-linked, not wound cord; albeit just as much so composed of Brainrock-Gypsium Godstuff; devic Godstuff dot-ditto.

And bowed, more like bowled – as in tea-cupped, nothing to do with bowling: concave to the in-coming; convex to those still beneath it. As such she'd rendered it akin to a mini Cathonic Zone or Dome. She twirled it, simultaneously raising it as if a Kevlar umbrella; impermeable not just over her, but over most of Diminished Dustmound.

She thus rendered it akin to a roiling, Aurora Borealis sunshade; a whirling dervish's flaring skirts, equally so. That would be Young Death's brolly. And she kept twirling it, maintaining its hoodie shape, ever so effortlessly. Of course, even if the third eye and lustrous, pseudo-brilliantine garment hadn't given that away already, she wasn't altogether Fish either.

Neither was she muttering to herself as if someone gone off her medications. She was talking – at times irresistibly fishifying – to the devil within her.

========

Well over two thousand years earlier, bygone Illuminaries of Weir named Harmony, the Unity of Balance as well as Panharmonium, Datong Harmonia. True, she had something of a temper; a Nemesis-aspect she couldn't always keep down like a bad dog. Ask biomage-made eidolon Herta Heartthrob about that, roughly fire hundred years ago, or Marut Kanin (Fitna Marutia, Kore-Discord, Strife), fifteen hundred years before that. Which of course you couldn't, due to said malicious, retributive proclivities and their tendency towards permanence.

There were those who claimed she was the first Master Deva to see the light of day all those ten-thousands of light years past; the light of day on the far-off world of long ago, thoroughly obliterated First Weir, that is. Thrygragos Lazareme concurred with that notion; was on record saying as much to, among others, the legendary 30-

Year Man, also 30-Beers, the recurring deviant who'd been chronicling devic history for something like two thousand years.

Lazareme should know, too. He was her father, prohibitively the last remaining Great God on the surface world; the one who, when he looked at himself in a mirror, saw a three-eyed version of the selfsame Male Entity currently on the Moon. (And it was Heliosophos who ordered Machine-Memory to burn First Weir's sun unto a supernova killing zone in the first place.)

Others claimed Harmony didn't need to possess a debrained demon to gain solidity much fewer millennia ago; that she was always much more than just a third generational Shining One; that she was living Godstuff. Aka Thrygragos Everyman – because, to almost everyone he came across, he looked like his, her or its idea (ideal) of what God should look like – may or may not have agreed with that.

There was no way of asking him, either. Not according to Jordan Tethys there wasn't and he, the aforementioned Legendarian, was on Tympani (Sedon's Eardrum, the Isle of the Undying One), in the midst of the Aural Sea (Sedon's Ear), yesterday morning. The consequential deviant's devic half-grandfather couldn't be found anywhere anyone looked; not even in his regular, between-space domicile there.

His absence additionally meant that there wasn't any way to find out if he even knew his most precious offspring was back, after half a millennium of virtual death, more than just moderately maddened and calling herself Freespirit Nihila. And she'd gone between-space specifically to tell him just that.

(Which was how Tethys found out no one could find him. She told him so, just before she conscripted him to play a part in the disastrous Goddess Gambit.)

========

For all anyone knew or figured the Great God had gone on vacation — perhaps to the Moon!

****

Tenth Moon: **Springing Forth**

========

Monday, December 8, 5980

As Maxwell and Memory were doing, so too were Professor Romaine Kinesis and the Quetzalcoatl of Cosmic Cuisine.

========

Kinesis, though, was having none of his nonsense. As far he was concerned this wasn't Heliosophos or even Heliopolis. This was his four years' younger, childhood-through-early-adulthood friend and relative, on his mother's side. Rom would be damned if he was going to call him anything but Kadmon.

(Hot Rox, the supra codenamed Slipper, married name Kinesis, was a Summoning Child born Roxanne Heliopolis. Her parentage wasn't absolutely certain. Aerobe nee Catreus died having her, yes, but her father could have been brother Agenor – who was Kadmon's father – their uncle Ulysses, or Agenor's father Belus.)

Their conversation rambled, much like it often did when they were together on Trigon in the Fifties and early Sixties. They covered a lot of familiar territory. Who were dead? A lot of their mutual acquaintances. Who were alive? Not as many as Helios might have wanted. And what they were doing now? It was only when they got around to discussing what they'd been up to since they last saw each other that the host started dominating the conversation.

Finally Kinesis had to interject. Despite what he'd experienced in the past eight days, particularly a week ago last Sunday when he encountered Devil Wind (the Byronic Nucleoid Illuminaries of Weir named Vayu Maelstrom), the professor wasn't one for fantasy. However, when it came to philosophy, he felt he could contribute something.

"Never was much of a Xuthrodite, Kadmon," Rom admitted. "Never saw the sense of it. If you're an atheist, which I'm not, though I am something of a proper anarchist, what's the point of having a god? Even Xuthros Hor — who was just a human, if I'm hearing you right. Sort of an oxymoron, if you get my meaning."

"Don't think of him as a god, Rom. Consider him an ideal. Don't think of him as the pious, put-upon-by-Unyielding-God, Noah of the Bible either. He was a brilliant, determined man. He caused the Flood, not just survived it. He did it to wipe devils off the face of the then still Whole Earth. Damn near succeeded as well. I aim to finish his job."

"Wipe out or simply have done with them?"

"You sound like Milady Memory. One's as good as another as far as I'm concerned. In some respects I'm darker than even Dark Sedon. I made him after all – at least so I've been reliably informed."

"How do you know so much about this Sedon-Satan character? You've already told me the Great Flood happened almost six thousand years ago. You've also said you've experienced a hundred lifetimes since you were killed and Trigon vanished. You going to tell me you were there or, even more incredibly, you were Xuthros?"

"Ah, but I was, Rom, after a fashion. Not there. I'd been killed five years earlier, ironically by Xuthros's father, Oriartes Ma, the Biblical Lamech, ninth patriarch of Golden Age Humankind. Hor was my ancestor, as he obviously is of everyone at least on the Outer Earth, but he was also my direct descendant.

"Let me tell you a little of where I've been these last dozen years; these last hundred lifetimes and five years of mine. Assuming of course that I wasn't in the Soviet Supracity, in the Ukraine, trying to understand the discoveries of Jesus Mandam until 1975 – and trying to bring his dreams into reality ever since."

"And if you were?"

"Then let me tell you about my dreams."

========

"You know about Trigon in October 1968. How I fled there together with some of my closest comrades in the Black Rose – my cousin Thaddeus Hyperenor, Echion Sangati, Rathegar Pelorus, Capnan Udaeus, and the Cypriot-Israeli, Chthlonius Tiecher. How another of my cousins, Demonites' bastard by your own mother, Dmetri Diomad, informed AMERICA of our whereabouts on Santorini.

"How our guests, Genial Jim and Big Max, with Loxus Ryne, our benefactor in the early Sixties, and Mikelangelo Starrus, recently also my guest here in the citadel, hounded the six of us back to Trigon. You know about the bomb Starrus dropped. That it hit an outcropping of Gypsium and Trigon promptly vanished. Out of sight, out of mind, I'm sure everyone thought, even if we left no bodies behind. Anyhow, that was the end of my first lifetime.

"I next came conscious something like thirty-five hundred years earlier, in the land of Canaan, Phoenicia, during Minoan Times. My name was Cadmus, which is virtually the same as Kadmon. I had a father also named Agenor, a mother named Telepassa, a sister named Europa – the same as my half-sister by Mnemosyne D'Angelo – and four brothers: Phoenix, Cilix, Thasus, and Phineas. They each looked remarkably like some of the people I was close to in my first life: my parents, sister, and my lifelong companions, the same Shoot, Itch, Bugbear, and Jackrabbit I called my Dragon's Teeth; presciently, as it turned out.

"As Cadmus, I had many adventures, some of which remain well known, albeit in mythological form. Relatively early on, I encountered Dyaus-Zeus, supposedly a god, though he acted more like a horny, old devil; was in fact just that, a devil named Varuna or Uranus, though I never really twigged on that. He kidnapped Europa and took her to Strongyne, an island in the Aegean Sea whose eventual eruption caused Trigon to rise in the first place, albeit hundreds of miles away.

"My brothers and I pursued them. Came across a dead-ringer for Tiger Tiecher calling himself Attis in the process. One thing led to another and, after a while, alone once more, I ended up in beefy Boeotia, founded Thebes with the help of the magical Spartae – Ti Tiecher and the other four back yet again – and married the exquisite Datong Harmonia, a golden-haired lookalike of Mnemosyne D'Angelo.

"Together we had a number of ill-starred children; so did the five Spartae. I was friendly with devils then, thought them gods. Was drinking with one when he, more so than me, inadvertently caused the eruption that destroyed Strongyne and, with it, the Minoan civilization – though some bits were preserved on nearby Crete.

"Mythology has it that Harmonia and I were turned into serpents. But mythology sometimes needs to be taken with a bucket of sea salt. What actually happened was I was killed. Took my Trigon, not freshly risen Aegean Trigon, with me back into the time stream.

"Almost a hundred lifetimes have blazed past since. You would have to ask Mnemosyne to delineate them. I'm sure she has a list stored somewhere in her memory cells. It was my fifth that I most regret; that has haunted me ever since. We turned up in the far off Planetary System of Old Weir, where the natives were called Utopians. They had been at war with machine-men for hundreds of years – Utopians sometimes lived for three or four thousand Earth years, if not longer – and they were winning.

"However, their leader, Cabalarkon, wanted both a final victory over the mandroids, as he called them, and their Machine Mother Moulder. Wanted as well immortality for his people. What I did, using one of his two eyes as a starting point, was create an entirely new life form, the devazur as it's now known.

"At first there was only one devil, Sedon, the big D Himself. I realized what I'd done, who I'd effectively engendered, almost immediately. I even tried to destroy him, albeit not immediately enough. He nailed me, instead." He paused to refresh himself with some retsina; a, for many, foul-tasting, pine-scented sauterne that he drank like water.

"I kept coming back, lifetime after lifetime, time and space after different spaces and different times – sometimes even before them. On more than a few occasions I came across Sedon and his offspring. At times there were only his partheno-geny around: the Three Great Gods and the Three Great Goddesses, Thrygragos and Trigregos. One of the former, I don't mind telling you, was even based on me whereas the latter three have formed a lasting bond with Mnemosyne and, to a lesser degree, myself.

"At other times there were just their offspring, the Master Devas, around. Once in awhile, long ago but time-wise far from now, we chanced upon their devic children, the fourth generation of solid devils, as opposed to the much, much more numerous azura spirit beings. We also came across variations of mandroids, homunculi, clones and planetary daemons, the likes of which once proliferated down below.

"As for the multitude of alien races we've come across during our time-tumbles, rather than time-travels, almost all had heard of us and, since we had brought devazurs into being in the first place, most had and probably still have reason to hate us. There were also times we ended back here, on the Earth. Don't ask me how many, I have no idea. Nor the when and the where. I doubt even Mnemosyne can answer that with complete accuracy. We've both been insane more than once; lost our minds, and with them our memories, dot that ditto.

"What I can say to you, Rom, is we're back, we're sane, and we aim to stay."

"Stay to ruin what you always championed, the planet and its people? Because it seems to me that seems exactly what you're trying to do up here."

"Ruin the status quo, yes," he admitted. "Rehabilitating the diseased minds that devils have fed upon for over six thousand years, yes. Reawakening humanity to its Golden Age potential, yes. But ruin the planet, its people, no, never. Witness Lunar Assault Crews One and Two, Johnson and Kulagin, American and Soviet: fifty men, hard-cases, now committed to our cause."

"You brainwashed them. Turned them your way, which is hardly the only way. You didn't give them a chance to decide for themselves. You did the same for us when you teleported us in from the Liberty. That's what you're doing to the populace downstairs with your thought-controlling beams."

"So Jimmy Aremar and his antique master, Loxus Ryne, would have you believe. My beams are thought-provoking, not thought-controlling. What I've done is give humanity an education, an opportunity to make an informed choice. Yes, they're choosing my way and yes as well, it is the way, the only way, the way of total, unadulterated freedom. Of course they would choose it. And they are. That's what is happening throughout the Whole Earth even as we speak. I give you the same choice, Rom. You and Big Max and the rest of the Liberty's men. Join us."

"And if I refuse?"

The Chef Seriously Sane simply shrugged. "Then refuse. I won't harm you. I'll even send you downstairs. No spacecraft, no re-entry trepidation. None of that discomfort. Basic usage of Gypsium, what you might be able to figure out yourself if you had a few more lives. You'll be lonely, though. Times are changing. For the better. And I'm the one changing them."

It was a dramatic statement, doubly or trebly emphasized by rumbling from one of the towers adjacent to the central rotunda beneath the dome where the feast was being held. Memory suddenly flopped into her intergalactic soup, vanished – which she couldn't have done if she was clone, homo or mandroid; if she was anything but humanized by a devil with a subtle matter (daemonic) body. Promptly became visibly one with the computer walls of the Lunar Citadel.

The Quetzalcoatl of Cosmic Cuisine deactivated his disguise. The man who stood in his place was bare-chested, wore only tights and had a golden pendant shaped like a lion's head with a flaring mane strung around his neck. He was as muscular and youthful-looking as Rom remembered.

He looked closer to the nearly thirty he was when he vanished than the just past forty he should be had he actually been held in some kind of stasis within the Ukraine's Supracity (where Jesus Mandam once made his base as the Conqueror). The main difference was that his previously dark hair was now shockingly white, thinning, and hung to his shoulders.

"You're going to have to make your decision right now, Rom."

Professor Kinesis filled out powerfully, began to glow with Gypsium; became the Doc Defiance of Centauri Island and Houston, rather than the pale approximation he'd managed the previous Sunday when he faced Devil Wind near Damnation Isle. He threw off the leather jacket he wore. Underneath it he had on an open-necked, Greek style linen shirt. Even though he no longer needed a canister on his back nor, strictly speaking, arm rods, two thin tubes ran down either arm as reminders of which hand did which.

"Guess I just have, Kadmon."

"What's going on, Defiance?" shouted the Indescribable Mr No Name.

Gone was OJ Maxwell. Even his clothing, sport coat, trademark turtleneck, jeans and shoes were subsumed by the great, lumpy mass of dough in a generally human configuration. Unless No Name had simply switched places with Maxwell like an image in a double-sided mirror that had just flipped.

"We're about to find out!"

Out of the dust of the collapsing tower stepped six devils – Day, Night, Fire, Winter, Spring, and Autumn. Day (Castella Thanatos) had red skin like her mother, though she was shorter, not quite six feet tall, and much more slender than the full-bodied motherly figure the generally masked Scarlet Sorceress presented to the world outside of Lathakra. She was dressed in a flimsy, yellowish, almost gossamer gown. Except for her skin colour, third eye and bald head, she looked surprisingly like Mnemosyne just had.

In addition to looking like a red-skinned Human Memory, had she either silvery blonde or supranormally iridescent hair and only two eyes, Day would have been a dead ringer for Gloriella D'Angelo, the Radiant Rider or, more simply, Rainbow. If the hair she didn't have had been stark white, she would have looked like Belificent D'Angelo Zeross or, if it had been red, she might have passed for Estrella, Star Dark, Gloriel's now twenty-seven year old daughter by Immanuel Dark.

Night, Ereba, was as tall and slender as her twin sister and also facially and physically resembled Human Memory – except her skin was blue, like her father's. However, unlike Day, but like her mother, minus the mask, she was entirely covered; albeit in shades of grey and black, not red. Even her hair was hidden by a skull cap and cowl. Just as Mnemosyne had in her days as the Queen of Spades, she wore a shadow cape, but this one undulated like ripples of water. Although composed of Brainrock, it didn't so much glow as sucked in light.

Acheron, Fire, was clad from head to foot in battleship grey iron, not so much like a knight of old as a coal-burning furnace with its grate the front of his helmet. Auraura, Winter, had no clothes but her skin was a shapely, opaque sheen of ice that shimmered like the northern lights with lots of blue, particularly in her facial area. Klannit Thanatos, when she occupied a rendered-ambulatory, Ice Maiden statue made by Sedunihas the Artist, looked very similar.

It was a toss up which of the other two, twins like Day and Night, looked more alien. Orinth, Autumn, had a peacock's head and colourful eye-dotted feathers covering all but her naked torso. She could have been something Max Ernst might have drawn — and probably did, at least in his fantasies. Constantin, Spring, wore only a bulging loin cloth, radiated masculinity, and might have passed for Dionysus, supposedly a grandson of King Cadmus of Thebes and his queen of the day, Harmonia, had he not two heads on two necks.

He wasn't a hydra – probably wouldn't grow another head if one was cut off – but he would split into another body, then another, like an amoeba. As he stood there, he began to sprout breasts. His heads developed more faces, both male and female, then multiple faces on the same heads. If Maxwell had not been No Name, he would have recognized some of them; might even have recognized the breasts.

He'd fondled them often enough in the late Forties and throughout the Fifties. They, like one of the faces, were identical to that of Trebleman Joan Smith.

In fact, had he been more with it, Max might have deduced that all six of the Thanatoids were the devic templates of a number of supras from nearly forty years ago. Two of them, Winter and Spring, empowered Claudia and Leandro D'Angelo, Winterlady and Amoebaman, from the moment they were exposed to their grandfather's devil-ray in April of '43 until their deaths a few years later.

Another of them, Night, briefly charged their eldest sister, Nita (Anita), who became Madame Midnight. Sometime after Nita's nearly immediate death, their aunt, Mnemosyne Heliopolis, gained the same attributes and started calling herself the Queen of Spades. (Superior Sorrow, Dolores D'Angelo Rivera, was among those who believed her niece didn't die then; that, rather, Nita became the otherwise never identified supra codenamed Headmistress.)

Again after exposure to Satan St Synne's devil-ray, Memory's brother Raphael was initially Fire. Somehow that changed later on. Howsoever briefly, he thereafter turned into the Avenging Angel. Subsequent exposures to both the devaray and Strife's equivalent, the Miracle Key, resulted in other supras having a variety of codenames but essentially the same abilities of Night, Fire, Winter, and Autumn.

Seizing the opportunity, James Aremar pulled out a gun and shot Heliosophos in the head. The bullet literally popped against his skull. Helios barely blinked. "You'll have to do better than ballistic bubbles, Jimbo. You don't really think I'd have brought you over here and left you fully armed, do you? Get rid of them, Mnemosyne."

With the exceptions of Doc Defiance and No Name, but including the fifty members of Lunar Attack Crews One and Two, over a hundred men were suddenly no longer there.

"Get rid of them too." Heliosophos demanded of the computer wall that was his Milady Memory. "Place them under stasis again or send them to the Black Hole after Lord Ordure."

"Can't, my love," squeaked the computer mechanically. "Something's overriding me." The wall went blank, then red. No face stared out of it but a voice spoke. It was female.

"Nearly four thousand Earth years ago, you controlled Thrygragos Varuna Mithras, my schizoid father and my lover. At the same time, your three-thing controlled me. Mithras is fifteen hundred years dead, irretrievable, and I'm nearly two thousand years without a permanent body. By jettisoning the future Erebe, all that has just changed.

"Now I'm in control of your three-thing and Trans-Time Trigon simultaneously, something I never managed to accomplish all those centuries ago. Bow before me, Wisdom Entity. Bow before the Great Goddess, Fitna Marutia, or you can join Dame Darkness and Lord Light in the Black Hole."

A woman appeared in front of the six on-coming Thanatoids. With an otherwise featureless, scarlet-skinned face, a single cyclopean eye and a geyser of red-hair spurting out of the top of her skull, she was wrapped in a muslin gown, like a coarse cotton sheet. It wasn't so much dyed red as blood-soaked.

"Strife!"

========

Finding themselves back on the Liberty, James Aremar raced to the bridge and activated all systems.

"It's back," he shouted to no one and everyone. "God-cursed Helios has relinquished control. Positions everyone. We're going to blow his infernal citadel to Kingdom Come."

"I think not."

========

It was Ned Johnson who spoke.

He and Leonid Kulagin were on the flight deck. They were pointing their guns at Aremar and were flanked by a dozen of their men, American and Soviet citizens both. The Americans in particular having been thoroughly indoctrinated by Helios over the course of a week, chances were they wouldn't be firing balloon bullets.

Johnson spoke again. "If Heliosophos has given us control, he has also given us a choice."

"Choice! What do you think this is, Johnson?" ranted Aremar. "A vacation whoring in the Orient? This is a military vessel and I am in command. Put down your weapons and you may yet survive a court-martial."

"Heliosophos does not punish. He educates. We are the vanguard of his way, the way. We cannot abide your continuing efforts to scupper him. You are clearly acting in ignorance. We suggest you back off. Wait until he deals with what's down there. If those creatures we just saw manage to defeat him then we will support your efforts to destroy the Lunar Citadel. Should it go the other way, which is no doubt what will happen, then you will thank us for urging restraint."

"Place yourselves under arrest, Mr Johnson, Mr Kulagin, you and all your men. See to it, Mr Domenis."

Luke Domenis walked up to the Liberty's commander and took away his revolver, which once again seemed to be his prized Colt. How it had shot bubble bullets, well, you might as well ask him if he really did eat those Jovian jelly-bellies. He'd deny it of course; might even convince himself his gun hadn't shot bubbles bullets, but it had.

"Please come with me, Mr Aremar. I shall escort you to your private quarters. Struggle would be pointless. A hundred plus men can't be wrong."

"You're telling me I'm alone, that everyone is against me. Who's going to be in charge?"

"You're still missing the point, sir."

========

"Kore-Eris," Strife was correcting Helios. "Who the ancients also called Kore-Discord, she of the Golden Apples of same; not those of the Hesperides, which I also once guarded. But Strife will do just fine. So would Marut Kanin, comes to that, or many another name, so go with your gut. Before I rip it out!"

Suddenly, almost as soon as she appeared, Strife vanished.

========

The computer wall cleared itself. Mnemosyne's face smiled out of it.

"Sorry, my love," she apologized to Helios. "Momentary interruption of service. Trying to do too many things at once. Circuits got a bit overwhelmed. I blipped. She took hold of me and got rid of the dark lady almost simultaneously. Right then, black hole it is for them as well."

Fire, Acheron, pointed his armoured arm at the wall. A blaze of flame burst out of it. The wall ignited, the computer screamed. So did he. In triumph!

"Forget it, machine."

"Wait," demanded Day, Castella. "Don't destroy her. Let me try something."

Shorn of her power focus, bald-headed Day was not entirely shorn of power. She expanded her being then vanished into the wall. The rotunda lit up blindingly.

"She's trying the same stunt Marutia did," crackled Mnemosyne through the airwaves. "I think I can handle her. Buy me some time."

"Help her, Seasons," commanded Night. "Leave these three to Fire and I."

As one of the two eldest Thanatoids, Ereba received as much respect as her twin, perhaps more since she still had her power focus.. (All the fourth generational Thanatoid devils were born in pairs; this in contrast to the third generation, who were born in threesomes.) Auraura, Constantin, and Orinth melded with the computer wall.

"Three?" fumed Fire. "I see only two."

"Now you don't see anything!" shouted Ereba, spreading her shadow cape. The entire rotunda was plunged into darkness.

"Christ, Kadmon, Max," screamed Doc Defiance. "Where are you?"

He sensed the heat more than saw the flames but managed to erect a Gypsium shield around himself in time to deflect, every which direction, the infernal gush thrown at him by Fiery Acheron. His respite was negligible; his shield almost instantly emblazed anew. Although protected for the time being, he felt the oxygen burning out of the air. Whatever else he was, the Gypsium Man was still just that – a man. He needed to breathe.

Helios felt the darkness harden around him. He touched the pendant around his neck. Suddenly there was light and it was coming from him. His head was instantly radiating rays of energy, like the sun's, like a lion's mane. Solar discs appeared underneath his feet and in his hands. He clapped them together. The darkness was banished in a veritable flash.

Ereba fell to the floor, sucked into it. Defiance spotted his assailant and directed beams of motive-retarding Gypsium at Acheron.

"Gravity feeds fire, fool," roared the living furnace, glowing red hot. "Keep it coming. I'll turn this entire place into slag."

"Sorry, wrong arm."

Clenching one fist, he opened the other. Beams of motive-accelerating Gypsium bombarded the being. It was too much. He blew apart. Flames sprayed everywhere then simply dissipated, leaving a charred patch in the floor where Acheron had stood and the rotunda smoking perilously. Automatic sprinkler systems responded immediately. Rain fell falling inside the Lunar Citadel.

"Christ, I'm good," grinned Defiance.

Helios glided above him on his solar discs. His skin now golden; his long, remarkably fuller hair, just as golden, stuck out like sunbeams. His face was moderately leonine. Water steamed off him. "Frivolity's wasted, Rom. We're no better off than when we started. All six of them are now in Memory. The first one must have realized that, if she can possess devils, they can probably possess her.

"Milady makes a formidable foe but she has a weakness for devils. They make her human and she likes that. I'm sure she can control one or two of them, probably best all six in due course, but I doubt she'll dispose of them as she should. And if Strife is still around, which she could easily be since she somehow found her way up here in the first place, she could overwhelm her again. Where's that nameless Boddhi when we need him."

"If you mean little ole me, I'm right here." A marble obelisk grew out of the floor. "And here." Another did as well. Then two more and two more until there were six in total. "And here and here and, oh, you get the picture." The obelisks softened, became doughy then fleshy; took human form as well as skin and bone.

Were dressed in the silver and black striped uniforms of the Cosmic Express, had darkish hair and darkish complexions, like the Iraryan Caucasians they were, and only two eyes. Three were men and three were women. They took one look at their surroundings, the massive, burnt-charcoal, domed room and, as a unit, promptly passed out.

"And here." The Indescribable Mr No Name warped out of Samsara; grinned as best a Doughboy – of the Bodhisattva, Samsarite or Multivoid persuasion, not the WWI American infantryman variety – could grin. Whereupon he resolved himself into Big Max Maxwell.

"Christ again – Max!" gasped Doc Defiance, allowing himself to relax and revert to Professor Romaine Kinesis again. "How'd you pull that off?"

"I take directions well."

"Almost as well as I give them." Still wearing a shadow cloak, Mnemosyne stepped out of the computer wall – fully human, super-human, again.

"What did you do to the devils, milady?"

"Got rid of them, just like you wanted me to, Herr Hellacious Helios. All except Ereba. Her I kept. Even though she's just a kid compared to the one I'm used to, she fits like a pair of comfortable old jeans. What would you do without a Moon Goddess to compliment your Sun God, Kad?"

"Gods and goddesses have no place in this brave new world we're forging. What you should have said is *what would I do without you?*"

"Point taken, my love." The two embraced warmly but Heliosophos was clearly still agitated. They broke off quickly.

"What became of the Strife Virus, disposed of her, too?" That seemed to stump her, an odd thing to happen to a computer programmed for maximum speed.

Wednesday night on WORLD's converted fish packer, Strife was sucked out of Balkis Mandam and into one of Demios Sarpedon's prison pods by Ramona Avar, aka most recently Lady Guillotine. Shortly thereafter, Memory brought Ramona, along with Crystallion and Aranyani Nightingale to her Shelter here on the Moon. She supposed she must have contracted Strife in the process. But that didn't make any logical sense – and Machine-Memory worked primarily by logic.

Ramona hadn't brought the orb containing Strife with her into Memory's Shelter; nor any other orb, for that matter. So how had she come to the Moon? It couldn't have been through All of Incain or Trans-Time Trigon. Both were primarily on the Head and Strife could not function there; would in all likelihood be cathonitized instantaneously.

The Universal Substance was the obvious answer. Strife subsisted between-space when she wasn't either trapped within a prison pod or inhabiting some unfortunate shell: a Sedon-spring, though not necessarily a female offspring of Sedon St Synne. Of course, before she could have gone into the Grey, Strife would have had to escape from the prison pod.

What if she'd done just that then? What if Thursday morning, sometime after she returned the three former Strifes to where she'd taken them from, Strife got into one of them again, learned that Memory was on the Moon, and decided to pay a visit? Memory prided herself on being in tune with Samsara. She should have detected her.

There was another problem. Even if Strife managed to spirit herself up here, how had she contracted her? She hadn't gone through Samsara since Wednesday night. Didn't need to, not in the Lunar Citadel. It was an extension of her. In many respects the Citadel was her. Finally, had what she'd just said, what she believed to be true, actually happened?

Did Strife jettison the Future's Erebe, take her place as Memory's humanizing agent, and did Memory herself then get rid of her? Or, rather, have the prototype Void scatter her and the other five through a multitude of voids? Did she keep Ereba, the initial Night? Did No Name disperse her? Or did she still occupy the one from the Future? Did she possess her or was she now possessed?

In either of the latter scenarios, had she been wrong about her being the future Ereba Thanatos? Was she someone, some thing, else? If so, what horror had they brought to this century? And what horror was inside Helios? No, there seemed only one sensible answer, one that would have to do for now. Strife was as Heliosophos characterized her — some kind of virus.

"Of course I did," she lied, hopefully convincingly. "Guess you were right, Kadmon. Should have taken my vitamins."

"Then you better start now! Strife has an annoying habit of coming back."

Helios himself came to the ground, touched his lion-headed pendant, and reverted to the Quetzalcoatl of Cosmic Cuisine. Mentally adjusting the equivalent of a Signaller's Splendour Unit that he wore within it, he became his most normal-looking, albeit white-haired self. He smiled like the Kadmon of old.

"Guess it's time we had more retsina. Think our guests would like to join us?"

"I'm sure they would," agreed Maxwell.

"After a shower and some real food," volunteered Kinesis. "Cheeseburgers, not Lesser Magellan toe-brains, thank you very much. Does Macdonald's deliver?"

"Not to the Moon, Rom. At least not yet."

========

"Ye gods!" James Aremar propped himself up in bed and gaped at the person who materialized in his quarters. "Christ and be crunched, I thought you were dead." He flipped on the overhead light. "Fucking hell! Not you too, Sean?"

"Suppose you mean this." Sean Smythe blinked his third eye then held out his hand. "Want one?"

****

Eleventh Moon: **Dustmound Disharmony**

========

Mithrada, Tantalar 8, 5980

So long as it fell from above – or, less frequently, was shot into it from below – the Fish-deemed 'in-swimming' ordnance did go elsewhere interspatially.

Did so once it struck therefore not Fish's fishnet but possessive-Nihila's thus personally-projected Gypsium Dome. Make that went wherever. Hopefully far out to sea in the west or south or far east coast, all of which were the Head's interior ocean of Akadan. Or, maybe, it went the other way, into the perpetually rain-swept Diluvia Mountain Range to the north.

That still left those underneath it to fend for themselves.

========

"Shouldn't we do something, um, more interventional than the conventional," she asked herself seriously non-fishifying for a change. (She did that whenever she was worried.)

"I mean the bream, some poor sole down there might know-the-shoal where they got to, Bat-bait and her tormented toady, they and the turbot-talismans." (Even when worried she couldn't stop fishifying for long. Which might be why most of her friends tried to avoid extended conversations with her.)

"I do," she responded, "First thing that goes are those Utopians, not the Dead Things, and I still hate killing. You do appreciate what will happen to the Trinondevs without their eyeorbs, don't you? Shark food, to use your term, except on land. Besides, those gargoyles of theirs used to be ever so cute, always worth a laugh."

"Guess if they're worth their sea-salt they'll make it through in one plaice," she agreed, in preference to arguing with herself anymore.

In the same series of events that resulted in Demios Sarpedon's incapacitation, Fish and Nihila had been one since last night, early this morning. Fish, though, had initially thought her captured in one of his prison pods when they tried to salvage the Susasword, which was then pinning Nihila to the back of Vetala's throne. Boy – or buoy – how wrong could she be (not in the sea).

Nihila's coercive talents, filtered through Fish, their ex-queen, had been one of the main reasons the Godbadians decided to attack Diminished Dustmound as well as, simultaneously, provide aerial support to those invading Valhalla many hundreds of miles to the west. That those who'd got under her Borealis brolly, either before she raised it or soon thereafter, were causing a great deal of the carnage below it now was a shame. But Nihila was right about the Trinondevs.

Their eyeorbs were also called prison pods for a reason. They could capture and hold onto devazurs, even those with power foci and subtle matter daemonic bodies.

It wasn't all they could do, provided their eyeorbs weren't full up, but Nihila knew of only one countermeasure. Take them out before they could take her out.

As for who invented them, on New Weirworld, no surprise there. Unlike, chances were, Thrygragos Lazareme, they were on the Moon.

========

Thartarre Sraddha Holgatson didn't want to fend for himself, not anymore.

He and his Brown Robes weren't cowards, far from it. Were fighters from way back; five hundred years back in terms of slamming heads on the Head with the Blood Queen of Hadd, her surrogate, Janna Fangfingers, their sharp-toothed vamps and dull-witted, azura-animated zombies,

Like everyone who arrived seconds before the Godbadian air force and the Cloud of Hadd, he just wanted to get away. The sudden appearance of Disharmony Fish, the sheer size of her, what she'd already done in terms of a Gypsium Dome that glowed like the Northern Lights, had a lot to do with it.

What could anyone do about something like that?

========

"Sraddhites," the High Priest, still distrusting the Crystal Skull-set radios his War Witch allies lent them, yelled as loudly as he could. "Eyes peeled. Vetala and her deadly dangerous soldier might still be around. Just stay low, spread out, find cover, if you can, pick your spots, if you can't, and, whatever else, don't bunch up. We don't want to make ourselves an easy target for anyone, devils or bombers."

If Nergal Vetala and her misbegotten cat's-paw truly were no more then there was no reason to hang about. He had to get away, with all those he came in with, too; all those left, that is. If he and they could, that is again. (He'd heard about her up there. Not Fish, they were allies — the golden one. Had she taken out their egress as well as Fish and everything else that glowed on Dustmound?)

There was no point ordering his Sraddhites to let fly their arrows at the vultures. Even if they struck and killed the birds, the Dead aboard them would hurtle down – as would the vultures' bodies. Which were anything but light. As in the past, as now, falling, mostly organic debris killed more of his people than Dead Things rising off or out of the ground.

Many of the Godbadian flying gunships remained aloft; remained shooting, too. Unthinking barbarians, more of his supposed allies acting as if lawnmowers. Even though their main target had become ... who'd have believed it, a WWII-era panzer tank division on the Head in 5980? ... the *spray* of their discharged weaponry wasn't so particular. On every battlefield so-called friendly fire often caused more casualties than the enemy.

And so his universally brown-robed, shaven-headed marksmen and skirmishers did: scatter, such that they wouldn't go down in a single blaze of infamy. Did seek shelter (though not under any corpses, obviously; not even those of their fellow monks). And did hope for yet another demonstration that the pen was mightier than the sword.

Or, put another way, that the Brainrock quill, in the right hands, had enough Brainrock ink left to draw them out of here.

========

Thirty-five years earlier, when Thartarre was still a child, Nergal Vetala cost him his right arm below the elbow. The Brown Robes' Curia-appointed High Priest, whose dark skin betrayed some of the same Utopian blood his heroic father had, now wore a sword-like prosthesis in its place. For him it was as much a weapon as a reminder of what she did not just to him but to his dear mother, yet another one once well-known to the fledgling Society of Saints of the late Thirties and subsequent war years.

Even though he, wielding the Amateramirror, had actually done the dread deed, the monk always figured the former Irache-Nergalid Fertility Goddess bore ultimate responsibility for killing their beloved Bat-Bait, as Fish still sometimes referred to her Outer-Earth-born friend. (His father, her husband, died taking her out that same horrible day. Unlike Nergal Vetala, though, he never came back.)

That, until he separated them via the mirror, they were one and the same made no never mind. Barsine Mandam was born with the Nergalid inside her and she would never have harmed him, her only child, if Vetala hadn't been coming to the fore. He was as sure of that then as he was now that staying on Dustmound was very likely a fatal mistake.

Parenthetically, Barsine (raised Mandam become Holgat-wife, once she found her way to the Inner Earth) was a Summoning Child. That made her one of dozens, even hundreds, of children who could trace their conception to the same time period, in and around the Spring Equinox of 59/1920. A remarkably disproportionate number of those born on the Outer Earth on or within a month after the Winter Solstice of 1920 turned out to be supranormals.

Superior Sarpedon, husband Demios, his twin Melina now Zeross, John Sundown, Furie-Murray and the Diver (Yehudi Cohen, but probably a von Alptraum by paternity) were among Barsine's many Summoning Siblings. So too, naturally, since they were brought up as twins, was brother Jesse, Wiccan Warlock in here, the long gone, mostly unlamented Conquering Christ of nevertheless enduring notoriety as much as renown.

Among the others born on the Outer Earth around the same time count Argiope nee Zeross (Kadmon Heliopolis's mother), Roxanne nee Heliopolis (Romaine Kinesis's mother) and Headmistress Mannering, who looked more like Jesse than his supposed twin did. Quite possibly the unknown parents of James Aremar and Mikelangelo Starrus were also Summoning Children.

Barsine probably wasn't the only one born with a devil inside her; just the only one for sure born with one inside her. Not that those here in Hadd would be aware – though some would have suspected it – two other nominal members of the Damnation Brigade, the adopted twins, Aires and Thalassa D'Angelo (Airealist and Sea Goddess), may have been as well.

Certainly Thalassa believed it the case. Which was why she left the Brigade before the rest of them, brother Airhead included, ended up on the Head (minus OMP, Obadiah Melvin Power, who'd preceded them) late Lazam-Friday night. Just as much so, the Parents Thanatos wouldn't have gone to such exceptional lengths to get hold of, first, wife Melina (once codenamed Illuminatus) and their kids, then Harry Ringleader himself, if they didn't believe it, too.

With respect to Nergal Vetala, she was a twelfth-born Mithradite. Her only acknowledged immediate sibling was Kala Tal, the arachnid devil whose protectorate, the Forbidden Forest of just that, Kala Tal (Sedon's Moustache) was west of Hadd. It was there Vetala had been more like subsisting than recuperating, for the better part of thirty-five years, until her soldier fell from the sky.

(Their third sibling might have been a theoretical devil bygone Illuminaries called Lamia despite no confirmation of her existence. According to the still prevailing wisdom, she'd been stuck in All of Incain, then better known as Ginny the Gynosphinx, since centuries prior to Xuthros Hor causing the Genesea.

(All that was pure speculation. Only Dark Sedon and the Great Gods had names in pre-Earth, antediluvian days and there wasn't any census, let alone consensus, as to how many invariably insubstantial Master Devas – as opposed to Great Gods – Sedon sent to the planet with Lazareme's Expeditionary Force or brought down from the moon himself some years later; in 669 Pre-Dome, to be precise.

(As a result no one knew who or how many got stuck and remained in All to this day. Or, if All did, she wasn't telling.)

Mater Matare, the Apocalyptic of Mundane Deaths such as murder or suicide, claimed 12th born status. However, most agreed she was just a lower born Gorgon, the Medusa to her probable sisters Euryale and Stheno, the Cockatrice and Basilisk, unless it was the other way round. Each having snakes for hair gave that away.

In contrast to Kala Tal or, if she was her immediate sister, Mater Matare, there was nothing of the monstrous about Vetala until she voluntarily became a vamp. Indeed, long, long before the Simultaneous Summonings she was a different kind of vamp, a drop dead gorgeous seductress.

So attractive, so willing and so fertile was she, that she regularly bore many more azura spirit beings than any other female Master Deva in the known world. Because of that, her fellow Shining Ones more often addressed her as Fecundity than her Illuminary-given name. (A Nergalid was a Mesopotamian god or demon; Vetala was Sanskrit as well as, not so oddly given their linguistic connections, Ancient Greek.)

According to Headworld mythographers, and at least one Legendarian, just before the onset of the 1000 Days of Disbelief, in order to cease being used as a one-devil fertilization factory for not just her two fellow Nergalids – Gravedigger and King Harvest – Vetala intentionally became the second and, until only moments now gone, lone surviving, non-cathonitized devic vampire.

Her recent re-empowerment and corresponding re-enthronement as the Blood Queen of Hadd lasted barely a week. Her azuras, who were otherwise immortal, couldn't function in a rainstorm. Such an atypically peculiar deficiency was common to all of her offspring by whomever. It was her only drawback in terms of being a much sought-after mother-always-to-be amongst devazurkind.

Many cited her absolutely astonishing birth rate as the reason for her progeny's unique weakness. It was indubitably why she was considered Mithras's main moon goddess. Until she became a demonic bloodsucker, she waxed on a monthly basis. But it was with azuras. When she waned it was because she was giving birth. Come the new moon she was back in full seductress mode, ready and raring to start anew.

Given her prodigious output in the birthing department, the likelihood of her being born again in a very much non-evangelical manner was eminently probable. Although Thartarre Holgatson and his fellow altogether Alive must have hoped it wasn't imminently so.

Hadn't someone said Janna St Peche-Montressor was pregnant?

=========

The Utopian clone, Golgotha Nauroz, and his all-male Trinondev Warriors of Weir linked orb-forged mind-shields and, as they had trained and often done before, rose as a group into the sky. Perhaps out of a desire to try something different they didn't collectivize themselves externally as a *'battalion-bat'* this time. Instead, they opted for a ferocious, not to mention enormous, Wyvern of the Weird.

On the Hidden Headworld wyverns were not fanciful, heraldic beasts with wings and a barbed tail. They were two-legged, flesh and blood, albeit usually not fire-breathing, lizards with, yes, wings and a barbed tail. Natives of the Lake Lands, the eastern, Satanwyck-side of Sedon's Sweat Glands, they additionally had a ravenous, approaching unquenchable appetite for birds, the bigger the better, So the choice of a communal gargoyle couldn't have been more apropos.

The Utopians' thrust was a little different than yesterday's failed offensive on Dustmound; different than overnight and this morning's at least temporarily successful defense of Sraddha Isle's ancient, but no less venerable monastery. It may have even been inspired by the Indescribables they'd been battling of late; especially the ones who were, in a manner of speaking, all stomach and no brains.

Rather than seeking to unhorse Haddit zombies and their, due to rainfall, vastly more numerous Valhallan reinforcements, they mentally en-globed their vulturous mounts then compressed them, beasts and riders, unto bloody gobbets. Needless to say their *'globes'* took the form of a multitude of long-necked, hence hydra-like, wyvern heads with yawning maws, serpentine tongues and a few dangerously long, really fierce-looking teeth.

The Athenans, too, had a new strategy. Using their agates more intelligently than the day before, they became akin to ghastly spirits. Ran insubstantially upon the same stepping stones Ringleader scattered across the plain yesterday; never came fully out of Shadowland. (Harry Zeross disappeared – make that *'was absconded'* overnight. Young Death knew where he'd got to, too: Frozen Lathakra.)

There from – and, but for the sloppy ones, without having to put themselves at risk – they spurted the Headworld's, Sraddha-Somata-discovered, version of Greek Fire out of their borrowed back-canisters and arm-hoses. Many a Dead Things went down rolling in the dirt, immolation impending.

Too bad the rain was so heavy it as often as not extinguished them before completing combustion. Still, it did slow them down somewhat.

=========

No, it wasn't his two-time killer. He'd do as an appetizer for his blade, though.

Unsheathing it (his katana, his great sword, it with its slavering Death's Head pommel), Warlord Mikoto swooped low his vulture and jumped.

=========

Less than two days dead but already killed again, Kronokronos Mikoto hadn't gone terminal; hadn't gone the way Alastor Molorchus just had due to Young Death and, to a lesser degree, his accomplice, Dead Dis L'Orca (Garcia, not Salvatore, her older brother, the nominal head honcho of WORLD beyond the Dome).

A different Sangazur had reanimated him a second time almost immediately. As a consequence with barely a concussion-like blip to claim for the deathly experience, the Temporite Warlord, the onetime, but still acknowledged Headman of the Pre-Tokugawa Era Cavern, had retained his thoughts and memories.

He recognized the Awesome Akbar from the air, possibly from his undiminished size and overabundance of facial as well as head hair; recognized him as heir-presumptive to the throne of Temporis. Hate spurred the recognition process. In the late Thirties, Devauray's resultant Kronokronos Supreme thwarted his then-latest effort to wrest control of Temporis from their mutual, albeit devic half-father, Dand Tariqartha.

A few years later, on Hektor (August) the Eighth of 5945 Year of the Dome, Mikoto thought he'd repaid him. Did so by luring Akbarartha and his lady-wife Takeda, the Warlord's own daughter (later the supra codenamed '*Crimson Corona*' after her tiara, what no one on the Outer Earth apparently knew was one of the Trigregos Talismans), to what he thought would be their inevitable abolition in the Hiroshima Cavern.

Obviously it wasn't. Would be now, though.

========

As leaps went, it went only passably well. He missed the Dand-Head of his target's Homeworld Sceptre. That was the good bit. He'd no desire to be blown up, especially not through sheer slackness on his part. Also missed his intended-to-kill downswing. That was the bad bit.

That wasn't like him at all. Blame it on being dead twice-over. He did manage to topple the near-giant. Did, equally so, manage to land atop him as if a cushioning heap; hence the passing grade in terms of leaps. Remarkably, both by-birth-deviants recovered top of the class smartly. Were on their feet in less time than they'd been on their asses.

"You!" gasped his comparatively elderly, though hardly in terms of devazur lifetimes, part-brother.

"Bye!" Mikoto replied, uncharacteristically flippantly for him. Must have been the Sang talking.

Akbar swung his Homeworld Sceptre. Mikoto blocked or parried his strike. His wasn't a devic talisman; Akbar's might have been, at least to a degree. Mikoto whirled, slashed upward on the back swing, caught it more centrally than sideways, and thereby sliced the sceptre's shaft in twain.

Supreme, a dishonourable dirty fighter from way back, did not even swallow a breath. Dropped its halves and, virtually with the same movement, grasped Mikoto by his exposed throat. The Warlord instantly went boggle-eyed. Had he seen something over Akbar's shoulders or was it due entirely to him already strangulating unto his third death in a matter of two days?

Had something spurted out of the Dand-head's capacious equivalent of Shadowland? Some things — three of them?

Mikoto was no Demon Land, no Vetala, no Trigregos Titan. Akbar snapped the Dead Thing's neck with nary a twinge of effort and even less conscience. Still not content, he proceeded to rip its head off its shoulders and contemptuously tossed it perhaps not far away enough. Decapitated, the Sangazur inside his shell's trunk battled on. Akbar struggled mightily against Mikoto's flailing arms and legs, one of which still wielded the Warlord's Death's Head hilted, great sword.

The old man, whose non-devic parents were Temporite faeries, was thus too busy to notice an even more bizarre event occurring just behind him. His foe's severed head, eyes wide open, was trying to stretch out its tongue, and thereby seek purchase in the dirt itself, such that it could muscle towards the remains of Akbar's Homeworld Sceptre.

Unless it was towards whatever (or whatever was the plural of whatever) had squirted out of its Dand-head. Which amounted to the same thing.

Not at all blissfully unaware of its head's futile misadventures in advancement, the Awesome Akbar gripped the fingers holding Mikoto's katana with his right hand; raised his left one and mentally called back the two pieces of his Homeworld Sceptre. First came the lower shaft-end then the upper part, it with the Dand-head attached. With a further thought, either he or the sceptre itself fused it back together again.

(It was a devic trick. That Akbar could duplicate it might indicate Lakshmi of Lemuria's efforts to acquire Dand Tariqartha's power focus – after their shared, but already self-cathonitizing half-father melded it with Akbar's sceptre – might not have been a hundred percent successful.

(Such a thus-unfounded conjecture ran contrary to what went down two days ago. If Lakshmi, Aortic Amphitrite's deviant daughter, didn't have the whole of Tariqartha's power focus, how could she have teleport-tossed him and the rest of D-Brig out of Temporis so apparently casually as well as so undeniably cruelly?

(Still, it would have made as much sense as anything else if OMP-Akbar himself hadn't already realized just how much more powerful he was in here compared to out there. Perhaps his sceptre could always repair itself. Perhaps it just never got around to telling him as much.)

The young for a faerie, but old for a man, even for a Utopian male or female, was about to pummel his foe's headless body into so much irredeemable mush when a number of the Two Thousand Dead rallied to what was left of the Warlord. As in life, so in death, Mikoto was their leader.

They raced across Dustmound towards him. Some copied their liege lord's lead and leapt atop him off vultures. Akbar got one good swing in, blowing apart the arm holding onto the katana, before they were upon him. Once again sheer numbers militated against him and for them.

D-Brig-4 – where had the Diver got to anyhow? – being otherwise preoccupied, and in the absence of their flight-minded so-called allies, Akbar had no choice but to take them all on by himself. Notwithstanding his impressive size and strength, or his even more outstanding weaponry, they were more than willing to take him on, too. With bullets and even spears or arrows for those that, wisely, didn't dare venture too close.

Hardly for the first time, he regretted breaking apart his regalia the week previous at Hideaway Damnation (formerly Crimefighter Central, within Grouse Mountain across Burrard Inlet from Vancouver city proper). Had he especially had his Cloak of Many Colours, what devils in here referred to as Lazareme's Starcape, he would not be just invulnerable but shape-shiftily so.

(He had managed to snag Mikoto's blade so now had what amounted to an howsoever unsatisfactory replacement for his mutable sword: the Cross of Mithras; the other Thrygragos Talisman being the Mask of Byron.)

His normal, as in more like supranormal, defense mechanism was, to say the least, counterintuitive. The Dand-head of his Homeworld Sceptre didn't repel bullets and arrows; it as good as collected them. In the merest of minutes it became akin to a pock-marked, globular pincushion. By contrast OMP-Akbar himself remained unscathed, if not entirely untouched by foemen who did get comparatively close-in, very, very briefly. What he didn't blow apart he slashed apart.

As for Mikoto's severed head, the lights finally went out in his eyes. Its last sight was of disembodied hands reaching out of the ground and grabbing ...

========

The Diver's dilemma was, not all that unusually for him, Solidium; what those in here, beneath the Dome, tended to call Stopstone.

Demons were full of the shit, what he'd decided would be better referred to as God-crud, as opposed to Godstuff.

========

On the Outer Earth it accrued in manmade things, buildings and roadways for the most part, the older the more profusely. Some supras had a knack for using it, too often against him. Pluman (Alexandros Kinesis, Rom's father) made a career of it. So too did Will Tombstone, the Texas-born, hence damn near quintessential American supra first codenamed Kid Cemetery in part because he could bend the flight of bullets.

(Which, the Diver agreed with Akbar, when the occasion allowed, was a particularly useful talent to have when someone was shooting them at you.)

Will wasn't additionally called the Solidium Kid because he was good with its counterforce, Gypsium; called Brainrock in here. Yet another Summoning Child, Tombstone (his real name) was already a member of the Allied supra-group known as SOS – The Society of Saints when the Diver was conscripted by, of all people, Magister Joseph Mandam, Jesus and Barsine's father of record.

(Axis supras were thought evil so Saints v/s Devils fit what passed for the Allies' internal party line. Next to needless to say, this was over fifteen – make that over forty – years before the Diver knew to equate devils with Master Devas, chiefly these seemingly universally malignant Mithradites.)

As the world turned, while Will Tombstone may have began his supra-career on the German-Jew's side, he certainly didn't end it there. Didn't, as they say, just fall into bad company; he fell into the worst company. Should never have married the Diver's unofficial half-sister, Brunhilde (*'Burning Hell'*) von Alptraum, for starters.

More to the point, the cocksure cowboy should never have followed her into the Conquering Christ's Supranormal Defence League, on to the King and Queen Conquerors, and thence, into letting The Rache pull his strings. Then again Will was something of a reactionary. He actually believed socialism was wrong-headed and that British-mandated Palestine should have never have been allowed to become the Jewish Home State of Israel.

(Burning Hell's father, the old Baron, yet another Tyrtod by given name, had by then become Steltsar, an ameliorated man; in supra-parlance as well as classification – in no matter how fantastical fact, dot-ditto – a mandroid. His transformation from mainly human to mostly machine was one of the most noteworthy (for the wrong reasons) accomplishments of the then anonymous Conqueror, whom the Diver always had difficulty accepting was actually Jesus Mandam.

(That Steltsar was still around on the Outer Earth, albeit as Sharkczar, may not have amazed him; after all Fish – a former lover, the initially untold mother of the Diver's firstborn son – was too. However, that someone with Brunhilde's supra-talents may be on the Moon might have; all the more so that he was a man. When it came to looks the old Baron's bronze-haired daughter was an absolute stunner.)

Falling in or out with The Rache, wittingly or otherwise, got a lot of folks killed; John Sundown's Solace born Sunrise (*'Sorciere'*) perhaps most tragically. (The Diver was always silently grateful he and wife Rachel had a girl as a result of the Equinox events of 1952 and not, like the Sundowns, a boy.) A lot of them died at the hands, and hooves, of the Cheyenne avenger and his equally bloody-minded Beauty. Will Tombstone was one of them. Steltsar was supposed to be another.

In his case only because, when Sundown killed the Conquering Christ, Mandam's death triggered the Soviet H-bomb he built and secreted on Salvation Island.

========

The Diver had been too slow to avoid Morg's Stopstone-blessed, or cursed, Indescribables. They didn't exactly overwhelm him. He hit the ground and did a dolphin (or dorado); kept on going. They dug after him, deeper and deeper; some even soil-swam. Fortunately they were neither as fast nor as manoeuvrable as he was.

They also weren't equipped with gorgon goggles, the *'magical'* eye-covering – what allowed him to see through solid rock – that he'd first acquired in Rome, Italy, during the Alliance of Man's colloquium there in January 1938. (He'd attended it as part of the von Alptraum family contingent.)

(That they as a unit might be a devic power focus had occurred to him of late. They didn't glow, so he dismissed the notion. Once again, being unfamiliar with Master Devas pre-Limbo, he had no idea that so-called Tvasitar Talismans didn't necessarily have to glow. Thalassa's Aqua Ankh or Water Wand and her twin's, Aires-Airealist's omega-shaped Aerod, didn't, not usually, and Devil Wind thought them power foci a week and a day ago on Damnation Island.)

(Good thing his gorgon goggles didn't glow. Otherwise he would have inhumed them by now.)

After some few minutes of evasive soil-swimming, he looked up and through them, spotted what for all the world looked like the somehow snapped-off top of Akbar's Homeworld Sceptre, gasped at what popped out of it, gasped the more as a Japanese man's severed head hit the turf not far away, and saw it … what? It snake out its tongue and strive for them.

This would never do.

========

"There," sort of shouted towering Fisherwoman seconds later.
"There's what the sprat?"
"Them, out of the corner of my eye I thought …"

"Mine or yours?"
"Forget it. Must have been my imagination."
"Our imagination."
"Oh, get real, Fish. I'm not that desperate."

========

Blind Sundown and Raven's tore down Diminished Dustmound. As they came at them, Sundown long-distance-roasted many of the Lost Legion's tanks with his Solar Spear; the two of them together absorbing many more direct hits within their barely visible nimbus. Moments more and they'd be face to face with von Blut; he atop his panzer, Sundown riding his earth-bound beauty.

It was still raining; rain still seeped through Freespirit Fishy's personal dome, put equally accurately. Then it was raining even more arrows, many of them lit up as if torches despite the rain. It wasn't that yet another wave of the Cloud of Hadd had slipped beneath it; especially not with Sangazur-animated, Dead Thing Archers riding them. There wasn't another wave of the Cloud.

No, what happened was Thartarre's brown-robed long-bowmen had just spotted something highly significant paces beyond the tanks and were very accurate shots. That also accounted for the fire arrows. They were used to using suchlike against Haddit zombies and, even in their absences, what the hell. Why waste a good bludgeon? It wasn't raining so hard the flames altogether went out before landing maybe 40% bang on the spiky button, as it were.

Arrows hurt; killed, too; all the more so fiery ones. (And did so regardless of any typically spurious argument that arrows didn't kill, it was the folks who shot them that did.) What they didn't, couldn't, do was kill devils. In part that was due to the fact that nothing was that easy when it came to Master Devas, not even idiotic ones possessed by a Guardian Angel with the same name as von Blut.

(If it was that easy they wouldn't be Headworld gods.)

So, yes, Mars Bellona got in the way of more than a few; more like, seeing as how arrows wouldn't harm him, couldn't be bothered to dodge them. No matter how deep they bit he didn't even keel over. Maybe he couldn't die, but surely a few dozen heavy-headed bolts should have at least knocked him onto his keister.

Not a chance in camouflage pants. He was a comparatively highborn, relatively recently decathonitized Mithradite, the Apocalyptic of War no less. Guardian Angel Tyrtod was not about to let him shame himself any more than he already had due to idiocy; especially not in front of his own azura offspring, himself included.

Bellona became more than just superficially akin to a humanoid porcupine. He became a well lit up, humanoid porcupine. This had unintended consequences. For one, make that two, even in their rush to deal with Tyrtod von Blut once and finally for all time, Blind Sundown and Raven's Head couldn't fail to notice him.

What had they done to Headless Ramazar and the very lowborn, but still devic Vultyrie in Temporis? Much the same they were doing to Mater Matare later on in the next cavern over when Raven ran out gas, really high in the sky. (Thanks be to Gloriel for the rainbow non-trout catch.) What had Raven done to Nergal Vetala two days later, all by herself, not that there was much left of her by then? His turn.

Sundown couldn't fly. But he could be hurled. Tyrtod von Blut likely couldn't believe his dead eyes as Raven, in full charge, bent her front legs at the knees and snapped her back legs simultaneously up. She thus slung Sundown into the air, flinging him as accurately as the Sraddhites' fire arrows over top his tank.

He might have laughed out loud at what happened next except …

Raven was still coming at him, unicorn-horny head lowered like a fucking rhinoceros for fuck's sake.

No, Bellona wasn't in his right mind; didn't have a right mind left. Cyborg Cerebrus, D-Brig's erstwhile, nominal leader, had vegetated that, at the cost of his own, in Subcranial Temporis. He wasn't just a simpleton Shining One either. Deva, the word, almost always capitalized, meant Shining One; devil meant little god. He was both. He was also possessed.

An internal puppeteer – a very special, if not necessarily unique Sangazur Spirit Being – animated him. He (if Sangs could have a gender) not only could think for himself, he could think for Bellona. What he thought wasn't all that different than what Thartarre had been thinking a few minutes ago. And what von Blut was about to wish. Only, when he thought about getting the fuck out of here, Bellona got the fuck out of there.

What von Blut would have laughed out loud about was Sundown arcing through the air, Solar Spear blazing with cathonitizing energy, on a perfect flight pattern to impale Bellona inversely, from top of spiky skull to bottom of belligerent butt. The sun might not shine in there but the solar spear would still be shining when it came out the Shining One's rear end.

Whereupon he, Bellona-Tyrtod, vanished. Too late for Sundown to do anything except hit the ground at what should have been devil-piercing speed but instead was just plain embarrassing. Also hurtful, though given his internally-generated nimbus – what he'd learned to term his exclusion zone decades ago now – more damage was done to his pride than to either his hide or his spear. And what was one more human-sized crater to the bullets and bombs' pocked plain below Dustmound? Barely a dent.

Raven piled beneath the cannon extending out of von Blut's gun-turret straight into the tank. She was so strong she didn't just drive it backwards; she got her unicorn horn stuck into it and, with a snap of her neck, flipped it onto is side, caterpillar treads still rolling uselessly.

Von Blut was the first to crawl out. His other two men escaped as well. They had their handguns drawn, took one look at who they'd have to shoot and bolted helter-skelter across the plain hoping to get away before they got stomped into it. Target-practise for the Sraddhite long-bowmen? No, fodder for the helicopter gunships still in the air and concentrating on the rest of the Lost Legion.

Strafing fire brought a couple of them down. And the Godbadians had rockets.

========

"God curse all Antheans. Their illusions and their spells!"

========

That was Dervish Furie.

Sundown couldn't believe his ears. He'd never heard Furie shriek before but he recognized the voice. No, wait, it wasn't so much Furie, the Dervish, as the Murray, maybe even the Jervis. And neither of the latter had hard hides nor exclusion zones.

But he was blind without Raven; the cry of frustration as much as anything else too far away for him to do anything about anything.

That said, or thought, he could place, in his mind's eye, precisely what Furie was doing just after he, OMP, Raven and he himself, Sundown, extracted themselves from the concreting efforts of the Indescribables. Had the where down just as much so – going after Morgianna Sarpedon.

Godbadians may have rockets but in his hands Sundown had a guided missile.

========

OMP-Akbar threw off the last of Mikoto's minions.

========

He was beaten purple, bleeding from far too many cuts. He'd been in pain before but, between his Homeworld Sceptre and his regalia (which he still may not have realized were the Thrygragos Talismans), it had never been this bad. Or was he just imagining that? He'd lived a long time by comparison to almost anyone except his devic half-father but there were time-spanning gaps in consciousness …

No time for that now. What he wasn't imagining was who had just appeared over there, not far from what the Morrigan – bringer of so much additional grief to Dustmound – was doing to … Gentleman Jervis Murray, onetime superstar athlete, ex-wartime battlefield medic and Wilderwitch's long time lover.

The witch, non-capitalized, he knew best as Superior wasn't doing something to Dervish Furie; she'd done it. He'd gone from the Dervish to the Murray to the Jervis in – despite the intensity of multi-sided struggles for survival going on all around them – seriously short order. Jerry was utterly ordinary; Morg wasn't.

Often described as ambulant adamantine, the hardest substance known to mankind, the alabastrine White Witch positively glowed white hot with health and concomitant vigour. There was only one explanation. The Athenan War Witch traitor – in that she'd allied herself with vampires as well as the Ambulatory Dead – had somehow made the Furie's life force, his vivacity, her own.

And in the process she was killing him!

========

"Almost there," Young Death gurgled broken vocally.

========

He, with the lone arm available to him, to Alastor Molorchus's corpse, reached for Vetala's moon-sickle. Someone got there first, snapped it up.

"I won't let you save her," Dead Dis L'Orca told him, holding it tantalizingly away from his grasp. So near, yet so far.

Garcia was on her feet, both of which worked just fine. In fact, despite having her heart ripped out of her chest the night before by a Berserker Bat, all of her worked just fine. He knew that because he'd been animating her until a few minutes ago. Death, as he'd had many an occasion to say, becomes her.

"She's my darling daughter."

"She betrayed her Sisterhood, my Sisterhood, what I gave my life for. She doesn't deserve a second chance."

"It won't be her second chance; it'll be her eight billionth, give or take."

"I said no. Not for her. I give it to you, you make its Brainrock yours, use it to save those others, the ones still standing. We should never have come back. Vetala's dead. So is her soldier. They're not going to rise again anytime soon. Leave it to the Godbadians to mop up. If anything we should be taking the fight to Manoa. That's where Second Fangs will be; her and her big-shot, big-toothed vamps."

"The Vampire Queen dusted Fangfingers and Manoa's fallen to the natives. Or hadn't you heard?"

(Irache natives had always outnumbered the Ambulatory Dead, most of whom were their ancestors, but had only recently joined the Godbadian-incited revolt against Second Fangs and her largely still Marutian, vampire elite. These last were based in the Gleaming City of Manoa, some distance south of Dustmound.)

"Whoa!" he suddenly gasped, looking up at her. Had a third eye just flashed in Garcia's forehead? He was sure of it.

"Fucking Hell, fucking Vetala's in her sickle. She's got you!"

"Never!" Dead Dis L'Orca slammed it into Molorchus's cranium.

Young Death had always said Garcia was a capable girl.

========

Sundown hurled his solar spear – something even Raven had never seen him do in the heat of battle. Distance notwithstanding it caught the Morrigan in her neck.

Akbar was wrong. Morg hadn't absorbed Furie's hard-hidedness.

========

Just as there must have been great power once within Morgianna, there must have been some vestige of power left in it, Sundown's spear. Morg released Murray past the cusp of becoming the Jervis. Her body started adding to itself, layer by layer, ravelling, caking, hardening.

(This was faerie trick. Morg was well-trained in most of the Sisterhoods. And, yes, she had been the Ants' Superior in the Fifties and into the very early Sixties, when she was forced to resign in disgrace, but that was on the Outer Earth. In here you had be at least fifty before you could become a Nightingale, an Ant elder, and even older before you could be nominated, let alone become its actual Superior.

(So Jervis Murray may have been mistaken when he cursed all Antheans. While it was the Superior Sisterhood, the trunk from which most of the other Sisterhoods branched, it wasn't the oldest. That distinction belonged the daemon-loving Hecate Hellions and Morg was its Morrigan, its Superior.)

(As for the faerie Sisterhood, they were known as Mariamnics. What they taught most faeries learned naturally; could do instinctively. What she was doing to herself probably accounted for the many time-spanning gaps in Akbar's consciousness — he'd metamorphosed, howsoever temporarily, into someone else.)

Murray had already recovered, was going the other way rapidly. The Dervish yanked the Solar Spear out of her. Seemed momentarily confused as to what to do with it. Considered driving it through her skull. Except he didn't do that sort of thing. (The full Furie might have, but he still hadn't let go that far.)

He dumped it on the pile of snapped and blunted arrows that had accumulated around him, around them, when the Hellion's Mother Superior was doing whatever she did to him that caused him to revert. Furie's hard hide did come in handy, he had to smirk, especially in a war zone, that was for sure.

Was what she'd done to him really an Althean Healer's trick, akin to an Alt taking sickness unto herself then dispersing it elsewhere, into a rock, perhaps, or someone who already had a natural resistance? Or was it something daemonic that Hellions discovered during the course of their training? Who knew, who cared? Not him, not now, answered both those questions.

Furie raced off, suddenly in need of working off angry energy again. Just as well there were still some Dead Things about; Indescribables, too. The Morrigan continued to increase herself. She was forming a cocoon, a chrysalis, about her body. Who knew, if given the chance to develop properly, who or what she'd emerge as — a Female Furie?

OMP-Akbar was doing much the same thing. Only he wasn't racing; plus, he had a very specific, well lit up target in mind. A yet blazing, humanoid porcupine had just materialized (again) out of the Blue. (More correctly the Grey, as witches called the same between-space Shadowland devils had as the Weird.)

Although he wasn't privy to anything that had happened to the Apocalyptic since, he'd had a crack at Bellona in Temporis on Devauray-Saturday. He felt confident he'd have finished the now relatively newly Sangazur-animated simpleton then, had not his brood brother and thus fellow Apocalyptic (Disease, Plague, Carcinogen the Leper) intervened. There was no Carcinogen now.

Incoming rockets, bombs and missiles made for a very hard rain indeed. Follow up strafing from the leftover Godbadian gunships were – or would be – no less fatal. No fools they, the Athenan War Witches realized not just they were in circumstantial dire straits.

Future-famously fortuitously, Nihila Nereid hadn't taken in all the Gypsium Godstuff contained in their *'bullet-pellets'*, as War Witches lamely called their stepping stones. Or, if she had, she'd returned it. At Janna St Peche-Montressor's command, spoken over the Crystal Skull-sets they used for internal communications, they took reverse measures, leapt between agates and shouted for the Sraddhites, Godbadians and Zebranid they brought in to "Come out, come out, wherever you, let's get the fuck out of here!"

They did (albeit nowhere near as many as came in with them), grabbed hold of their teleporters' hands and buggered off. Some were hit as they retraced their witch-stone steps. These joined the already carrion crowd that would never make it back to the Sraddhites' monastery, at least not immediately and definitely not in one piece. (Those that did would be the lucky ones; the unlucky ones would be the enemy.)

Others were drawn there by the Legendarian (Jordan Tethys), finally awake to the meaning of Thartarre's frantic arms-waving; what he'd been signalling since moments after he sent them there; slightly fewer moments after Freespirit Fisherwoman appeared so impossibly gigantic over top Diminished Dustmound. That he could follow what was going on so many miles away was another of his, or its, knacks. Back on Sraddha Island his devic half-father's Brainrock quill drew what was going on there as if animation cells.

That'd be, according to him anyhow, Rumour of Lazareme's Tvasitar talisman, as effectively powered by Godstuff gemstones thereby rendered powerless. Something else it could do was draw folks back and forth. In other words, what Tethys could draw one way, to Diminished Dustmound, he could draw back to whence he'd drawn them from in the first place, Sraddha Isle.

All his quill needed was a Brainrock-Gypsium inkwell. All he needed was their permission. Draining intentionally left behind witch-stones satisfied his quill's dip-stickiness; that they'd given him permission to go one way, he assumed meant they'd given him ditto to go the other way. He couldn't do dots in the ditto department for Morg and D-Brig-5, though. They were on their own. So was Fish.

Nihila's chained lightning was awfully colourful.

========

Akbarartha, rightful Kronokronos Supreme, tromped toward Mars Bellona.

========

Blood-drenched as he was, gore-splotched as his sceptre and Mikoto's Death's Head-hilted katana were, he must have looked an absolutely gruesome sight. Did Bellona just smile in amusement? Could a fire-arrow-festooned, spike-fringed, bearded skull smile, amusedly or otherwise?

The devil was ready for him. That had to be why he looked so smug. Must be thinking: *'An easy target, at last.'*

Was this his destiny writ large: *'An approaching two hundred year old, wrongly exiled Kronokronos Supreme who tore up his celebrated regalia while under the possessive influence of decathonitized Apocalyptics and their devic Allies on the Outer Earth succumbs to twin barrages from the Mithradite War's cannon and Gatling gun forearms?*

No, too verbose for a fate. Or a headstone, for a that matter. Might have made a succinct obituary. Then again, maybe not. Too much of a run-on sentence.

Akbar paused, pointed his Homeworld Sceptre behind the amalgam devil, grinned gorgon-grimly. Made him look, too. (All right, so his was more in relief than grimly.)

The wyvern of the Weird was definitely smiling. Might have been hungrily.

========

It wasn't prickly with arrows stuck in, some of them still ablaze; it was prickly with eye-staves sticking out. Most had already open eyeorbs atop them; solitary eyeballs, at the elongated end of prehensile tendrils, glaring. Meaning they were newly replaced or reloaded, otherwise empty.

For about a heartbeat.

That heartbeat wasn't quite enough for Guardian Angel Tyrtod to think Bellona elsewhere. Eyeorbs captured Sangs, too. Didn't quite so visibly tear them apart, so his fate, seen large, was less spectacular than that of his simpleton shell. His unmanly screech was just as shrill, although those who heard it might not have realized there were two screeches for the price of one. It was endgame them.

The wyvern developed Golgotha's face. (D-Brig referred to the 80-year-old clone as *'Black Skull-Face'* due to the fact he was so thin his head resembled a skull with a Utopian male's skin covering.) He didn't have to grin; did, though, in satisfaction. The Wyvern of the Weird gave him a thumbs-up. Or what passed for one since, being a proper wyvern, it didn't have arms or thumbs as such. It did have expressive talons on its paws, however.

He looked up, way up. Akbar could tell what he had to be thinking. *'Got Bellona, got plenty of empty eyeorbs left, and that's a biggie, a firstborn up there.'*

Akbar shook his head. He and the Witch (Wilderwitch, Fisherwoman's nine years younger sister in more than just Flowery Anthea) encountered Nihila two days earlier in the Faerie Garden. She hadn't killed them then; hadn't even drained their vitality overly much. Called him cousin and left them with a suggestion to the effect that: *'You know what? Wilderwitch might even be my incarnation.'*

(Curiously, the Witch's devic half-mother was once Mariamne Dawnstar, long Krepusyl Evenstar. A second-born Lazaremist, she was the devic goddess of Twi-light, previously Daybreak; was therefore only a breed down from Nihila in terms of strength and authority.)

Almost everyone liked Harmony. As a result of his experiences in the Faerie Garden, OMP-Akbar even liked Nowadays Nihila. Golgotha, the main mind be-hind the collective gargoyle, didn't. For Utopians, all devils were their enemy. He did, in all likelihood, recall what she did to eyeorbs yesterday: Blew them apart with bolts of self-generated chain lightning replete with her integral superabundance of Gypsium-Godstuff.

The ground began to rumble. Was that her way of saying *'get lost, Trinondevs, or get dead'*?

========

"Now what?" gasped the shell-shocked, oversized fuerie, as much in exasperation as exhaustion.

========

"Run!" shrieked someone; the High Priest from the sounds of things. "This was Dustmound. The whole area around it's a mass, and I mean massive, burial ground. The rain's dissolving the zombies. It's going to collapse even further in on itself. Run, I say!" he repeated even more loudly. (Crystal Skull-sets amplified.)

Akbarartha whipped around just in time to see ... yes it was Thartarre. The High Priest ran all right, straight into the arms of ... What was her name? Right – Janna something or other; something or others. She had two last names. She was Superior Sarpedon's replacement as the War Witches' just that, Superior.

Something like that anyhow. Hadn't someone mentioned she was pregnant Devauray (Saturday) night, after Rings brought them to Sraddha Isle? She gathered up Holgatson as if a laundry bag of filthy brown robes, tossed an agate in front of her and stepped them both out of sight between-space.

"Superior?" Akbar said out loud, as if mulling it over abstractly. Chanced a glance. What had she done to herself now?

The ground around her crumbled. She – whatever she'd done to herself – slipped into a sinkhole. He almost did, too. Would have as well, a really deep one, had not the wonderful Wyvern of the Weird clutched him by his shoulders and taken off, all thoughts of taking on Disharmony Fish seemingly dismissed for the nonce, if not forevermore.

As big as he was, he was heavy for it. Maybe too much so. The earth seriously imploded this time; wide and widening cracks formed in the ground. Raven's Head swooped out of the sky. Blind Sundown reached off her back and hauled in the Kronokronos Supreme as if some sort of lightweight baton in a relay race.

The Wyvern was more of Weir or the Weirdom than the Weird. Couldn't access between-space. Instead flew off eastward, toward Sraddha Isle, at speed. Sundown didn't; rather, Raven didn't. Swept around. Going for Superior? No, Akbar realized from his undignified position, belly down across Raven's back.

Sundown was going for his Solar Spear, what Furie had inconsiderately discarded as if a chunk of worthless driftwood, and what he'd just seen slide underground. Oh, he can do that too. Reached his free hand out for the spear to snap upwards and into it, his hand. Not so long ago OMP-Akbar had done much the same thing with his Homeworld Sceptre while battling Mikoto.

"Raven can fly!"

"To the moon if necessary, old man."

Far below them, they saw a streak of humanity steeple-chasing over nature-dredged ditches, earthquake-expanding culverts, and around newly-sunk canyons. It was Dervish Furie and, though it was too misty to see who, the Wildman was carrying someone.

Had to be the Diver!

========

"I told you they wouldn't needle-nose need us," said Fisherwoman.

"Oh, do stop making things up, child."

"I tuna-belly will, as soon as you release me. And stop calling me child. I'm over sixty years old. Besides, I told you, Miracle Memory's my mom; half-mom, I mean."

"And who do you think I am … minced meat?"

"I'd have said fishmeal."

"Fine. Into which fishing hole should I dump you?"

"I'd have said fucking fish-hole."

"Fucking fish-hole then."

"My fish-lair will do finny fine."

Endgame her, the externalized half of her.

****

Twelfth Moon: **Draconic Endings**

========

Demetray, Tantalar 9, 5980

King Cold ripped his war-axe, his Labrys, off his back and swung it at Melina born Sarpedon and her children, Zerosses the three of them.
Daddy-Hubby Harry gasped in impotent horror!

========

Distances on the Hidden Continent of Sedon's Head were impressive. From its tip, more like the rounded, blistered, gnarled or knobby pate that was Sisert (Sedon's Bald Spot), to its toe, more like the flat of its foot or nether regions of its ponytail, the Prison Beach of Incain (Sedon's End), it measured somewhat north of six thousand miles.

From its easternmost reaches, what was now Samarand (formerly Sedon's Tongue) to its farthest west, what was now Crepuscule, the Grey Land of Twilight (formerly Daybreak, the Headworld's Land of the Rising Sun) a crow, or Raven's Head, would have to fly almost four.

The somewhat Crete-shaped, still volcanically active, but otherwise Frozen Island of Lathakra was once a formerly itself, that of Sedon's Horn. As such a legitimate tip, not a rounded pate, it reached much farther north than Sisert (short for the Silent Sands of Cathune Bubastis) ever did. At the time it might have struck galactic sightseers with the wherewithal to see through the Dome as akin to the Aleutian Island chain. Except Sedon's Horn curved north, not south, from its respective mainland base.

It wasn't that anymore for the same reason neither Samarand nor Twilight weren't where they started out after Xuthros Hor's Genesea drained the Archipelago of Pacifica. Their resident Master Devas at the time of such a radical rearrangement of geographical immensities – King Cold (Tantal Thanatos) of Lathakra, Byron's Dragon (Yati) of Samarand, and Lazareme's Venus (once Mariamne Dawnstar, now Krepusyl Evenstar) – simply got too big for their proverbial britches.

The Hidden Continent wasn't Tantal, Yati or Mariamne's Head.

========

From Aka Godbad City on the Gulf of Aka, where he started out on Sedonda-Sunday, Alpha Centauri's Protector, Cromwell Necator, and his mainly Sangazur-animated Valhallan flight crew would have to cross two thousand miles to reach the Prison Beach of Incain.

(In Outer Earth terms that was roughly the same as crossing the Soviet Union from Murmansk, on the Barents Sea in the Arctic Ocean, to Tbilisi, the capital of Georgia SSR, in the South, or the United States from New York to San Francisco.)

As advanced as the Corporate State of Greater Godbad was in 5980 Year of the Dome, it had nothing in the way of long distance strike capacity, no aircraft carriers and, in fact, not much of a deep sea navy. A good chunk of that had to do with its devic overlord, Thrygragos Byron, who hated to waste the lives of potential worshippers in pointless warfare.

CE (Centauri Enterprises), the daddy corporation of the Corporate State, didn't sink a lot of Godbad's abundant resources into manufacturing much in the way of big boom arsenals mostly because it already backed the most Outer Earth modern military on the Inner Earth.

That CE's nominal Centauri was, in his non-bulbous teen years, an Outer Earth born survivor of its Second World War contributed to that moderately pacifistic attitude. (If Great Byron hadn't possessed him that fateful day in August of its 1945, Alfredo Sentalli would have died fighting it.)

The Interior Ocean of Akadan, which lay between the subcontinent and the Cattail Peninsula, was the domain of mostly water-breathing, *'renegade'* Akan Piscines, pockets of whom had never joined Greater Godbad despite the absorption (as in forced assimilation) of their more complacent brethren in the Gulf of Aka itself.

They'd been around seemingly forever, these Akans. Thus more than just fairly sophisticated, their submersibles were extraordinarily fast and deadly. Supposedly inspired by – if they could be believed – a crustacean, the mantis shrimp, they used what was technically known as supercavitating effects to propel their undersea crafts and the torpedoes they shot out of them.

Mastery of supercavitation meant they had knowhow – which Godbadians to this day couldn't recreate on anything man-sized, let alone man-carrying – sufficient to create a bubble of gas inside a liquid large enough to encompass an object travelling through said liquid, thereby greatly reducing the skin friction drag on the object and enabling achievement of very high speeds.

That they couldn't duplicate the achievement outside their native environment, the sea, was what kept Godbadians safe from reprisals to their minds warranted by the Corporate State's incursions on or under their marine realm. Nevertheless, thus emboldened these piratical, absolutely ruthless, CE-deemed enemies of the state tended to sink Godbadian merchant ships that didn't pay a toll to cross over or through their undersea territory.

As for Godbadian warships, suchlike Akans were so wholly inimical to them, they rarely even bothered with the niceties of accepting howsoever exorbitant bribes.

(The famously fabulous, but altogether real, Fisherwoman, once Godbad's Queen Scylla, but nowadays more usually addressed as Lady Achigan, was a Melusine Piscine. They were amphibious. Some were even mermaids, able to keep their fishtails between-space when they weren't using them. Equally entirely not legendary Garudas could do the same thing with their feathers.)

(As alluring as she remained to this day – as alluring as she presumably remained when not being possessed by Harmony's latest and already most enduring Nemesis-persona, Freespirit Nihila, that is – Fish was no mermaid. She was, however, Aortic Amphitrite's step-sister and very much sympathetic to her Lemurians' anti-devic stance. And it was Amphitrite's deviant daughter Lakshmi who had been ruling Subcranial Temporis as its promulgated, Dand-anointed Kronokronos Supreme since Devauray.)

Non-flammable helium had been produced in Godbad ever since it was a vast but concentrated archipelago, just one more insular chunk of the overarching Archipelago of Pacifica, the Places of Peace. Since those selfsame pre-Dome times, its living Blimps actually fed on the stuff.

For multiple generations so-called Blimp Wranglers domesticated these immense windbags. They then sold their services as, in effect, East Indian mahouts riding or driving aerial elephants in order to provide high altitude transport in the mountainous, but six thousand years' long ago, terrestrially united subcontinent.

In the loftiest and hence most remote areas that remained the case. However, enterprising Royals (originally from Bandrad, which also had living blimps) mastered aerostatic flight (lighter-than-air vessels) early the previous century, thus making Blimp Wranglers, or as they sometimes styled themselves Blimp Lords, largely redundant.

Once Centauri Enterprises – to the victor go the spoils – took over virtually all of the Royals' commercial ventures, it introduced actual airplane travel. Speed thereafter provided a major plus; producing fuel, in New Iraxas, site of Godbad's only petroleum deposits, became a vastly greater environmental minus.

Due to a not-yet-avoidable shortage of airline fuel, Godbad's commercial flights were mostly limited to the subcontinent itself. For the time being only, that is, pending payback for its military's supportive role in the Iraches' revolt against Second Fangs and her vampire-elite in neighbouring Hadd.

Indeed, with an eye to the future, CE had relatively recently inaugurated an increasingly popular run across Akadan. It hopped from Godbad City to Krachla City to the Island Nation of Shenon and thence to the various city-states on the sub-continental-sized peninsula. Again however, Godbadian water and airborne vessels of war were forbidden access to either Krachla or Shenon, both of which were fiercely independent nations.

(Shenon, Witch Isle, was an extreme matriarchy, where according to some men were treated like cattle. Krachla, for its part, was a mercantile Thalassocracy jealous of Godbad's ever growing influence, particularly in the southeastern areas of the vast and very wealthy Cattail Peninsula — areas resource- and food-poor Krachla regarded as its private breadbasket for something like twelve hundred years.)

Cromwell Necator didn't have time to waste on diplomatic niceties. Fortunately there was another way. The Vanlan Confederacy, part of what had, since ancient times, been called the Pastures of Plenty, was the Corporate State's greatest ally on the Cattail.

(All of the Pastures had once been a part of Greater Godbad; as had Krachla, Iraxas, the Inner Earth's El Dorado, and the high plains of Bandrad, east of the Pastures, whence came Godbad's now deposed royalty those selfsame twelve hundred years ago. There was even a Lake Byron in the Pastures, though the Great God hadn't resided there for even longer.)

Necator and his Valhallan Select flew a thousand miles south of Aka Godbad City to Arborealis, one of the largest metropolises in Goatwood (Sedon's Beard). Originally a tree city, it had been cleared along the coast and an international airport built. (Djerrid Ruin, ex of the Untouchable Roderick Paraja, was Goatwood's most popular devic god; hence why it was also called Djerridam.)

Leaving Arborealis Mithrada (Monday) morning, it was another thousand mile flight, this time across the broad, broiling breach where normally calm Akadan met the invariably tempestuous Ocean of Psychron, to Vanalana, the confederacy's capital. There, as part of a friendship treaty between Godbad and Vanlan, a large military installation had been constructed over an old pear tree orchard permanently manned by Godbadian regulars.

Shortly before noon Demetray, Tuesday on the Outer Earth's Centauri Island (there was one on the Headworld as well, one of the Panic Isles that dribbled across the Gulf of Aka from Krachla to the subcontinent), two dozen bombers took off. They had enough fuel to make it to Incain, dump on All, and return to Pear Port.

Shouldn't be a problem.

========

Tuesday, December 9, 5980

Obscured, like a character out of Al Capp's Lil Abner cartoon strip, by its own self-generated mini weather system, the Phantom Freighter re-emerged from the Sedon Sphere around dawn Tuesday morning. After satisfying herself that her altogether un-natural dragons were still sleeping off their most recent meal contentedly, Crystallion came above deck. Sharkczar was already there waiting for her.

"Good hunting?" He grinned as best as an anthropomorphic hammerhead could.

"Some of the best. WORLD's traitors are eliminated. Their boats and bodies made for fine feeding but Centauri's planes were even better. It felt satisfying to be in action at last. Even war planes are no match for my technopomps. But that was Sunday. They'll be hungry again soon. When are we going to destroy the island?"

"The main reason we have been waiting just swam by."

========

Crystal St Synne was now Crystallion. The Old Baron, Tyrtod von Alptraum, was not so much Steltsar as Sharkczar. Neither had much left of their humanity. She now referred to herself as a *'technopomp'*, a name she adapted from *'psychopomp'* since she was more a technological horror than a psychogenic one.

She was also more a maker than a carrier of the dead, though her nuclear fire-drakes did carry Hell's Horsemen. By contrast he was a *'trinary'*, a tripartite being: part machine, part mantel, part man: a cyborg with the still-functioning brain of the Nazi Nightmare and a body Tariqartha replicated in Temporis that he, long Steltsar, had artificially reinforced with robotics, some of which were his own design but most of which were leftovers from the anonymous Conqueror when he dwelled in the Soviet Supracity.

Steltsar had reshaped his latest body to suit his new nomenclature. It was based on a grotesque parody of a hammerhead shark; hence just that, Sharkczar. Its head resembled a claw-hammer more than anything natural. He'd had himself given an oversized mouth and three layers of sharp teeth. Nearly ten feet long, he stood on legs like a man but his feet were webbed and disproportionately long. His arms doubled as pectoral fins. His hands had long, spindly fingers that ended in talons.

He had a pronounced dorsal-like fin that stuck out of his spine from just below his neck to his tail-bone. His entire body was armour-plated more like that of a rhinoceros than a shark. His skin was dun-coloured and inlaid with a grey, metallic mesh that took the place of clothing.

It was a body built for battle; there wasn't much it couldn't withstand and not much that could withstand it. He could breathe underwater as well as in the air but was most comfortable in the ocean. Plus, it retained all the qualities its predecessors had in terms of being both a machine master and Solidium in-swimmer.

The handpicked group of bio- and technomages who helped put him together this last time had known their business. Of course it helped that they themselves were Old Weir style mandroids. They weren't just based on degenerate Utopian scientocrats from Samarand (once Sedon's Tongue). Were, for the most part, built by and of degenerate Utopian scientocrats from Samarand (what was now on the Head's East Coast, where Daybreak, nowadays Twilight, was once situated.)

The same mandroid craftsmen, now based in Quarter Queen Amphitrite's Aorta on the heart-shaped island of Shenon, had also done a job on Crystallion. A striking-looking child, she had grown into an attractive teenager. Her mixed blood – her mother was racially Japanese while her father was half-French, half-Ainu – looked to give her tremendous beauty as an adult.

Unfortunately, shortly after sisterly exorcists got Strife out of her in '65, at the age of nineteen, her life started to fall apart. She began to lose weight at an alarming rate. Her skin jaundiced. She became palsied. Her mother, Corona Power, had been in Hiroshima when the Americans dropped the A-Bomb. Even though Corona didn't become pregnant until the next year, some sort of belated reaction to its thoroughgoing irradiation might have had something to do with Crystal's condition.

After the ordeal of being 1965's Strife, she deteriorated rapidly. As Headmistress Virginia Mannering, who had virtually raised her since Corona (birth-name: Takeda Mikoto) withdrew to Hiroshima a dozen years earlier, and ex-Superior Sorrow (Dolores born D'Angelo become Rivera) were forced to admit, the young woman was beyond the help of even the Superior Sisterhood.

The Steltsar of the late Sixties found out about her plight and recognized a kindred spirit. In a bizarre case of déjà vu, he kidnapped her – just as an earlier Steltsar had seventeen years earlier. From then on they were practically inseparable. As he suspected, her mother was a child of replicates and therefore virtually, but not quite, human. After ascertaining that, deducing the rest of their story wasn't too difficult.

Unlike his original self, the Steltsar of the mid Forties, neither Corona nor Crystal were man- or machine-made. They were devil-made; specifically, in an oblique fashion, by Dand Tariqartha, the devic lord of Temporis. That subterranean realm beneath Sisert, the Silent Sands of Cathune, on Sedon's Head, was populated by mandroid-like versions of real men and women. (Technically replicates were mantels, tellurian men, rather than mandroids, who were mostly machinery, but the difference to the unwashed was negligible.)

Her mother's beginnings as an enhanced half-life, added to the fact that her father, Sedon (once Satan) St Synne, was biologically normal, made Crystal at least three-quarters human. Her tellurian quarter made her akin to an earthborn daemon. Which explained why she could hold onto Osiraq, a possessive devil, rather than the other way around.

(Osiraq, unless it was Tammuz, was one of the Idiot Twins held within All of Incain since the 49ᵗʰ Century of the Dome. Tammuz, unless it was Osiraq, was the other. Their story so far, as ineluctably meshed with that of the Death's Head Hellion, Melusine Master Morgan Abyss, ended with the atomic ruination of the Elysian Fields and the corresponding generation of the Ghostlands in the Upper Head circa 4825 YD.)

The post '65 Steltsar couldn't cure her but did manage to get Strife into her again. That kept her going until 1970, when AMERICA finally crushed WORLD for the last time until this time. Even though Amphitrite of Lemuria and All of Incain rescued them; even though he was out of action yet again; even though Countess Ramona Avar (born Meroudys Maenad, but nowadays better known as Lady Guillotine) was once again made to take the fall; Crystal St Synne immediately reverted to her deteriorating state.

Steltsar could and did save her but at the cost of what little humanity Crystal had left. As he was rebuilt, she became something that could be rebuilt; became Crystallion — an altered, almost Jungian animus who lived in a radiation-containment suit. Her helmet even looked like a Japanese demon's mask.

She amounted to a homunculus, a homun being. In consequential collaboration with All of Incain, who held onto them both since the time of the Death's Head Hellion, her makers adapted Crystallion specifically to house the atomic elemental named either Osiraq or Tammuz by Illuminaries of Weir during the course of the Inner Earth's fourth millennia.

(In the Mithraic tradition on either side of the Dome until Thrygragon, they were Thrygragos Varuna Mithras's heraldic torchbearers. As Cautes, one held his torch up to symbolize either Sunrise or the Vernal Equinox, whereas the other, as Cautopates, held his down, symbolic of Sunset or the Autumnal Equinox.)

In certain mental meanderings into the philosophical as opposed to scientific field of cosmology during medieval times and earlier, psychopomps were supernatural beings who conducted souls safely to the afterlife. Equally often they were described as mystical horses that shamans rode to the underworld in order to commune with spirits or retrieve the souls of the sick.

Technopomps had horses, too, but they weren't mystical: they were nuclear dragons. And Hell's Horsemen didn't ride them to the underworld.

They used them to send others there.

========

"Give your mandroid Mounties and firedrakes a few more hours rest," Sharkczar instructed her. *"But I want them up and fully charged by ten. You strike at noon. I'm on my way now. Even though Great Byron and his Nucleoids managed to elude us, by today's end I'll have given All a dozen more Master Devas to keep her company on Incain. And you'll have made it impossible for any more to leave the Hidden Headworld."*

"Did all the cosmicars make it to the Head as Daemonicus planned?"

"That, my dear, is not our concern."

"And if my drakes collapse the Dome?"

"I can swim. They can fly, you on them. It's cry havoc time, Crystallion."

"Hope it doesn't rain."

========

Sharkczar had no trouble covering the distance between the Phantom Freighter and the now abandoned submarine nest built deep beneath Centauri Island.

He knew enough of this place to understand it was necessary for the Fatman and his Headworld transients. Wouldn't do to bring the likes of Samarand's most trusted technicians, Sentalli's Untouchables and the Valhallans of both Necators, father and son, straight through the Nag Gap and onto Centauri Island without some reasonable explanation. First they had come through the Nag Gap from Aka Godbad City without anyone seeing them. Then they had to leave the island via submarine, only to come back via standard methods such as planes, private boats and commercial ferries.

Centauri Island was just three isolated peaks linked at low tide when Tyrtod von Alptraum effectively died in 1944. Similarly so, the Steltsars that carried his mind until '53 had no idea it even existed. The Steltsar that was rebuilt by All and the Lemurians on Shenon in '54 was brought to Godbad later that year to fight alongside the Frog Folk and their various allies, many of them eldritch earthborn like those Second Fangs employed over in Hadd until just recently.

For four years he battled dutifully away, completely ignorant that in Aka Godbad City there was a link between the Inner and Outer Earth. That held true for the virtually idiotic Steltsar of the early Sixties, the one Moe Two fashioned mostly out of Solidium and whose mind Major Mind managed to get functioning at far less than one hundred percent.

Although that version was on Centauri Island in '65, he lived and died (courtesy of Pluman, Alexandros Kinesis) in equal ignorance that the other side of the link between the Outer and Inner Earth was thereabouts. In terms of awareness that there were two sides to the planet, the late Sixties' Steltsar was far more with it than his predecessors.

For example, that one knew of two ways to pass through the Cathonic Dome. Used both of them – from the He-Sphinx in Egypt to his pre-Flood mate, the She-Sphinx in as much as on Incain; and the Hir Gap from Hiroshima, Japan, to the Hiroshima Cavern in Temporis. Yet that Steltsar, the best one ever in some respects, still hadn't been cognizant enough to figure out the secret of Centauri Island.

Things were different now. For the first time since his template, Tyrtod von Alptraum, exposed himself to his colleagues' devaray in 1943, he had a mind completely his own. No more Phantast, Baphomet, Grand Inquisitor or Hypnosis King telling him what to do. No more Pluman telling him what not to do. No Judge nor Wiccan Warlock, St Synne or King Conqueror, no nascent System, nor yet another Daemonicus holding him back.

Oh, he still had to deal with Lemurians, a couple of Master Devas, and All the Invincible, but they weren't pulling his strings anymore; had finally come clean – told him the truth about Centauri Island. They also told him what to do with it. And Crystallion what to do about it. Truth was he couldn't be more delighted.

Other than it was confined within the island's three peaks, they hadn't told him exactly where it was, though. It might even wander like this SAG Gap he'd heard about, but couldn't access because its stationary entrance on the Head was surrounded by molten Brainrock, and he was philosophically opposed to melting.

While he only knew in general terms where the Nag's entrance and exit were in either place, Sharkczar expected that was about to change for the better. He'd find out very soon where it was on this side specifically. In short order thereafter he'd discover precisely where it came out over there.

The last of his voices may have ceased confusing him a week ago last Sunday after Phantast escaped the Sedon Sphere. But Sharkczar still retained links to a former voice: that of Signal System's never altogether dead-headed old corpse. He'd promised to guide him to it through his superhuman link to the Signalmen, one in particular, who could traverse the Weird physically, not just mentally, and consequently who was already on the island.

He'd known Crystal's conceptive father, Sedon St Synne, for virtually all his existence. As Steltsar he'd also known him as both Wiccan Warlock and as a previous Daemonicus. He also knew why the Witches of Weir, through their surrogate, Tereza D'Angelo Lancz, kept him on life support at System's Stanford University headquarters in Palo Alto, California.

The old corpse may not be an actual corpse but he was last living Sed-son on the Outer Earth. Without him the Sedon Sphere would collapse.

========

Hours after Sharkczar saw her swim by Sea Goddess was back.

========

The shark thing was long gone by then. The Phantom Freighter wasn't. Then again, it hadn't been anywhere near here the last time she was in the vicinity, still following Aires or whomever's sending. Couldn't have been. She wouldn't have missed something that big, that rusty, that scummy, that beat up; that, yes, ship ghostly.

It had to have come from somewhere, presumably under its own steam since it was still afloat but, given the shape it was in, it couldn't have come from anywhere too far away. That suggested it had rather emerged from somewhere. It probably wasn't from the bottom of the sea; at least not too recently, as in the last few weeks.

To judge from the smoke engulfing it, the fires and explosions wracking it, that's where it was heading before too much longer. Hush Mannering had been right to trust the six Signallers she'd transported over to it via between-space in hopes of sinking it before its targeted occupants could get off. Scuttling, like sinking, were S-words. So was successful. Unsuccessful wasn't; at least it didn't start with an 's'.

Off in the distance Sea could readily make out what Hush meant by dragons. About thirty of them were flying towards the coast of Centauri Island.

The very place she'd just come from!

========

They were huge; glowered, more so than glowed, with a fire that seemed vaguely familiar to her – Emperor Energy's monstrous offspring? Could his Headmistress (not the Virginia Mannering, once aka Ginny Gemstone, Headmistress) have borne something that frightfully unearthly? Surely not.

They had long necks topped by heads like frigate birds or pictures of pterodactyls (whom Sea, howsoever whimsically, was certain would eventually prove to be, hence never rendered extinct, oversized frigates). Their bodies looked metallic. Enormous wings beat against the sky audibly. Even from her remote, wave-riding vantage point, she could hear them.

If those weren't dragons, how else would you describe them? All that was lacking was visibly fiery breath, though she had little doubt they came fully equipped.

Hush spoke to her just then, out of the agate mounted in the ring Thalassa wore on her finger. "I wish you'd come along earlier, Sea Stuff. I got the Signallers there too late. If we could have sunk the freighter before the dragons, or whatever they are, left it, we'd have nullified them. I doubt firedrakes and the ocean mix."

(The Silver Signallers were Shelter, Sharpshooter, Selene, Stiletto, Stupendo and Shadowswirl. The first three were System Seers, meaning they'd helped design their state of the craft body armour and built-in micro weaponry. Either Shelter or Shooter was leading them. Obviously the former, whom the others called House-Head due to his quirky headgear, wasn't quite as certifiable as most reckoned him.

(Unless he was a she, that is. Signallers were supposed to be anonymous; went to extraordinary lengths to keep themselves that way. Being human, they couldn't be sexless. Their Silver was deliberately unisexual, no bumps or bulge giveaways, and they all sounded the same when they spoke. Every Signaller also had to have an S-name. They even made Hush assume one. It was, naturally, Shush.)

"What about Aires?"

"Don't worry about him. He wasn't on it anyway. Your abilities are better suited defending the island."

"Why should I?"

"I think I know where Aires went."

"You always have, haven't you, trickster?"

"I've always known the drakes were out there, too. And I like that island. Tell you another thing for free. You don't save Centauri, chances are you'll never see your precious twin again." It wasn't like the forever seven year old to issue barefaced threats, even if they were, in this case, barefaced thought-transmissions.

And Sea Goddess should know — as General Huff 'n' Puff Jollity, Hush was hers and Aires' occasional trainer in supra-doings back in the mid to late Thirties.

========

"We're getting visuals now," shouted Dolph Dulles. "I don't believe it. They are dragons. Must be thirty of them. Big as biplanes. There's someone riding each of them."

His Enormity responded just as urgently. "I don't care if they're Norse Gods playing Swan Maidens to the tune of Wagner's Valkyrie, Mr Dulles. Take them out."

========

Heat-seeking missiles found their targets. Some exploded on contact – amazingly to no effect. Even more amazingly, others were swallowed whole. The firedrakes kept on coming; the ones who had been hit larger than earlier. The island's jets homed in on them. Strafing fire riveted the dragons and their riders. More rockets, more dragon food.

The jets blazed away, out into the Pacific. The helicopters also backed off over the ocean, though whether they had enough fuel to get to another island was more a matter of guesswork than gauges. The dragon-riders ignored them entirely and whipped their unnatural beasts onwards.

========

"No use, sir! Don't see as we have any other option."

In the absence of O'Ryan *'Big Max'* Maxwell – who was either on the Liberty or in Helios's Lunar Citadel – Adolph *'Dolph'* Dulles was the youngish chief of security on Centauri Island. Like a number of others, Barb Black's *'Little Hitler'*, as Colonel Jock Maxwell used to refer to him (his still unacknowledged son) when he was growing up in Vancouver, was hunkered down within the dubious protection of the largely manmade island's underside bunker.

Those there were watching everything that had thus far befallen up top on closed circuit television screens and video feeds.

"All right." Sentalli flipped open his armrest and began clicking in a code only he and Dulles, of those alive and still on the island, knew.

They were flying abreast of each other – strung out across the skyline like blazing beads on a nuclear necklace – their massive wings almost touching. Then there was a flash. Six of them vanished. Fifteen of them swooped back out over the ocean. The remaining nine simply hung in the empty air: gargantuan grotesqueries caught in an invisible spider's web.

From out of Mounts Heliopolis, Zeross, and Kinesis, Alfredo Sentalli had just raised the Gypsium Curtain.

"Will it hold?" demanded the patriarch, Loxus Abraham Ryne.

"Damned if I know," admitted his Enormity. (The Fatman was known by his birth name, Alfredo Sentalli, out here but as Alpha Centauri on the Inner Earth. Not that anyone who was there that minute besides himself knew of its existence, let alone that one of the few reliable ways between the two sides of the Whole Earth lay not that far away from the bunker, as the rock or concrete mole bored.)

"You know what Professor Kinesis always said about Gypsium. Any idea how the dragons suck in everything we fire at them?"

"Look at the way they glow," said Spherus (Cecil Mayhew, under the globular silver helmet and exoskeleton he wore). According to some the world's first Bubble Boy, since being recruited for Signal System at an early age the hence severely immunities-deficient genius had made a study of supranormals.

(That in itself was no mean feat. Those few governments and corporations who knew about supras never, ever, let any information about them or the Supra Wars get out. So he must have had exceptional security clearances. And he did, particularly when it came to the annals of the Alliance of Man. His father, Theodore Mayhew, was one of the Great Man's closest aides throughout the Thirties and well into the war years.)

"Back during the latter stages of the War there was a supra by the name of Emperor Energy. He literally fed on explosions. We never did learn much about him, but Raphael D'Angelo thought he was an archangel sent by the Lord Above. Then again, he was convinced he was one, too."

"Emp En did a bunk after the second Atomic Bomb was dropped over Nagasaki," the Great Man, Loxus Abraham Ryne, provided, possibly selectively. "Either it was too much for even him or he figured the war was over, his job done. Good thing you had that in reserve. What does it do?"

(There were many who reckoned Ryne knew a whole lot more about Emperor Energy and his mate, the non-Ginny Headmistress, than he ever let on.)

"What Gypsium usually does, I guess. Whatever that is."

"Six of the dragons went poof," said (presumably no longer) Doubleman Johann Schmidt, the last of the Psychic Siblings now that his confrère, Sean Smythe, had reportedly expired under the usual ever-so-mysterious circumstances aboard the UNES Liberty. "From what Sean told me before he died, something similar happened to one of the LAC Squads on the Moon more than a week ago."

"Fucking Hell!" swore Spherus, who'd been left behind by Shelter, Sharpshooter and the others not because he was too valuable as a System Seer to risk but because his fellow Seers, House-Head and Bullet-Brain in particular, judged him useless in a fight. "It's fading."

"Didn't put enough oomph into it," figured his Enormity, fidgeting with the controls built into his wheelchair in faint hopes of bolstering it. Wasn't to be.

"Got any more tricks up your sleeve, Al?" muttered Ryne disconsolately as the Gypsium Curtain vanished with the nine dragons and their riders caught in it.

"There's still fifteen firedrakes left," the Space Age Spartan noted with remarkable, almost fatalistic calmness.

(He, Gus Soldakis beneath the Silver, had been the Signallers' field leader for as long there were fields in which to lead them. Then he dared challenge one of House-Head's decisions. At least the madman, or madwoman, beneath the Shelter Silver, hadn't caused his to constrict painfully, if not fatally, as punishment. Spartan, though, would have loved to help scupper the Phantom Freighter. Another ex-operative of the Black Rose then AMERICA, he was an action-oriented warrior at heart.)

"They're massing again, sir," yelled Dulles.

"Don't worry about it, Dolph." Hush Mannering appeared off one of her agates, either the one Ryne or Sentalli wore as a ring inlay. "Got it soused!"

She giggled at her own little joke.

========

Spouts of ocean shot up. Hit the technopomps. Fire met water. Steam dissipated both. Only one of the atomic dragons got through. It landed on the airport tarmac.

========

Crystallion leapt off it, seemed to sniff the air, dropped a Hellstone at her feet and went through the Grey to confront the perpetual seven year old and the rest of those gathered in the underground bunker with her. Once there she just ignored/absorbed all the ordinance being blasted at/into her by Dulles, Spartan and Schmidt.

Tearing off her demonic helmet, thereby unveiling the featureless face of scarlet-skinned, geyser-haired Strife beneath the transparent radiation mask she always wore, she spat her venom. "You little monster," she screamed at Hush. "I should have killed you years ago. But I've got you now. Die!"

Crystallion shook-shoulder-shivered. Then her suit began to glow.

"Gloman!" someone shouted.

"Nuclear!" screamed someone else.

"Sluts for nuts," the trickster nattered inanely.

========

Cromwell Necator did not believe in missions impossible. The way he reckoned it, bombing the Prison Beach should have been done a long time ago.

========

Incain was the domain of All the Invincible, the semi-legendary, she-sphinx-like, multi-millennia old Machine Master Moulder. A mandroid monster maker from way back – on both sides of the Dome as well, from what he'd heard tell – All was also the inspirational leader, if not necessarily the actual fount, of the hated mandroids.

A quarter century ago, had the Republicans – including Alpha Centauri and the likes of his father Godfrey or New Irache Governor Ferdinand (Weird Ferd) Niarchos's father Gomez – planes capable of it, the Godbadian Civil War would have been over in matter of months instead of the nearly six years it took.

Lemurians were nothing without their tellurian (earthen), often All-manufactured servants and mandroid militias. And, without them, the much more numerous, but poorly equipped royalist forces loyal to the Bandradin Royal House of Achigan Auranja proved themselves next to nothing up against the Outer Earth modern equipment and hired guns of Centauri Enterprises.

Although he'd been warned that Incain was just a long, apparently empty stretch of sandy beach, it was still a disappointing sight. He wished there'd been a prison complex or massive monument similar to the Giza Sphinx on the Outer Earth. Instead, there was no sign of any habitation, nor any inhabitants, whatsoever. He had his orders. Saturation bombing was the strategy and that's what he did.

He was on the first plane that dumped its load on the beach. Its mission completed, he returned to Vanalana, refuelled, stocked up again, and went back over the Whiplash Range and the High Plateau of ancestral Bandrad to Incain. For the next six hours, with no opposition and no losses, Incain was hit and hit again.

This was crazy, he was thinking after his third jaunt. Who ever heard of wasting ordnance on sand dunes? The bugs probably wouldn't even be impacted.

Likely he never realized that bombing Incain did more than just distract All the Invincible. It was probably all that kept the Phantom Freighter from disappearing into its own version of Shadowland yet again. Thoroughly sabotaged by the six Signallers, who barely broke a silver sweat doing so, it was finished off by American fighter planes.

With its destruction went Hell's Horsemen's escape route through the Sedon Sphere back to the Inner Earth. As for All, being largely within the dark-grey, universal substance of Samsara, it, she, was mostly unaffected. No devils escaped but the same could not be said for the factory.

Constructed, mostly by All herself, beneath the beach and extending into the Head's eastern ocean, Tempestuous Psychron, that was where All, Aortic Amphitrite, her Lemurians – amphibious women and purely water-breathing males – and themselves artificially reproduced biomages fashioned the dragons and horsemen.

It shuddered under continuous bombardment. Mandroids shut themselves down. Frog Folk fled for their lives. Seals cracked and burst. Psychron reclaimed its own. And Amphitrite? The Summoning Child born, Quarter-Queen of Shenon, as well as full queen of the Frog Folk, was in the far north, beneath Sisert, Sedon's gnarly bald spot, in Centurium, Replicated Versailles.

Barely three days gone, on Devauray (Saturday) the 6th of Tantalar (December), her deviant daughter, Lakshmi of Lemuria, celebrated the day after her eighteenth birthday with the stunning takeover of Subcranial Temporis. Through her, in the former protectorate of Dand Tariqartha, and in neighbouring Absudyl (Minius), Amphitrite held the tellurian heartland.

Forty-five hundred years earlier, her ancestors had almost put devils out of business on the even then, long hidden continent of Sedon's Head. Within a couple of years, the Frog Queen was now certain, she would succeed where her predecessors failed. Then, with the help of her inspirational Mother on the Moon (as well as in Minius, where Trans-Time Trigon settled five years earlier), they'd go beyond putting them out of business on the Whole Earth.

They'd drive them to extinction everywhere!

========

Thalassa D'Angelo, Sea Goddess, whose water spouts had extinguished Hell's Horsemen, came out of Samsara off the same agate first Hush, then the other one, Strife's latest shell, had mere seconds earlier. She pointed her Aqua Ankh at the faceless, even eyeless redhead as she neared critical mass; thereby inundating Crystallion's radiation suit with seawater.

"Get everyone out of here, Mannering!" she shrieked, already realizing there wasn't enough time. Sea didn't so much explode as the icy depths of the Pacific burst out of her. Thoroughly immersing her with her own aqueous substance, she took Strife-Crystallion with her.

And then it was all over!

****

Thirteenth Moon: **Prayer Power Powwow**

========

Friday to Tuesday night, December 5-9, 5980

Dreams have obsessed, more like distressed, sentient beings since time immemorial. And not just sentient beings either.

========

While it may be something of a stretch to call them sentient – except in the sense that they have senses, some more than five if one includes instinct – many animals dreamed, too. Most believe they are self-generated mental exercises in sorting out the day's muddle of thoughts. A few think they are sent by God or something similarly, but only seemingly, supernatural; devils or supranormals, for example.

In terms of Master Devas, Phantast Thanatos was rightly called the Dream Weaver. Born in the same litter as Lathakra's Tantal and Mythland's Methandra, whilst he was active even his own kind feared him. Until the Thirtieth of November 1980, he hadn't been active for a very long time. Along with most of his underlings and co-conspirators in the Crimson Conspiracy, the Moloch Sedon cathonitized (catasterized) him circa 4000 YD in there, around the time of Jesus Christ out here.

Although no longer the case, he was still languishing in the Sedon Sphere when, thirty-seven years prior to his escape, his attributes were extracted from Cathonia. With Strife's collusion, Satan St Synne imparted them to Tyrtod von Alptraum via his devaray. As a result, the Nazi Nightmare could thereafter transmit dreams.

Some subsequent incarnations of the old Baron – the Steltsar destroyed on Salvation Island in '53, the one who fought on the royalist side during the Godbadian Civil War, and the one who made the rounds so brutally in the late Sixties – at least partially retained that ability. The Russian supranormal Boris Gagarin, codenamed the Sleeping Giant, was a quadriplegic who literally dreamed up his supra-self, a giant who could do much more than just physically grow.

In his prime, and long beyond it, Sedon St Synne could send his dream self to those either of his own blood or with whom he shared blood, cut to cut. Reputedly, albeit as System, he still could. Indeed, there were those, particularly on Apple Isle, who said Judge Warlock (Cybele, the Korants' long time Miracle Maenad's father) walked the Headworld to this day.

Thanks to the Conqueror's life support system, as rebuilt at California's Stanford University's campus in Palo Alto, St Synne was technically alive. Shaman Manitoulin (*'Shamanitoulin'*) was not; hadn't been since the Solstice of June 1953. In his lengthy day, the Cheyenne medicine man (who helped raise Sedon St Synne, Louise born Riel St Synne, John Sundown and Solace Sunrise) was, however, another dream-sender.

Like St Synne, his foster son, he too could do more than that. His Dream-Sent Man not only walked the Head when he breathed, some claimed his spirit still haunted an abandoned village in the northeast corner of the Iraxas (Hadd) mainland. Even though there was no such thing as magic per se, just different ways of doing things, conjuring daemons, the stuff of nightmares, was something that could be taught and hence learned.

(One of Manitoulin's familiars was Horny Head, a narwhal psychopomp native to an estuary off the Aural Sea of Sedon's Ear that stretched into Satanwyck, Sedon's Temple. His ghost, perhaps both their ghosts, he riding her, could also been seen once in a while, particularly on very dark nights, frolicking in the frothy, phosphorescent waters of the Straits of Jaag, what separated the Aural Sea from the Interior Ocean of Akadan.)

A few gifted witches, be they Antheans, Korants, Afrites or whomever, were adept at dream-casting. The ancestors of today's Mariamnics first worshipped Mariamne Dawnstar in the Land of Daybreak. They kept the name once she became her Grey Lady self, Krepusyl Evenstar, when Dark Sedon moved Daybreak some four thousand miles to the twilight side of his Head.

They positively revelled in dream-casting. Of course they were in near daily contact with faeries, some of whom could not only appear and disappear in someone's dreams but could do so physically over distance.

From Sunday night until he transferred himself, minus his regalia, to the Head on Lazam-Friday, OMP was busy sending selected folks dreams via his Homeworld Sceptre. Much to the horror of those of his D-Brig fellows who found out what he doing too late to stop him, he was letting them know the King Crimefighters were back and unaged, albeit as the Damnation Brigade.

(Obadiah Melvin Power was latterly revealed as Akbarartha, a very long-lived faerie-sort born in the 58th Century of the Dome. He was – and, as the Fates would have it, remains – the eldest surviving, hence deviant half-son of the Lazaremist, Dand Tariqartha, and the Byronic, Malar Tzigame. Largely due to Lakshmi of Lemuria, he was no longer the Kronokronos Supreme of Temporis.)

Among the recipients of those dreams was Erech Avar Ryne, which was why he wasn't entirely shocked to find whitecap-haired Thalassa sitting next to him on the plane from Vancouver to Los Angeles Friday night. OMP's ex-wife, Corona Power (born Takeda Mikoto); his foster daughter, Corona's birth-daughter, Crystal; her, eventual Crystallion's birthfather, Sedon St Synne; plus Erech, Psycho and Cerebrus's father, Loxus Abraham Ryne, may have received them, too.

One who did, on Gloriel's behalf, was Sophia born St Synne D'Angelo.

========

What should have been a wonderful weekend, the occasion of the Family D'Angelo's latest five year reunion, had mostly been a disaster.

========

Friday night, both Sophia and Raphael encountered what appeared to be Gloriella (whom they called Gloria or Glory), alive and unchanged after a quarter century. As a consequence of Gloriel's ill-thought-out visit, Papa Rafe suffered a minor heart attack (if there was such a thing) and was taken to hospital for overnight observation.

The next *'impossible'* thing Mama Sofa belatedly heard was that John Paul, Anna Maria, her three children (by Bruce Dre'Ath) and Tereza's Sapphire Lancz had seen and spoken to David Ryne, as well as saw the adopted twins, Aires and Thalassa, earlier that same Friday night at the airport. (They were waiting for Teri's flight to arrive from San Francisco.)

Until then, even though she'd long held suspicions otherwise, she believed the Terrible Twins died in 1943 and that David was killed, along with Gloriel (her then eldest surviving daughter), in a plane crash on Christmas Day 1955. Mama Sofa, as some of her more disrespectful children called her when they were growing up, was big on belief. Nevertheless, even decades later, some things struck her as unbelievable.

(Her Roman Catholic faith surpassed even that of Raphael, once a highly influential lay adviser to the Pope. Circumstances, including a rift with his ordained rivals, as well as not just his hatred of Fascism, forced the Family D'Angelo out of Italy for Scotland before the War. After the War, lousy weather and worse food thence took them to Canada; where they'd been ever since.)

Saturday morning, Colonel Jock Maxwell – a slightly older, long time family friend who retained highest level connections with the local constabulary as well as the Royal Canadian Mounted Police (RCMP) – phoned to let her know Estrella Dark, the real Gloriel's twenty-seven year old, unrepentant wild child of a daughter, had been arrested for attempted murder at a downtown discotheque.

According to old (Auld) Jock, she was disco-dancing in nothing but her panties when a couple of bouncers tried to evict her. Star, as she liked being called, tossed a glass full to the brim with brandy at them. Whereupon she flicked her Bic (plastic lighter), as the current saying went, thereby severely burning them.

The story, to Sophia's mind, reeked of cover-up. (Big, bruising bouncers, a brandy snifter, an itty-bitty lighter pulled from her panties? Pull the other one, Max.) Being well-respected by the police (at one time he'd been the RCMP's chief commissioner), Auld Jock was nevertheless in the process of getting her released.

To further begin the day on entirely the wrong foot, as riots intensified throughout the city, Sapphire, their punkish teenage grandchild, was told to prepare herself to fly to Hawaii with the rest of her father's Signallers. Fortunately, again because of the riots, that was delayed. Also for the same reason, the three men – Gloriel's husband and Star's father, Immanuel Dark; Tereza's Simon (Lancz) and Anna Maria's Bruce (Dre'Ath) – were unable to join the rest of the family for their reunion.

Needless to say, though Rafe was out of the hospital, Estrella out of jail, and Sapphire still in town, Saturday's celebration was a muted affair, ending early. That night Sophia prayed Raphael to sleep then tried to do the same for herself. Hers was fitful at best, troubled as she had been all week by visions, and visitations, from the past. It was worse than that actually.

For the first time since Virginia Mannering, unless it was someone else (couldn't have been a jolly little blonde no more than six or seven), gave her amnaesthetics almost a quarter century ago, she began to remember the so-called Secret Wars of Supranormals. (The Supra Wars, which lasted roughly seventeen years, from early 1938 until late 1955, were no secret to those contesting them.)

Both sides of her family, the D'Angelos and St Synnes, including her father's foster brothers and sisters, had been intimately involved in them virtually from their real Day One – the Summoning of February 1920. Along with her *'Nubian'*, Ubris Nauroz, not yet sister-in-law, Celestine D'Angelo, had actually called it.

(Ubris, Morgianna's grandfather, was blacker than the Ace of Spades whereas Morg herself, Superior Sarpedon, wasn't codenamed the White Witch because her skin wasn't white-as-bleached-lightning, to quote another long gone old friend, Yehudi Cohen. As for Papa Rafe's eldest sibling, Mama Sofa remembered Celestine as a radiant, silver-haired, yes, human angel.)

In Scotland, forty years and eight anniversaries earlier, all but the child, Marcello, *'Nino'*, who had died the previous year, were alive. Sure, Raphael's parents (Michael and Leonora), his eldest sister (said Celestine, who, at the time of her death, was the Antheans' Celestial Superior), her father (Sedon St Synne, albeit only supposedly) and, like Raphael's kin in 1920, her mother (Louise nee Riel) and her then only "official" sister (Cybele) had all vanished by then.

(Spookily – as would be the case with Gloriel, maybe, and the Terrible Twins, for sure, a dozen years before her – not a single one of them left a body behind as proof of their passage. Sadly that wasn't the case for all their other lost children. Something of an Earth Mother of the Church-approved barefoot and pregnant variety, counting the adopted twins and Marcello, who really wasn't hers, there were thirteen of them. Only three remained.)

Tereza was just a baby. Anna Maria, Belificent, and John Paul were still to come. But everyone else – including Raphael's two surviving sisters, Dolores by then Rivera, who yet lived, and Mnemosyne yet to become Heliopolis – was together. They were celebrating the family's relatively recent escape from fascist Italy, an event their subsequent gatherings continued to mark.

Five years later, Mnemosyne (Memory), Anita (Nita) and, apparently, both Aires and Thalassa were dead. Peter (who never liked Pietro), Leandro, Claudia and, again supposedly, her father would be before the next get-together in 1950. By '55, so too would Gabriel. Gloriel would die in an upcountry plane crash after being called away from their fifth reunion right here in Vancouver.

(She did leave a corpse behind but, by the time they found the plane, the bodies were so badly deteriorated that she, once the consensus most beautiful woman in the western world, the founder of Radiant Rainbows Fashion Emporium, could barely be identified. Neither she nor Raphael even asked see it, again choosing to leave everything to Auld Jock and the Great Man, Abe Ryne, who'd lost his two eldest sons, David and Saul, as well as the exceedingly eccentric Xuthrodic spokesman, Obadiah Melvin Power, on the same flight.)

Beginning Saturday night and continuing for the next three nights, thoughts of her lost ones dominated her dreams. Then, towards dawn Tuesday, her dreams became a nightmare. The wild child whose genes Star Dark might well have inherited, the unabashed hussy whose wanton ways Raphael came to regard as his staunchly Roman Catholic family's greatest embarrassment, appeared before her, in their bedroom, with Raphael asleep right there in the bed next to her.

Mnemosyne wasn't a ghost, though she looked much as she'd done when Sophia last beheld her, easily three and half decades gone by. She couldn't be a ghost;

not even some supra-sent manifestation. She spoke to her in a sane, considerate manner. Proper ghosts never spoke like any of that. They wailed, mournfully.

"It all comes down to Strife, doesn't it, Sainted Sophia?" Memory of the Angels – of the Devils, according to Papa Rafe – insisted. "It wasn't your long lost sister Cybele who ruined your life and that of your family. Sed's sorely misused Red didn't wittingly draw you, your husband, and your children, to your by then satanic father's Vichy laboratory in '43.

"She was but a possessed pawn, an occupied husk, a seized, severed-of-self shell of the terrifying spectre who watched, so dispassionately, to see who you got once he exposed you to his devil-ray. It was Strife by then manifest, not Cybele by then thoroughly subsumed, who strove against Nita; Strife who forced your lovely dark-haired Summoning Child to sacrifice herself so most of you could get away.

"Peter, Leandro, Claudia and Gabriel might still be around but for her. Strife killed me, my original self, painfully, cruelly, mercilessly, in 1945. Then, fifteen years later, Strife did the same to Joan Smith and your beautiful Belificent, an incarnation of my most miraculous sister, the Celestial Superior, if ever there was one.

"Strife tried to finish off Bel's new husband, Harry, and my stepson, Kadmon, that same horrible Witch Week in 1960. Strife was responsible for the disappearance and eventual deaths of Alex and Roxanne Kinesis, of my daughter Europa and my triplet granddaughters, potential Great Goddesses all three of them. How many more lives has she claimed over the decades? Far, far too many.

"She's still around, Sophia. Father John Paul must have told you what happened to the Cosmic Express. He's Centauri Island's papal nuncio; the island Catholics' father-confessor or whatever suchlike are called. Well, Strife was behind that; her and her latest Daemonicus, the same emanation of evil that so twisted your thereafter unfairly demonized father into Satan St Synne all those decades ago.

"He's been dealt with, hopefully forevermore, but I'm on the lookout for her. And I'll find her. Don't worry about that. But who can hold her? Who but you, with your saintliness and hitherto unprecedented prayer power? Are you willing to try?"

In her delirium, she said yes.

========

Seventy-four year old Sophia D'Angelo was at supper early Tuesday night. By then, with the rioting mostly a bad memory, at least in Vancouver, Immanuel Dark, Simon Lancz and Bruce Dre'Ath had flown to the naturally beautiful, but depressingly wet and dreary, Rain Forest city. Unfortunately, and for the same reason — calm in the streets as well as the runways in Hawaii — Sapphire had already left it.

As was the family tradition, they held hands around the table while she (Raphael being confined to bed upstairs) said grace.

Of her children, the three scientist-husbands, her five grandchildren (only four of whom were there), and three guests, Jock Maxwell, Bunnie Galvin, and TJ Maxwell (who had actually been knocked down by Gloriel as she fled her parents' house on Friday evening), only the priest, John Paul, was particularly religious. Nevertheless, all of them bowed their heads respectfully.

By then, they had heard from various ports.

========

Erech Ryne had phoned from Houston, again apologizing that neither he nor his father could be at the reunion. He didn't say anything about seeing white-cap-haired Thalassa, her lookalike or, in some views, her clone, on Friday; did mention that his mother, Ramona Avar-Ryne, seemed well on her way to a full recovery after her transference to the Houston Academy of Man for treatment.

(Mama Sofa may or may not have found that good news since, regardless of her guilt, Ramona took the fall for killing both Joan and Belificent in May 1960. As a result mostly of that, she'd spent the next twenty years – until he collected her in Budapest last week, in fact – confined to one mental institute after another.)

On the negative side, Erech put to them, the person most responsible for that, to him undeniably welcome turn of events, Aranyani Nightingale, still hadn't been seen since her (latest) mysterious disappearance the previous Wednesday. No one, not even her colleague, the third Moses Callion, had any idea what had become of her. However, given the Man in the Moon was still up there, and given his father's obsession with bringing him down, he frankly feared for her life.

(He thought Aran his half-sister, not – among many another – mother Ramona and Sophia's dot-ditto. He knew she was Big Max's estranged wife and Timmy's mother. He may or may have known those there believed her daughter Firenze, whom she kept to herself, was TJ's full-sister. No one disputed Aran was a pharmaceutical wunderkind, though, and it was in that capacity, as his Mama Ray's saviour, he was referencing her.)

Erech, especially for a Ryne, was neither very bright nor particularly respectful of others' feelings. Timmy loved his mother much as Erech, whose twin had died on the Cosmic Express, did his. But Sophia was a mother many times over. She loved all of her kids and grandkids equally. That being the case, she was no more happy to hear about killer-sister Ray's recovery than life-loving sister Aran vanishing, this despite what she'd done to Timmy, crippling him in the cradle, all those years ago.

More bad news was forthcoming from Centauri Island. Adolph Dulles phoned just before supper. Like Bruce, Simon, Big Max himself and son TJ, the elder Maxwells all but raised Dolph. He couldn't say much and mostly spoke to Auld Jock – though he professed not to know it, his actual father – and John Paul. Even to them, he was guarded in his comments.

The island had come under some kind of attack. Again not mentioning Thalassa, he implied Crystal St Synne was behind the assault. Yet another of Sophia's half-sisters, her an official St Synne and seemingly the latest Strife, would not be behind anything anymore, he guaranteed them. (Jock had lived through the Supra Wars and hadn't been wiped; John Paul had been thoroughly briefed during the years he spent studying at the Vatican.) He couldn't say with the same certainty that Strife wouldn't be back of course.

He then spoke directly to Tereza, the most austere, even unattractive, of the D'Angelo brood, either sex, any generation. He did so primarily to assure her that Sapphire was fine. Finally he asked to talk to Simon Lancz, who didn't seem to have much use, let alone love, for his punkish daughter. When Signal System's Strategos picked up the phone, it was Gus Soldakis, the Space Age Spartan, who came online.

"I'm sure they died well," Lancz said just before he hung up.

The news that three of his Signallers (Solano, Savant, and Sub-System) were definitely dead, and that seven others (Shelter, Sharpshooter, Shadowswirl, Stupendo, Stiletto, Selene, and Subitor) were missing and presumed dead, would do little for his appetite. That two others, Sheriff and Sebastion, had deserted their posts just as the attack began and, through their negligence, possibly cost their three charges (Yataghan Sentalli, Connie Lindquist and George Hannibal) their lives only further soured his mood.

Even though he didn't know said charges from Adam or Eve; suspected, like Big Max did, they were closet supras; and was secretly happy to hear that Shelter and Shooter might have gone the way of Solar, if perhaps not Styx and Sasquatch; Simon expressed a politically correct desire for their ultimate survival.

"Let's hope the others came through as well as the patriarch and Al Sentalli did. Tell Spherus I'll be expecting his report, and yours, in Palo Alto come tomorrow afternoon. Tereza and I are flying back there in the morning. Oh, and Gus, if Shooter and the others don't show up, pick another six for frontline assignments.

"Not Sapphire this time. That was a mistake. Teri may never talk to me again because of it. And while that may be a relief personally, System needs her. So does her grandfather, the old corpse. No one knows how to keep him clicking – rather, the life support thingies he's wired into – like her."

"Six? Don't think we've got that many left. Fact is I'm sure we don't."

"Well, we better have. Bruce Dre'Ath is in town and his botch-up, the new Mammalian and his Manimalians, even if they aren't were-creatures this time, need prejudicial attention hereabouts."

Soldakis-Spartan ventured they might need more than seven howsoever inexperienced Signallers to handle the Beast Master anyways. Truth told, he reiterated, doing the math, if Sheriff and Sebastion were stripped of their Silver, as they should be for abandoning their post, he couldn't even count up to the minimally mandatory S-number of six.

Not without Sapphire and Spherus, who had no aptitude for fighting, he couldn't. In the continuing absence of the Seers Styx and Sasquatch, he only had four: Sapperstein, Static, Sonora and himself, assuming he was reinstated. Plus, he reminded his boss, there were also the King Crimefighters, be they clones or the real thing, and conceivably, if Sentalli hadn't nailed him with his Maser effects, Steltsar to consider.

Might Lancz be considering donning the Strategos Silver for real instead of just pretend on the parade ground? It was supposed to be quite advanced, right up there with Shelter and Shooter's according to Spherus. Lancz laughed at the that; said they'd talk more about it tomorrow. Without recycling any of the wrecked ones, or rebuilding any of the lost ones, System had a few more Silvers up its sleeve, he assured him. And the potential Signallers to wear them.

After signing off, Simon returned to the table to fill in the others with what he dared share of Soldakis's information. Mama Sofa took in everything stoically then began to say grace. Dr Immanuel Dark, Bunnie Galvin and Jock Maxwell, not one of whom anyone had even tried to wipe, not successfully at any rate, devoutly trusted her prayer power was as effective as it had been in the Forties.

"Let us thank the Lord," Sophia intoned, "For father's recovery. For the survival of our beloved child, Sapphire. For the continued health of the patriarch, Abraham Ryne. For our old friend, Johann Schmidt, in his distress; for the Tedesco girl Maria, who may have survived only to fight another day; for our godson, Alfredo, who has just lost his only son; and of course for the boy himself, no matter how oddly chlorophyllous he was."

Maria Tedesco, the Signaller who wore the Sonora Silver was a relation of the D'Angelos through Papa Rafe's sixty years' dead mother, Leonora nee just that, Tedesco. Yataghan Sentalli, the Fatman's exceedingly strange son by Emeralda Plantagenet, Dolph had told them, was among the missing and presumed deceased.

"Let us also pray for O'Ryan James Maxwell and Romaine Kinesis. May they succeed at whatever they're doing, wherever they are. Let us not forget the salvation of your soul, dearest Estrella, and that of our absent ones ..." Her voice trailed off. She looked upwards, as if to the heavens, and seemed to go catatonic.

She remained physically in their presence but her spirit essentially flew to the Moon. When she returned, she broke the chain of hands and, blaming the week's strains, took to her sewing room upstairs, across the hall from Papa Rafe and their bedroom. After pecking at his food, John Paul, her only surviving son, chaplain of Centauri Island and confessor to Roman Catholics aboard the Cosmic Express, went to see her in what had once been his bedroom.

Despite the fact that he was only thirty-six, he was already an adviser to the Pope of the same name. (His father, though never as a priest, held a similar role with a different Pope, Pius XI.) Nevertheless, regardless of his success in that and nearly every other endeavour he put his mind to, he had long placed last in terms of his father's affections. Whatever resentment he retained for Raphael's attitude towards himself didn't extend to Mama Sophia, however.

"Mother?"

"It's better this way, John Paul," she said. "No one else can contain her. No one else has the fortitude."

Reawakened to their reality after transfigured Memory's visitation, she suspected that, in his capacity as confidante to the Pope, he had much more than just some slight glimmering as to the reality of supranormals, of Strife in particular, and of their long ended Supra Wars; not that, obviously, they were long ended anymore.

She further reckoned he knew more about what was actually going on in this world of theirs than anyone else in the house save, perhaps, for Dr Dark and, almost for sure, the elder Maxwells (not that Jock and Bunnie ever married). After all, his intellect was as prodigious as his faith was ferocious, so very few of the Church's myriad secrets would have been kept from him.

"But you're too old," he said, confirming as much.

"Then pray for me. It's always better to be prayed for than to pray for. I leave it to you to see that neither your father or I are abandoned."

"You can rely on me, mother."

========

Strife had been troubling Moon's Angel since the night before.

========

The tripartite being that was Miracle Memory wasn't satisfied with any explanation she could come up with as to how Marut Kanin – as Fitna Marutia the one-time mate of her Great God father Thrygragos Varuna Mithras, if that was whom Strife (Kore-Discord) was – came to possess her, no matter how briefly.

However, as she told her (currently) beloved Heliosophos, she was confident she had finally got rid of her. "I would have thought of it myself except my template, Mnemosyne Heliopolis, Memory of the Grey, of the Angels, was killed before Strife became much of a factor. If you think about it, it's obvious. Fitna Marutia, under whatever name, is the devil Classical Greeks knew as Eris, she of the Golden Apple and the Judgement of Paris."

"Eris almost rhymes with Ares, the Olympian God of War."

"Who's her brother, at least according to some sources, but regardless of that, just so. She's an affinity for females connected to Sedon St Synne. That includes me, though I – that is to say my original self – only slept with him. Generally speaking, we're an imperfect lot: impulsive, even compulsive, rather than resolute; less reflective than convective. Except for Sophia, my namesake's sister-in-law, that is.

"Wisdom of the Angels is so spiritual, so intrinsically good, I doubt even the epitome of Discord can corrupt her."

"Just what I needed, something else to celebrate."

========

Sea Goddess vanished on the agate one, Hush, then the other, Crystal, had appeared upon seconds earlier. She hauled Strife-Crystallion with her. Both were suddenly deep beneath the ocean. When Crystallion self-detonated, Strife no longer possessed her – Memory was waiting for her within Shadowland, what passed for her own personal Witch Shelter – and Thalassa was fully in her watery form.

Only Crystal St Synne died that moment.

========

Or, rather, what Steltsar (Sharkczar), All of Incain, Quarter-Queen Amphitrite, her Lemurians and mandroid biomages in the onetime Weirdom of Shenon, by exploiting her genetic heritage, had made of her that died. (When, pre-Genesea, Sedon's Head had been the Archipelago of Pacifica, Eden's Zoo, the even-then heart-shaped island of Shenon had been the Edenite zookeepers' headquarters.)

The real Crystal had probably ceased to live, in terms of having her own free will, the first time Strife, with the connivance of her cancer-riddled, pain-ridden and embittered mother, Corona Power, took the then thirteen year old over during Witch Week 1960 (Witch Night, Walpurgis Nacht and/or Beltane Eve, April 30th, being its start) — in particular the day Crystal strangled Belificent by then Zeross with her riding crop.

Even changing to water, Thalassa might have shared her fate but for one thing. Using his teleportive Brainrock rings, Ringleader transported Methandra (Hot Stuff, Miss Myth, the Mistress of Mythland), from one side of the Dome to the other.

(By now, as per usual when dealing with outsiders, masked and robed or gloved in various shades of red such that neither her face nor even her hair was visible, she'd been following Thalassa's actions via the scarlet fumes of her purloined cauldron. Indeed, as Klannit explained to him because her mother wouldn't speak to those she judged lesser beings, Methandra had been sending Sea the vision of Aires that led her to Centauri Island in the first place.)

With her mind-over-mind abilities as much as her sorcery, Lathakra's Crimson Queen rendered Thalassa forcibly solid again. Gathering her thought-daughter up bodily, Rings returned them through the Sedon Sphere to the Frozen Isle. Massive Tantal was waiting for them atop his glacial palace in the Labrys mountain range.

"Your wife and daughters are safely back in Cabalarkon, Dr Zeross," King Cold told Harry, deigning to speak to him directly.

(So long as they had a power focus, devils could travel through the Weird at will. Some, like the Thanatoid Devalord of Lathakra, had a flare for the dramatic. Liked to use their talismans to slash great gashes in the sky itself preparatory to hauling themselves and those they carried to their destination.

(Ringleader was still hoping nobody would notice just how piss-pants horrified he'd been when the gigantic icicle-bearded firstborn had done just that for himself and Harry's family before vanishing between-space earlier in the day. The wetness of the ocean depths, which he couldn't altogether avoid even though he never emerged from his between-space teleportal, did provide something of a face-saving excuse.)

"I see you have made your first downpayment on our beneficence."

"Extortion, more like," Rings pointed out. (Devils could only slash themselves elsewhere beneath the Dome. They needed him to get them through it.)

Methandra handed the still-stunned, codenamed Sea Goddess to her fellow firstborn, her immediate brother and husband. Suddenly she grabbed her forehead. Someone was communicating with her telepathically. Unmindful of Zeross's *'inferior'* presence, she exclaimed out loud: "It's Artist. Mirrors had found the others."

(Artist was Sedunihas, their eleventh, fourth generational child. He was a deafmute who could make himself understood through sign language as well as telepathically, though not always altogether coherently like most true devils. Mirrors was Klannit. Somewhat similarly to Heliodromi like Irisiel Mercherm, the world's first known azura occasionally acted as her mother's messenger and/or interpreter.)

"By the Triplet Goddesses, they're on the Moon!"

========

"Bloody wonderful," muttered Harry, entirely exhausted from his exertions. "Oh well, at least I can't say it's the last place on the Whole Earth I want to go."

It was a line that would have done the Diver proud. If he was still alive.

****

FOURTEENTH MOON: **Loose Endings**

========

Tuesday/Demetray, December/Tantalar 9, 1980/5980

It wasn't the Untouchable Diver that Dervish Furie carried back to Sraddha Isle. It was the sliced-and-diced, but not altogether disconnected, and amazingly still mobile, remains of Alastor Molorchus. By the time they arrived it was late Mithrada (Monday) evening. Even with Young Death still inside him — and Vetala's Brainrock moon sickle nowhere in evidence — there didn't seem much point in questioning him then.

Everyone who had survived the final battle on Dustmound had much better things to do. Primarily sleep!

========

Come first thing Demetray-Tuesday morning, about all that had changed was the ghostly pale, one-armed man had finally succumbed to his wounds.

In some respects fortunately, his corpse still lay in the large tent outside the monastery that the Sraddhites had turned into a hospital; the very place Furie left him with instructions to some of the Godbadian and Zebranid guards posted overnight that he, the dead man, was not to be disturbed.

The mostly monkish medics weren't too happy about that then; still weren't when dawn arrived after a significantly incident-free night. They were there to treat the large number of Athenan War Witches, Godbadian regulars, Zebranid volunteers and their fellow monks, who either made it back by themselves or were brought back on orders from Quentin Anvil, the Hadd-born, Godbadian general in charge of the subcontinent's Haddit operations.

Corpses, by definition, were beyond treatment, they loudly complained. Their diseases, what may or may not have killed them, could still spread to their immunity-compromised patients. It was only a matter of time before he started to seriously stink. Oh yeah, even if the Living had won a famous victory yesterday on Diminished Dustmound, this was still Hadd.

So wake up and smell the coffee, folks. Or whatever else was brewing. Molorchus wasn't an Irache. Was from all reports an Outer Earth Greek conceivably related to Barsine Holgat-wife and look who she turned out to be all those years ago. In any case, not being a native son, it was highly unlikely he'd be invited over for tea and crumpets by any of his still living relations in the near-neighbourhood.

Summoned down from the heights of the monastery in order to deal with the issue, another one-armed man, Barsine-Vetala's son Thartarre agreed with his medical team. Anvil didn't. The Wildman — who, looks deceiving, wasn't a hated, demonic Indescribable — had left instructions the body shouldn't be disturbed and the Living owed a great deal to him and this so-called Damnation Brigade of his.

Of course, as the Sraddhites' High Priest, Thartarre had far more authority on the island than the Godbadian general. He wanted Molorchus's body taken to the huge crematorium beneath the monastery and immolated immediately. It was Tantalar after all, only the tenth but usually coldest month of the Sedonic Year. (Appropriately so, given who it was named after: Tantal Thanatos, Lathakra's old King Cold.)

And, no matter how distasteful non-Sraddhites found it, the Brown Robes used physically burnt-out zombies to supplement their monastery's heating fuel.

Cold as it was, Raven's Head preferred sleeping outdoors to either stables or tents so Blind Sundown had done the same. (Having come through what they'd come through, what was one more hardship? Besides, they had their cosmic aura to keep themselves warm.) The commotion woke them up.

She wasn't averse to entering tents, either. Which only annoyed the medics even more. Moments later Kronokronos Akbarartha and Dervish Furie himself joined her and Sundown. So too had a few others by then: Golgotha Nauroz, Janna St Peche-Montressor and even New Iraxas Governor Ferdinand Niarchos, among them. Molorchus, though, still lay not just dead to the world but resolutely dead, period. Which for D-Brig-4 was less of a nasty surprise than a major league disappointment.

In the absence of Ringleader, who brought them to Hadd between-space, and the Legendarian, who, Thartarre informed them, had stepped out for a beer, or thirty, the night before and hadn't returned, they'd lost their ride home. Or at least back to Golgotha Nauroz's homeland, the Weirdom of Cabalarkon, where the Brigade's three other, hopefully still surviving members awaited their return.

St Peche-Montressor, the War Witches' perhaps pregnant, acting field chief as well as, not at all contradictorily, a love-loving Afrite, had a suggestion. "Because of his mother's curse, and his sister's perceived disloyalty to himself, if perhaps not to the Weirdom, its consensus Master, Saladin Devason, doesn't allow witches of any affiliation in Cabalarkon."

"Save that of Althea Brand," Golgotha interrupted. "But that's only because his High Illuminary, the other Dr Zeross, is a natural-born witch-healer and he relies on Mel to handle most of the day-by-day nuts and bolts of running the Weirdom." (D-Brig-4 had already heard that Demios's twin sister, Melina nee Sarpedon Zeross, the woman once codenamed Illuminatus on the Outer Earth, was an Inner Earth born Utopian.)

"It follows," St Peche-Montressor carried on, unfazed by the correction, "That he won't allow our stepping stones there either. That means, as much as we might like to, we can't help you get there directly. However, as everyone here knows all too painfully well by now, dead on the Head does not necessarily mean ever after inert. You and your men sucked in plenty of Sangs on Dustmound, Golgotha. As did we with our psycho soul grenades, as someone dubbed them. We could revive him."

"But I saw him moving," objected Dervish Furie, the faunish (Woodwose) more so than werewolf-like Indescribable-type. Despite a decent night's sleep he still hadn't reverted to Jervis Murray; this additionally despite the lack of any apparent, imminent threats, let alone immediate danger.

"Hell's bells, he signalled me over; called me *'son'* like he always does and said he could get us the fuck out of Hadd if I hauled his sorry-ass carcass – that sorry-ass carcass – out of there. So I did. It's not like I needed the exercise. I've seen the bastard in action. He's a teleporter. He'd just gotten rid of the Dis L'Orca dame with that arm thing he does."

(D-Brig knew Garcia's father Hadrian, yet another Summoning Child, from the Supra Wars, when he sided with Generalissimo Franco in his native Spain. They didn't like him, the Hypnosis King, also the Grand Inquisitor, but never managed to nail him for collaboration with Axis devils during WWII or The Rache after it.)

"Not any more he isn't," Golgotha noted. "And I've no intention of releasing anything into anyone, not after all we went through over there. One was a Master Deva, recall. Big fellow, Death's Head, lots of spikes. Besides, if I did, I'd rather try to raise up some of my fallen Trinondevs; they weren't all purebloods. Not only that, not all the azuras we captured were Sangazurs. And they're the only ones who can raise the dead compos mentis, as they were, right?"

"There is that," Janna acknowledged. "There is one other solution."

"So there is," agreed a samurai Dead Thing, recognizable as one of Mikoto's Two Thousand. He walked into the tent flanked by a half-dozen male and female Brown Robes. "Perhaps I can be of help." The zombie collapsed. Out of it stepped a superficially seven year old, black-skinned Voodoo Child.

It was Young Death (Augustus, son of Golgotha's template Ubris Nauroz, father of Saladin Devason and the reckoned late Morgianna long Sarpedon). Over thirty years ago – for two, more than forty years ago – on the Outer Earth, the Brigade members knew Thartarre's chief revenant as Auguste Moirnoir, the Black Death.

He was wearing black, shin-high pants, hot-weather, open-toed sandals, a glossy golden smoking vest but no shirt, a black waist coat and a top hat. All his clothes looked new, Godbadian-made, mostly because they were — he had a fat closet. (There was a reason Gentleman Jervis Murray made a point of dressing so well. Even if he wasn't – the Godling, Joshua Murray, was Jerry's father – the Black Death always called Furie son; hence it was a matter of like father, like son.)

"Sorry, son," he apologized to the Wildman, whom everyone simply assumed was the Gentleman's supra-side. "Should have mentioned I preferred my own bed to a mortuary slab. Then I got called away early to ream this guy out for Daddy Bang-Head there."

He turned to Anvil (Daddy Bang-Head). "Okay to fire him now? He was there when Byron's Nevair Neverknight, Nowadays Nihila and then Carcinogen-Plague and Bellona-War got into that humongous hullabaloo outside the walls of Sanguerre Devauray afternoon, but it's probably nothing your Daddy Gomez hasn't already reported, Ferd."

(Gomez was a Godbadian hero, the Fatman's main man in Valhalla. Main dead man in Valhalla, put better; main, still fertile dead man in Valhalla, put even better. Governor Niarchos was called Weird Ferd in part because he had so many children, especially for a supposedly gay guy married to a gay gal. Not many knew that most belonged to Gomez, post-mortem. Obviously Young Death was one who did.)

The Godbadian General nodded. The Voodoo Child gave the Brown Robes the go-ahead to cart the dead samurai downstairs for disposal. As they bent to their task, he lit a cigar. No one bothered to tell him smoking was bad for his health. No one ever did. Why bother? Young Death killed himself – or had others do it for him – in order to get about through the Weird.

St Peche-Montressor did grimace, however. Was presumably worried for her unborn child's health; this after battling Dead Things in a torrential downpour with pin-cushioned vultures and their already dead riders dropping out of the sky; spears, arrows, strafing fire, the occasional exploding rocket and cannon shell going off all around her the day before. The Fatman's daughter-in-law was just that kind of devil-may-care babe with a blade.

"You might have told me, Gush," grumbled Thartarre. "You do know I run things hereabouts, not Nanny Klanny's brassy boy."

(Tvasitar Sraddha Quentin-son, called Anvil, was Holgat Sraddha Thartarre-son's predecessor as the Sraddhites' High Priest back in the Thirties. Janna Fangfingers turned him into a vampire. His wife was Klannit Janna Anvil-wife, Thartarre's Nanny Klanny. Vetala tossed her off the monastery's uppermost balcony a few days ago; endgame her. Their son was the Godbadian general.)

"Never catch me disputing that, Daddy Bossy Pants."

"I'm wearing a robe," Thartarre objected. "How do you know what's under it?"

"We would like to talk to him," Janna intervened. "I know she was your daughter but Morg has brought the Athenan Sisterhood into hopefully not permanent disrepute and he was her right hand man. Of course he only has a right hand but you get my meaning — her Number One."

"Hey, happy to oblige. Anyone want to finish my cigar." No one flinched so he handed it to one of the Brown Robes who came in with him. "Keep it warm for me." At which point he strode across the floor to the mortuary slab, slid onto it beside the corpse, rolled over and rolled into it (merged with the corpse, not the mortuary slab).

Molorchus suddenly sat bolt upright; screamed, in his own voice, as if terrified, then started waving his lone hand around as if grasping for something to hang onto. The Brown Robe, who'd clearly done this before, gave him back his cigar. After a couple of long puffs Molorchus, who may or may not have been a smoker in life, calmed down appreciably.

"Ah, I always feel better after the first nick-hit of the day."

This time it was Young Death's voice. He took another pull, inhaled, paused, as if savouring the moment, exhaled. Those familiar with his routine realized he was more like taking a look inside the skull – its brain, more specifically – to see if there was anything left and, if so, whether any of it was worth reporting.

"Right, start firing away." Some of the others exchanged quizzical glances. "I mean with the questions, not the flames."

Now the glances were more like quizzical as to who was going to start the quizzing. "Be that way then," said Young Death. "I'll do it myself." Equally eerily he switched voices. Now it was Molorchus doing the talking.

"What answers would I have anyhow?" He didn't sound happy, certainly not in any mood to cooperate with an inquisition. "I've been on the Head for twelve years. In all that time, I doubt I've been allowed an original thought. I'm just a pawn of the rebel Anthean-cum-Athenan-cum-Hellion, Morgianna Sarpedon, and the vamp called Fangfingers.

"What they were up to, I have no idea. And they're both gone, so you can't ask them, though chances are they wouldn't reply anyhow. Anything else?"

========

D-Brig-4 had only heard of Second Fangs in passing after their arrival on Devauray night. She was a 500-year-old bat; an undying enemy proper Sraddhites deeply desired to dust, once and for all time. The others there knew her as Janna Somata, Sraddha's twin sister in life. (Sraddhite womenfolk were given her first name for their middle name. Janna's St Peche parents gave it to her as a first name possibly just because it sounded nice.)

Devauray evening, just before Ringleader drew D-Brig-then-5 to Hadd, to this very tent actually, then used as command central for the Sraddhites and their allies, Jordan Tethys had used his miraculous quill to draw what turned out to be her fate as it happened. Vetala and her soldier did the Sraddhites' job; they dusted her. As if to congratulate them, Tethys drew them on fire.

It didn't do them any long term damage; that was left to D-Brig themselves, yesterday, after the Diver managed to free the four now here from their own death-like confinement in the Amateramirror. Fangfingers, though, hadn't been seen since Devauray evening, neither in person nor via Quill Tethys's drawings.

And, according to Thartarre, he'd apparently tried to draw her up a few times since then. It wasn't on his behalf, either. The High Priest did look like her twin brother Sraddha and admitted that, as a result, Second Fangs rather fancied him. But, no, Holgatson insisted, it was purely of his own volition.

Alive and dead – make that undead – Tethys and Fangs had known each other for a very long time. Not just biblically, nor altogether in the distant past, Thartarre quickly qualified. The two thousand years' recurring Legendarian hadn't been un-dead any time, let alone any lifetime, recently. (Jordy had been a woman. Just don't get him going on that. He could get long-winded; not to mention vituperative.)

As for Superior, Sundown riding Raven, with OMP-Akbar rather undignified slapped across her back, belly down, hadn't gone back for her. They'd gone back for Sundown's Solar Spear, the in effect guided missile that presumably killed her just before she could finish off Jervis Murray. They last saw her hardening, mummy-like chrysalis slipping into a crevasse or sinkhole then newly forming on what was left of Dustmound.

When Golgotha, who considered himself not just a Sarpedon family friend. but her grandfather, told her about her mother's demise, Andaemyn shed nary a tear. Her mother had saved her from her uncle Sal, true. Had loved her as much, maybe even more than she did her other, much older daughter, Tsishah Twilight, she of Shenon, also true. But would she cry for her? No. Did that mean she wasn't dead, that she'd be back and that Andy somehow sensed it? Probably.

For her father's part, despite the fact that he was barely able to walk, Demios – whom D-Brig-4 recalled best as Blackguard or the Ace of Spades – was already working on the Godbadian General, Quentin Anvil, to send a helicopter to Dust-mound in order to retrieve her Mariamnic cocoon, her in it. Not that the Brigade survivors cared overly much about that. Morg was a traitor to not just to the cause of the Living. She'd betrayed them, her old comrades. Which, to their minds, was as bad or worse.

They hoped she'd be happy with her dead friends. Assuming all of them hadn't been dissolved in the now seemingly endless rain falling over Hadd.

=========

Raven whinnied a query, one only Sundown completely understood. "She's asking about the Diver."

"No idea," Molorchus said. "Neither of us have any idea," said Young Death, out of the same mouth. "Morg's Indescribables were ploughing him under the same as they were you three when I came through via Garcia and took over Al here." (Dual personalities were only slightly more prevalent on the Inner Earth than they were beyond the Dome. In here, where devazur possession was comparatively commonplace, they were just more often like duelling personalities.)

"Garcia got the Sang that had hold of him," he added, unbidden. "She shouldn't have needed it but Fish took hers for being a bad girl. More like for not letting her know about these psycho soul grenades you War Witches have developed. Fish trained as a War Witch herself, in case you didn't realize It. And she doesn't like being kept in the dark, not unless she's doing it herself."

"Not letting me know either," said Janna, who'd been forced to take Dis L'Orca's place as the Athenans' makeshift chef de guerre in yesterday's embarrassing, though as it turned out, final battle for Dustmound.. "How long had Garcia been dead anyways?" she asked, seizing on the opportunity to satisfy her curiosity.

"That isn't our immediate concern," snapped Furie, so toothily it all but confirmed what most of those there reckoned already: That he was an albeit welcome, howsoever beneficent Indescribable. "I clawed out of that gloop and went straight for Morg. Johnny and Raven roared off to take on that undying Nazi's Lost Legion, wherever the fuck they came from …"

"Sanguerre, New Valhalla, Sedon's Inner Nose," said Niarchos. He – Weird Ferd, as 30-Beers sometimes called him – got glared at, balefully. Of the four it was a toss up which was more scary. Akbar was big and awfully hairy, like a Godbadian Yeti or Cattail Barring, but he'd dealt with fucking faeries before and they were more dangerous to themselves than anyone else.

Raven's was unnerving. There was no denying that, all the more so with that still glowing horn of hers. Which had no more subsided than Jervis Murray had came back to the fore of his joint being, if that's what it was. Said not-yet-reverted Wildman and the blind Irache could-be, though, theirs looked positively life-threatening — to him, not to them.

Niarchos decided it was the latter. All those beads making up his blindfold glittered like mini-eyeballs. Some had just winked at him. He also decided to shut up.

"What about you, old man?" asked Furie, in a tone indicating a civilized man yet lurked inside him somewhere. "You came up the closest to where he went down. Any idea where he went?"

"Are you cranially crackers, coconut? The rain was pelting down so hard I could hardly see anything, not even the big buggery buzzard that dropped my ex-father-in-law – and much younger quarter-brother – down on top of me. After that things whipped by so fast and furiously I barely had time to stay alive. Which obviously didn't much matter to Mikoto, him being already past tense. Plus, I wasn't getting any help."

"You did get his head, though," said Young Death. "Not that you kept it."

"I would have, " said Diego de Landa, Thartarre's Number Two, who was a big game bat-hunter as well as an amateur taxidermist.

"And his great sword," Sundown reminded him.

"What about us?" Golgotha protested. "Or doesn't a Wyvern of Weir count?"

"Wasn't you or yours I was thinking about, Skull-Face."

Thartarre reckoned this last was directed at him. After all, he and his Sraddhites were comparatively nearby; did have fireboxes and arm-hoses; were old hands at using them; and both demons and Dead Things were highly flammable, even in the rain. Unfortunately, figuring the day lost before it really began, they were already ducking and running for cover when OMP-Akbar came up swinging.

Rather than try to belatedly justify their cowardly actions to the old man, the High Priest chose to deflect the discussion back to where Niarchos left off. "Your wyvern's dinner was Mars Bellona. The Bloodlands became his protectorate sometime after the Idiot Twins rendered the original Valhalla part of the Ghostlands well over a thousand years ago. They're about a thousand miles north of Godbad, probably twice that from here, in case you care anything about Headworld geography."

D-Brig didn't. He wasn't done yet, though. "I did know that fellow Mikoto you mentioned, Akbar. In life, too, years before he came back dead the first time, Devauray night. He and his band of mercenaries, Molorchus here and Andaemyn Sarpedon among them, were looking for the Trigregos Talismans; heard we had one. He wanted it to get to the others in order to turn them against his devic half-father, Dand Tariqartha. Once he got rid of him, he planned to take over Temporis."

Golgotha picked up Thartarre's thread. "Tariqartha exiled Mikoto and his two thousand. A few years later – we're going back thirty of them here – they marched on my homeland, the Weirdom of Cabalarkon. Came at us through the Ghostlands. Guess their radioactivity didn't affect Temporites."

"Or they were too dumb to know any better," provided St Peche-Montressor.

She wasn't born thirty years ago but knew her Headworld history due to an osmosis-like gleaning of her prohibitively immortal, oft-times occupant, Aphropsyche Morningstar, over the years of sharing her being. Unbeknownst to SPM, APM All-Eyes was among those Gush's Hush captured not so very long ago on the Outer Earth's Centauri Island.

(Janna and her burgeoning family spent more than a few vacations on the Inner Earth's namesake in the Panic Isle. Gudrun, hers and Yataghan's daughter, the Fatman's lone granddaughter, loved it there. The island itself was owned by her father-in-law and boss, the selfsame Fatman: Alpha Centauri in here, Alfredo Sentalli out there.)

"Your Nazi's Lost Legion did, too," Golgotha continued to relate. "The ones who were already dead did anyhow. Saladin Devason took credit for breaking the sieges on all four sides; sent the lot fleeing for their lives. Or at least their existence, for those who didn't have proper lives anymore. Used the opportunity to claim the Mastery for himself and promptly booted Morgianna and Demios Sarpedon out of Cabalarkon."

"Seems like everyone's after those things," said Furie, momentarily distracted from his inquiries.

"No doubt about it, son," said Young Death, still talking out of Molorchus's damaged mouth. "Demios and Morgianna were, too. And, especially in the case of my Morg, more so for herself than each other. Dr Zeross wants them as well, though his wife sent him to collect them on behalf of the Master. The Trigregos Talismans are symbols of power in Cabalarkon, except they've only Brainrock copies of them."

"Quite so," said Golgotha. "If the Sarpedons had the real things – even if they divided them up, with Andy getting whichever one her parents didn't want – they could use them to conquer the Weirdom. Actually, with them in hand, they could probably waltz in and take it with next to no opposition. Saladin is not particularly popular in Cabalarkon; just thought necessary for its survival."

"So much for another Utopia," muttered Furie. "This Master of yours," he said to Golgotha, "Might be dead too, though his wasn't among the bodies we found after the Sunday morning attack. That being the case, does that mean our old sparring buddy, Blackguard, becomes the new Master by default?"

(Old was a relative term. As they'd already found out, Utopians tended to age much slower than they did – not that that applied to the absent Elemental Twins, Airealist and Sea Goddess, who had not aged in any way whatsoever since the early Forties. Raven didn't seem to age either; hence Sundown sometimes teasing she'd been on Noah's Ark.)

"Hardly," Golgotha replied educationally. "In order to become Master one has to answer the Challenge of Weir. Thirty years ago, Morg and Demios were a year shy of adulthood so they couldn't compete for the privilege. I could. And so could Fish, strange as it sounds. She was Master Kyprian's protégé but Saladin beat us both — not least, I'm sure she'd tell you, because of why we call him Devason."

"Just not to his face, I imagine," Furie imagined.

"Just so. But, to answer your question, it's speculative but I'd say the inside favourite right now would be Demios's twin sister Melina, Dr Zeross's wife and the mother of his three delightful daughters. They're sort of like royalty up there, far more so than Sal and his brood of cock-a-hoop bastards."

"Speaking of Harry, where'd he go?" wondered Akbar. Vetala's Soldier having captured D-Brig-4 within the Amateramirror on Sedonda-Sunday resulted in them missing out on much of the news since then.

"I'll put my hand up for him," said Young Death. "I'd put up one for Al, too, except he's only got the one for the pair of us." This was only news to D-Brig-4, who hadn't been around when the Voodoo Child made his dramatic return to the monastery after, as he'd informed Thartarre and some of the others there, a Lathakran iceman gave him an icicle enema at his request.

"It wasn't so much Harry or me as leaving Mel and those selfsame darling daughters of theirs to the never-tender mercies of the Family Thanatos. It gets really, really cold in Lathakra and I had the wherewithal needed to convince old King Cold to bring them back to Cabalarkon. Rather, Molorchus did and he was dead."

"And you're good with the Dead," said St Peche-Montressor, whose Athenan Sisterhood nominally worshipped Hot-Stuff, Methandra Thanatos.

"That I am, Janna Banana."

"So," snarled Furie, "Discounting Fisherwoman, White Witch and Blackguard for the moment, it seems we may have lost two more Crimefighters — and we only came across Kid Ringo again Saturday. More and more, Damnation Brigade seems a real loser name for our merry band of abject twerps."

"Look on the bright side, son," said Young Death distinctively; though for most of those there it was still understandably difficult to distinguish which one was talking when. "Maybe Fish and Diver are off reacquainting themselves somewhere wet and wild. They were an item forty odd years ago, I seem to recall. Didn't she have his child?"

"All I can say," said Akbar, "Is I hope you're right about that."

Fish may not have been a Lovely Lady Afrite like Mnemosyne D'Angelo was then or Janna St Peche-Montressor was now, but she was no shrinking violet either. Plus, as Young Death knew better than they did, not being from in here, when it came to fish fry Fish had been fay-fairly-fruitful. So much so that, as she only found out long after their apparent deaths, fays had stolen them, one by one.

Notwithstanding that, no one could answer yay or nay as to whether she had a child by the Diver; not with any certainty anyhow.

(She did: Chthlonius *'Tiger'* Tiecher, one of Kadmon Heliopolis's Spartae or Dragon's Teeth. Rather than risk bringing him inside to raise herself, she fostered him out to a Greek family on Cyprus; hence the non-fishy names. Since she was married to King Achigan of Godbad by then, having to explain how his queen's bastard came to be living in the palace would have proven awkward.)

"I guess the next question is what's next," said Sundown, as bluntly as ever.

"You are of course welcome to stay here," offered Thartarre.

"It's tempting. Except we'd fit much better on the mainland. And chances are that would make us enemies, wouldn't you agree?"

"He's a point," said Anvil. What he didn't add was that his Godbadians, more specifically CE (Centauri Enterprises), also had designs on Hadd. Sundown, though, would have figured that out already. "And without Dr Zeross or Bodiless Byron around, you can forget about getting back to the Outer Earth."

Janna and Alastor Molorchus exchanged glances at that but no one picked up on it. Or, if they did, no one challenged Anvil's assertion. Quite the contrary.

"We definitely wouldn't fit in there," said Sundown. "Already tried haven't we, beauty." Raven cawed her accord in that unmistakable, if mostly unintelligible, whinny of hers.

"Then you better come with us to the Weirdom," said Golgotha. "Thanks in no small measure to you four our task down here is largely done. Mind you, without Dr Zeross and his miraculous rings, it could take us the better part of a month to get to Apple Isle and even then there's no way of telling when, or even if, we can catch a boat the rest of the way to Cabalarkon."

"The way things are going we could probably arrange to fly you to Sanguerre," said Anvil, who shared the insiders' gratitude for what D-Brig-4 accomplished on Diminished Dustmound. "Wouldn't be able to get you much closer to Ap Isle, though. Time Quakes are a reality beyond Valhalla."

"True enough," agreed St Peche-Montressor. Like Young Death she knew about the Nag Gap. Wasn't about to volunteer that information any more than the

Voodoo Child was; not in present company. "Anywhere on the Head, outside of Godbad and the lower Cattail Peninsula, transportation's pretty primitive. All the more so since, from what I understand, you've been relying on Harry, witches and devils to get around ever since the Nucleus brought you inside."

"Raven's all the transportation we need," Sundown claimed. "You'd have to spare us a guide and it would be an indignity for her to carry too many at once."

"Seems to me the obvious answer's sitting right here." Akbar turned to the one-armed man. "Molorchus, you're Gypsium-gifted. Can you send us to the Weirdom?"

"I doubt it," he answered in his own voice. "Something happened to all the Gypsium on Dustmound. I reckoned the Diver stole it. I'm skint."

"Then what'd you do to Dead Dis L'Orca?" said Furie, evidently somewhat hard-of-discerning. "And why'd you say you could get us away if I hauled you here?"

"Because that was me doing the talking," came back – no surprise – a moderately different voice out of the same mouth, "Not Al. He took such a thumping good clunk on the old bean bag in order to get charged up again, it amazes me he's not still oozing brain matter instead of just blood and bone."

The one-armed amalgamated man tapped himself on the noggin, indicating the terrible-looking crack on the top of his skull (Vetala's power focus, as delivered by Dead Dis L'Orca), not the bullet hole in his forehead. "Then again, maybe he didn't have any little grey cells left to ooze by then. In any case, he's no self-teleporter and Garcia didn't have a mirror on her."

"You sent Garcia away to get a mirror?" St Peche-Montressor sounded aghast.

"Not the Amateramirror?" questioned Thartarre. After so many decades, even centuries here, albeit hidden, he probably believed it belonged to the monastery.

"Couldn't have," said Furie. "OMP destroyed them. Right?" All eyes turned to Old Man Power (Akbarartha, rightful Kronokronos Supreme of Temporis).

"Must have. I gave them everything I had."

"Any old mirror would have done," said Molorchus, though it obviously was not him speaking. "She was supposed to come back on a Hellstone, or whatever you War Witches call your agates. Except, what with you running amuck again, son, and what with the little that was left of Dustmound collapsing in on itself, I didn't feel like hanging around until she did."

"So you can get us away from here."

"You heard me," answered Young Death. "I never said I couldn't; that was Al. Made up your minds where you want to go yet?"

========

Radiant Rider was the first to greet them after they came through the Weird into the Weirdom's vast central square. She was still severely shaken up from shielding herself, Furie and the Diver beneath a solid rainbow coverall while the Byronic and Apocalyptic Nuclei were busy obliterating each other above Sisert last Devauray afternoon. But at least she was on her feet.

"You're back," she exclaimed. "You're wonderful."

It wasn't lost on the other three that the first of them the silver-haired radiance tippy-toe-hugged was Old Man Power.

========

Kronokronos Akbarartha, Wildman Dervish Furie, Raven's Head and Blind Sundown were also on their feet, or hooves; were steadier than she was, truth told. They didn't have to emit tangible rainbows to help prop themselves up either, which she did. They also couldn't fly on them, which was how she got to the square almost as soon as word reached the Masters' Palace, where she was convalescing, that they were arriving.

Golgotha Nauroz and many of his surviving Trinondevs were just as on their feet, if not their toes. Of the latter, those that weren't were being carried in cushiony bubble beds projected from their eye-staves; individual and/or house gargoyles proudly projected around the eyeorbs atop them.

Young Death had promised to send up those judged still too much in need of medical treatment to travel, even next to instantly through Samsara, in due course. He made the same promise with respect to their honoured dead. Would, it went without emphasizing, first ensure they were thoroughly and professionally dispossessed, if they hadn't been purebloods.

Hadn't needed a guide to transport them unerringly, via Alastor Molorchus, to Cabalarkon. He'd been born there. Not in the square, true, but it hadn't moved in thousands of years. Probably couldn't, certainly not like a flying carpet or some such. (The Byronic Master Deva, Pretty Parsis, had as her power focus just that, a flying carpet. She was another Byronic Gush's Hush took out not so long ago.)

As for where he acquired the Gypsium he got for Molorchus to use, after her penetrating encounter with Raven's unicorn horn the day before it wasn't as if Nergal Vetala needed a moon-sickle anymore. It also wasn't as if, after altogether assimilating it within the still Gypsium-gifted, one-armed man's ambulant corpse, it could readily be expelled again.

So, if she did need it, she better head for Sedon's Peak and beg the devic Anvil, Tvasitar Smithmonger, to make her a new talisman.

========

"How's Cerebrus?" ex-Supreme asked Living Rainbow, after she finished embracing the other three.

(Not that the yet-Wildman, as he was right now, nor Sundown, as he almost invariably was, were eminently embraceable types. Raven was; so long as you didn't offer her an apple, a sugar cube or any other typically horsey treat, that is. You did, you'd get a swift rejection and a soppy snort as thanks.)

Gloriel D'Angelo shook her head sadly. "Doesn't look good. The scientocrats have immersed him in a tub of what they call Cathonic Fluid. That's where they place their incurably ill. Like they say, though, or should, incurable today could be curable tomorrow."

"And Witchie?" asked Furie, knowing full well she'd never go to bed with him again so long as he stayed in Dervish-mode.

Gloriel smiled slightly. "The scientocrats wanted to amputate her leg but the Witch wouldn't have it. She's an Ant after all. Said she was born knowing more about medicine than any man could ever hope to learn. And those were her exact words. She could be off her feet for the better part of a year, though. And, if you say that's the way you like her, Dervish, so help me, you'll have a seriously hard-handed rainbow smack wiping away your simpering smirk."

"So long as it's not most of my face."
"That could be arranged."
"Any sign of the Diver or Ringleader?" queried Sundown.
"No."

========

Not in the Weirdom of Cabalarkon, there wasn't. She was right about that.
****

Fifteenth Moon: **Memory Of The Demons**

========

Monday, December 8, 1980

"Ye gods!" James Aremar propped himself up in bed and gaped at the person who materialized in his quarters Monday night on the Liberty.

"Christ and be crunched, I thought you were dead." He flipped on the overhead light. "Fucking hell, not you too, Sean!"

"Suppose you mean this." Sean Smythe blinked his third eye then held out his hand. "Want one?"

In his palm were four eyeballs, all of which glowed with Gypsium intensity.

========

"Billowing bazookas, what are those?"

"Devic eyes! This Amoebaman has amazing abilities. During the tail end of the war – that's World War Two, not 'Nam – I had only a smattering of his talents. He not only can create duplicate bodies of himself or other people. He can go right into other people and possess them body and soul. If they are supras, he can use their powers, yes, but he can also usurp them, make them his, their knacks.

"Amoeba Prime, let's call him by his real name, Constantin Thanatos, or his attribute, which is Spring, as in bursting out all over, can go into mortals like the cosmicompanions downstairs – across the hall, more like, on the Moon – and take out the devils possessing them. That's what these eyes are, hornless devils.

"I bet I could make you become Fire." Smythe smiled at his next thought. To Aremar, who no doubt still hoped he was hallucinating, it seemed like his lieutenant had two mouths, one superimposed on the other, both grinning. "Wonder what would happen if I stuck one of these others into your skull, instead. Fancy being a female, Jim? Maybe Winter, or have a peacock's head like Orinth?"

"Crush them, man. Or dump them down the loo. Toss them into space, just get rid of them. The one in your forehead foremost."

"Believe me, that's exactly what I'd like to do. But I've somehow found a way to sort of control this Spring and his abilities. Rather, we seem to be working together. He's a bright boy; must come with having two heads. He figured out what Helios's combo computer was up to when she dragged Big Max's Bodhisattva into her. The Boddhi took the cosmicompanions out of her but I took the devils out of them; all but Ereba, that is."

"Ever heard of outer space?"

"How did I get back here is what you're really asking." Aremar allowed as to the accuracy of that statement.

"The simple answer is I teleported; but that's not exactly true. Sean Smythe died on this ship. Only he didn't quite die. He was reabsorbed into Amoebaman, his original self, over there. There was a bit of a byte left of him here, though. It helps if you think of that bit as being a focal point or maybe the equivalent to a witch's stepping stone. So, when I needed a place to go, I homed into it and became Smythe again."

"How nice for the pair of you."

"Know what he, Spring, wants me to do now? Commandeer the Liberty or one of the shuttle craft and head to Earth. He says his parents would know what to do then."

"Devils have parents?" The idea struck Aremar oddly.

Every living thing had progenitors; presumably so did every non-living thing. Which was why so many believed in God. The progenitor business had to have started somewhere and, by definition, God was the only one who hadn't had to start anywhere. Nonetheless, the concept of devils, alien to his rational mind in the first place, having parents had never occurred to him.

"What a bizarre notion. Maybe you should ask these eyes of yours if they know where I can phone for a few angels. Think the two would cancel each other out?"

"Getting a bit whimsical in your middling age, Jim?"

"Billowing bazookas isn't whimsical?

"You've been using that as long as I've known you. Some pretty blonde kid in your neighbourhood taught it to you, didn't she?"

"Okay, so you are Sean Smythe after all." (Despite the way he sometimes treated him, Doubleman was the closest Aremar came to having someone he could talk to like a friend.)

"And what if I wasn't? What would you do then?"

"Roll over and go back to sleep."

"In your dreams. Haven't you figured out what I've got here, Jimbo? These eyes are like St Synne's devil-ray or Strife's Miracle Key. Only they don't just transmit their powers, they contain the beings themselves. These things are somehow still alive. I bet I could do exactly what I said I could: Turn them on our men and have them take over their knacks, just like the ray or the key did all those years ago.

"I doubt they'd be able to control them as well as I do Spring. More than likely it'd be better to return them to the original possessors, if that's the right word. They've shared a degree of familiarity already. To that end, I'm maintaining a mite more than a byte to Anon Sasarian. He doesn't realize it but I can see and hear exactly what he does.

"When the time comes, I'm going to go back into him and have these eyes repossess their initial hosts. Whether the devils takes command or the companions do, I'll turn them against Rom, Big Max, Herr High and Mighty Helios, and his three-thing, who's sort of a third my aunt and three-sixths Spring's mom."

"Herr Helios? Three-sixths, not one-half."

"The other three-sixths is his devic mom; his half-mom, in other words. Mnemosyne is his other mom, but she's actually three beings in one, So three-sixths makes more sense. One-third of that sixth seems to be Mnemosyne D'Angelo, so that fits too. I remember her from Leandro's youth. She was a real corker, as Smythe would say. And one way or another I'm still Smythe."

"Herr Helios?"

"Yep. Spring reckons he's his half-father, too, but he isn't Kadmon Heliopolis. Rather, he is and he isn't. Helios dies, he comes back, somewhere; has more lives, sometime. Only he doesn't start them as a newborn. He starts them in his late twenties, at the same age Kadmon was when you and AMERICA did him in the first time.

"He's in his hundredth now, but Spring reckons his devic dad possessed him in one of his much earlier lifetimes because that's when he became his half-father. At any rate, whichever lifetime it was, he got up to all sorts of hell-raising horseshit. He was the anonymous Conqueror; not Jesus Mandam. Jesse only took over his work after whichever death in the very early Fifties.

"And you know what his work was, still is? To get rid of devils, Spring's own people. That's why he got involved in the Summoning thing in 1920; that's why he helped out Hitler, when it suited him; that's why he went over to the Soviets after the Nazis decided devils were more their cup of tea than he was. And that's where the Herr Helios came in; Herr Hel Helios, to be precise."

"And that's where you and those evil eyeballs come in, too. You want to hasten Herr Hel on to his hundredth and first."

"So do you, Jim. So do your, our, paymasters planet-side. One way or another we will destroy the Lunar Citadel and those in it. Sure as we shit in the morning, as soon as we do the Man on the Moon and his buddies will return to being figments of everyone else's overly fertile imaginations."

"What did you mean by *when the time comes*? Seems to me it's already come and gone. Helios and his buddies clearly knocked you and your eyeball-pals ass over cup of teakettle over there. If you, your Leandro aspect, hadn't been hit by St Synne's devaray back in the Forties and had some glimmering of the powers this Spring gives you, then you and the cosmicompanions would have been toast before breakfast.

"What you say about him being the anonymous Conqueror, and how much trouble he caused until thirty-odd years ago, is all very interesting. I'm sure the Great Man downstairs – way downstairs – would be fascinated. Even I know Jesus Mandam was his nephew and that plenty of his gear went into the Liberty. But it being Helios's all along only makes me more discouraged. I don't see how anyone can stop him.

"Hell's hellacious teeth and gums, he's turned my own men against me. And I'm supposed to have a natural gift for instilling loyalty. We return planet-side, it'll be flower power all over again. Too bad the original Heliopolis didn't live long enough to witness Altamont or the deaths of the big three, Hendrix, Morrison and Joplin, not to mention a few thousands more O-Deed peaceniks. He might have concocted a more sensible vision of Heaven on Earth."

"Heliopolis was never a hippie, Jim." Smythe pointed out. "He was a brilliant man in many respects, but he was also a serious revolutionary. Extreme violence was second nature to him. And his Black Rose was as vicious a band of mad bombers as any of his grandparents' anarchists had been around the turn of the century.

"If it wasn't for that punk kid of Demonites Zeross, Dmetri Diomad, failing to assassinate the Prime Minister of Greece in August of '68, Kadmon might have successfully ousted the Colonels and taken over the country. As it was, the PM survived long enough to call on Ryne and AMERICA to help him wipe out the Rose. We did it then and we'll do it again now. Sure you don't want to become Fire?"

"No fucking way."

"Sleep on it, Jimbo. Because that's what I'm going to do. Fact is, no matter how many I have, I can barely keep my eyes open. This supranormal shite isn't all it's cracked up to be. Guess I'm just out of practise."

"Out of your mind, more like."

========

Tuesday, December 9, 1980

Shortly after noon Tuesday, Crystallion, Crystal St Synne, mounted on her nuclear firedrake, was the last to leave the phantom freighter.
She wouldn't be back.

▬▬▬▬▬▬▬

As Crystal-Transmogrified flew off on her dragon, Shelter spotted American planes zeroing in on the freighter from above. Never one to panic, he super-hardened his Silver just as the first rocket hit the freighter amidships. He reckoned it past time to do that hockey thing and get the puck out of here.

Activating the teleportive aspects of his armour, he figured to go back to Centauri Island. He vanished but found himself in the hold on one of Crystallion's Hellstones or Korant Kernels. (Not that Shelter knew anything about the Hidden Continent of Sedon's Head but Crystal's half-sister Cybele, Sed's Red, was, at seventy-plus, the Korant Corn Queens' Miracle Maenad on Apple Isle.)

Something was definitely wrong. Two more steps through the Grey and he was still on the ghost ship. Clearly there were too many of Crystal's kernels scattered throughout the boat. Unless it had something to do with the lump of only faintly glowing Gypsium he spotted in its ruined hold. Too much of a good thing? Had Gypsium turned on him? It was supposed to be somehow sentient; prone to fickleness. For whatever reason, he couldn't get off the doomed freighter.

The planes continued to bombard the boat until it was a blazing wreck pocked with holes and three-quarters on its way to the bottom. The strangest thing of all, none of its surviving crew, who'd put up a valiant fight against the six Silver Signallers, tried to leap overboard. They must have been content to go down with the ship.

What they'd done, he realized, almost too late, was shut themselves down.

========

Centauri Island looked as if a tidal wave had washed over it. In some respects that's exactly what happened. Sea Goddess had awesome abilities. She virtually domed the Island with the Pacific Ocean, rose it up then let it drop. It was as if the firedrakes had been drowned upwards — except they'd been vapourized instead.

Largely because of the occasional cyclones and more common, but far less devastating, Pacific weather systems, the island, especially the leeward town, the two resorts, and its much more meatier, underground installations, had an efficient drainage system. Even though parts of the underside structures were already affected by Alfredo Sentalli opening the locks at its deepest level, the system was still mostly up to task.

Perhaps because it was more like a heavy, extremely salty, tropical rainstorm rather than an actual tidal wave that hit the island, there were no casualties and less damage than a bad squall – at least to the buildings on the surface. The last dragon, mindless without its rider, just sat dumbly on the runway as it was cooled unto shrunken extermination.

Around sundown, the clean up already begun, the Space Age Spartan and a number of those who had been in the bunker when Thalassa took herself and Crystallion elsewhere, gathered in the hotel's private dining hall. By then he'd spoken with Sheriff and Sebastion about deserting their posts. He had also heard that the doctors, Paul Creel and Angus Skullian, had been seriously affected by Sonora using her sonic scream to escape Sharkczar earlier in the day.

They had both suffered nerve damage and Creel, certain he was now deaf, was injecting himself with steroids in hopes of reversing it. (In some respects that was morbidly ironic since Skullian, not Creel, had a deaf parent and consequently already knew sign language.) Even though it had been his decision to let them go along, Spartan decided that Sonora had to be disciplined for indiscriminate use of her Silver the same as Sheriff and Sebastion, albeit for not using theirs in any way, shape or form whatsoever, sonically included.

As a result, of the eighteen Signallers who'd been on the Island, three were dead, seven were missing, and four others were no longer wearing the Silver. Of the latter, only Sapphire Lancz had taken hers off voluntarily. That left four in armour: Spartan, Static, Sapperstein and Spherus. It was an unlucky number but eighteen had been even worse. Which of course was down to Shelter. He should have stayed behind in whatever cesspit he customarily hung his house-head-helmet.

Adolph Dulles, who'd been out and about in order to assess the extent of the damage, had an opportunity to consult with his chief lieutenants: Mugwump, Marsh, and Tadpole; native Hawaiians the three of them. By then also, he'd phoned Vancouver and let Spartan speak with Strategos. Entering the dining hall, he was met by Mug, who whispered something in his ear.

Face even longer than earlier, Dulles walked up to his Enormity (aka the Fatman, sometimes even by Yataghan raised Montressor, his own son); told him the bodies of said son, Centauri Island's last thought healthy doctor, Connie Lindquist, and George Hannibal, the Fatman's omnipresent legal adviser ('*the Human Cheque Book*', according to some) had been found. A barrier wall had given way on the next to lowest level of the island and the waters from the flooded submarine nest roared in. They'd apparently been crushed before they drowned.

Hush Mannering, back to calling herself Dorothy Dodgson, obligingly broke into an impressive sobbing fit, accompanied by a cascade of crocodile tears, when a sombre Sentalli announced the news. After briefly eulogizing each of them, his Enormity asked Dulles to take him upstairs to his suite. Before the acting security chief could oblige, Loxus Ryne started laughing.

"Why?" snorted Ryne derisively. "So you can get away too?"

"That isn't fair, sir," snapped Dulles defensively.

"Isn't it, indeed," mocked the octogenarian. "Figure it out yourself, Dolph. You and Max, even Sean Smythe before your time, had a list of Al's Untouchables. Doesn't it strike you as odd that Alfredo is now the only one of them left alive? Wouldn't surprise me if his corpse turns up in his bed tomorrow morning."

"And just where do you suppose we get all these fake bodies from, Mr Ryne?" Sentalli protested.

"Same place you got Demios Sarpedon and your stinking albinos. Big Shelter, of course." The Fatman shot Hush a nasty glance. "Not her fault, Al. She's been re-dacting me, editing my memory, every chance she gets since I got here last Monday. Still hasn't figured out why I talk to myself all the time, though."

He opened his coat and pulled out a pocket-sized tape recorder. "It's so damn simple. Too simple really. Makes me think I've done it before, probably whenever she's around, but she always makes me forget it. This time, though, we've got some pretty serious technology around. It doesn't take a supranormal to send what I've sent to, say, oh I don't know ... Groundbase Houston, for example.

"I've a few other failsafes up my sleeve as well and none of them have to do with supras either." Not that the patriarch mentioned him by name but one of those was Dr Angus Skullian. He had an amazingly precise eidetic or photographic memory. As was no longer much of a secret, he'd inherited it from his father, Mycroft, the deaf Skullian.

(Angus Dre'Ath had four Summoning Aged sons, by four different women, none of whom were his wife Gilda nee O'Ryan, Bunnie sometimes Maxwell's sister. The elder Dre'Ath, who was named after a Celtic love god and acted the part, claimed their mothers were fay-fairly-stunning sisters whose last name was Skullian.

(Hush could have told him, and probably did, that, first of all, they were fucking faeries and that, second of all, that wasn't their surname. It was where they were from: Skullian = Skull = Head = Sedon's Head. She wouldn't have let him remember what she said, though. Even proper Godlings like good old Angus – the Godling Guild being the precursor to today's Alliance of Man – couldn't be trusted with the truth about the Hidden Headworld.

"So do we," announced Spartan, not really giving away any System secrets. What he was about to say only stood to reason. Signal System was one of the most advanced outfits on the planet. "And not just voice recorders. Silvers automatically videotape everything that happens near them. And from a number of angles."

"When Sub-System was around they were sent via satellite directly to Stanford," Spherus elaborated. "Even after Hartwig was killed, his devices continued to operate and, of course, the others never stopped. We'll have to thoroughly analyze the data but one thing is irrefutable. This little witch and you, Mr Sentalli, are the key to damn near everything that's gone on here. What you two don't know probably no one does."

Whether he was the Mayhew Bubble Boy or not, Spherus was a System Seer. When he spoke, one could almost here Simon Lancz speaking. "I propose the Alliance and Signal System join forces, take both of them into custody, and keep them there until we squeeze every last bit of useful information they have out of them. We can do it here or stateside. Up to you, Mr Ryne."

"Don't even think about it, Dolph," warned the patriarch as Dulles made a motion for his weapons. Eyeing the two Silvers, Spartan and Spherus, he held off.

"It's all right, Mr Dulles." His Enormity sounded resigned to his fate. "We don't need any more dead people."

"Sure you won't reconsider, Daddy Rhinoplasty?" Hush asked Ryne, somewhat flippantly considering he'd never had anything wrong with his nose, let alone any surgery to correct it. He didn't even have a particularly big beak. The Great Man shook his head firmly. "A shame. Too bad, Daddy Homunculus. I was growing to like you."

"I was growing to like me too." His Enormity slumped forward. He was dead and Hush was just an illusion of herself before anyone else in the hall could move.

"I'm holding you responsible for his passing, Daddy Dickhead," the illusion informed the patriarch. "Autopsy to your heart's content, any of you. The Untouchables are dead and you have the bodies to prove it. You'll never find out if they were the real things or not. Never learn anything more about Big Shelter either, least of all from me. Or from anyone else here; not now anyhow.

"Don't forget about Panharmonium, though. It's coming. Sooner than you think. Sooner than anyone but me and four or five others realize. I hope you get the Man on the Moon. He's almost as out of line as WORLD, most of you lot and, especially, Daemonicus and Strife. See you around, daddy."

"How about Christmas?"

"Sounds good. Just remember you're the turkey." She vanished into the Grey.

"Don't worry about it, sir," said Spherus, making a mental note of Ryne's invitation. Christmas Day was exactly a week before the Great Man's eighty-first birthday and someone as egocentric as the tiny trickster wouldn't be able to resist making an appearance. The meant neither would the Signallers, howsoever clandestinely.

"Sapphire captured her aural emanations in one of her manmade witch-stones. They double as soul sinks so we can track her anywhere in the world."

"Afraid not," admitted the punkish looking teenager. "She caught me washing my face a few hours ago. Was on me like the little monkey she probably half is. Did something to my mind with one of her agates then made off with all of mine. She's free as a bird. Too bad. Maybe she'd have trained me to become an Ant."

"Caught you without your helmet on!" Spherus was outraged. When on duty, Signallers were always supposed to wear their helmets.

It protected them from mind control, specifically that used by the Superior Sisterhood in the days when the disgraced Morgianna Sarpedon – Demios's wife, he also being her companion/bodyguard from much longer ago than that, since at least the late Thirties – was still their Mother Superior. Seems hardly anyone, least of all System's Seers, ever trusted the onetime White Witch.

"That's why I resigned," Sapphire confessed. "I'm just not ready for the Silver."

"But you had such a knack for our artificial agates."

"Sorry, Spherus. I fucked up. Call me again in a few years."

"Don't worry about it, youngster," assuaged the patriarch. "We would never have been able to hold her anyhow."

He'd known Hush seemingly forever. He might have even met her when he was Sapphire's age or younger. Which conceivably meant he'd have met her before she went from normal to transformed victim of, according to some, a faerie's curse. He'd definitely met her parents, if they were her parents, albeit without realizing it.

(His gun-toting, suffragette mother, Athena born Kinesis, of the American side of the globe-roving Gypsy Family Kinesis, was friends with Celestine D'Angelo. The silver-haired Anthean adept was occasionally seen with someone named Pandora; might even have been her daughter, albeit not by her Nubian, Ubris Nauroz.

(When not casting glamours about herself, Hush looked more half Asian than half black and, whilst it was rare for Ubris to be seen without Celestine around, and vice versa, he wasn't called her Nubian because he was part Asian. Or if he was, then he was as good or better at disguising his appearance than the tiny trickster.

(Then again, years after they were last seen, Demios turned up with Melina – who, like Morgianna was white as bleached lightning – and announced they were twins. Until then hardly anyone out here realized something like Celestine having a white child by Ubris was both possible and perhaps not all that rare.)

(In terms of the twins, it had to be an extreme form of super-fecundation, also called hetero-paternal fecundation. Morgianna, though, as white as she was, had a year older black brother named Saladin, the same as westerners called the Saracen conqueror of Christian Jerusalem in the 12th Century of the Current Era. In Amsterdam, beginning in September 1938, they'd attended the inaugural class of the first Academy of Man together.

(Everyone just assumed they had different fathers and neither Sal nor Morg disabused anyone of that notion. Of course again, none of those on Centauri Island after his Enormity's passing had any idea an originally extraterrestrial race known as the Utopians of Weir shared the planet with top-of-the-food-chain humans.)

"What's a homunculus?" Ryne asked, looking at pseudo-Sentalli's body not at all remorsefully, as if it was just a slab of beef. "Some kind of Chinese figurine?"

"Don't exactly know," Spherus had to admit. "A dwarf, I think."

"Biggest bloody dwarf I've ever seen," mused Ryne, who quickly became all business again. "Have one of your men get that out of here, Dolph. Add it to your pile of Untouchables. And take pictures. Order autopsies for everyone you find in the morgue. Bring someone in from Maui if you have to."

As Dulles briefly left the dining room to delegate duties to his men, the octogenarian turned to nowadays Singleman Johann Schmidt. "Guess it's finally safe to leave Centauri, Johann. That said, I'm loath to go. Too many mysteries left to solve. Nevertheless, make sure my plane's ready to take off. I'll fly back to Houston with the rest of my SPACE contingent tomorrow afternoon.

"I want you and fifty of the Alliance's two hundred to stay behind and set up shop. Leave Centauri's security folk and Samarand's scientists to carry on with their work. The locals trust the former and the test tubers could care less about anything except just that, their work. But you're to go through this whole island with a fine tooth comb."

"To what end, sir?"

"Every end, Singleman. Every nook and every cranny. I'm not exactly sure what we're looking for, other than it's called the Nag Gap according to Spherus here – more secret passages in all likelihood. Start at the bottom and move to the top. I'm sure Signal System will provide you with as much help as you require."

"Can't, sir," regretted Spartan. "We'll wait for the other seven as long as we can but, come first light, we've orders to return to our home base in California."

"More renegade supras?"

"You should know, sir. Against his brother-in-law, our boss's best advice, you financed Bruce Dre'Ath's diddling around with nature at the Academy of Man in Amsterdam. As a result, it seems a veritable Island of Dr Moreau has transferred its franchise to British Columbia. Then there's the Crimefighter clones – and Steltsar, if that, um, thing didn't nail him."

"I'm sure we did," promised Dulles, as a couple of his biggest men wrangled Sentalli's massive body onto an oversized gurney and wheeled it away. "But don't forget Strife or Crystal, whatever she was, the little witch, and the Sea Goddess clone, assuming it was a clone. They could still be around. So could the albinos, I suppose. Not to mention the dragons and their riders.

"By my calculations, Sea Goddess only got half of them. The rest, well, God knows what the Gypsium Curtain did with them. It is bloody teleportive."

"I goddamn hate loose ends," complained the patriarch. He hadn't just financed Dre'Ath's experiments at the Amsterdam Academy. He'd financed his daughter Aran and Moe Three's attempts to clone not just the Crimefighters at the Houston Academy. "And there's enough of them left to keep a wig-maker in raw material for years. I suppose we can only do what we can. My main concern is still Helios on the Moon."

"As to that," put in Schmidt, "I still can't shake the feeling Sean isn't dead."

"Then he probably isn't. Guess that means I can call you Doubleman again. All right, Johann. Assign some men to go through Centauri's suite then join me in mine. Stick with me, Dolph. Oh, and by the way, I don't blame you. I've been sucked in by the dotty Dorothy more times than I care to admit. Or that she's let me remember, put better. You'd think after nearly fifty years of knowing her I'd have learned how to resist her."

"Not sure what you mean, sir."

"No? Of course you wouldn't. She'd have already redacted you. Works quick, the little witch. You have to admire her for that if nothing else."

========

Sleep was precisely what Sean Smythe needed. Anon Sasarian and the rest of the cosmicompanions from Cosmicar Two in Lunar Trigon did, too. Heliosophos didn't seem overly concerned about the cosmicompanions, not outwardly. Left monitoring their condition to the always multitasking Mnemosyne Machine.

If only to kill time, he was happily showing Rom and Max the latest pictures he – rather, his computerized better half – had somehow taken of the planet below since the riots began Saturday morning in Tokyo.

Times had definitely changed.

========

"Do you still doubt me, my friends?" he asked, not just bordering on boastfully. He wasn't gloating, though. Not yet, at any rate. "Want to see the statistics from your favourite New York Times, Max? Since Sunday, when my thought beams altered subtly, there's hardly been any murders in the entire city. Too bad John Lennon wasn't one of those spared but it's nevertheless a stunning statistic."

(Remote viewing was a witch trick but they usually did it live, through the eyes of their familiars. It wasn't clear how Machine-Memory pulled it off, other than if it was broadcast she could relay the signal for rebroadcast on her own internal systems up here. A lot of what they saw didn't look like commercial television, though. Did she employ robot rats with head cams?)

"Don't see how we can trust Memory's eyes, whatever or whosever's they are," argued Maxwell, finding it easier and easier to stay himself when his Boddhi side wasn't immediately needed. "Given everything else she can do, there's no reason to believe she can't make movies too. Sense Seer, Homer Skullian, could – and the only camera he had was in his head."

Homer, father of the weak-eyed Signaller known as Selene (after a much later, as in post-Mnemosyne, Greek Goddess of the Moon), was only blind when he used his external eyes. When he used his mind's eye – his pineal gland, some said – he could "see for miles and miles and miles", to quote The Who's hit single from a dozen years gone. He could also save and later on project what he saw on a wall or screen or some such.

"Afraid he's right, Kadmon," agreed Kinesis. "The only way we'd know for sure is by going down there ourselves."

"Oh we will, Rom. In another couple of weeks. As a matter of fabulous fact I was thinking of making my first public appearance in Bethlehem on Xmas Day."

"Oh, Christ," groaned the professor. It was his habitual cuss word but the double meaning wasn't lost on Helios.

"I said Xmas, not Christmas, cousin. 'X' as in Xuthros Hor, the Biblical Noah, not the Chi-Rho, which was a Mithraic symbol in any case. So, are you with me?"

"Already said I was," confirmed Kinesis.

"And you, Max?"

"Hate to admit it, but I'm leaning that way."

========

A few minutes later, Mnemosyne told him what she'd done about Strife. He gave her a flip remark about having something else to celebrate. It was a hollow crack. He'd have been a whole lot happier if he was 100% convinced she was with him. Hell, he'd have been happy if he was three-quarters' convinced.

One thing irrefutable about one-third machines was that the other two-thirds could lie very persuasively.

========

Following tracking signals sent out by the six missing Signallers, Subitor, in his flying car-boat, found himself hovering over an empty ocean. Just when he was about to switch his transformative, state-of-the-twenty-first-century-art of a vehicle into undersea retrieval mode, the Pacific spewed forth silver waterspouts.

Whereupon Shelter, Sharpshooter, Selene, Shadowswirl, Stupendo and Stiletto burst upwards on their in-house boot thrusters. Two were carrying one of the others. Their Silver had protected them from both the American bombardment and drowning, but their armour could only do so much.

None of them were entirely unscathed. Nevertheless, Shelter, who was permanently damaged anyways, at least mentally, stuck out his thumb.

Nowhere in System's operations manual did it say not to pickup hitchhikers.

========

Returning to Centauri Island well after dark, Spartan and Spherus met them. Spherus was particularly glad to see Selene. Probably only Subitor knew they were man and wife. Then again, probably only the two of them knew his real name was Jubal Skullian – the same as his father's before him. After all, she (Sheila), like Ryne's doctor Angus, were his cousins.

After greetings were exchanged; Selene, Subitor and the others, along with the Space Age Spartan, dismissed to rest; Spherus led Shelter and Shooter to Paul Creel's smallish and now thoroughly overloaded morgue. He opened the drawers tagged as containing the bodies of Joe Hartwig, Oussama Modise and Terry Teller – Sub-System, Solano and Savant. They were empty.

He next took them over to the tables where the covered corpses of Dr Lindquist, the Fatman's Human Cheque Book (George Hannibal, actually a lawyer) and Sentalli's son lay. Removing the bed sheets one by one, he asked his fellow System Seers if they noticed anything unusual. Shelter spotted them almost immediately — tiny Anthean Agates stuck in their mouths. Extracting them, it came as no surprise they turned out to be Hartwig, Modise and Teller.

"Seems the trickster's become a jokester as well," observed Shooter. "Where were they found?"

"In a flooded chamber, second lowest level down."

"Where you brought me just before we encountered the shark thing," Shoot recalled.

Shelter whistled in a mechanical way. "Guess we just located the Nagasaki Gap it was talking about."

"I teleport on agates, too," Spherus reminded them. "I went down there as soon as I realized what she'd done. Of course it's been drained – otherwise Dulles's men would never have been able to pull out the bodies – but it's also been blown. Whatever this Nag Gap was, it's history."

"Is it?" Shelter queried, knowing full well that the first man known to use witch-stones was Jesus Mandam. "I wonder. Clearly we're dealing with some kind of Gypsium-based teleportal to this Big Shelter we keep hearing about. Two other things we know: the Godstuff supposedly has a rudimentary mind of its own and this island's three peaks have no longer molten craters full of it. Tell you what, Shoot. After we get Sasq and Styx away from Mammalian, we may have to move here."

"Only if you promise never to wear a bikini over your Silver, Shell."

========

As far as he was concerned today had only arguably been the longest and most fraught day of his eighty dangerously lived years, It wasn't over yet, either. Approaching midnight Loxus Abraham Ryne was still wide awake. Not so arguably he'd decided that, when it did arrive, just this once it wouldn't mark the Witching Hour.

He reckoned he'd already had about eighteen of them in a row.

========

He had received a report from some of Schmidt's two hundred from the Alliance of Man. Perhaps not surprisingly, an elevator shaft had been found behind Alfredo Sentalli's roll-in closet. The elevator car had been ruined; call it sabotaged, as it was in even worse shape than almost anywhere else on the near tsunami-swept island. However, they were able to trace it to one of the lowest levels of the largely artificial island.

Come morning they'd start to in effect excavate the chamber in which it ended up. The report did make it clear that it was in the same area Dulles's men had found the bodies of Yataghan and the other two. By then, he had also been told what Spherus had discovered; that they weren't really their bodies.

The trickster had disguised the corpses of three dead Signallers with some of her agates. Which meant he'd been wrong to assume Hush had ensorcelled Dolph into body-building the corpses. Which, in its turn, meant he still had no proof Dolph had somehow gained Amoebaman's abilities after some twenty-seven years of Norman Normalcy. Presumably she'd remotely destroyed the Nag Gap as she made her getaway but, like the Silvers, Ryne wasn't so sure.

That was another mystery he'd solve some other day. Right now, he had other fish – actually a Man on the Moon – to fry.

========

Even though the Liberty remained incommunicado, Ryne had other links to it; at least he had until Sunday.

On Saturday night, Dolph had picked up Sean Smythe's cry of distress to Johann Schmidt; the one wherein Smythe claimed Amoebaman was alive, was some kind of three-eyed devil, and described him as a hydra. More reliably however, just before Smythe faded out of sight, Schmidt had been psychically listening in on his conversation with Big Max.

"So," summed up the patriarch, going over the notes Schmidt made while he was still stuck in Pearl Harbor on Sunday, "Smythe said Amoebaman was real. He's a devil like the two I encountered Saturday and in possession of one of the cosmi-companions now on the Moon."

(Ryne's devils included one of the two Professor Kinesis, prior to him assuming his Doc Defiance persona most of a week earlier, saved Max from just after Hiyati Samarand hastened the Cosmic Express's countdown so abruptly. Her Illuminary-given names was Aphropsyche Morningstar, more commonly *'APM All-Eyes'*. Ryne's other devil was Damon Goldenrod, Byron's Apollo, who'd been inside Yataghan Sentalli when the Indescribable Mr No Name first appeared.

(They were immediate siblings, third-born Byronics, members of that Great God's Secondary Nucleus. Freespirit Nihila encountered the third member of their brood's threesome, Nevair Neverknight, on Devauray outside of Sanguerre's walls in New Valhalla. He, Byron's Paladin, was now a star in the night's sky shining not far from his father and the latter's second-born, Primary Nucleoids: Vayu Maelstrom, Sedona Spellbinder and Chimaera Glimmenmare.)

"Smythe also telecommunicated to you," he said to Schmidt, "That five of Amoebaman's siblings were with him there." He paused, fixed the prohibitive Singleman firmly in his as yet unfailing eyesight. "Johann, you're all that's fully left of Septupleman. Dolph, you're the son of Quintupleman Barb Dulles. Together there's got to be a way you can reach what's left of Sean. Work on it. Hold hands."

"You've got to be joking," reacted Dulles.

"Just do it!" demanded Ryne, using his voice to its coercive fullest. They did.

"Christ on a stick, Ryne," gasped Schmidt, after a few moments. "I was right. Sean is still alive. He's inside Amoebaman."

"Then go to him, Singleman," insisted the Patriarch. "Get him going. Get the rest of them going." Johann Schmidt vanished.

Ryne turned to an astonished Adolph Dulles. The twenty-seven year old was looking pasty-faced, about to pass out. "Stay the course, Dulles," demanded Ryne, his voice raised a notch higher, to command mode – something he hadn't tried since he convinced the Ringo Kid to abandon the King's Own Crimefighters to the tender mercies of the Magnificent Psycho on Damnation Island almost exactly a quarter century ago.

"What are you experiencing?"

"It's no good, sir. Something's stopping me. I get the sense of a woman in a black cape."

"Sounds like Madame Midnight or the Queen of Spades – probably both the same creature. Concentrate, man!"

========

Wednesday, December 10, 1980

On the Moon, a full day had passed without further incident.

========

Heliosophos had spent most of it showing off his citadel. *'This too is what I can bring to the Whole Earth'* was one of his most frequent comments. However, as very late Tuesday became comparatively early Wednesday over the planet below, he invited Kinesis and Maxwell into his dojo.

(Out of convenience, as well as for regulating regular shuteye periods for his guests, he had reset Lunar Trigon to operate on Houston time rather than Hawaii time. He did so mostly because the Liberty did. It was still in stationary moon orbit above the citadel and showed no signs of leaving, with or without Big Max and the professor.)

"This is where I practice. Want to practise with me, Doc Defiance?"

"That isn't fair, Kadmon," protested the professor, yawning. "I told you I'm not your enemy."

(Despite all the space and time-zone travelling he'd done recently – as in since the 30th of March, when he discovered that, via between-space, Gypsium-Godstuff allowed him to cross tremendous distances, in a comparatively short few minutes – he was a Centauri Islander through and through. After so many years on the tri-peaked islet, that wasn't going to change with Helios or Machine-Memory herself twirling a few knobs on her control chronometer.)

"What about you, Max? Your Boddhi want to come out and play for a while?"

"Told you what I think about that too, Helios." And he had. The way Maxwell had it figured, Mr No Name only showed up when he, Max, felt threatened. It wasn't altogether accurate but he used Gentleman Jervis Murray's other side, Wild-man Dervish Murray, as an example of a similar supra-phenomenon.

(Furie ramped himself up, ferocity-wise, as needed. It was almost as if he had a built-in adrenalin accelerator. Furie, though, could also ramp himself down. Max hadn't determined if he could do that yet. Or, the more he let him out, whether he was becoming increasingly in danger of giving himself irretrievably over to the No Name thing.)

"Then let me show you something."

Heliosophos, who hadn't been other than his fit, howsoever prematurely white-haired self all day, went into a cupboard and pulled out a long, rectangular box. "Seen something like this before?"

"Blackguard, Demios Sarpedon, carries one of those with him. Always has, and I've known him for nearly forty years."

"Known of him, more like, Max." Helios unlatched, but didn't open, the box. "Made of a Solidium composite, this is," he said, rapping on it. "Devils, and not just devils, call it Stopstone to Gypsium's Brainrock. Like yours with respect to Furie – whom my father was never particularly fond of, Demonites used to tell me – it's an imperfect analogy. But if you think of it as the lead to Superman's Kryptonite, you won't be far off."

(Kadmon Heliopolis grew up idolizing Demonites Zeross, who was born most of a decade before him, but lived on Aegean Trigon where Dem's parents, Angelo and Megaera nee Kinesis, raised him, Kadmon, and so many others. Of these, one, Meg's nephew, was then currently in the dojo with him and Max.)

"Remember what I said about having had a hundred lifetimes? In the last one, I supposedly occupied a future version of the Lord Order I was telling you about. He called himself Vajra, after the lightning bolt wielded by one the Hindu Trimurti – Brahma the Creator, I think. Shiva the Destroyer had a trident, as I recall, whereas Vishnu the Preserver had a lotus blossom or some such, which probably made him a woman.

"I said supposedly because this Lord Order calls himself Yajur, the same as every other Lord Order I've come across in my past. Which, my past, should include those days yet to come for everyone except Memory and I. And that's the point. Vajra's days are all according to Milady Memory. I don't remember them."

"What are you getting at?" queried Kinesis.

"Just this. Mnemosyne says I possessed this Vajra jerk in my last lifetime. I'm not saying I didn't, but I am saying that I didn't come into this one still possessing, or possessed of, him. If I had I wouldn't have died the last time. See, devils are immortal. They take on a shell, that shell can't die, again according to her, so long as the devil's still inside it. With me so far?"

"I'll take it as a given," allowed Maxwell. "What's in the box? Something like Sarpedon's staff and eyeorbs I assume."

Helios flipped it open. Inside was a long sword with a glaringly sharp blade shaped like a ragged lightning bolt. "This is Vajra's power focus. It's the future Order's talisman. Proof, Memory tells me, of her version of Number Ninety-Nine's occupational hazard. Except ..." he said as he touched it tentatively, uneasily, like one would a dead snake that might not be. "Well, see for yourself. It isn't."

Kinesis sucked in his breath more reflexively than disbelievingly. Max cursed: "What the flying fucking hell ..."

Neither of them should have been as surprised as they looked and sounded. They'd both been around witches and what passed for their witchcraft enough in the not-too-distant past to have expected no different. Then again, maybe like Strife, witches didn't leave memories behind.

What was now inside the Solidium, casket-like oblong was an evidently metallic shaft or long staff just, as Max had speculated, like Demios Sarpedon's eye-stave.

Helios opened one of a series of pouches in the lid. "This is an eyeorb," he explained. "They go by a number of different names. Eye-egg comes immediately to mind. So does prison pod, though ringots like Harry got hold of, mostly from his father, Angelo Zeross, the first Ringleader, Ringkeeper more like, are a bit different.

"In some respects they're just oversized Anthean Agates. As such, they can be used to change outward appearances via what some might describe as coronal or aural manipulation. That's why photographers can't spot a face-dancer; it's an external, as in physical, not a mental, as in mind-over-mind, trick.

"Mnemosyne must have glamorized one to make the stave look like a lightning blade. To put it bluntly – that's not a joke, by the way – she used it to convince me I still held the future Order inside me."

"Shh," cautioned Maxwell, "Can't she hear you?"

"Of course she can. But what's she going to do, kill me? Devic possession, if she is devil-possessed, only preserves the life of someone altogether alive already. She isn't. I go, she does too."

"I don't get it?" complained the professor.

Heliosophos pulled out the stave and attached one of the leathern prison pods to its top. A disembodied eye poked out of it. Both Kinesis and Maxwell leapt backwards. Helios laughed out loud. "Nifty parlour trick, eh? Make that parlous, albeit only if you're a devil." That said, he detached orb from stave, placed them carefully back in the box and closed its lid.

"Among many other things," he put to them, "What those things can do, in case you haven't figured it out yet, is suck devils out of those they're occupying; suck out their subtle matter, daemonic bodies and power foci, too. This one didn't. Ergo I, and both of you, aren't devic hosts, who are usually occupied willingly, any more than we're their unwitting shells.

"Unless, that is, it's a devil so strong the things don't affect him, which no Yajur/Vajra ever has been that I've met or even heard about. Ergo again, if I had a lifetime in your future, my immediate past, wherein I had hold of this Vajra, or vice versa, I no longer do."

"Then neither does Mnemosyne," realized Maxwell.

"Yet she was, or claimed as much anyhow," Helios pointed out. "By a future version of Ereba Thanatos, no less; one with an *'e'* instead of an *'a'*. Recall, Strife said she was a devil. That she jettisoned the future Night. I don't think she did. I don't think there is, or isn't anymore, a future Night. I don't think Mnemosyne was possessed by a devil at all. I think whatever was humanizing her left her. Left a vacuum that first Strife then, Ereba now, filled."

"Then what was it?" demanded Max.

"A demon's my guess."

"What's the difference?" wondered Kinesis.

"Generally speaking," shrugged Helios, who'd been dealing with demons since his first lifetime, "One's skyborn whereas the other's earthborn."

"Skyborn? You mean extraterrestrial?"

"Heavenly. Got to have fallen from somewhere and you don't fall upwards."

"Devils are extraterrestrial."

"That they are but, beyond that, I don't know precisely. I'll bet, whatever she was, her name's Lilith, though"

"Was?" Max sounded stunned. Memory had mentioned the name to him at dinner recently. According to her Primeval Lilith was the mother of no less a figure of fable than Cain; that Cain, Slayer of Abel. And, yes, she'd even admitted that Lethal Lily could humanize her.

"I think something's happened to her. I think she's history."

"Thought that was you," said Kinesis, who'd spent most of the same Monday night dinner talking with Helios, not Shelios.

"So did I, Rom."

"Just one question," Maxwell asked. "Have you tried pulling out the devil now inside your three-thing?"

"Devils aren't the only way to humanize her, Max. Have you ever tried making love to a mandroid? Need a drainpipe for a sheath."

The other two flinched at the metaphor. Max allowed that he hadn't, not that he was absolutely sure that Joan Smith didn't qualify as one. When it came right down to it, Amoebamen had to have come from somewhere and so did mandroids. He further felt obligated to point out the obvious: "I'll take that as a no. I gather you've no idea if this doohickey's a dud?"

"There is that," Helios grudgingly had to admit. "They take out demons, too. Suck in subtle matter I should have said. Plus, there are few more where that came from; which is to say right there in that box. Besides, it's no big deal for Memory to make more anytime she pleases. Her Mother Machine aspect did invent the whole eyeorb/eye-stave binary weapons' system.

"Tailor-made them for an elite cadre of Utopian warriors she called Trinondevs for some reason," he said. Something must have struck him because he paused, briefly, then added: "I suppose I could have tested it out on the cosmicompanions when they were possessed but I didn't think it was necessary. Memory seemed in control of the situation."

"You'll pardon me," Maxwell said, not that he was about to say anything that needed pardoning, "But, given what you've told us, don't you think your machine woman's in control of just a wee tad or two too much? Ask me, about the only thing you're in control of, Mr Called Sophos the Wise, is your bowels."

"I can shut her down with a word; less, a mental command. Course, I find it difficult functioning without heat and gravity, not to mention air. How about you?"

"Android Dulles, Mr Automatic, could control machines too, Helios. But he got killed by a human tree, Mandasoma Plantagenet, as I recall. You ever seen *'2001, A Space Odyssey*?"

"Thanks in fair measure to you, I got killed before I had the pleasure. But I've heard of it. What are you suggesting?"

"That we advance your second coming."

"How?"

"By taking the cosmicar up to the Liberty and going downside. After you shut her down!"

"Interesting notion. Been thinking of it myself, as it happens. Trouble is I'm not sure I can fly it. Then again, we know six who can."

========

On Centauri Island, Johann Schmidt was no longer physically in the patriarch's suite. Dolph Dulles wasn't much there either, though he was mostly lost in dreams. The octogenarian had finally fallen asleep as well. Although, tossing and turning as he was, it was more of an aerobic nap.

At his age, there was the constant dread of not waking up again. What would be even worse, though not for him if he did die in his sleep, was if Helios actually won.

****

Sixteenth Moon: The Trigregos Sisters

========

To Tuesday, December 9, 1980

"Two LAC Squads have just been sent down from the Liberty," the computer-wall said to His Story.
"So deal with them, milady. Do as you've been programmed."
"As I've programmed myself, you mean."
"Same thing!"
It wasn't.

========

For many centuries, the Antediluvian Sisterhood of Flowery Anthea cherished the goal of Panharmonium. Even though the name was identical, they insisted their version of it should never be confused with the Panharmonium that Lazaremists – more like Datong Harmonia, the Unity of both Balance and just that, Panharmonium – imposed upon the Inner Earth circa 5000 YD. Imposition missed the point.

Then again, being free-wheeling anarchists, Lazaremists almost always did miss the point; had an aversion to them, much as snakes did kids with pointy sticks. (Even Lord Order didn't believe in rules or rulers, didn't think there was any need for either/or, especially when he was around.)

Witness how their version of Panharmonium ended: With the Disunition of the three Unites of Lazareme, the consequential abolishment (if perhaps not the definite death) of the incomparable Harmony, the subsequent Thousand Days of Disbelief and, at its end, the termination of their Age, if not their father per se, in 5495 YD, over a thousand years after Thrygragon saw off Thrygragos Varuna Mithras.

What even Harmony – the devils' best and brightest, whom Miracle Memory purported to base herself upon as much as Human Memory – failed to grasp was at the vital heart of Panharmonium. The inception of the Ants' version would mark the day when the inbred-patriarchal, devazur race finally joined other fully sentient races on the Whole Earth as equals, not overlords.

To accomplish that, a gender balance had to be restored. Which, in their view, meant the Trigregos Sisters either had to be reborn or else lured to the Whole Earth. For most, not knowing if the three sisters still existed, the former was the only option. It required generations of selective breeding that didn't start bearing no matter how as yet bitter fruit until the early part of this century.

Despite their successes, and the support of other sisterhoods as well as more than a few female Master Devas, events conspired against the Superior Sisterhood such that their goal often seemed as far off as ever. For one, though, the latter option – luring them to the planet below – was just a matter of time and persistence.

That one didn't know if the Triplet Goddesses would return as pacifiers or would-be avengers; only that they would return. When it came down to dust – whatever kind of dust you'd care to mention: stardust, faeriedust, dirt dust – it wouldn't much matter howsoever they did.

She fully intended to destroy whatever was left.

========

"I have secured the SAG Gap, anchored it in near-space. We anticipated devils might become involved in our designs. We have prepared for it. Kindly let us carry on with the plan. To do otherwise, to do what we have so often done during your previous lifetimes, to improvise, to make things up as we go, that's the recipe for continuing failure.

"Do you really want another hundred lifetimes when we're so close to your first? What did you say to me less than an hour ago?"

"Let's get it right this time!"

"Exactly!"

"You're right, milady. We can handle this ourselves."

That exchange, like the previous one, happened between the Wisdom and Memory Entities on the Moon, in Lunar Trigon, the tri-towered citadel where they still were. If they'd been on Sedon's Head, it would have been Sedonda, Maruta 30, 5980 YD.

What Mnemosyne didn't tell Heliosophos was that his Black Hole and her SAG Gap were one and the same. It wasn't just anchored in near-space either, though it was that. Via between-space, the Grey, the Weird, howsoever you preferred to call the dark-grey universal substance of Samsara, it was linked to New Weirworld.

Where dwelled the Trigregos Sisters.

========

"Your petition is denied. You shall dismantle your apparatuses forthwith and present yourself to the College of Astronomers, who will determine whether your genes are worth preserving."

So declared the Visionary of Weir – there being no other Weir as far as he was concerned – on the equivalent of Sunday, November 30, 1980 AD.

The self-named Ubiquitous Uncle Universe exercised his rights and demanded to know the Visionary's rationale for his decision. There were a number of reasons, but the crusher was the integrity of Weir.

"There is the strong possibility that this wormhole of yours is not some kind of cosmic accident. I have seen that it may not just be a way for us to go in pursuit of devils. It may be the devils' preliminary way of going in search of us!"

The Astronomer accepted the verdict; went away to dismantle the galactic gateway between his basement and the proximity of the Whole Earth's Moon.

Even if he'd wanted to, he didn't get enough time to complete the job.

========

"We believe the hole in the wall of your basement was an effort by the Dual Entities to educate us. We have learned. We have destroyed the hole."

So said the Trigregos Sisters – three speaking as one, unless it was one speaking for all three – on New Weir to Uncle Universe two days later, on the equivalent of Demetray, Tantalar 2, 5980 YD. They didn't knowingly lie; they just hadn't anticipated the lengths to which the Mnemosyne Machine was prepared to go in order to ensure her vision of Panharmonium.

Of a cosmos without devazurs save those humanizing her.

========

Thunder and Lightning leapt to his feet, not so much oblivious to pain as he felt betrayed by his own obtuse gullibility. Honour was lost on the Wisdom Entity: "Should have known you would cheat, human. This is your environment. You set the boundaries. Why don't we go outside and see who is really the master?"

The wall fired. Yajur found himself being sucked, inexorably, into a Black Hole. Miracle Memory never informed her male counterpart that the Black Hole she sent him into was the no longer wandering SAG Gap; this mostly because she reckoned she might need him, Lord Order, again.

That was late Thursday, December 4, 1980.

========

The work crew had been at it for two days, clearing up the mess Yajur's expulsion from New Weir had made of an astronomer's house. One of the workers was overweight and out of shape. He had a stubble beard, a crew cut, and wore loose-fitting clothes.

Up until two days ago he had been the Astronomer and this had been his house. Now he had been stripped of his rank and authority, reduced to the status of a non-person, while the College of Astronomers sat in council trying to decide what to do with him.

There was much to consider beyond whether his genes were worth preserving. Was he worthy of being an astronomer? Was he worthy of preserving period? Was he a traitor? Should he have been allowed out of his development tank eight centuries ago in the first place? If not, then why was he? Was the process corrupt and, if so, for how long?

Was the damage already done now that his family had fled the planet and the devil he brought to Weir World expunged? Or was it ongoing? Had every man and woman who stepped out of a development tank in the last, say, thousand years been polluted with Trinondev genes? Were they Dystopians rather than Utopians?

As his fate was being determined, the self-named Ubiquitous Uncle Universe engaged his body and tormented mind in manual labour.

(Ubi wouldn't have known this but, back on Earth whence Lord Yajur came on the planet's 30th day of its last month, Demios and Melina now Zeross were members of what was once termed the Sarpedon underclass. Until comparatively not so long ago in the Weirdom of Cabalarkon, Sedon's Devic Eye-Land, the Idiots of Weir leached off them. Consequently near drone-like in their slavish embrace of duty, they did most of the hard work that kept Cabalarkon functioning as a Utopia for the majority of its inhabitants.)

The top two floors of what had been the former astronomer's designated domicile had been bulldozed. A crane was now digging out the rubble that filled the basement area wherein he'd surreptitiously constructed his home laboratory. Someone shouted for help. Looked like there was a woman down there.

Universe rushed forward. Maybe his consort, his private wife – who called herself Atomaunt, though he called her '*Tom*' to his '*Ubi*' – hadn't got away after all.

The mistake was instantly apparent. All women in the Utopia of Weir, all pureblood Utopian women anywhere, were white-skinned. The opposite – rather, all colours combined instead of the absence of any colour whatsoever – held true for the men, who were black as coal.

The workman had seen a brownish, but nevertheless light-skinned person and naturally assumed it was a woman. It wasn't.

It was Thunder and Lightning Lord Yajur.

========

Mikelangelo Starrus could see that there were gigantic black men and almost as large, but contrarily white women in the room with him.

========

He was not sure what day or, other than it wasn't the UNES Liberty, where he was. It certainly wasn't the Lunar Citadel he'd revealed to those on the Liberty what seemed only a few minutes earlier. Indeed, about all he knew for sure was that he still had a third eye, couldn't suppress it, and was wearing his uniform.

As for his companions – more like observers – gigantic was a gross understatement. Those below him were proportionately at least twenty times his size. The only reason their voices didn't deafen him was that they must have somehow sonically dampened his immediate environment.

Additionally, men and women might be misnomers. Though humanoid they definitely weren't human. Besides their skin pigment, the only way he could differentiate their sex was that the whites had more pronounced protuberances in the areas of their breasts. Finally, no more amazingly than anything else he supposed, he appeared to be sitting in a birdcage.

Was effectively the bird.

========

"Remarkable."

The blindfolded Visionary returned the weapon and its sheath to the bailiff. It was a kind of sword, actually more like a lightning bolt attached to a hilt. Its scabbard was equally remarkable in that it seemed to be composed of a substance somehow converse or countervailing to that of the blade.

"They each seem to be some kind of unusual metal. Your insights are requested, Mr Metallurgist."

"Not metal, sir," testified the particle scientist, a woman whose otherwise alabastrine skin was a patchwork of variously coloured substances. "Not as such. Spectrum analysis confirms two principle agents. These are Brainrock, in the case of the blade, and Stopstone, in the case of the hilt and sheathe. Their manufacture has been forsworn on New Weir for multi-millennia, likely on the recommendation of the Dual Entities.

"The latter is associated with the mandroids of ignominy; the former with devils of near equal disrepute. What seems equally true is they appear to be mutable, albeit shape-changing rather than state-changing, though perhaps they could do that too, in the right hands, Which mine aren't.

"Subtle matter is a term that comes to mind. We know it from our exceedingly, um, circumspect dealings with the so-called Celestial Sphere. Remarkable does not. They are beyond remarkable; perhaps even beyond knowable. They defy analysis. In theory they are antithetical; in some respects comparable to matter and anti-matter. Which is to say they should disintegrate each other.

"However, in this case, they seem to compliment each other. In other words, what the sword can do, it couldn't without the hilt to hold onto and the sheath to guard it when not in use. It's even possible they're so mutable they, dependent on their uses, amount to the same thing.

"Call it Brainstone, perhaps, or Stoprock; call them the complimentary substances of between-space then drop the plural. I can't describe it adequately. Not today. I'm not sure I ever will, could, can." She farted deliberately. "Listen to me. I sound like an idiot. But I'm not. No one in this courtroom is an idiot, saving perhaps your idiot savant self," she added, obligingly. "And our guest here. Perhaps he would be in a better position to describe it."

"In due course." The visionary dismissed the scientocrat and turned his attention to the outwardly reinvested astronomer.

Uncle Universe had been allowed to appear before the court in his professional persona: tall even for a Utopian, bulbous, with white tattoos of comets, stars, nebulae, planetary systems, and clusters plastered over his night-black skin. His genitals were sucked into his mass and he had only the barest etchings of a mouth and nose. His eyes and ears were completely obscured by a Saturn-like halo of light ringing his temples.

"Mr Provisional-Astronomer-Again, you picked up this sword when you discovered the male devil lying unconscious under the rubble of what had been your basement." Universe nodded. "And when you held it away from the devil, it altered into the tiny creature we have before us." Again Universe agreed. The Visionary next addressed another witness.

"This, however, is not a devil, Mr Physician."

The physician was another night-black Utopian, this one with the white tattoos of his trade – muscles, bones, internal organs, teeth, and nerves – etched on his skin. He looked like a walking transparency, a living anatomical model with his innards externalized, albeit only in two dimensions and no colour. He took the Visionary's statement as an invitation to re-address the court.

"Despite its extraordinary tininess and feminine skin pigmentation it appears to be a primitive form of male Utopian. It has intelligence and speaks in a language easily comprehensible once properly amplified. As for its size, the best I can venture is that it comes from a microverse. It calls itself, himself, a human being. I am prepared to accept that as a fact except, by its, his, own admission, humans do not have three eyes.

"As a consequence, I believe it – he – is indeed some kind of devil and, as such, probably should be exterminated."

"I shall make the judgements here, Mr Physician," cautioned the Visionary.

For the next while a number of other scientocrats stepped forward. Another physician, this one addressed as Mr Veterinarian, confirmed that Starrus was indeed human; speculated he came from somewhere on the far side of a cluster of galaxies conceded to be under the generally benevolent jurisdiction of the Celestial Sphere. Such not-so-alien life forms were prevalent there, one Mr Spaceman confirmed.

As to his size, there were spatial distortions, as a Mr Terrestrial Traveler testified from firsthand experience. Had the exotic arrived through ordinary methods it wasn't as preposterous as it sounded that he would have grown proportionately. Presumably this meant he came directly through hyperspace.

Less contentiously a Mr Constable suggested that, based on innumerable sightings of Lord Yajur two days earlier, devils had no problem altering their size. In fact, just before he inexplicably vanished, there were those prepared to swear he was not only walking on the air but was much larger than the average Utopian.

After listening to the submissions of some exceedingly elderly Utopians addressed, for clarity's sake, as Mr Illuminary Cranky, Mr Illuminary Doddering and Mr Illuminary Almost Infantile, the Visionary concluded the procession of expert witnesses then began summing things up.

"It is a known fact that, but for their progenitors and an obscure, fancifully named being referred to by two of the Illuminaries as VAM, the Amalgamate Abomination, devils were spirit beings. These selfsame antique individuals did add that, in their view, there could be more than one VAM; that in certain conditions devic spirit beings could congeal, for want of a better word, and thereby form solid individuals akin to their aforementioned progenitors, whom they refer to as the six Great Gods.

"However, they ventured further, they'd be very rare and likely extremely short-lived due to the development of distinct personalities and subsequent incompatibility with the other spirit beings making up suchlike joint beings. In their view it is even possible the six Great Gods may have encouraged congealment of their offspring in order to provide them with entertainment in the form of athletic competition or sexual variety, among other things.

"That noted, I am inclined to classify this last as either purely speculative or a product of befuddlement wrought of our witnesses' admirable but extreme age. In short, I give it no credence. By and large, therefore, consensus suggests that, while they could possess most non-Utopian, but nevertheless sentient beings easily enough, they had no physical presence of their own. At least such was the situation countless millennia in the past.

"It is clear, however, that such is no longer an operable statement of facts. Whatever else he may be, this Yajur was definitely a solid being. This in turn has led some of our Evolutionists to propose that, as you might suppose given their fields of expertise, devils have evolved.

"A number of other experts in various fields suggest there is a link between the lightning blade, including its scabbard, and Yajur's undeniable physicality. As you can see, the sword, if that is indeed what it is, is of a size and weight such that only a Utopian or someone larger could lift, not to mention wield, it with any effectiveness. As for this matter of mutability, it does not just defy logic it apparently defies demonstration. In any event, mutability is moot, irrelevant to my determination.

"Six days ago, this Court judged that Mr Provisional-Astronomer-Again should dismantle his link to the solar system where Yajur came from two days later. He says he was in the process of doing just that when the devil showed up on our world. His private mate and the developmental children they were responsible for bringing up have vanished and their house was mysteriously wrecked.

"Subsequently, a thorough search has failed to detect any sign of the galactic gap. Ergo, Order travelled through hyperspace. However yet again, his host, for that is how this exotic has been characterized, cannot grow as the devil did. The significance of this appears twofold. Firstly, it can be safely concluded that devils remain essentially spirit beings. Secondly, devils do not always dominate their hosts.

"Beyond these deductions, though, there are outstanding questions that lack satisfactory resolutions. Specifically I shall have to consider whether Lord Yajur can only gain physicality when in possession of this diminutive alien. Yet, as is evident by the man's third eye, the devil is somehow still within him. Quite conceivably, he is also simultaneously inside this weapon, its scabbard, or both.

"Allowing for the likelihood of a symbiotic and/or catalytic relationship between this Lord Order and our three-eyed guest, should he-slash-they regain contact with the devil's weapon, presumably we would be contending with Yajur Rampant and not this meek, fragile curiosity of otherworldly mortality.

"I would further venture that slaying this specimen would not necessarily rid us of the devil. Anecdotal attestations from great antiquity aside, there is no guarantee a thusly evolved Yajur cannot possess one of us. Then again, when it comes down to it there is no guarantee that he is even still around; the third eye may only be a passing vestige of the devil's occupancy. Finally, if dispossessing the devil of his weapon left only this mortal offworlder behind, then it is not for us to abolish him.

"Mr Human Devil, I will hear from you now."

"About time," protested the man in the birdcage, his voice amplified so that everyone in the courtroom could hear him yet, as before, modulated such that he didn't damage his own hearing. "I am not a devil. Though not without sin, there is nothing intrinsically evil about me. You are, however, right in stating I am a mortal human being. I am Cosmicaptain Mikelangelo Starrus."

"So I have been given to understand. Rankings, save for purposes of sensible listings, are immaterial whereas names are an entirely private matter in Weir. Kindly do not abuse the court's aural capacity with their utterance. You are Mr Human Devil until I rule you otherwise. In the meantime, pray continue to elucidate. Begin by explaining to this court how you came to be possessed of a devil."

Thus allowed leave, if not carte blanche to ramble, Starrus went over nearly everything that had happened to him since the launching of the Cosmic Express on Sunday the Thirtieth. He did so succinctly, not intentionally leaving anything pertinent out, but at the same time trying not to volunteer anything that might compromise Earth defenses. (Not that they'd amount to much in the way of beanhills to such an impossibly advanced society.)

When he was finished, the Visionary consulted the Ys before, what seemed like hours later, rendering his decision. "There is much more knowledge to be gained from this wee homunculus of a human being. It would therefore be remiss of me to declare him a non-person and warrant his annulment. However, there is the paramount security of Weir System to consider. Mr Butcher, your theory as to how to deal with this unwelcome phenomenon strikes me as meritorious. Please repeat it."

One of the previous witnesses, a female with the black markings of her craft, a variety of cutting implements against typically bone-white skin, stepped forward.

"At your suggestion, sir, while researching my presentation, I consulted with some of our once-venerated ancients at the College of Illuminaries. At one point in time, we Utopians suffered from something called disease – infestations which, more often than exceedingly old age or mortal injury, contributed to Imminent more so than Immediate Death. One of the most pernicious was cancer. The usual treatment, as barbaric as it sounds, was to cut it out."

"Very well. Proceed!"

"No," protested Starrus. "You don't know what you're doing."

He was quickly proven incorrect.

========

On the equivalent of Sedonda, Tantalar the Seventh, Starrus awoke on a bed in a sanitary-smelling room. Weird, these enormous, ungodly Utopians, was his first thought. They operate on you in a courtroom then take you to a hospital. He felt his forehead. Nothing. No third eye, no hole, no sutures.

He wondered vaguely if he'd dreamed the whole thing. Then the roof of the room lifted off. As was now certain, he was in the equivalent of an oversized shoe box. An alabastrine Utopian – a female of the species, he now knew – placed what to him was a hot tub, but to her was more like a thimble-sized, coffee mug beside his bed. He took the hint and, never having been shy, not like Nidaba with her background, had a bath.

When he was finished and dressed in his laundered uniform, the door to his shoebox studio opened and in walked a half-dozen tall, but hardly gigantic Zulus complete with grass skirts. They carried long spears with bulbs, not blades, attached to their shafts. In that, and with their blackness, they vaguely reminded him of Demios Sarpedon, whom he occasionally saw on Centauri Island before the launching of the Cosmic Express.

They were the same size as him and were flanking the space man – as he thought of the man with space-scenes tattooed across his skin – Mr Provisional-Astronomer-Again, as he had been called in the Courtroom of the Visionary.

"I trust you are feeling better, Mr Human Being."

"Had a visit from the White Rabbit?" cracked Mik.

"Rabbit?"

"You know, from Alice in Wonderland; not the one on the moon who mixes the elixir of immortality. Though I was thinking more in terms of the Jefferson Airplane: *'One pill makes you larger; the other makes you small; but the ones that mother gives you; don't do anything at all.'* No, I guess not. Still, the song was hard to avoid a decade or so ago where I came from."

"You're asking if I've miniaturized myself. Perhaps. In a manner of speaking. Ever heard of Virtual Reality?"

"Like television?" That Universe understood.

"After a fashion. We have perfected a wide variety of devices that cast our consciousness. Even though most aren't, some, like the one I'm using, are visual – you can see me as well as myself and these constables can see you. Indeed, this one also provides tactile sensations. Just before the surgeon put you under the knife he had one of these on."

"So you're not really here."

"I did not say that. Not exactly."

"Can you whip up something like that for me?"

"Not a question of having to whip one up, Mr Human. In terms of size, you are not as unique as those in the court might have implied. In our travels, particularly near spatial boundaries, we have often encountered diminutive species. Some do grow as they enter our realms; others are naturally tiny. Do you have fairies on your Earth?"

"Never seen one but, yeah, I guess we do."

"Though you're much larger than a thumbling, that shall be our analogy. You did not respond to my initial greeting. How do you feel?"

"Mixed up but, if you're wondering if I've any sense of being possessed by Yajur, or anyone else for that matter ... No, not any more. Your surgeon must have known his stuff."

"Excellent. For once the Visionary was right. As he suggested, and I'm now convinced, Yajur amounts to a trinary being. He is fundamentally a spirit that manifests himself in a third eye, but one who needs a host and contact with a talisman such as his weapon in order to gain both physicality and his extraordinary abilities. I further believe he can no more possess Utopians than his ancestors could. That's assuming he had any and isn't parthenogenetically immortal, which I also believe."

"In other words he might have been around millennia ago, either as himself or as part of one of those VAM Entities the Visionary dismissed as speculative."

"Precisely. And full marks for perspicacity. Ergo, deprive you of his eye and his weapon, he's an insensate entity – little more than a harmless curio. His blade and sheathe I have been allowed to keep as trophies. The Visionary now has his eye in a fishbowl filled with Cathon in his bedroom."

"Why didn't you destroy it?"

"The Visionary could not envisage any way to do that with certainty. However, he has seen that Cathonic Fluid, the stuff that makes up our development tanks and where we lay those suffering from Imminent Death, neutralizes devils. It is a clear liquid that tastes remarkably like apple cider. In fact it is distilled from the golden apples that are partially responsible for our incredibly long lives. By your standards, not the Sisters."

"I don't mean to sound ungrateful but what am I to you? I mean, you're an astronomer. I hope you don't do double duty as a vivisectionist."

"Experimenting on animals is strictly forbidden in Weir System. Which isn't to say we don't enjoy eating or even hunting them once in a while. To answer your question, you have been released into my care. It seems that, partially thanks to you, I have been rehabilitated. We have been granted a domicile in the very tower of the Visionary. We shall share our lives."

"Oh, really!"

"Oh, yes. You see, because of Yajur, I have recently lost my family. Seems I have adopted you as a kind of substitute."

"Then let's not be so formal. Call me Mik and I'll call you Pa. Which is short for Provisional-Astronomer."

"Ubi will do fine. Though not in public, understand?"

"Hardly anything, to be honest,"

========

Ubi came through with a miniaturized version of the Virtual Reality device. Thus Starrus was able to walk around the Utopia apparently the same size as everyone else. His actual reality was completely different. A levitation gadget was supplied such that he could be part of his enlarged image.

Perhaps fittingly, he took up the area where a human's heart would be. On Earth an avid reader with, some might say, esoteric interests, he began to think of himself as precisely how he was described in the Courtroom of the Visionary; as a homunculus, a comparatively minute man that folktales speculated was contained in the spermatozoon or ovum. He refrained from shortening that to homo, though.

Two grown men, both of whom had recently lost their beloved wives, well ... There was already enough talk about him.

========

Theirs was a comfortably large – Brobdingnagian, when he wasn't attached to the VR thingamajig – two bedroom apartment on one of the lower levels of the tower. It had a splendid view of the parklands of Weir City, some of which also came on different levels, ones with artificial mini-suns on their undersides. Some were so large they even had woodlands. A different kind of woods dwarfed them: Utopian-built skyscrapers.

Quite sensibly, Utopians grew their cities upwards rather than outwards. Urban sprawl was urban spiral throughout the planetary system of New Weir. There were many Utopians, claimed Ubi without a hint of humour, who never touched the ground in their entire lives. In fact, reverse-vertigo was a serious problem here. Ground Zero gave a lot of Utopians severe headaches and fear of falling objects was one of their most common phobias.

As he learned over the next few days, there was a great deal more that distinguished Utopians from Earthlings.

========

Mithrada-Monday – the very day, notwithstanding Helios's thought beams, one of his musical idols, the former Beatle John Lennon, was shot down in cold blood – Starrus was taken on a tour of the tower. One section, which seemed much like the hospital he'd been in, took up two levels of the massive structure.

There were about a dozen of what had to be sperm tanks since they contained motile nucleated cells with tails swimming around in a semi-clear liquid. What particularly struck him was that the sperm were all blackish.

Nearby, behind a series of glass windows, were slates of honeycombed, fleshy egg cartons. The ovules inserted within the receptacles were marble white and looked just as hard. Milling about the room were a large number of black or white technicians with charts and various paraphernalia with which they were conducting tests.

"Everything we need, from birth to death, is contained within this edifice – as it is within most towers in the city. This for example is the Nativity Ward. Here we are bred, our genes selectively knitted together according to the needs of the tower, of the city, of the planet, and of Weir System, in that order."

Starrus made the mistake of asking why every tower needed its own Nativity Ward if Utopians live so incredibly long, worry-free lives. After all, they suffered no wars, disease, famine, droughts or other, for Earth commonplace curbs on its population. Wouldn't have, if this was a true Utopia. It was a mistake because Universe liked to explain things in tremendous, almost excruciating detail.

As was his wont, Ubi launched into an extended discourse on figures and quotas and suchlike. It boiled down to a matter of keeping the cycle flowing; of always being ready to fill in the gaps should disaster or skirmishes in the border worlds cause a temporary lapse in manpower. And, he assured him, nothing was ever wasted.

He was still on the subject when Starrus finally got him to move onto the next sight – ADHD (Attention-Deficit Hyperactivity Disorder) was a common enough human trait even among the adult population. Folks like him got antsy without activity designed to keep them moving. Given what it was, Mik wisely kept his mouth shut. He didn't like thinking of his host as being a cannibal, though the conclusion was hard to resist.

"Every level of the tower has food processing stations. From what you tell me, most of your species eat lesser species. This is the definition of barbarism to us, not that we deny ourselves the occasional blood treat. Helps to keep our wits about us, you understand. Unhealthy to stray too far from your natural, If otherwise redundant roots. Millennia have conditioned us to be satisfied with a juicy drink prepared onsite, taken once a day.

"As I told you earlier, it is called Cathonic Fluid and, with bulk supplied by plant fibre, it's all we need to live long and very contentedly. Some of us do augment our diet; unnecessarily, as I am a perfect example. Some drink other liquids, use stimulants, smoke soma – the same substance Visionaries use to channel their Y-visions – but most consume only the fluid and fibre.

"Sleep is not particularly important to us, though of course we do indulge; again because we were born to sleep. Sex is for animals but not expressly forbidden. In fact, the word forbidden is not part of our common parlance. Work, dharma, our duty to further knowledge, is our primary reason for being. Relaxation is work; work is relaxation."

Starrus was under no chauvinistic delusions. Humanity was in its infancy compared to these Utopians, but he couldn't help wondering what more a civilization in existence for at least two hundred thousand years needed to learn. What more was there? Godhood? He confined himself to more mundane matters and, too late to catch his tongue, asked about their daily lives.

"Your years are somewhat analogous to our days. Based on what you told me I have lived around two hundred ninety-two thousand of your days, yet I am barely your equivalent of twenty-nine. Put another way, when I reach my first millennia, I would be approximately thirty-six and half. What would seem a hundred years in your terms would, at an age of over three thousand six hundred and fifty to us, be the start of our late middle age ..."

That was also just the beginning of his verbal ramble ...

========

On the equivalent of Demetray-Tuesday – Utopians had different names for days – Uncle Universe took Starrus on an aerial tour of the city. It was only after they were back in their shared apartment that Ubi finally asked the question that had been bothering him since first encountering Order the previous Tuesday.

"I have shown you my readings and yet you tell me there is no such thing as a Hidden Continent in your North Pacific Ocean. Of course, by definition, if its existence was generally well-known, it would hardly be hidden, would it. Notwithstanding suchlike ocular substantiation, you further discount my assertion that devils live there. How then do you account for Lord Yajur?"

Starrus pondered for a while. He didn't have a Y-vision and, as a man of action, wasn't one for philosophizing. Finally he responded about as reflectively as he could muster. "I can't. Not in any rational way. If they are possessive beings, as is obvious now, that sort of negates any need for a hidden continent, wouldn't you say? I would. I guess devils are devils, which is to say they are evil.

"I had always thought evil just a part of the human condition. It frankly never occurred to me that evil could be ascribed to the influence of alien beings. I still have trouble coming to grips with that broad a conclusion. Surely you have murderers, money-mongers, people who abuse your system or you and your fellow Utopians."

"Accidents do happen, but deliberately? No, never. Harming another Utopian is not the Utopian way. Evil, as you said, and is probably equally true for all your fellow, natural human beings, is a wholly alien concept. In eight hundred years of life, insulated as this planet is well within Weir System, the only really bad thing that ever happened to me was last week.

"And that was directly attributable to Lord Yajur — or whomever attached the galactic gap to my basement in order to facilitate Order's arrival. While I have my theories about that last, it seems to me that the major reason we Utopians, and you humans, differ so much is that you live on a planet polluted by devils."

"Which was the point I was trying to make. However, are your Trigregos Sisters, your deities, not devils as well?"

"It would further seem," Universe quickly added, "That your Earth's devils are male, or at least paternally dominated, whereas our deities are female and answer only to themselves. Besides, we don't actually worship them, not overtly. We don't worship anyone, except perhaps knowledge. They simply live here; do no one any harm and so are allowed to persist, howsoever they subsist. Starlight, most likely."

"Having only consciously," Starrus caught himself. "No, that's not quite the right word," he reconsidered. "Given that I was conscious only of Yajur's domination of me ..." He thought of a better way to put it. "Having only experienced one devil, that might be overly presumptuous. Could it be, for the sake of argument, that your Triplet Goddesses are the only beneficent devils that exist?"

Ubi mulled that over in context with his brief conversation with the Three Sisters a week ago. "An interesting way of putting it. Beneficent, as in doing good? Yes, precisely. Although it is difficult for a Utopian not on one of the border worlds to fathom, doing good might actually require doing harm.

"In this case, as the Trigregos Sisters implied, to non-female devils. They further suggested that my family – Tom, me, Son-shine, and Star-baby – may be the progenitors of a new breed of Trinondevs. But they also talked in the long term; a couple of millennia, not even hundreds of years.

"Frankly, I don't see the problem. These devils aren't so very difficult to handle now that we know how. If Yajur's any example, all one has to do is remove what we are beginning to refer to as their power focus and they become a three-eyed human.

Furthermore, as our physicians predetermined long prior to the first incision, the third eye doesn't wire itself into your brain. It just sits there, between skull and skin, as if a fully functional, yet entirely separate entity unto itself.

"Removing it does no damage to either of you; at least not as yet it doesn't. For it, there's no apparent symbiosis. Whereas for you, removing it appears have the advantage of leaving you altogether human again. Taking it a stretch further, it seems reasonable to presume that if you could find a way to destroy the third eye, you would destroy the devil. Of course presumptions are akin to theories. If you're wrong, what's next?"

"That sticks in my craw. Why didn't you try to incinerate it? Better yet, disintegrate it in one of your power sources or bombard it with this Stopstone your metallurgist mentioned in the courtroom. I mean, why keep the lightning blade mounted on your bedroom wall? And why does the Visionary keep Yajur's eye in a fish bowl on his nightstand? Even that bothers me. Why do Utopians need bedrooms or nightstands if you don't sleep much."

"I did tell you that some of us do indulge ourselves with these human-like appurtenances. There is such a thing as gratuitous pleasure — even for we Utopians. Myself, I do some of my best thinking lying down with my eyes closed. As for Visionaries, they are a highly specialized breed.

"They have to sleep, that is keep their eyes shut or blindfolded. They don't even dream, I'm told. Understandably, I suppose. For the sake of their sanity, such as it is. When they open their eyes, they see not just what is in front of them, but billions of things that are possibly in front of them; both immediately and into the far flung future."

"So you don't sleep so much as benefit from a little shuteye, a bit of a catnap, now and then?"

"Very nicely put. *'Sticks in craw.' 'Shuteye.'* Do all you humans have a such an idiosyncratic way with words? We Utopians tend to think much more concretely. Our vocabulary is to the point compared to yours." A lack of idioms isn't the only thing idiotic about you Utopians, Starrus was thinking. If Yajur hadn't been so out of it, how easy do you think he'd have been to handle?

Out loud he asked about the wormhole. "Is it still in your basement?"

"Not that anyone can detect, but we're pretty sure it's still around. Which is part of the reason I've been rehabilitated. It seems the last Visionary saw things more my way. Of course it might have been the first Visionary. To an untrained eye, they all look alike. Mind you, so do we astronomers. And our eyes are trained.

"Anyhow, I believe he was as impressed as I was at how easy it was to neutralize Yajur; that, chances are, we're more dangerous to devils than they are to us. You see, part of our heritage – you might say our genetic makeup, certainly our conditioning – is to think of devils as almost as bad as mandroids. In fact, the only reason they're shone in a slightly better light is because it was Sedon, the first devil, the Sisters' eldest brother and conceivably even their creator, who finally rid Old Weir of mandroids and their Mother Machine.

"Visionaries rarely have second thoughts to go with their second sight but it now seems that ours is seriously considering doing what I suggested in the first place. Which was, and again is, to use the wormhole, assuming we can locate it, as a springboard to your universe. The idea is to help your race wipe out devils. And for you to act as our go-between."

Starrus suppressed a yelp of joy. He'd been hoping an offer like this would be forthcoming. At least there was now a possibility he'd be able to return to Nidaba.

"It seems the noble thing to do," the Provisional-Astronomer continued. "But would your people appreciate our efforts? That's why I was asked to take you in. To assess your qualities as a reliable representative of another highly intelligent species. I don't mind telling you, I like what I've seen of you thus far."

"Why thank you, Ubi. I like you, too," Starrus added, hoping he sounded genuine and not sarcastic. "But I'm not entirely sure you'd like a lot of humans. They may well be devil-touched, though it is unlikely very many of them are as thoroughly devil-possessed as I was. There is even a man, ancient by our terms though he's only a tenth your age, whom you should meet if we returned to the Earth.

"His name is Loxus Abraham Ryne and he is the patriarch of the Illuminated Faith of Xuthros Hor. I don't understand much of its precepts but the mortal they call Xuthros was known as Noah in our Holy Book — one of them, the Bible. The story goes he caused a worldwide flood that washed the planet clean of evil. Conceivably, what he washed the planet clear of was devils like Yajur."

"Washed them onto a hidden continent, you mean."

"Let's not get into that again. It's a fable, a metaphor of some sort. There is no geological evidence for any Great Flood, nor anything particularly close to one; not a worldwide one at any rate. And mankind's as evil as ever. About the only correlation I can offer you is that certain Creationists, call them biblical scholars for the sake of politeness, have traced the Flood back about six thousand years.

"Back in the Seventeenth Century of modern times, one of them, an Irishman named James Ussher, fixed creation at exactly four thousand and four years before modern times began. If you take that date as when the Flood happened instead of our actual creation, it roughly marks the beginning of known civilization on Earth."

Universe found this remarkably interesting. "If my readings are correct, devils arrived in your planetary system approximately seven thousand of your years ago. Give them a millennium or a bit less to establish themselves as more noticeable than just a fundamental flaw, an irritating nuisance, a glitch in human makeup, and it seems I wasn't far off."

"How did you arrive at these readings, by the way?"

"According to our far-too-long neglected College of Illuminaries, devils emit a certain radiance. This somewhat corresponds to Cathon, what provides our apples with their life-extending qualities, and the related substance we know as Brainrock, but you tell me is called Gypsium on your world."

"Wonder if it's related to Vitamin C."

"C as in Cathon? It does sound strangely likely doesn't it."

"To you and me both, now that I've mentioned it."

"At any rate, it is a strangely unpredictable material but, if it remains stationary for, say, a few thousand years, it decays at a calculable rate. The planetoid, your Earth's moon, has been stable for multiple millennia. Approximately seven thousand years ago it was infused with an inordinate amount of this Gypsium; much more than could be ascribed to a particularly large meteor shower, for example.

"Ergo, devils arrived there in great number about that time. And if they could get there, they could easily transfer to your planet. The anomaly I detected globing the northern half of your Pacific Ocean is of a similar makeup. Hence my conclusion that it encloses a hidden continent or, perhaps better put, a separate dimension contiguous to that area."

"Sorry I asked."

"I would go slightly further than that, if I may." Without waiting for a response, Universe carried on. "We have a notion of what might be described as interspace. It's far more than a notion actually. We wouldn't be able to travel the vast distances of Galactic Weir without a thorough understanding of faster-than-light, hyper-speed transit.

"We refer to between-space as the Universal Substance, or, more mnemonically, the Grey; Dark Grey Matter, to put it yet another way. Gypsium can cut through it. Which is what your Lord Yajur, with his Brainrock weapon, may have done on your Thursday, when he returned here after being away for two days and we found him the next morning. Unless he never went away, that is."

"The Sisters told you they ejected him and destroyed the wormhole. Unless, as you believe, they were wrong, he clearly found his way back."

"But it can't be as straightforward as all that, you see. If this Yajur can simply slash himself unerringly through the Grey to my ruined basement, why haven't devils reappeared on Weirworld millennia ago? Since they haven't, we're left with only a very few reasonable explanations.

"That the Sisters didn't get rid of him is the most logical, which suggests that the Galactic Gap was sealed externally, presumably by the Dual Entities. Then again, if they did eject him, they couldn't have destroyed the wormhole. Otherwise how did he return? And that in turn begs the question of where it is now.

"Finally sealed? Then why wasn't it before? Is it still around, either elsewhere on this planet or somewhere in nearby space? It must be. Which again points to the Dual Entities. Surely you can appreciate the dilemma. That this Yajur is much more powerful than he seems doesn't fit observable facts."

"I was just wondering about that. Your seemingly superior attitude to him doesn't make much sense. From what you told me of your first encounter with Yajur, he wasn't easily handled at all. I gather that if it wasn't for your devils, his mothers, he'd have had things pretty much his own way.

"More to the point, how often do you think you'll come across a devil lying unconscious, as if after running into the spatial equivalent of a brick wall?" Universe continued to marvel at the little man's perceptiveness. Even if they were addicted to Atomics and afflicted with devils, there might be hope for this human race of his.

He wasn't sure he liked that notion. The mere facts they were addicted to Atomics and afflicted with devils suggested they should be left alone to ruin themselves. But what if they muddled through long enough to develop faster-than-light travel or some sort of mass-productively wormhole workaround. Would they then ruin everyone they came across afterwards?

"You did say something about a pair of Entities," Starrus further speculated. "It's obviously occurred to you that they may have caused the Gal Gap to appear in your basement. That they could therefore do it again, any time they pleased. That you could waste decades looking for it only to have it appear next time they felt like ditching a devil they didn't like in Weir System."

"The Gal Gap – another interesting term! That would imply the Female Entity; the Sophia to his Sophos, as they themselves taught our ancestors. Perhaps it might even explain the attitude of Trigregos to their brothers and male offspring. Might Female Supremacists and Male Supremacists not clash? Might they mellow each other?"

"It might also imply the collusion of this Entity and your deities. Maybe that's why the Visionary couldn't see any way to destroy Yajur's eye. Maybe the Sisters controlled his vision. Maybe they're deliberately keeping Yajur on hold, as it were, though I don't quite see why right now. As a backup perhaps?"

"For all we know, he may have been abolished already," Universe was quick to respond. "Then again, it could be Her Story – as the Sophia is also contrasted to the Sophos's His Story – is guiding us in her own obscure fashion," he speculated. "It seems you are a veritable font of inspiration. Wittingly or not, you're extremely insightful. Yes, you were well-worth preserving."

Starrus took the hint. "Hope that doesn't mean I better keep on being worth preserving but, just in case it does, here's another thing for free. If devils do live on a hidden continent that we, um, therefore Outer Earthlings know nothing about, how to you propose to get there? Shoot a few rockets or drop some bombs that aren't there either?"

"Properly speaking flippancy belies as well begets ignorance. I should ignore you. And I will. Suffice it to say that once we locate and stabilize the Gal Gap, as you so aptly named it, it shouldn't be much of a problem."

"And once you get there, I'm sure you'll find it not much of a problem deciding what to do then."

"We will be guided accordingly. As I've repeatedly advised you, Utopians do not have deities as such. However, if we did they wouldn't be the Trigregos Goddesses; they'd be the Dual Entities. The fact is, as every Illuminary not verging on senility – and most of them that already are well past it – would tell you, the Entities are probably the Triplet Sisters' deities as well."

"And they'll be on the other side waiting to hold your hands."

"It would seem so. Rather, it would see so."

Starrus shook his head in amazement. He wasn't as shocked at Ubi's credulity – his peculiarly contradictory faith in good and bad devils, his belief in deities of deities – as he was at his ego, his almost insufferable overconfidence. It wouldn't surprise him if Universe and crew turned on Trigregos or the Dual Entities the moment the likes of this Demon Sedon, his sons and grandchildren such as Yajur were vanquished.

Mind you, given the wherewithal, he'd be strongly tempted to do that himself.

"I'll grant you one thing, Ubi. You and your fellow Utopians definitely seem to be immune to devil-possession. Otherwise Yajur would be out and about again – assuming, like you said, he's still around at all. Maybe that comes from your pristine lifestyle. Maybe it has something to do with the Sisters or the rules, rather the lack of them, that your Entities gave you.

"Nonetheless, getting rid of Earth's devils certainly seems a matter worth pursuing. I'm one human who'd love to help."

"And there's much you can help us with as well, Mik. Now, I know how much you need your sleep. I too could do with a little – how did describe it? – shutting of the cat's eyes for awhile myself. I've much to think about. Fortuitously, I've plenty of time to think about it."

"Hope I'm still alive when you wake up."

========

"What a rude thing to say. You are in no danger from me nor any Utopian."
"Not Utopians I'm worried about, Ubi."

****

Seventeenth Moon: Cosmi-Crunch Time

========

Wednesday, December 10, 1980

Sleep came, sleep went.

The morning after the night before, Heliosophos and Humanized Memory hosted brunch for Romaine Kinesis, O'Ryan James Maxwell and the six finally awake as well as, presumably, now devil-free cosmicompanions: Nidaba Starrus, Enan and Anon Sasarian, Viraf and Ahura Mazda, and the lone bachelor among them, Xerxes Alchaemid.

With Memory around, learning how to fly a cosmicar was not on the agenda. Riding a Terror Donna might have been mentioned, albeit only in passing.

========

Having lost a week of their lives, and after just wasting something like thirty-six hours in the sack, the cosmicompanions weren't exactly with it. But neither were the professor and Big Max. Their problems were slightly different. For one, they hadn't so much lost more than a week as they felt in danger of losing their individual identities. Were Doc Defiance, aka the Gypsium Man, and the Indescribable Mr No Name becoming more them than them?

More to the point, albeit oppositely so, were they even around any more?

"And that's about the extent of it," Nidaba finally finished recapping all that had happened to her and the other five survivors of Cosmicar Two since the Express was launched a week and a half ago. (Presumably because she was named after the Sumerian goddess of writing, in addition to learning and the harvest, it fell to her to tell their story.)

"Mik developed a third eye, spotted something wild on the monitors and literally went through the cosmicar's hull to go after it. I gather you or Memory brought us over here and stuck us under with drugs or light beams or some such. Next thing we know it's Monday night. Now it's Wednesday morning. We all feel fine, fully ourselves again, yet you tell us we had third eyes, like Mik, and that we were possessed by devils, which you also call Master Devas."

"That we do," confirmed Helios. "And that you were, though I suppose fourth generation devils might not count as '*Masters*'. Plus, given your Zoroastrian background, I expect you consider Devas devils. Yet, thanks to Milady Memory and Big Max here, you're no longer occupied with anything except the pleasures of having a proper breakfast. You sure none of you will have a drink? If you don't like retsina, we can provide almost anything else you want, firewater included."

"Water minus the fire will suffice for me," said Anon Sasarian. "And it was the Magi before Zarathustra came along who worshipped fire."

"I'll have some more of this excellent juice," requested Enan, Anon's wife being Nidaba's sister. She had no interest in being drawn into a religious discussions; not now, not when hypothetical gods of ancient mythologies had proven themselves definite devils of modern age reality here on the Moon.

(Enan was short for Inanna. Hubby Anon didn't approve of it for a very simple, if superstitious, reason. Inanna was yet another Sumerian Goddess, that of sexual love, fertility and warfare. Mnemosyne instantly liked her; all the more so when she pointed out that Inanna's nominal mother was Sin, a Moon Goddess the same as Titanic Mnemosyne, who was more famous as the mother of the Muses by Olympian Zeus.)

The other three, Viraf, wife Ahura and Alchaemid, in the absence of Nidaba's husband Mikelangelo Starrus technically their cosmicaptain, also stuck with juice. There was a wide variety of it as well, hardly all of it made from fruit grown on the Whole Earth. Not so Maxwell and Kinesis.

Both men were throwing back retsina as quickly as Helios could refill their glasses, which was almost as fast as he refilled his own. Lady Memory, too, was well into her cups. The two Greeks, the German-born Scotsman, and the semi-one-third-Italian weren't falling over drunk yet but they were well on their way.

"Perhaps you might explain to us what happened to these devils," enquired Alchaemid. (Xerxes had initially been tipped to be Two's Cosmicaptain, with Mik Starrus Cosmicommander. Then the now late Colonel Sol came along and, for reasons of his own, Sentalli made him the Express's overall chief officer.)

"Max's nameless alter ego," began Memory, whose early morning physical drunkenness shouldn't impair her computer third's functionality, "Seems to have found a way to lose them in the Weird without losing you. An impressive bit of work. You should be grateful. I was about to chuck you into a black hole."

"Like you did my husband?"

"I'm afraid Cosmicaptain Starrus was no longer an issue," Mnemosyne tried to console Nidaba. "He'd been consumed by the demon-devil, Lord Yajur. Helios and I have had dealings with him in other lifetimes, some far in his future, and couldn't risk having him around in this one.

"Even though I don't quite see how, he must have survived in order to have far futures, but there's little chance your husband could have. It's unfortunate that Max's Boddhi wasn't here on Thursday to save him as he did you six. That's just the way of things. You'll have to accept that I had no other choice."

"With all you can do," snarled Nidaba, angrily yet perspicaciously. (Enan might have got the warrior name but her sister got the warrior attitude.) "No, Memory, I can't accept it. You wanted rid of this Yajur because, for whatever reasons, you need him to have a future. You couldn't have cared less about my Mik. Expediency is not a virtue."

"Neither is stupidity," retorted Mnemosyne, emptying yet another glass of the foul-tasting sauterne. "Mik Your Dick was gone. Irretrievably! I thought you six were as well. You're <u>lucky</u>, underlined. Starrus wasn't. If you cannot go along with that, fine. What say, Kadmon? It seems our guests aren't enjoying themselves. Perhaps they would be better off on the Liberty. Shall I send them there?"

"I wouldn't." said Maxwell, suddenly sounding sober and very worried.

"Why not?"

"I may not know much about what I can become but I do remember what No Name did – and it was on your instructions, Memory. I flowed into Samsara and through it, into your computer-self. Brought some kind of substance akin to Solidium out of it and encrusted their spirits; all but the dark one you appropriated."

(Memory made no secret that she'd kept Ereba Thanatos for herself. She liked being human. For one thing computers couldn't drink retsina without short-circuiting. Being named after a moon goddess also implied an affinity for darkness. More to point, when Satan St Synne exposed her template, Human Memory, to his devaray and she thereby found herself a supra, in all likelihood it was Ereba Thanatos she acquired. So, in some respects it was akin to putting on an old friend.)

"When I came out, it was with them and, I assumed, with the devils possessing them as well. Yet it seems what I brought out were six perfectly normal men and women; six folks who couldn't have been inside you without being possessed by supernatural beings. Seems you assumed I got rid of the devils and I figured you'd disposed of them."

"Meaning they're still around?" Kinesis put down his glass. "Where? In who?"

"No one in this citadel," insisted Memory, realizing the import of Max's information. (Sobriety came quickly when only two-thirds of you were drinking.) "I scanned everyone before I came out. You're as you should be. No Name must have got rid of them without you knowing how."

"These devils are called Thanatoids." Max thought out loud, a habit he'd picked up from years of working alongside Loxus Ryne. He had finally figured out what should have been obvious to him Monday, even if he was Mr No Name at the time. (It also helped that Helios had explained the difference between Human Memory and Humanized Memory yesterday.)

"The one inside you is the same one who was inside the first Memory when she was the Queen of Spades. It's just the effect that's different: she was human, you're not; at least not altogether. The one who was inside Leandro D'Angelo in the Forties, when he built Septupleman, was responsible for taking back Sean Sunday. He's the actual Amoeba Prime – Constantin Thanatos."

"Sean heard you," grasped Kinesis, remembering catching Maxwell talking to himself shortly after the Laird of Lethal Letters left the Liberty. "You were trying to communicate with Smythe's spirit and he heard you. Did what you wanted him to do. Unless he's an it by now, never been too sure about spirits."

"Wasn't your mother, my paternal aunt, called the Living Ghost, when she wasn't called Slipper?" inserted Helios, significantly not offering anyone another drink; nor finishing the one he'd already poured for himself. "Don't recall her being an *'it girl'*, though. Actually, now that I think about it, she was, absolutely. You don't get a nickname like Hot Rox without being an *'it girl'*, as in *'the girl's got it all'*."

"And believes in sharing it," muttered Kinesis, who well-recalled his mother's reputation. He was looking at the very someone who brought it out of her, too.

(Human Memory was Roxanne born Heliopolis's mentor as well as her brother Agenor's eventual husband. She was a decade or so older than Rox, who was a Summoning Child. Both became Lovely Lady Afrites at an early age by today's standards. They thereafter dedicated their lovemaking to the Great Goddess Aphrodite. By all reports both were also very devoted.)

"Yeah, so I heard anyway. Well, Max …"

"I'll go with he," Big Max decided. "And just like I thought he could, he broke this Thanatoid out of whatever holding-contraption Ms Memory here whipped up for him. Then either Sean or the devil broke out the rest of them, cosmicompanions and all. Later on, when he realized what No Name was doing, he did something similar. This time though, instead of taking you lot out, he only took the devils."

"Christ, Kadmon!" swore Kinesis. "Do you think they somehow got to the Liberty? It's full of folks they could take over."

"And come back here," appreciated Maxwell, glaring at Humanized Memory. "To get their sister."

Helios stood shakily. "It seems our celebrations were somewhat premature, ladies and gentlemen. Get back in the wall, milady. Scour the Liberty with your scanners. If you find out who they're possessing, Black Hole them. I don't care who it is, I want those devils out of our way. That includes the one in you,"

In terms of reaction time, when only one-third was sober, majority often rules.

========

"I said I'd wait for the right moment, Jimbo. Seems like it's now or never. I can see right through Anon Sasarian. Helios, Memory, Max and Rom are drinking retsina even as we speak. They're three-quarters plastered and the cosmicompanions are Iraryans, brought up in a Moslem culture. They don't drink. We'll stone them when they're stoned. Didn't Bob Dylan say something like that?"

"Wouldn't know Bob from Thomas to be honest, Sean. But, if I understand your abilities correctly, might I suggest a slightly different approach."

He did. Smythe liked it.

========

"Too late, Kadmon."

Rom Kinesis was on his feet. His body shook visibly; became the inordinately muscular Doc Defiance – only now he had a third eye. Just as he had a week ago last Saturday on Centauri Island he imbrued the surrounding area with motive-retarding Gypsium. No one, not even Mnemosyne, could move. And if she couldn't move, presumably she couldn't get into her computer side.

"Amazing power this," the professor commented in a voice not his own. "Mine as much as the pro's. Remember me, young Heliopolis? Don't bother trying to speak, you can't. I'm sure Max does since he as much as accepted paternity for my son, even though Jock Maxwell was the real father. I'm the supra once called Amoebaman.

"That's right. The real life bodybuilder, the one who could split his body into many bodies. Split his mind into others' minds as well. Which is what I'm doing now inside Rom. Max would tell you that when Leandro D'Angelo was killed he left behind seven distinct individuals. Initially we all had abilities similar to Leandro's but they wore off. Something like seven years later, one of us, Barb Black, had Adolph Dulles.

"She wasn't the only one of us with children, of course, but seemingly Dolph is the only one who has inherited any of our abilities. Collectively we were Septupleman, the Psychic Siblings, but only a very few people remember that. By '60, we were just Trebleman: Schmidt, Smith and me, Smythe.

"So here we are," said Doc Defiance, beaming despite himself, "But for the Iranians, one big happy family. Me, once Leandro; me, once Joan, once Barb; and me again, now in possession of Rom Kinesis. He's your cousin, right, Heliopolis? Roxanne was your father's sister. And Agenor married Leandro's aunt barely a year after your real mother, Argiope Zeross, died having you. Now you're sacking Aunt Memory's what? Living memory!

"That's good, isn't it? Living memory! What do you think, Jim?" He paused for a few seconds. "I'm also up here on the Liberty by the way. James Aremar says I should get on with it. So does Johann Schmidt and Adolph Dulles. He's with Loxus Ryne on Centauri Island while Schmidt's sort of betwixt and between. Mr Ryne says hi by the way. Hi and goodbye. Dolph was just asking if I can't set Schmidt up to possess you, Heliopolis.

"I explained that, at Jim's suggestion, I tried to do that myself before settling on Rom. Even tried to get into your three-thing of a computer-woman again. Couldn't do it. Spring says you two are already possessed by devils: her by his sister, Night; you by someone he thinks, even if you don't, might be Lord Order. He's a legend in Spring's mind despite this Yajur fellow being cathonitized hundreds of years before Constantin was even born in our Twenties; his too, come to think of it.

"That's funny as well. Not the matching timelines — their Year Zero is four thousand years before the West's Year Zero. A dyed, then died, in-the-wool anarchist like you possessed by the embodiment of Order? That is funny, eh wot. Apparently Max is already spoken for too – by something beyond his ken, mine, and probably the rest of yours as well. The whole thing is pretty damn complicated. Fun, though."

Doc Defiance opened his hand. In it were the four other devic eyeballs. "These are yours." The orbs vanished; third eyes appeared in the foreheads of the four cosmicompanions whom the Thanatoids initially possessed. Only Anon and Nidaba remained unadulterated. They stayed motionless in their chairs.

"I want to try something else." Defiance closed his third eye briefly. When he reopened it, Sasarian did as well. A third one. "What an interesting situation. Anon is now possessed by me as well. Let's see, that makes Sean in the Liberty, Schmidt in between spaces, Dolph on Centauri Island, and Defiance here. Guess I shouldn't count Dulles, though he has a sliver of my talent. Hope that doesn't qualify me as a scatterbrain."

It was difficult to determine which was more offensive, thought Max, unable to speak out loud for a change: the devil's ego or lame wit. The latter, he decided.

"Have we been formally introduced by the way? Can't remember. Anyhow, I'm Spring, Constantin Thanatos. I'm a fourth generation devil. That is my brother Fire, Acheron, and those are my sisters: Castella, Auraura and the lovely Orinth, my twin – Day, Winter and Autumn. Ereba, Night, is the one in Memory. Like I said, the other guy's Spring too. We're sort of bursting out all over, aren't we?"

Once again, Defiance chortled involuntarily. Whatever part of his being was Smythe — or, rather, this devil that was presumably in charge of their joint being – thought himself a regular comedian. The rest of Kinesis wanted to throw up. If he could move he'd stick his fingers down his throat. But only if could throw up Sean-Constantin.

"Now here's the real tricky bit," proposed Spring, through the Gypsium Man. "Night's going to teleport the five of you possessed by my brothers and sisters up to the *Liberty*. Then she's going to transfer herself to Mrs. Starrus and leave me in charge of the computer. I'll send her to the ship.

"Listen up, you six – I'm talking to myself and my siblings now, so the rest of you don't have to pay attention; not that you've much choice in the matter. You're going to have to suppress your third eyes and appear to be cosmicompanions. Aremar will be the only one who knows the truth but he won't hassle you because, once you're safely out of here, I'm going to use *Defiance's* Gypsium to wipe this citadel off the face of the planetoid.

"It'll probably mean Smythe will be killed but, as an acceptable trade-off, so will Helios, Memory, Max and the poor professor. Shame about our three but what the hell. Amoebaman uses up bodies like hermit crabs go through discarded shells, so Sean was never really alive anyways. As for Max and this me, the over-and-under-me, well, they knew the risks.

"Plus, we – the other this me, the one in Sasarian, and the rest of us – we decathonitized devils won't have to worry about killing lesser beings anymore.

"Let's get things rolling shall we. Over to you, Night."

========

He, Defiance, screamed suddenly. "Christ, what the fuck's the matter with you, Jim? No, you bastard. Stop it!"

Clutching at his throat, Defiance crumbled to his knees.

========

On the *Liberty*, James Aremar was in the process of throttling Sean Smythe. "You're the fucking bastard. Talking to yourself like a fool. You think I'm letting a bunch of self-proclaimed devils loose on my ship, let alone bring them to the Earth? Forget it! I'll figure another way to deal with God-cursed Helios."

Although they were virtually the same age, at least in terms of being alive, and equally well-trained, Aremar was physically about twenty years younger and much more determined. Scatter-brained as he was, Smythe wasn't about to give up without a struggle. Then he wasn't alone. Johann Schmidt came fully out of interspace, grabbed Aremar by the shoulders, and ripped him away from his psychic sibling.

Bursting into Aremar's quarters, Leonid Kulagin and Ned Johnson spotted three apparently unarmed men struggling furiously. One, Sean Smythe, only now with three eyes, they'd heard had died on Sunday. Another, Schmidt, was vaguely familiar to Johnson from his apprenticeship at the Alliance of Man; looked a lot like Smythe, and had at least a glimmering of a third eye as well.

Neither Johnson or Kulagin particularly disliked Aremar. Helios had gone so far as to excoriate him as exactly what this brave new world he promised didn't need. Still and all ...

"Shoot them, you imbeciles!" This from Aremar, typically non-endearingly.

Kulagin and Johnson didn't have much choice. Better the devil you knew than two other devils you didn't want to know.

========

In Ryne's suite on Centauri Island, Dolph Dulles suddenly shrieked, waking the Great Man in the process, and clutched at his chest. Blood spurted out between his fingers. Then he twirled like a top spun by an unseen hand and went down in a heap. He was now bleeding from a head wound as well.

"Get a doctor," Ryne shouted to the guards standing outside his suite.

In his early morning befuddlement, he'd momentarily forgotten that Connie Lindquist was apparently dead and that the other two he knew enough to trust, Paul Creel and Angus Skullian, were tragically nerve-damaged – Creel now deaf. Nevertheless, his cry was answered almost instantly.

Dr Aristotle Zeross stepped through a teleport-hole.

=========

Suddenly two-eyed again, the Gypsium Man released his throat, took a quick look around, and let everyone move again. Anon Sasarian threw back the chair he was sitting in and tried to leap to his feet. Instead, he fell to his knees and grabbed his chest. Blood gushed between his fingers. Then he whirled like a Hebrew dreidel or poltergeist's bobbin and went down in a pile. He was now bleeding from a head wound as well.

OJ Maxwell collapsed almost simultaneously. Memory's body vanished. Her digitized face reappeared in the computer wall. Helios was ready to punch someone. The third eyes of the other four possessed cosmicompanions began to brighten perceptibly. As far as he was concerned that rendered them as good a place to start swinging as any.

The computer wall that was Mnemosyne pulled a Doc Defiance, shot immobilizing bolts of Gypsium radiation that froze the four of them in their seats yet again. Anon groaned, looked at his hands and wiped his brow. Barely a spatter of blood. Otherwise nothing. Zilch! It was as if he had never been bleeding.

Helios fixed that – kicked him in the head, cracking his jaw in the process. Memory froze Sasarian like she had the others then, for good measure, did the same to Romaine Kinesis and Nidaba Starrus. Feeling only moderately better after giving Sasarian the boot, Helios was still itching for a fight.

"Even if they are our half-children from a different lifetime I've had it with these dickhead devils. Free up Max, milady. Maybe his Boddhi can dispose of them like we thought it had."

"I never immobilized him in the first place. What's wrong?" Helios went over to Maxwell, looked him square in the eye, and felt for a pulse. "Well, I'll be damned, eventually. I believe our Mr Maxwell had a heart attack and died while we were twiddling our thumbs listening to Spring ramble on about how wonderful he was."

He gently laid Max on the floor and closed his eyes. "Sorry, mate. Even if I never much liked you, you were a worthy ally of my father and many of his comrades in his Black Rose back in the Big Bloody. The idiot devil didn't realize Mnemosyne's always partially connected to her computer self even when she's humanized. He thought he'd immobilized us with Gypsium too.

"Us! Gypsium protects us, always has. In many respects, we are Gypsium, leftovers of the Godhead's Big Bang, nothing less than the stuff of Godhood and all that non-rot. It was like using a fire hose to stop a flood. Good tool, wrong job. All we wanted was to get the rest of the devils back here where we could deal with them properly. Guess we fucked up royally, eh?"

"Gotcha!"

The Indescribable Mr No Name rolled out of Samsara; rolled Helios into the right half of his made-glutinous body. His toe touched Maxwell's body. The phony corpse sucked into it, as if a balloon through a siphon, filling out No Name even further. Gander and goose, the analogy worked for what he'd just done: namely, an Amoebaman. Except Boddhis didn't need amoebas.

"Now, Milady Memory, unless you think you can free your boyfriend before I snuff him, be good enough to release my esteemed colleague from whatever's holding him in place. In case you haven't noticed, parts of my Solidium substance are stuffing up Helios's ears, nose, and throat already. I could expand real rapidly."

Heliosophos gagged something unintelligible. If Machine-Memory understood it, she gave no indication. "Don't harm him, Void," came back the computer wall, using an alternative term for what the onetime Callion Clone had become apparently after receiving twin blasts of devic eyefire on the 30th. "I'll turn Kinesis loose but, be forewarned, he's powerless. I've drained the Gypsium out of him."

The all-white mass of mostly the Grey pulsated briefly, as if it was laughing. "Think I've got enough powers for both of us, Memory. Wouldn't you agree?" As soon as the computer wall released the professor, it was OJ Maxwell who had Helios in a stranglehold. "Hey, pro, back with us?"

"Seem to be." Kinesis slumped into the chair, hefted the bottle of retsina, and, not bothering with a glass, took a healthy swig. "Where's what's-his-name?"

"Around and about, I imagine." Max didn't need to be any more of a mind-reader than Memory was to catch the reference. "Guess that's why he's considered a Multivoid, capitalized. No Name exists in a multitude of voids; spatial pockets of next-to-nothingness. He's also a suspicious type. Figures both Helios and Memory know how to get rid of him. Doesn't want to give them a target."

"You going to break his neck?"

"The thought had occurred to me."

"Don't do it," warned the computer wall. "You kill Helios, Trigon, this whole place, rips back into the time stream — me with it. I don't know if those six will survive. The devils might but Nidaba will perish almost immediately. So will you, professor; more than likely you and your Boddhi-side as well, Max.

"If I'm reading things right, he's more part-you than you're separate beings. So why don't you ask yourself this instead: Want to take the chance? We're still on the Moon. This citadel goes, you'll be in a much more permanent void, if you get my drift. And if you don't, well, I just told you what'll happen."

"Then why don't you teleport us to the Liberty? I'll leave the devils for you to deal with."

"He's turning purple, Max," noted Kinesis with a scientist's acuity for the bleeding obvious.

"Do it, computer."

"Then you'll snap his neck for sure. No, I think you better release him first, Max. Then we'll deal."

Helios finally found the leverage he'd been struggling for. He flipped Maxwell over his shoulder almost effortlessly, kept hold of one arm and rammed a foot onto Max's chest as soon as he had him down. He looked plum out of patience, if not even slightly out of leverage of his own. Dislocation could follow; a this time, heart-stopping heal-thump reapplied, much more likely.

"Rather you deal with me one-on-one," he challenged the physically much older-looking man. "Or would you prefer to send your Boddhi out to play?" It wasn't the first time he'd tossed down that gauntlet. This time, though, play meant slay. He wasn't talking Crazy Horse either.

Today was a good to die. For a lot of folks to die. None of them him.

Releasing him with a parting jerk, he touched the lion mane pendant under his shirt. As had happened before, there was light and it was coming from him.

"Either way, I can't wait!"

========

Maxwell came up ready to fight, took one look at his foe, a veritable Sun God now, and thought better of it.

"Bit of a non-starter that," he muttered.

========

Holding up his hands in a gesture of surrender, he joined Kinesis at the table and accepted the bottle of pine-scented sauterne.

"Wise choice keeping the Nameless Nobody hidden, Max," congratulated the professor, taking the bottle back. "No question it's the right one. Kad and his Living Memory are just toying with us. Have been all along. The moment Doughboy shows, they'll turn him into Gypsium shortbread and eat him raw."

Kinesis gestured toward the five, three-eyed companions still sitting motionlessly across the table from them. "What are you going to do with them by the way, Kadmon? Pen them up until you're ready for more sport?"

"Black-Hole them, Memory. All eight of them!"

Just that second the entire citadel, except for Helios who hadn't changed back, went dark. "Something's screwing with my power again," they heard her swear.

The lights went on again. Dimly. Kinesis and Maxwell ducked under the table – and not just because they were still halfway hammered. Five devils – Fire, Day, Winter, Autumn and two-headed Spring – were on their feet. Bald-headed Castella, she shorn of her power focus, was in their midst. The other four stood protectively around her.

The sixth one, Night, Ereba, appeared beside Helios: Machine-Memory re-embodied but externally, yes, Madame Midnight, the Queen of Spades, reborn as one.

Nidaba Starrus, the only one of the cosmicompanions left with two eyes, ran across the room to embrace a similarly-dressed newcomer. He glowed like the Lightray Lunatic (as someone, probably Helios himself, once styled the Male Entity) and had a third eye. Neither Max nor the professor needed to hear her cry her husband's name to realize who he was. They'd helped train him for his mission to the stars.

That he now had a former star inside him, well, that seemed likely.

========

On Centauri Island, Harry Zeross took one look at Adolph Dulles and pronounced him fine. "Got to go, old man. Say hi to Megan and Pauline for me."

Ringleader was gone before Loxus Ryne remembered his last set of twins were Harry's nieces; that their mother Oriani died of cancer due to overexposure to older brother's Gypsium rings.

He'd have rather first remembered which pocket he kept his Beretta. By then it was too late for that, too.

****

Eighteenth Moon: **Noodling Nihila**

========

Wednesday/Birhym, December/Tantalar 10, 1980/5980

Sedonda-Sunday in the upper reaches of Frozen Lathakra's glacial palace, Laza-reme's female Heliodromus or Messenger of the Gods (Angelus to devils; Irisiel Merch-erm to Illuminaries), ran straight into … Well, she remembered when Tantal Thanatos finally came to release her late this Demetray-Tuesday night – she'd run into someone, hadn't she?

Maybe she'd just been clumsy. Run into something anyhow. A wall made of black ice, perhaps? More like a mass of really, really thick darkness.

With a pink face and an unwavering smile? Nah, couldn't be!

========

"You may go, Angelus." King Cold used the word in its older context, as in envoy. (Her Illuminary-given name came from a combination of mythological messengers of the Classical variety, including Iris, Mercury and Hermes.) "We have Aristotle Zeross now. He can traverse the Dome, which we devils can't, and he's already brought us our daughter, Water. Soon the rest of our children will be back with us."

The devic courier shook her arms, restoring their feeling. A dark-skinned, chiton-clad, Mediterranean or East Indian looking daughter of the Libertine, she was used to warmer climes. To her mind, the Frozen Isle was no place for even a Master Deva. It bewildered her how the male Thanatos and his sister-wife, her now-former friend, Tantal's onetime Scarlet Empress, survived here.

"This whole episode is beneath you, Cold. I shall be speaking with Father, Thrygragos Everyman himself, about this. Be assured, none of his sons or daughters, my brothers or sisters, will ever support you again. Nor will any of their loyal adherents and he's a world full of them. Myself primarily!"

The enormous Viking shrugged his shoulders. "I said you may go. Of course you are welcome to stay, should you so desire; restraints reapplied, your option."

The Lazaremist deigned not to respond. On winged feet she raced out of the Glacial Palace, down the Labrys mountainside eastward, through the domain of Tantal's Fire Kings, across the Sea of Clouds, up the Cattail Peninsula, across the Gypsium Wall, once long lost Harmony's preserve, and into the occipital regions at the back of Sedon's Head. Even though she could have done it faster, had there been any perceived urgency, shortly after dawn Birhym (Wednesday) she was on Tympani, the Isle of the Undying One (arguably Lazareme himself).

Her Thrygragos of a father, the last Great God on the Head proper, remained elsewhere; most likely still half-drunk and sleeping it off in the Dinq, Doinq, Danq

Cavern Tavern, on the northern slopes of the Diluvia Mountain Range, where it hadn't stopped raining since the Great Flood.

He often went there, meticulously incognito, in order to relax and, as he put it, indulge his human side. (Lazareme looked in a mirror and saw a three-eyed version of the Male Entity currently on the Moon looking back at him. He did so because his Father Sedon creatively based him on Helios.)

One who wasn't there, between Hadd and Marutia, because she was right in front of her here and now, large as life on the comparatively much larger landform in the middle of the Aural Sea, was the DDD's long-time former owner. And she was based on the Female Entity. Unless she was her hived in twain.

"Harmony?" Irisiel hadn't seen her in five centuries. She looked appreciably different: darker, somehow less golden-glowing than golden-glowering.

"Call me Nihila." Oh, oh, Irisiel thought, but didn't say, she's in one of those vengeful snits of hers. "Good to see you again, too. I have a mission for you."

"Yes?"

"Find Order!"

"Find him yourself, Balance," yawned the courier, deliberately not addressing her eldest sibling by what was clearly a Nemesis-name. No matter where she'd been, or whatever had happened to her half a millennium in the past, it wasn't good to encourage suchlike acting up.

(Well over 1600 years earlier, the lone female Unity found her sleeping with their mutual father right here on Tympani. She promptly tossed her in All the self-proclaimed Invincible She-Sphinx, on the Prison Beach of Incain, as punishment. Left her there for decades, too; until Thrygragon's aftermath, as it happened. Irisiel thereupon found out that, after ditching her in All, Harmony went back to sleeping with him herself.)

"I've had enough running around to last me for a momentary eternity. Wake me in a couple of years and I'll see what I can do."

Mercherm walked toward her private pavilion. Nihila hailed her again. The Messenger of the Gods turned, as much warily as wearily.

"Where should I start?"

"Don't ask me, Harmony. His star's not in the Sedon Sphere. That much I can tell you. Hasn't been since the thirtieth of last month. Although, now that I think about it, I guess you might not even be aware he's been stuck up there for almost as long as you've been gone; since Chaos vanquished him at the end of the 1000 Days of Disbelief, as a matter of fact."

"Him, too?"

"Ah, then the Legendarian was right about what happened to you."

"What happened to me was wrong. So was Chaos. What became of him?"

"Never got as far as the night's sky. Committed devic suicide."

"Cut out his third eye?"

"Know or any other way? Except he survived to tell the tale, when Author wasn't around to do it for him, that is. Too bad for many, many others over the ensuing centuries. Mind you, he always was something of a demon." (Occupying debrained daemons, either spelling, is how Master Devas started becoming solid individuals ca 2000 YD.)

"Tell me about it."

"I'd rather tell you about this: There was a bloody bright battle going on upstairs a week or so ago. Except I can't, not for sure. As near as any of us could make out from down here, Order had come back from wherever he'd got to and was taking on Granddad himself in the night's sky. Author would be the one to ask. He's always full of answers. Lies as well, so watch it."

"And where might he be?"

"Probably drinking with Dad at the Danq." That said, Irisiel entered her tent and tied down the flaps.

========

She was right; in the sense of not being altogether wrong.

========

Nihila found the recurring deviant, Jordan Tethys, at his favourite table in the Cavern Tavern. (It had been his favourite table five hundred years ago, too. Even on the Head some things never changed.) The grizzled Legendarian, he with the tee-tee tails pasted onto his mostly bald head underneath his cap, and whom devils tended to call Author, was absently doodling in a sketchbook – his famous splotch pad. Was doing so with his glowing Brainrock quill; what had been brother Rumour's power focus until he vanished as Phantast Thanatos's Crimson Conspiracy ran its mass murderous course most of two millennia gone.

(Regardless of the fact that virtually all of the unnecessary deaths attributed to him took place on the Outer Earth, Dark Sedon ill-starred, or cathonitized, the Mithradite Dream Weaver. Served Phantast right, many said, for attempting to make himself a Great God beyond the Dome. Was hardly the only one the Mighty Moloch mostly in the Sky cathonitized back then. He'd have done for Fitna Marutia, Mithras's myrionymous Ewe for Aries, which had just ended, but Harmony, in one of her nastiest Nemesis states ever, got to her first.

(Hurled her into the lava lake filling the Peak's caldera with molten Brainrock. Watched as she swam toward the subsurface cave that contained the then stationary SAG Gap. Her debrained, daemonic body must have been mostly Red Salamander or Lovely Lady Lava Lout because damned if she didn't get away, albeit minus her power focus, her Golden Apple of Discord. Which melted out of existence like Harmony hoped she, Strife, would.)

It was still quite early in the day so he was sipping foul-tasting Cathy instead of the Danq's heavenly pilsner. (Harmony's own concoction, albeit mostly according to her, from long, long before there ever was a deviant Legendarian, if perhaps not a DDD.) The oohs and awes engendered by her arrival snapped him out of his reverie.

Having more than just come across her on Sedonda-Sunday – on Tympani, as it happened – he shuddered visibly, as if in dread, and flipped to a pre-drawn emergency exit page. Something else that hadn't changed in five hundred years, she supposed. (Not a lot could change in Sedon's Cheek, what Mithras himself named after Marutia. It did, the Time Quakes he started on Thrygragon just knocked them back to where they'd been.)

Consequently not at all ignorant of what he was about to do, the darkly golden-haired, butterscotch-skinned former Unity – her with the Brainrock necklace, stern, oval-shaped face, fresh green tunic, it covered with a mesh of glowing chain mail, and metal-shackled wrists, they with only a couple links of eminently extendible chains dangling off them – smiled benignly, as if in reassurance.

Almost every man in the vicinity – and not just men – sighed involuntarily. Their longing suspiration didn't quite suck all the air out of the tavern but it was almost humourously audible. Not a one withered in her presence, though. Quite the contrary. No one melted either, except perhaps figuratively. (Fortunately for the non-casualty count, none of Tantal Thanatos's icemen were around.)

Harmony had always had that effect on people, and not just people. If her father was thought of as Thrygragos Everyman because everyone who beheld him when he wasn't wearing a disguise somehow perceived him as his, hers or its idea of Godhood, then Harmony was everyone's ideal of feminine loveliness. Seems, despite her atypically grim demeanour, Freespirit Nihila had much the same effect when not acting ferociously.

For his part, Tethys scratched his sandpaper beard and changed his mind about buggering off. She'd only just find him again and, what the hell, she'd been lost for half a millennium. It wouldn't wreck his day to be sociable. Even though he'd known since Devauray where she'd been all that time and why – his daughters from a previous lifetime, Katatribe and Yomikune, had been part of Mikoto's band in the Crystal Mountains – there was bound to be a story or ten here somewhere.

Besides, his cup of Cathy was still warm and he hated being wasteful.

"You left me in something of a lurch, Jordy," she told him, taking a seat across the table unbidden.

"A lowly deviant leaving the first Master Deva ever born in a lurch? Pull the other one, Harmonia, or Nemesis, or Freespirit Nihila, or whatever you're calling yourself this morning. Seems to me you were well on your way to becoming Trigregos Demeter by the time I drew myself and Saladin to safety. You did tell me to keep an eye on him; something about Sal being the last surviving Sed-son on the Inner Earth."

"I meant pinned to Vetala's Brainrock throne by the Susasword that night."

"That night I was having a fay-fairly-fine old time in the sack with a Lovely Outer Earth Lady up in Cabalarkon. Next time I saw you, albeit not in the flesh, you were in Lady Achigan's flesh. Except, you'd made her impossibly huge for some reason. What was up – and I do mean up – with that, by the way? You weren't doing much besides towering above everyone looking superior."

"Bombs were falling but they weren't landing, not on Dustmound. Or did you think that was Fish's doing?"

"Not really. So what can I do for you today? And don't ask me to draw the terrible talismans. Every time I do that my splotch pad goes up in flames. So does whoever has them. Which smarts like a dropkick dickens if you're not a Master Deva or, apparently, her soldier. Besides again, I saw what happened to them."

"You did? What?"

"Just before you showed up inside of Fish, another of my drinking buds from a few lives back, the big faerie fuck who nowadays hangs out with D-Brig, blasted them out of existence; the Trigregos Talismans, not the supras. Rather, his Homeworld Sceptre blasted them all the way to Sedon's Peak, whereupon they must have melted out of existence. Endgame them, at long last."

"Seriously? That's what I was going to do with the cursed things. How did he know that's the only way to destroy them, to destroy any power focus?"

"He didn't. And it isn't. One of those D-Brig types I told you about actually ingests Brainrock, even in the form of Tvasitar trinkets from what I've heard. And it was Kronokronos Akbarartha's Homeworld Sceptre that did the knowing. It's special. Carved from the Garden of Eden's Tree of Knowledge."

"You're joking. There's no such thing; never was."

"Dust to dust, fire to fire, then. Only common sense. I told you it was smart. So was your brother, Tariqartha. He replicated the Garden of Eden as it was supposed to be in one of his caverns and then fashioned Akbar's Homeworld Sceptre out of the copycat Tree of Knowledge he grew there."

"He replicated Adam and Eve in Temporis."

"The very same; the original pair. Not Alorus Ptah and Trishtar Thrae, they're the second set."

"I know. I met them. Fact is I possessed her near the end of her life for a while; dad did too, possessed him, for a lot longer while. They were the Dual Entities."

"In his 61st lifetime, I heard that too. From Granddad. Was their son, Anti-Patriarch Cain, really Heliosophos in his 1st lifetime?"

"Not hers, that I can tell you. Cain's mother was the Demon Queen, Primeval Lilith. Correction, not hers unless she was possessing Lilith, which I suppose she could have been. It's the daemons that humanize her, not the devils. Be that as it may, in a fit of jealous rage Machine-Memory built the male and female sphinxes to contain her and Daemonicus, her Demon King, the one before Granddad took his place after Ragnarok a couple of hundred years before the Genesea."

"That'd be your half Great-Grandfather – on both sides of the bed – if you really aren't Brother Rumour. Him up there," she gestured.

"I know who you mean." At the merest mention of the Moloch Sedon the scar tissue in the middle of Tethys's forehead began almightily itching. Scratching it, he reflexively signalled for a pilsner. For him there was no such thing as *the hair of the dog that bit you*. For him also it was never too early to start biting back.

"We've met. He eye-fried me into another life once; thought I was bagging Pyrame Silverstar's shell when it was his turn."

"I remember that. You were. The Death's Head Hellion."

"Master Morgan Abyss, yep, but I was only in her bed when he walked in. She was outside having a swim, I think. Whatever. He didn't have to roast me. I'd have moved." (Truth was that Morg, unless it was Lilith inside her, knew he was coming and laid a trap for him. It was Mithramas, after all. And he always visited his thought-father, Cabalarkon the Undying Utopian, on Mithramas Day; still did.)

"Killing you doesn't warrant ill-starring. And you can't cathonitize Grandfather Sedon. Even he can't cathonitized himself. He is Cathonia."

"Even so, no matter how many times, or how many ways it happens, getting killed always hurts. 'Must have hurt her, too, and she doesn't come back. She may well have been Fish's ancestor but Fish isn't her mindful reincarnation, not like I am of all my previous selves. Yet you killed her – that Morg, not Fish – in one of your, um, transitory conditions and got away with it."

"Like Nihila."

"You said it, not me. Didn't you – killed her, not Sedon?"

"Killing equals in self-defence is no capital crime, especially when they're full of Lethal Lily. Or didn't you know that?"

Tethys let that slide with a noncommittal grunt. He was sort of friends with Pyrame Silverstar, another who hadn't been in the night's sky since the Thirtieth, and she always insisted she hadn't acquired Primeval Lilith during the many centuries of her pre-Flood incarceration within Future All, then Ginny the Gynosphinx.

If she never had Lilith in the first place, how could Master Morgan have kept her when she duped the Pauper Priestess into a ringot that long gone Mithramas Week of 4825 YD? He never pressed perhaps pal Pyrame on that, so why start with Nihila Nastiness, particularly when she was being so nice?

In both cases it was that obvious. That obvious, just as much so, that Sedon sought out Pyrame in order to half-father his Sed-sons on her, her shells, because she had hold of the evidently indestructible Demon Queen. (He was skyborn; she was earthborn. 4,000 years of accumulated evidence confirmed that the results of their unions, their Sed-sons – so long as one was alive on either of the Head at all times – did somehow or other mystically maintain the Cathonic Zone.)

"So," he asked, dismissing that line of inquiry as futile, "How about I verbally step back a few paces and start again? Anything in particular I can do for you this fine wintry morning in the land of everlasting rainfall? So long as it isn't helping you try for Great Godly Goddess Hood again, that is?"

"Like I told Fish, I'm over that." Nihila grew briefly silent, as if formulating an appropriate response. "What I'm not over is what's become of me. I'm a mite lost, sooth said. You called me Harmonia, Illuminaries of yore named me Datong Harmonia, both of which mean the same thing: Harmony, me. Winged Booties, your flapper-footed former sister, also called me Balance, as in the Unity thereof. But what is there to balance if Lord Order isn't back as well?"

"And Abaddon."

"Angelus told me what became of him too, after he catasterized Yajur. Am I to leave him in charge of the mess the Headworld's become in my absence?"

"He isn't; at least not in the way you're thinking. Chaos may reign but that's just a figure of speech; that's not him. He's in the Land of Nothingness — after your time; way, way after your time. Think of a dimensional rift letting an Anti-Matter Universe leak into this one without actually vapourizing anything and you wouldn't be far wrong. Best leave sleeping dogs lie is my best advice to you."

"And their hair biting you?" she asked, as the waitress brought him his first mug of frothy suds for the day. Like just about everyone else in the Danq was still doing, howsoever obsequiously – and had been since her arrival – the waitress openly gawked at his tablemate.

"Smile," he said to her. She did; had nice teeth. He told her as much, then added, "Nice normal teeth; not long nor sharp at all. Thanks. Want anything?" he asked Nihila. She shook her head querulously. "Had an infestation of bad battiness here last week. Your dangerous daughter's doing; may she rest in dust to the wind."

"Oh." (Harmony was Second Fangs, Janna Somata's devic half-mother.)

"Sorry, what was that again?" he refocused on the immediate. She repeated her observation. "That's not the figure of speech I was referring to."

"No, but it was the one you were thinking about a few minutes ago."

"Doggone it, Nihila. It's impolite to read minds. Harmony never did. Or, if she did, she'd never tell you she had."

"That's my point. Even if I wanted to go back to the way I was before – back to my birthright, in other words – I couldn't. I'm supposed to stand between my brood brothers; supposed to balance them off each other, Chaos and Order. Yet you say the big thrice-cussed brute who laid me out all those centuries ago is in a different universe. Plus, you're dodging the whole Yajur issue. Can you or can you not help me find him?"

"I can draw him as I remember him, sure, but I don't see why I should. Don't see why you'd want me to either, quite frankly."

"As a favour."

"I drew Chaos as a, shall we say, forced favour for Janna Fangfingers last week and look what became of her. I told her then what I'm telling you now. Leave him where he is. Which isn't another universe as something like another universe. The Land of Nothingness is on the Cattail, his long time sphere of influence from your latest last time, when Thrygragos Lazareme didn't want your brothers and sisters to have their own protectorates.

"I guarantee that wouldn't continue if Order's back in the picture. Uncle Abe would find out about it somehow and, suicide or not, they hate each other. Goes with the territory; their born-to attributes, if you prefer. After whatever talismanic madness possessed Chaos to get rid of you all those centuries ago, they ruined three-quarters of the Headworld in a three-year, single-minded effort to expunge each other.

"They, not Vetala, nor anyone else, not even you by your absence, were the direct cause of All Death Day, when there were more Dead Things Walking than Living Folks Breathing. So no, I kind of like the way things are right now. Maybe you should go have a nap. Make it a long one, okay. Another five hundred years sounds about right."

"I don't appreciate your attitude, Author. Last Devauray this world lost its reigning Thrygragos, Great Byron. You'd think Father would jump at the opportunity to take his place but, no, he seems even more unwilling to do that than he was when Mithras got himself stoned then chipped unto keepsakes on Thrygragon, his own damn birthday. He is still out of existence, isn't he?"

"Unless you count his head. I heard Granddad smashed it up and has been using it as a pillow since Thrygragon; hence where the name Undying One came about for Tympani."

"Be that as it may," she said, not denying it, "Back then it fell to Order, Chaos and I to keep things humming along in dad's stead. Now it seems he's gone on an indefinite vacation; no forwarding address, as you modern types put it. Or is he in one of the back caves with some trick of a treat indulging his human side?"

"Couldn't say. He wasn't here last night. Neither was Holy Hetaera. Not that I noticed anyhow – Granddad, not your sister – and we're drinking buddies. He'd have at least said hello." (There were those who claimed the Whore of Babylon was the lowborn Lazaremist Illuminaries named after the singular of *'hetaerae'*. They were Ancient Greek courtesans, not the Mithradite highborn Beguiling Belialma,

Lady Lust, whom the Libertine claimed was second only to Jordy's tablemate in terms of treats for trysts.)

"But you are saying I should try to carry on without my immediate brothers."

"You've declared yourself a free spirit, Nihila," he confirmed. "Why don't you act like one. It could be the smartest thing you ever did."

"You'll pardon me for ignoring the advice of a guy I used to call 30-Beers."

"Guy?"

"Gal, too. Throw in the towel, Tethys. Do as I say."

"Old buggery," he muttered, almost in resignation. "I never could say no to Harmony and even if I now know I should have said no to you on Sedonda, when you put it like that, how can I say no now?" He flipped a page and quickly drew a sketch of Yajur as he remembered him from five hundred years and howsoever many lifetimes ago. "Don't say I didn't warn you."

The page blackened, obscuring the image almost immediately. "That's about as clear as mud manifest," she upbraided him.. "You better not be doing that."

"Hmm," he reflected, more in concordance than denial. "If you can find Order in all that, you've got better eyes than me. Which of course you do, three of them. Except he's supposed to be the Thunder and Lightning Lord. He's supposed to be bright; like a star in sky, not like some whizzbang Brainiac in the head, on the Head. That's why everybody called him Sparky, albeit never to his face."

"Angelus told me about the brilliant battle in the Sedon Sphere last week," she considered. "I got the sense it came close to making night time daytime."

"Hey, aren't I supposed to be the taleteller?"

"Draw dad then. My dad, if you persist in pretending you aren't the Rumour who cut out his third eye in hopes of getting away from Phantast Thanatos."

"I'm not. Plus, I'm sick and heartily bagged of hearing that from folks who should know better; not to mention folks I used to like. Rumour's my half-dad; your brood-lower sister Metisophia, Titanic Metis, Wisdom of Lazareme, is my half-mom; hence my exceptionally with-it deviancy. So stop with the innuendos. And, no, I didn't muddy him up deliberately. Shit happens."

"My dad, Jordy."

"Just like that? Mind explaining how I'm going to draw someone who looks like God to everyone that, you know, *'beholds'* him, including me?"

"Then it's hopeless."

"Never say never, Nihila," he alliterated, which he sometimes did even when he wasn't in fairyland, let alone when he was speaking to one or the other of the faerie tricksters, Young Life or Young Death. "I've just had a thought. Didn't ask for it either," he added, sounding somewhat puzzled this time.

"About time someone besides me did. What is it?"

"There's a reason I called you Harmonia. Think back, Balance, to what you used to tell me about your rivalry with Divine Coueranna, Kore of the Many Names, and Miss Myth, Methandra Thanatos, Mediterranean Athena or Cretan Athana, on the Outer Earth. Think back thirty-five hundred years to how your so-called Goddess Culture ended out there."

"The Atomic Triplet Novadev got drunk; blew the heart of Strongyne into the stratosphere. Its fallout, that of the Island of Strong Woman, ended the Golden Age of Minoan Crete and, unless you've changed your theory in the last five hundred years, simultaneously instigated the Twelve Plagues of Biblical Egypt."

"Ten."

"Ten, then. You aren't just Author; you're the Legendarian. What of it?"

"Got drunk with?" he goaded her.

"My husband, King Cadmus of Thebes."

He sketched Cadmus, Phoenician Prince, bringer of the phonetic alphabet to Europe, brother of Europa, who gave it its name, founder of Grecian Thebes, leader of the mythological Spartae or Dragon's Teeth, destroyer of Strongyne. He didn't have to have known him; would have had to claim he didn't because, to admit otherwise, would all but confirm he was once Rumour of Lazareme — and devils couldn't lie.

No, he didn't have to have known him because King Cadmus of Thebes was the Male Entity in his 2nd lifetime. And this time, as the background filled in by itself, it didn't black out. Which ordinarily meant … Wait a minute! First it showed where he was at that minute, eating brunch with a number of others, then it panned back as if on a camera dolly to the hall they were in, then out further to outside the building itself, and finally to where it was situated.

"Cadmus is on the Moon!"

Even though she had only been a spirit being in those days, she recognized it at once. After the travails of the Celestial Sphere, it was there the Sedonshem finally settled; there where their not-as-yet regally daemonic All-Father – he who composed said Sedonshem – recuperated for many years thereafter. (Until 669 Pre-Dome, to be precise, when he brought it down on top of Droch Nor, the Sixth Patriarch of Golden Age Humankind and therefore the Biblical Enoch, in Kanin City.)

While he did so, recuperated on the Moon, he sent Thrygragos Lazareme and his expeditionary force downstairs to explore the planet below. They were nameless then but their number included her, her immediate brothers (the eventual Unities of Chaos, Unholy Abaddon, and Order, Thunder and Lightning Lord Yajur) and Pyrame Silverstar, among many another Master Deva.

"That's impossible," he said. "Look what just happened to my drawing of Sparky Sibling. I can no more draw anyone on the Outer Earth than I can anyone between-space or in an area shielded by Stopstone. Not if I want the background to fill in, which it just did. I do, it's just from memory; just an ordinary drawing."

"Your turn."

"Huh?"

"Not that, what you said. Repeat it: *I do draw him, it's just from memory.* Capitalize Memory."

"She can't do that." Until then he'd been sipping his pilsner. Now he threw back what was left of it in two great gulps.

"Don't sound so befuddled. What just happened is hardly beyond your ken. Nor your kin. Master Devas can; so can our fathers. Devils humanize the Mnemosyne Machine. She's got one; she can do whatever they can. And I should know. I've had her more often than even your pal Pyrame. Hell's Temple, I'm more her than Memory is herself."

"From the Moon?"

"Look, in this case I'm betting looks aren't deceiving because, as sure as you're about to order another beer, it looks like she just did. Ergo, she wants me to find her. It's a bit of a leap, ha, ha, but I might be able to travel up there through the Weird from the other side. The real question is how am I going to get outside?

"Kore of the Many Names collapsed her volcano after the Horrites discovered its link from Strongyne to the Head. Rather, once we realized Cadmus was the Male Entity, we did it for her. We did a ditto for those Tholoi Beehive Guest Houses I used to use to traverse it after we found out I was bringing in Outer Earth diseases whenever I came back. And I'm not going to waste years trying to track down the SAG Gap if it's wandering again."

"Not to mention trying try to swim to it if it isn't. Not like Strife did, in order to escape the Moloch Sedon cathonitizing her."

"Or try to go through All, not in this condition. She might eat me."

"I doubt that. Still, perhaps I can be of some service after all."

"How?"

"Outside of the Cheeklands some things do change on the Head."

He drew Alpha Centauri's towering domicile overlooking the Gulf of Aka. He thereupon drew himself and Nowadays Nihila in its outdoor, Georgian garden. Which, like a long gone Holy Roman Emperor's folly in today's Nuremberg, were intentionally reminiscent of Nebuchadnezzar's Hanging Gardens of Babylon.

Except, Centauri's weren't built on a lofty hill not far from where Albrecht Durer lived in the late Fifteenth Century out there. (Tethys and Harmony had both been to the German garden. Indeed, when Tethys was '*Q for Squiggly*', Janna's pre-Fangfingers paramour, he and her twin, Sraddha Somata, took the boy Dire back there, along with his dog Drang, such that he could grow to adulthood and became Tethys's favourite artist besides himself. He did so on Sraddha's half-mom Harmony's instructions.)

He looked at her meaningfully. To his delight the honey-brown stunner clearly remembered what he could do given her permission. She nodded acquiescence; smiled as she did so. Even after all she'd been through, it seemed to him that not even the Sun itself was more luminous than her face when she smiled.

With a flourish he signed and dotted his name to the drawing. Consequently drew themselves to Centauri's sky-high Babylon.

========

"An indefinite vacation … No forwarding address … So can our fathers …"
Some things bore repeating.

****

Nineteenth Moon: **All Hell Comes Calling**

========

Wednesday/Birhym, December/Tantalar 10, 1980/5980

Ginny the Gynosphinx didn't call herself that anymore. Never had. That was just the Dual Entities being cute. She did sometimes sport Memory's face, however.
Especially when she went on the prowl.

========

Birhym (Wednesday) morning, Pandora *'Hush'* Mannering was finishing her yoghurt and granola breakfast in the rooftop solarium atop the Fatman's (not to be confused with His Enormity's) well-fortified Aka Godbad stronghold. It was on the sleeping side of Centauri Enterprises' unofficial headquarters in the still a-building city. The *'interior'* ingress-egress to the now sealed shut Nag Gap was nearby.

Much closer were those sharing more than just a meal with her: the real Alpha Centauri (who shouldn't be confused with Alfredo Sentalli because they were one and the same), Connie Lindquist, George Hannibal and Yataghan Sentalli. Having come back from Hadd the day before, Yat's wife, Janna nee St Peche now Montressor – the surname hubby used on the Inner Earth instead of Sentalli or Centauri – was there, too.

They had already traded news — the Fatman being particularly pleased with how things were turning out over in Hadd and exuding a confidence bordering on certainty that Cromwell Necator had been successful on his mission to Incain. They also exchanged views on whether the Nag Gap should remain closed; whether, in fact, they had any future out there. In that regard, the consensus was they did.

After all, no one really knew if Big Shelter existed; not for sure. There was no ocular proof to shake a spear at, said Hush, sort of quoting Shakespeare.

What insiders were still outside – the Valhallans who'd sabotaged the Houston Academy of Man last Friday morning; the Infernal Twins (Balkis and Solomon evidently Mandam), Aranyani Nightingale, Ramona Avar and Magnifico (Saul *'Don't Call Me Psycho'* Ryne), who must have read a few of their minds by now – would likely continue to keep the Head's existence to themselves.

When it came down to it, with the exception of the onetime Magnificent Psycho, why wouldn't they? It was part of their conditioning. And, if both son Cromwell and father Godfrey Necator's albinos could come and go via the submarine pen with impunity – God in '65, earlier as well as later; Crom, most recently, last week – surely they could come up with some reasonable explanation as to where they'd gone yesterday.

Antheans, as Hush was and Connie had ambitions to become, if she ever had a daughter – right now she was only an Althean, named after Lazareme's female healer, Amal-Althea – were notoriously resourceful. Cleverness, trickiness more like, was an Ant trait. Lying wasn't but, hey, Hush would say, it isn't a lie if you believe it's the truth and creating self-delusions weren't just an Ant speciality.

Devils, who supposedly couldn't knowingly lie, were masters at constructing elaborate, alternate histories, particularly if it cast them in a better light. As Jordan Tethys was among the many who suspected it, a case in point was the Pauper Priestess, Pyrame Silverstar, vis-à-vis Primeval Lilith.

It was indeed her, Lily – not her, Pyrame, her witting holder, with very few exceptions, until 5950 – that the Moloch Sedon really needed to father Sed-sons (such as Saladin born Nauroz in here and Sedon St Synne out there) in order to maintain the Sedon Sphere, the Cathonic Zone separating the Inner from the Outer Earth for nearly six millennia. (When Mother Earth makes deals, Mother Earth keeps deals.)

Their conversation inevitably returned to Crystallion, Hell's Horsemen and their nuclear dragons. (They had no way of knowing that these last were a pretty good reason why they shouldn't be overly worried about Aranyani, the real Ramona – not the Callion Clone recovering in Houston – and Psycho telling anyone about the Hidden Continent of Sedon's Head. Atomic firedrakes fed on destruction, including helicopters seeking to flee WORLD's converted fish packer the previous Thursday.)

To no one's amazement, Hush figured she had her own version of a reasonable explanation for them. And maybe she did. Equally so, as was well-known to those there, she liked to hear herself talk. Presumably in order to illustrate whatever she was about to begin pontificating on, she reached into her bottomless beach bag and brought out what appeared to be a toy facsimile of one of the creatures.

"No toy this," she asserted. "This is the one Crystal rode and abandoned over there. I grabbed it from the tarmac before I came across the last time."

"Come again?" disbelieved Centauri.

"It's mostly made of Solidium, what's usually called Stopstone in here. Daddy Yati could tell you all about it if I felt like letting him loose. Which I don't, due to strongly held personal objections to being eaten alive. So you'll just have to believe me when I tell you it's a substance counter-indicative to Gypsium, yet of a just as much so unknowable constitution; non Fourth of July variety.

"Crystal must have been a supra as much as she was a freak. Her abilities, at least those of her drakes and horsemen, were somewhat reminiscent of the old-time supra Emperor Energy. She generated her own innate energy and funnelled it into these things, made them huge; trained or more likely had made Hell's Horsemen to ride them.

"None of them survived, I'm afraid – the dragon riders, I mean – but I bet you a brick shithouse in Shenon I'm right about that. They were mandroids, like the crew of the Phantom Freighter undoubtedly were. If you're interested, I think I can see how it all came about."

"Goes back to Jesus Mandam, the King Conqueror," guessed the Fatman. "Everything else seems to."

"Goes back even further than that, I figure," ventured the perennial child. "Certainly to the Summoning of 19/5920 that my maybe mother, Celeste Mannering, the Celestial Superior, called. And remember that all of the Conqueror's technology was lifted from the ruins of Weirdoms dotted throughout the Head. Recall also Steltsar was a leftover of the old Baron von Alptraum, the Nazi Nightmare.

"I stayed with him in the late Thirties at Castle Nightmare. Actually, I more like stayed with his mother-in-law, Hulga Faust always Volsung, and Two's template, Moe One. That's because he was as often as not in Hamburg being a ha, ha, hot shot in the aerostatic engineering and manufacturing business; dirigibles and such like.

"A few years later, during the Outer Earth's Second World War, he and the second Moses Callion routinely whipped up unthinkable monstrosities like this little feller here. Long before his first and what should have been only death, Tyrtod claimed it was something he learned when he, along with many other Godlings, most of whom were his elders, was lost in the Himalayas sixty odd years ago now.

"Then there were the Orientals. I'm thinking specifically of Ching Li, the Manchurian Mandrake, although he was just the last of them. Perhaps because their civilization is so ancient – Stopstone accrues in manmade objects – oriental supras were good with Solidium."

"I remember you saying way back in the Godbadian Civil War," said Centauri, "That the Steltsar we were dealing with then wasn't so much an altered von Alptraum as a mantel-replica from Temporis freed by the Conqueror. Replicates, tellurian mantels, are all mandroids, which is to say they're composed of Stopstone, correct? The Gypsium Curtain interacted with the Solidium in these things. Cancelled each other out."

"Disintegrated each other, more like," said Hush. "I can just see god-awful Daddy Abe or doting Daddy Dolph Dulles, who's getting up there in terms of Amoebaman abilities, wondering if the dragons the Water Witch didn't take care of would suddenly pop back out of Shadowland and finish what they started." Got glared at for that.

"It won't happen," she assured them, in response to their unspoken shock. "When you think about it, given what they've become, it's a tremendous irony that Big Max Maxwell and Rom Kinesis are such good friends. As they almost found out a week ago last Sunday, had Kinesis continued to bombard Mr No Name with Gyps he'd have wiped him out. Mind you, if No Name had the sense, he'd have continued to draw Solidium into himself and eventually snuff Doc Defiance, as Kinesis fancies himself nowadays."

"I don't have your encyclopaedic knowledge of supras," acknowledged the Fatman, who no more used Sentalli when he was on the Inner Earth than he did Centauri on the Outer Earth. "But didn't the same hold true for Rom's parents? Pluman's abilities were based on Solidium whereas Slipper's were based on Gypsium."

"Holds true for Master Devas and mandroids too, Daddy Do Right Sometimes. Given enough Stopstone, tellurians can encase devils, imprison them on the spot. Which makes Dand Tariqartha even more remarkable. Whatever else they call him, he's Lazareme's Earth Magician – Persian, to use the Mithraic term. That makes him probably the only devil left who can control the stuff."

"So what are the chances either Sea or Crystal came through it in one piece?"

Hush had to think about that. "Reputedly, in 1943, Thalassa D'Angelo was caught up in the North African campaign. A couple of the Axis supras the Desert

Fox, Field Marshal Ervin Rommel – himself an old Godling – was working with then were Wolfgang Shekmet and Seth Kephren."

"The first Mammalian and the Sphinx," remembered Centauri, from much more recent, not to mention personally verifiable history.

"Whatever," granted the little girl. "As you might assume, the desert's not the best place for an essentially aquatic animal like Sea Goddess. Apparently she turned to water one day and, if you can believe it – we're talking supras here, so you should – actually evaporated." Somewhat involuntarily she started giggling. Centauri, more so than the others in the room, anticipated she was about to make one of her notoriously corny jokes.

"Enter Dolores Rivera, Superior Sorrow. By the way, because both Thalassa and Aires bore a distinctly D'Angelo family look, I've often thought she was the twins' mother. Conceivably," she chortled – that was the joke, the Fatman feared, though he did not think it particularly witty: "She was impregnated by either Abe Ryne or his father, Charan, during the Summoning, because they almost always had twins. So did Mary Magdalene, namely Barsine and Jesse."

(The patriarch's sole exception on record was Aranyani always Nightingale eventually Maxwell. And she didn't have twins either.)

"Also just by the way, after talking to Sea. I've revised my opinion of her and her twin. Now I don't think they're two-eyed devils. I think they were either Sorrow's kids, whom she kept hidden for her own reasons, or they actually were street waifs. What happened is they found the Thanatoid children's power focuses, the Aqua Ankh and the Aerod, and that's how they got their powers.

"I figure the same thing happened with Gloriella D'Angelo. Only she didn't find Castella's hair; she was either born with it or, more likely, acquired it when she was exposed to her grandfather's devil-ray back in '43. But that's neither here nor there any more, is it?" She finally returned to her narrative.

"In any case, Sorrow went to the same place Sea vanished with a tanker truckload of seawater. Lo and behold, who do you think reformed but Thalassa. So, yes, I think there's a good chance she came through just fine. Afraid I can't say the same about Crystal St Synne, though."

"Why not? Steltsar always has. AMERICA even had his body in 1970, according to Big Max."

"There's something nearly unique about him. Like Strife, he may be a spirit being or, like devils have been known to do, he could have found a way to externalize not so much his soul but his mind. Crystal's a different kettle of conundrums. I mean, sure, she's a daughter of Sedon St Synne and probably was born with a caul covering her face, just like Strife supposedly has to this day, but that doesn't make her a spirit.

"Sure as well, superstition says cauls protect folks from drowning, so that might help her against Sea Stuff. Then again, they're also supposed to bring good luck — and Crystal's never had an ounce of that in her life. Besides, that's just it. She is – or was – altogether alive. If she blew up, that'd be it for her.

"Another thing about her, if she's anything like Pluman and sucks in Solidium, caul or no caul, she'd be helpless in the middle of the ocean. Which is where

Thalassa would have taken her. No, I'd say Crystallion has breathed her last. Probably for the best, too. She was a tormented little horror.

"And don't any of you say I'm the same. I'm nowhere near as fucked up. I don't kill people for one thing, not even myself. Never have."

The reference was to Hush's Gush, Young Death to her Young Life. Janna St Peche-Montressor left him still arguing with Thartarre about whether to shovel Al Molorchus's corpse into the monastery's crematorium. For Janna, in a week and a half filled with too-often-unaccountable tensions – starting with the as yet unexplained rat attack on Lazam the 28th – it was one too many for her to handle.

Understandably, Moirnoir was arguing with one one-armed man on behalf of another one-armed man from inside Molorchus himself.

"But you think," Centauri said, "If I'm reading you right, that Steltsar will have survived. That my homo, God rest whatever soul he may have had, didn't abolish him."

"Highly unlikely, especially since your island is largely manmade. You won't remember but, back in '65, when we thought we'd dealt with Strife and Daemonicus – them for hardly the first time, I should add – Pluman presumably finished off Steltsar just before he had his heart attack and died. I think Steltsar not only survived then, too, but likely was the one who released the two possessive beings from the agates or ringots we dumped in Mt Kinesis.

"I guess it goes without saying they're still around as well, though we shouldn't have to worry about them in here. My take on Strife is that she'd be cathonitized the moment Dark Sedon became aware she'd come through the Cathonic Dome. Same goes for Daemonicus, though I still can't figure out how he came into existence in the first place. It'd be real scary if I can make my worst imaginings real, wouldn't it?"

"All in all then, an extremely unsatisfactory end to a piss-poor ten days."

"Who said anything about it being over?"

"The last week and a half's all I meant."

Someone rapped on the transparent glass wall to the outdoors; made a drinking motion when they all looked. Even though they were at least ten stories up, with no external staircases or ladders anywhere to be seen, no one was surprised to see the male of the two, all the more so given the drinking motion. Even Lindquist and Hannibal knew the legendary 30-Year Man.

Only one there recognized the woman with him. It wasn't Hush; was the actual youngest one there, Janna St Peche-Montressor. Even though she had been in Hadd when Hush captured the Byronics she still showed no signs of releasing on Centauri Island, for Janna it was akin to an internal lightbulb going off; one she didn't realize was even inside her.

It was Hush who sighed, however. Then again, she'd already suspected she hadn't nailed all of APM All-Eyes.

Aphropsyche Morningstar had a knack for scintillating herself.

========

"Ah, Jordan," said the Fatman, once Yataghan let them into the breakfast solar off the rooftop garden. "Have a pill."

He regarded the Legendarian's companion closely for the first time.

========

"And who's your charming-looking friend, pal?" he added, determined not to be cowed by whomever's gloriously gorgeous, 3-eyed presence.

Like Hush, he'd seen the look in Janna's eyes. Only two of them were visible but the third wouldn't be faraway. APM was a third-born Byronic, one who often possessed Janna, at her Thrygragos of a still missing father's insistence. That she'd obviously left a functional piece of herself in Janna while she more wholly occupied Connie on the Outer Earth didn't surprise the Fatman.

What did surprise him – and he'd met her face to kaleidoscope-eyed face on many occasions – was her in effect blowing her cover so blatantly. She was rarely impressed by anyone; other than her father and she herself, that is. Yet, to judge from her face, this was someone super-special. Had to be one of the true biggies.

He was pretty sure he'd figured out who it was, too. This wasn't just a biggie. In terms of Master Biggies, this was the first.

"Here I thought devils made your scar tissue itch," he put to his grizzled, beer-smelly friend, who did indeed have a scar in the centre of his forehead, about where a devil would have a third eye. "So what are you doing hanging out with one? Especially one with glowing chains? Never pictured you into bondage."

"Hoping you could cure me of that, Al," said Tethys, grabbing a beer out of the ever-present cooler beside the Fatman's wheelchair. "Or you, Young Life."

"We haven't time for this, Author," warned Nihila, eye-balling those around her not so much nervously as warily.

Even if there wasn't much more than a flake of her inside the one she remembered from Dustmound, she sensed APM's presence – they were familiar with each other since pretty much forever. The others all had devic residues about them, too. Most were Byronic; the obesity in the wheelchair, who seemed to run the place, reeked of Bodiless Byron himself.

As for the little girl ... could it be? Had to be. Fitna Marutia (myrionymous Strife) had been inside her not all that long ago.

"Oh, well," this one muttered, very much nervously.

(Hush had already guessed her identity. Wasn't much of a guess, sooth said. Brainrock necklace, glowing chains, body beautiful, everything about her beautiful, including the unmistakable, if muted, rage she couldn't help but exude: Who else could it be?)

"Without their father or his Nucleoids around to help me, I doubt Trala-lorn would convince easily to return me to my rightful age anyhow." Most witches were materialists, as in make-ether-real. No witch, ever, could materialize whom she could. "Besides, there's never a dull day when you're seven instead of seventy-seven; not even when you've been seven for sixty years."

Young Life produced a batch of eyeorbs out of her bottomless beach bag. A dozen other Byron Spawn – the next-door-to-fullness of Aphropsyche Morning-star, her third-born brood brother Damon Goldenrod, heroic Hektoris Headcase, cow-faced Vach-Hathor, the bowman Djerrid Ruin, the temptress pretty Parsis, elephantine Ganesh, Monk-eye (Tau Hanuman, he of the Bazooka Banana power focus), All-Merciful Kannon, Scorpio Hala Sadrapa, Petrogod and Kunta-Kintu Mawulisa – immediately surrounded Nihila.

Even Yati, the Dragon of Byron, but for his third eye still appearing to be Project Centauri's human overseer, Dr Hiyati Samarand, came out of Samsara. In all likelihood he wouldn't be humanoid for very long. And this dragon, while presumably not nuclear, was no mandroid. He might actually have eaten Hush alive.

"Balance them, babe," challenged the little girl.

Empty eyeorbs begged for refilling. Small as she was they barely amounted to an armful for in here's Young Life. She flipped them in the direction of Freespirit Nihila. They were opening in midair when, with nary a shrug on their target's behalf, miniature jet-streams of Borealis lightning (Northern Lights) immolated them like a disconnected wreath of firecrackers more like fizzling than exploding.

As the smoke rose and the dust settled, the Byronic Master Devas regarded each other as if hoping one of them, Goldenrod perhaps, would signal whether they should fight or flee in fear for their continuing, non-starry persistence. No one did, not definitively, though APM did step backward a few feet. The other twelve immediately followed her lead, none quicker than her brood brother; Byron's Apollo not always being a cocksure ignoramus, as Tethys thought of him.

That left an unimpeded pathway between the onetime Unity, also of Panharmonium, and the Ants' 60th Century cat's-paw, the now tiny trickster who was supposed to give birth to three Great Goddesses 60-odd years earlier. The former glared at the latter. Hush smiled weakly, opened the palm of her hand and let drop an Anthean Agate. It never reached the floor. Went poof before Hush could go ditto.

Escape denied her, she let herself slump in her chair. When faced with the likes of a firstborn – the first born of the firstborn; the first born of the first born Great God – it seemed the sensible thing to do. After all, what would any self-respecting seven year old do at this point except sulk. Too bad the whiff of Strife and her subsequent actions had already alerted Nihila that she was no ordinary child. Still …

"Can Huff have a puff?" she asked, materializing a cigarette.

Nihila lit it for her. Rather, she extended one of her chains and its end lit it for her.

"Oh, good, a party," chortled Centauri. "I trust devils drink beer."

========

Jordan Tethys certainly did.

Which was one reason some called him 30-Beers. Most of the reason for that, though, was because he was also known as the Thirty-Year Man due to a *'faerie curse'* that had been afflicting him for something like two thousand years. That's how long he lived, at the max, again and again and …

Even though he strenuously denied it, most believed he was once a devil; a very specific devil, Rumour of Lazareme. (Not to imply that either Thrygragos Byron or Thrygragos Varuna Mithras had a Rumour to call their own. They didn't.) The real Rumour, Jordy's half-father in his account of his history, hadn't been seen since circa 4000 YD (Year Zero AD).

According to the once-a-devil version of his origin, Rumour was driven mad by Phantast Thanatos (the dream-weaving brood-brother of the Thanatoids of Lathakra) and cut out his third eye; hence the Legendarian's scar tissue. According to Tethys's account, shortly after his first birth faeries stole him out of his crib, leaving a glamorized log in his stead. Devic daddy Rumour promptly went after him, where-upon his fay kidnappers consumed him completely.

It took Baby Tethys twenty years to find his way out of the faerie mound or knoll (as correctly called a *'knowe', 'sidhe'* or *'shee',* among many another term, and not just on the Inner Earth). In part because he used, and thereafter kept, Rumour's power focus or Tvasitar talisman, a Brainrock quill, to facilitate his getaway, he managed to avoid recapture for fully thirty years, to the day, of his initial escape.

Relentless faerie trackers finally hunted him down, again. This time they got hold of Rumour's quill before he could use it to draw himself elsewhere. Defiant to the end, he reputedly willed himself dead rather than allow himself to be forcibly returned to the knoll.

Remarkably, a few years after this first death he found himself consciously in control of a twenty year old man's body. Thirty years later, again to the day, that man – his own son, no less – died, this time of altogether natural causes. When the pattern was repeated, albeit in his granddaughter, he realized he'd become some sort of supranormal deviant. (The mortal offspring of possessive devils were always called deviants on the Inner Earth.)

He, or she, didn't always last thirty years. In fact, she or he rarely lasted that long. Nor did his or her offspring necessarily die when he passed on after what amounted to a thirty year shared occupation of hers or his body. He or she didn't always come back – take over hers or his latest incarnation – when he or she turned twenty; just never before she or he turned twenty.

Indeed, most of the times he, as he preferred even when he was a she, came back was after an extremely bad, very much life-threatening accident or some other sort of near-death experience on the part of whomever he came back as, besides himself. He did, however, always come back in his offspring or their offspring. And on most of the days he was back, he did guzzle upwards to thirty beers.

The Fatman could care less whether his drinking buddy was originally a devil or a faerie crossover, a daemon or demon even. He did know of his thirty year deviancy, however. Hard not to: Since coming to the Head in 5945, he'd met three Tethyses. While they all shared the same memories and personality, one of those was indeed female, Sister Jordan. (She, as him, hadn't lasted anywhere near thirty years.)

Seeing whoever he was with; seeing the Byronics cower away from her once they realized her identity; seeing how effortlessly she'd ignited Hush's Sarpedon-gen-erated eyeorbs – that wasn't chain or sheet lightning she'd streamed; that was (not that there was much difference) the Northern Lights given irruptive violence; he was frankly worried about this one making it beyond the next few minutes.

In the absence of Thrygragos Byron to protect him, the Fatman wasn't about to make any predictions regarding his own ability to do a ditto.

Then she said: "Sure. I used to own the DDD."

========

Tethys realized he'd taken a chance coming to Alpha Centauri's upper floors suite atop Aka Godbad City's unofficial headquarters of Centauri Enterprises.

The Fatman could have been in a number of places: the Outer Earth's Centauri Island; the Head's privately-owned island of the same name, which lay in the Panic Isles that dribble-drabble-dripped between Krachla and the Subcontinent of Godbad; or CE's official HQ in downtown Godbad City, where he could keep a close eye on Greater Godbad's already winding down military thrust in Hadd.

(Hadd, old Iraxas, was the shaft to Krachla's head of the Penile Peninsula, Sedon's Mutton Chop.)

Regardless of where he was, drawing himself hither hadn't been the chance he'd taken. (Such were his talents that he could have found him wherever, virtually anytime he pleased.) Bringing Nihila (the newly released Nemesis-aspect of Datong Harmonia) with him had been.

Centauri was intimate with Unmoving Byron and his tribe; couldn't help but be since the subcontinent was their collective protectorate whereas the Great God himself oft-times possessed the Fatman. Byronics, Lazaremists and Mithradites weren't always kissing cousins.

Something like eleven hundred years earlier, Harmony and her brood brother, Thunder and Lightning Lord Yajur, fought alongside such highborn Mithradites as Belialma of Satanwyck, Geld Neargon of Androgynia, and Dandset Typhon of Moorset to halt the north-westerly advance of the Empire of Lathakra into the vast plains of Marutia (Sedon's Cheek).

Consequently the Thanatoids and their allies, including hers and Order's brood brother, Unholy Abaddon, the aptly designated Unity of Chaos, opted for the south-to-north route up into the Cheek-lands. That meant they first had to cross the Interior Ocean of Akadan from one peninsula, the Cattail, to the other, the Penile, where Byronics also held sway at the time. Iraxas fell easily and devils had long memories.

"There's no need to be so unfriendly," Tethys calmly told the Byron Spawn. "Nihila's no threat to you."

But someone else was.

========

Sharkczar came out of the hardwood floor and swallowed Samarand whole.

========

"Then there's the Crimefighter clones," The Space-Age Spartan (Gus Soldakis) reminded the Great Man (Loxus Abraham Ryne) not so long ago on the Outer Earth's Centauri Island. "And Steltsar, if that, um, thing didn't nail him." (By thing he meant his Enormity, Sentalli-Centauri's homunculus, homo or homun being.)

"I'm sure we did," Dolph Dulles assured them, as a couple of his more muscular men removed his nominal boss's body.

He was wrong. His Enormity hadn't nailed him – not enough of him at least. Nowadays Sharkczar had gone into the floor of the submarine pen after Shelter and Sharpshooter disposed of his physical, for want of a better word, extrusions. Sensing the walls electrifying, he'd gone up a couple of floors. Awhile later, as he contemplated how to get back at Judge Warlock, System, for setting him up like that, he heard an elevator coming down from somewhere up above.

Connie Lindquist, George Hannibal, and Yataghan Sentalli (as Centauri's son was known on the Outer Earth) stepped off it; made their way to what looked like a blank wall. The female of the three stepped on something and a trans-dimensional tunnel opened out of nowhere. The Nagasaki Gap at last!

They went through it unhindered. But before it closed he was part of the wall. Even later the little witch appeared on the same thing, obviously a stepping stone of some sort. She was dressed for the beach, even carried a beach bag. Out of it she took three agates, laid them on the ground. Three dead bodies formed out of them.

After arranging glamours such that they seemed to be the three who preceded her – the same as three of those with her now in the Fatman's solar – she opened the between-space tunnel or tube again. This time he followed her through it to the Hidden Continent of Sedon's Head.

He'd been with her ever since — as part of her left sandal.

========

The hammerhead distorted grotesquely, became akin to a human-sized, though no longer humanoid technopomp akin to one of Hell's Horses. Yati, the Dragon of Byron, must have become his totemic self inside the mandroid monstrosity. But was it too late? Could Sharky hold it, Yati, inside its Sharkczar self?

Tethys could care less. He flipped a page, having already prepared the sketch in case the first one he'd done drew a blank, and flourished his quill. "With your permission …"

Nihila and the Fatman nodded, the latter frantically, all but begging for Jordy-style deliverance. Before Hush could shout *'Hey, what about me?'*, he signed and dotted his name, thereby transporting the three of them between-space to the Fatman's office-conservatory even further up and on the business side of Centauri Enterprises' local headquarters.

"What was that?" demanded the Unity.

"An old nightmare," Tethys answered. "Nothing to concern yourself with."

"And what's she?" After the Legendarian introduced her as Nihila once Datong Harmonia, the Unity of Balance, Centauri wiped his brow and acknowledged he'd heard of her. "Matter of fact, Jordy was telling me about you only the day before the launching of the Cosmic Express. So how come you're still alive?"

"Hardly the most relevant issue right now, Al," Tethys told him. "Think the Byronics can handle the mandroid?"

"A dozen against one? Yati will have probably turned him inside out and swallowed him by now. Still, I owe you a debt of gratitude for getting me out of there. Hope Hush and my son, not to mention Connie and George, don't get damaged in the crossfire. Janna can look after herself. Either that or APM can look after them both. Anything I can do for you, besides offering you another beer, that is."

"Depends. Sure you still want to go the Moon, Balance?"

"Stick with Nihila, Jordy. And yes."

"Then maybe you could show us how to access the link you use to get outside."

The Fatman hesitated. And not just because he'd didn't like her new name. Nihila sounded malicious, wicked-bad. "Wouldn't do you any good. Before she came over Hush destroyed the gateway. She clearly didn't do it in time to stop Steltsar-scum-Sharkczar coming through but I can't reopen it from here."

"If it's intact enough to get me through the Cathonic Dome, I could draw her to the Moon even if I'm still between-space on that side."

"Then I could seal this side, leaving you both stuck betwixt and between. Want to take the chance?"

"You wouldn't do that to an old friend."

"Wouldn't I?"

"I could offer you a one-way trip to, say, Satanwyck or the Forbidden Forest of my old paramour, Kala Tal."

"I'll take her, Daddy Do Dick." Hush Mannering manifested herself on an Afrite Bulb.

"What happened back there?"

"Riddle me this," the female trickster said by way of explanation. "What has the wings of a demon, the head of a Gorgon, the body of a hellcat, and the breasts of a beautiful woman except her milk is bile?" She reckoned casting her answer in the form of a riddle might give it away. She reckoned wrongly. Maybe Harmony, or whatever she was calling herself these days, had never heard of Oedipus Rex.

Which would have been odd given her effective immortality and the mythological fact that Oedipus's mother Jocasta was a direct descendant of King Cadmus of Thebes and her, Datong Harmonia, via Agave, one of their four daughters. Then again so was his father Laius, albeit via their only son, Polydorus.

(Oedipus killed Laius prior to marrying his mother. Betwixt and between times he managed to solve the famous Riddle of the Sphinx, a be-winged, hence female man-eater. Which in turn was why Thebes' regent, none other than his uncle Creon, Jocasta's brother, invited him to marry Jocasta in the first place.)

Nowadays Nihila had seen a grotesquery like that on Thrygragon in 4376 YD. Long before that, in the days when Master Devas could only become whole by amalgamating with each other, her-then-not-yet-named Harmony self had been part of the same creature not once but many times.

"The Unnameable!"

"Close, Balance. Answer's the Gynosphinx. The real one, Ginny, not the one that got blown away on the Outer Earth's Centauri Island fifteen years ago."

"All of Incain," appreciated Tethys.

"Oh her," said Nihila. "She doesn't have a gorgon's face. She has mine."

"Regardless," grinned the apparent little girl. "My guess is All will get a severely serious case of indigestion trying to devour all those Master Devas at once. She'll either blow up or have to go home to settle her stomach. I'm afraid you're going to have call in your architects, though, daddy. Your solarium's a muddle of rubble."

"Yataghan, Janna, Connie, George?"

"I didn't hang around to find out."

"Tell you what, Alpha," offered Tethys. "How about I buy you a beer? At my companion's old establishment no less: the Dinq, Doinq, Danq?" The Fatman shrugged. Tethys took that as a yes and drew them both back to the cavern-tavern on the lower north-easternmost slope of the Diluvia Mountain Range.

As always he was delighted to discover it hadn't collapsed. Yet.

=========

Back in Centauri's office Hush gave Nihila an enquiring look. "Are decathonitized devils still bound by their oaths?"

"I was never cathonitized."

"Can you get to the Moon without Jordy?"

"If you take me beyond Cathonia."

"In that case, there's something you've got to do for me once you get there."

"Name it."

"Master Devas are genetically bred to obey their fathers, right? Well, man-droids are a little like that. And All has a mother."

========

Hush had lied.

As Abe Ryne once told Dolph Dulles, tricksters were prone to doing just that, lying. A lot. All, the self-proclaimed Invincible She-Sphinx of Incain, had indeed come out of the Universal Substance in order to aid Sharkczar. Had devoured the Byronics and destroyed that side of CE's Aka Godbad HQ.

But the She-Sphinx hadn't a bad case of indigestion. She was energized and on the rampage. The bastards who'd bombed her beach had to have come from Godbad; had to have been sent by the felonious Fatman. And she knew where Centauri Enterprises had its actual headquarters.

Then her tummy did start gurgling Farting wasn't an option, especially considering what might come out besides gas.

Whoever had said this wasn't over, not by a long shot, was bang on the button.

****

Twentieth Moon: Talking Headgames

========

Wednesday, December 10, 1980

That night, unless it was that morning, while it was still dark at any rate, and not for the first time since he arrived on New Weirworld, Starrus thought he was dreaming. As he quickly realized – not that he could do anything about it – he wasn't so much dreaming as he was being thoroughly probed.

His life was an open book. It had three readers. Not one of them needed glasses; not even ones with three lenses.

They could close it at any time. Ah, but would they close him at the same time?

========

'I do not approve of relying upon a Visionary, Mind. Not only are they conservative, even for Utopians, they are barely grounded in the present. Have virtually no consideration of the past. How can we trust their direction towards a future commensurate with our best interests? With the Cosmic Dream of Panharmonium?'

'Which is why we have seized upon this opportunity to examine the thumbling, Soul. All the better to judge for ourselves. Is that what I think it is?'

'Indeed, sister. It certainly looks like Trans-Time Trigon. What's he thinking? Did I do that? Dropped the bomb that caused it to vanish twelve years ago as he counts time. Within the realm of possibility. Brainrock, which the Dual Entities are blessed with more so than even us, is still mostly beyond our capacity to comprehend, certainly to its fullest extent. Could it be the Entities were from this tiny planet originally?'

'Even though it sounded like the Earth was but their most frequent stopping point, the Memory Entity never explicitly said otherwise. Then again, as it pains her to admit, she only follows after Wisdom and Trigon; doesn't have any choice in the matter. No destiny of her own. It could therefore be only his starting point.'

'Barbaric, these wars of theirs, the way they so self-righteously slaughter each other. And their weapons. All that brainless use of nuclear power without realizing how safe it can be. Is this what our children have made them to be?'

'That faceless redhead. The one who appears to be running this WORLD Starrus and his AMERICA are fighting against after Trigon. There she is again. Could that be one of ours?'

'He's bounced ahead. This is just recent. Look at that craft. Most impressive. Yes, I too detect loads of Brainrock and this Stopstone stuff the metallurgist talked about at the hearing. Mik Starrus calls them Gypsium and Solidium, but he's not a scientist. He knows virtually nothing about them.'

'That notion of his, that they were two sides of the same thing, Stoprock or Brainstone, the mutable matter of between-space, may not be so farfetched.'

'Another deliberate explosion. These humans certainly enjoy their pyrotechnics. Wait. What's that? A big eye with a mouth in the middle of it. It's sucking in the Cosmic Express. Now it's spitting it out.'

'The man out there, the one Starrus is trying to rescue, look at the image in his mind. That's one of the lesser entities, one of what Wisdom called his Dragon's Teeth, Trigon's Spartae – Chthlonius, wasn't it? Whoops! So much for him. Ah, there's Ambassador Yajur. Manifested himself right out of Starrus and is standing in outer space; on outer space. Missed what he said.'

'Now he's back inside Starrus. And Starrus is back in his dinky craft. Cosmicar. Has a third eye. And that must be his lovely Iraryan wife — Nidaba, right? Looks a little like you, Body.'

'We all look alike, Soul; indistinguishable. Ah, here's where we come in. I'm still not certain we should have sent Yajur back out there. I know we agreed that with all that thunder and lightning at his command, all that rage at what had become of him, he had the best chance to overcome Brother Sedon, but are we absolutely sure that's what Memory wanted us to do?'

'Of course it wasn't. Not precisely. She was obviously so annoyed with us she re-inserted what Starrus calls the Gal Gap in the Astronomer's basement and sent him back.'

'She wanted us to assess him; see if he was still salvageable and, by extrapolation, whether the rest of our offspring might be as well. Even at this advanced point in time, if we judged he wasn't, and we did, we were to let him go such that he could develop into a true Sedon-slayer. Which is apparently what he will become, if Memory and the Visionary are even close to right.'

'We did let him go – but back to slay our eldest brother now. Why wait, we reasoned. What he might become, he must already be. Otherwise how could he become it? Sure, as Memory said, he was cathonitized for five hundred years but, after something like seven times that of solidity, he's hardly a child. If he can't slay Sedon now, we figured, he'll never be able to. His potential can't be limitless. Could we have been wrong, sisters?'

'Visionaries do not ask questions. They provide answers. Better not question ourselves and do the same. We have masked the Galactic Gap. Even, as seems apparent, we can't destroy it, we should be able to reject it, and eject him, again, at any time. I do not anticipate this becoming an endlessly repeating cycle. Sooner or later, Memory will understand we're as displeased with her as she may be with us. Besides, her rationale for sending him back here strikes me as faulty.'

'Agreed. What does she, should she, care if a young Yajur has to be given the opportunity to develop into the one she believes is possessing Wisdom now? The whole notion of controlled time-travel is preposterous. Given her story, she should realize that more than anyone.'

'Quite so, sister. They just stumble and bumble as they tumble into and out of their various lifetimes. If they could control where they end up, you'd think they'd go back to Old Weir and never create Brother Sedon in the first place. She must know something we don't. There's no other explanation.'

'There is some sense to that. By her own admission, the Male Entity only knows what she lets him know. It also stands to reason she can't know what she hasn't experienced. This sending Yajur back here may well have been a calculated move — one predestined, as it were. We're supposed to let him go.'

'But what if we don't. I see nothing wrong with giving her new experiences. She is, after all, based on the Mother Machine of Old Weir and therefore no one-hundred-percent-true friend of either us or our Utopians.'

'By that logic it doesn't matter what we do, Soul. Whatever it is, it's already been predetermined, hasn't it? Whether we do what she wants or try to foul her up, it won't make any difference. At least so you'd have us accept. Let's not dwell too much on the ineffable and continue our scan of this mortal's life. There may yet be a clue, an indicator, such that we can forge our own destiny.'

'I concur, Body. When it all comes down to dust, there's too much of it. Who's to say whatever Future-Memory's experienced will necessarily happen? Think of it another way. How can something that's already happened occur again? Certainly there are lessons to be learned from history. But from His or Her Story? I doubt it. What's past has passed. What's yet to come is, by definition, yet to come.'

'The eye-mouth again, Mind. No doubt about it. That's what's become of Brother Sedon. Fight him, ambassador. No go. Order's no match for his uncle. Not in that ostensibly primitive state at least. Memory may not be infallible but she's obviously right when she says he isn't ready to slay Sedon yet. There's Starrus again. Inside another of his planet's spaceships; one much more elementary than the Cosmic Express.'

'And there's her Hisness. Looks almost identical to the first time we rendered Memory wholly human. What's that instrument? Ghastly sound. Yajur doesn't much like it either.'

'Another fight. Wisdom against Order. There's Memory's face on the wall. Here he comes. Zoom. Back through the wormhole – back to us! That's about it.

'Does this human hold none of Yajur's other memories? Something we can use against our three Brothers, even if it's just a hint that Great Byron and Yajur's father, the libertine Lazareme, are still around? That either Varuna-Ahriman-Mithras, abominable amalgam of our first born by the Moloch Sedon that he is, or Demogorgon, the Devil-Eater, can still be made into a factor?'

'You have seen all we have. He does not. What do we do now? Meld Starrus with Yajur again and try to read him?'

'We have already tried to meld Yajur with the Visionary and other Utopians. He doesn't take hold. Like they always were in the past, Utopians remain immune to devic possession. If we try to meld him with Starrus, he might not just take hold. He might take over. Is it worth the risk?'

'Order needs to develop, Memory claimed, in order to become a genuine Sedon-slayer; in order to have a future such that Wisdom can possess him in his last lifetime and carry him into this one. But what if it's his shell that needs to develop? Memory never said anything about this Starrus having to survive as well.'

'In other words, the mortal may have nothing to do with how Yajur eventually becomes Vajra. What say we make it so he does?'

'Either way, it's certainly worth a try.'

========
Starrus awoke in the middle of the night.
========

Without bothering to turn on the Virtual Reality device, he easily crept into Ubi's bedroom. As he had suspected, the astronomer was sleeping soundly. He wondered how many other lies Ubi had told him. Somehow he couldn't ascribe deliberate maliciousness to the plump Utopian but Universe may be acting under instructions; possibly, just as he was now, from the Trigregos Sisters.

He activated the levitation device, what allowed him to assume the heart position of his hologram self, rose and touched the lightning blade hooked onto the bedroom wall. Amazingly, it instantly vanished into his body. Suddenly the room was full of light and it was coming from him.

That's when he realized Ubi wasn't just sleeping; no one could have slept through the inadvertent display of brilliance that Starrus was suddenly emitting. No, he was in some kind of artificially-induced stupor. Utopians had no doubt perfected pharmaceuticals for every occasion but he sensed his host's condition had nothing to do with drugs.

'No good, sisters. Starrus has Yajur's abilities but none of his memories.'

'Maybe that's the key, Body. What we've been missing all along. Yajur possessed Starrus; now Starrus has possessed Order. Can he survive the plunge back through the Gal Gap?'

'The Visionary foresaw he could – but not as he is. We'll have to guide him to the eye.'

Starrus blazed out the window and up ten flights to the Visionary's resting quarters. He had the eye and it was in his forehead just as the Visionary awoke.

This one, in all likelihood, had only been feigning sleep.

'Something still doesn't make sense, sisters. Starrus should revert to Yajur. What's he done? Absorbed the ambassador along with his abilities but still without any of his memories?'

"No, deities." It was the Visionary who spoke. Clearly his mental acuity was at such a highly functional level he could overhear them talking amongst themselves. "He has done exactly as I envisioned. This Yajur of yours is not what he once was. I believe he is much like a shade or spectral revenant, one dead yet risen, more spirit again than anywhere near as whole as he had been.

"He was weakened by his five centuries containment within what we must call the Cathonic Dome – probably permanently so. He needs to possess a shell but, once dispossessed and now repossessed, it is he who is the possessed. Starrus is dominant and Starrus is a devil-slayer. Care to try him out? On yourselves!"

'You play a dangerous game, Visionary.'

"I do not play games, sisters. You are devils and Utopians owe it to the cosmos to destroy devils. Will you challenge my vision?"

'Would you have this mortal challenge us?'

"That is up to him. My recommendation is this: Even though all devils will be destroyed, you three shall be the last to go if, and only if, you return him to his universe and seal the wormhole behind him. This time do it in reality, with no subterfuge or, in a matter of mere minutes, you shall be the first to fall."

Although still no more than disembodied voices with no form whatsoever, it must have seemed to the Visionary that the sisters were silently ruminating amongst themselves. Finally one – unless it was the air again – spoke: 'Even if we were suicidal, which we're not, we couldn't do as you suggest. We can get rid of the Galactic Gap but we can't seem to destroy it. The Wisdom or Memory Entities could just reattach it to Weir World.'

"Then you must eliminate them. You know how that is done. Before he slays his first devil, Starrus must slay Memory's mate!"

Mikelangelo Starrus wasn't asked his opinion.

========

The three sisters brought the hollow tube that was the Gal Gap – in reality the sometimes Wandering SAG Gap – into the Visionary's bedroom.

It sucked Starrus into its midst and promptly vanished through the Grey.

========

"A wise choice, Sisters," applauded the Visionary. "Weir isn't ready to lose you three just yet. I would suggest you take your leave shortly, though. A farewell tour of Weir System is my recommendation. That should take a few hundred Earth years. You should also take your mutant astronomer with you just in case. He certainly won't be able to continue on as he has been here once the truth of his manipulated birth is known.

"Maybe catch up with his family. They can't have got too far; probably not anywhere near the cosmic boundary between our macroverse and his microverse. Unless, I suppose, they got through the Gal Gap, which I somehow doubt. In any event expect no help from the Entities. They hate you, your brothers, your sons, daughters, and grandchildren with as much vehemence as we Utopians do."

'They've been with us before; will again. Right up to our last days. And theirs!'

"I'm afraid that is even less than probable. It is in reality a very minuscule possibility. The vast majority of Ys I perceive indicate that Starrus will kill them before he even starts on the Moloch Sedon and your devazur descendants. Kill them, I say; not wipe them out altogether. As you're well aware, the Entities don't stay dead like proper mortals. But, by the time they tumble this direction through time again, the devazur race will be history, not His Story.

"Like humans think dinosaurs are, they shall be extinct!"

========

Not every human reckoned dinosaurs extinct. For one, Thalassa, raised a two-eyed D'Angelo, but maybe born a three-eyed Thanatoid, wasn't alone in thinking frigate birds were small pterodactyls. Indeed, the prevailing wisdom on the Outer Earth was that dinosaurs evolved into birds; that they therefore weren't extinct in any way whatsoever.

Of course had the Visionary – or Thalassa, for that matter – spent any quality time beneath the Cathonic Dome, he might have learned to ride one of the Hidden Headworld's Terror Dons or Terror Donnas in the Floodlands. (Which weren't to be confused with flightless Phorusrhacids, aka Terror Birds, who were wholly birds, not just birdlike; weren't extinct either, not on the Head.)

And what were Terror Dons or Donnas except oversized pterodactyls?

****

Twenty-First Moon: And, When Helios Dies ...

========

Wednesday/Birhym, December/Tantalar 10, 1980/5980

Helios might have been dreaming from 1968 to 1975.

========

Then again, presumably by subliminal, as in brainily subcranial methods, he could have been learning the secrets of Jesus Mandam, the King Conqueror or equally self-proclaimed Conquering Christ. That would have been within the Soviet Supracity in the Ukraine some distance north of Kiev.

If that was the case then he would have been under the watchful eyes of the simpleminded Callion Clone, Caliban Kopf. Herr Kopf was the second Headsman. The first was The Rache's Baphomet Headsman, whom Jesse disposed of on Salvation Island, Christmas Day 1953; was one of many including, he went to his death believing, none other than the Moloch Sedon himself.

More reliable eyes than Herr Kopf would have belonged his employer, the not so young any more Baron, Günter von Alptraum (Somnambulancz, as the also not-at-all-simpleminded techno-designer was rather inventively codenamed within Signal System). Almost exactly like OJ Maxwell (initially named Victor Richter), von Alp was a closet clone made by Moe One in collaboration with the perpetual child known as Joli Blon in the late Thirties.

Almost two decades later Kopf was formed out of DNA strands left by the original Baphomet, Donar Lancz. As agreed upon by Loxus Ryne and the various principals of the Alliance of Man in '54, he may have been the first clone Moses Callion the Second didn't accelerate. (He started accelerating them again after he went rogue in the Sixties and joined WORLD.)

On the other hand, perhaps Helios was made by Moe Two, like some of the other non-accelerated, but now matured and (arguably) leading Silver Signallers currently on Centauri Island. However, regardless of whether Kadmon Heliopolis had actually gone through the hundred or so lifetimes Memory claimed he had; whether the real Heliopolis had died on Trigon in 1968, died and stayed dead; there was a Male Entity.

He may even have been the Adam Kadmon, meaning *the original or primordial man*, hypothesized in both Ancient Greek and Cabbalistic traditions, to name just two sources of the belief. Much more immediately certainly he was the Entity called Heliosophos (Sophos = Wise).

To judge by what he had his female counterpart do to Weirstar all those multi millennia in the distant past, he was probably the first of a multitude of mad gods.

Right now, though, Helios on the Moon was the maddest of them all.

========

"Mik, Mik!" cried Nidaba Starrus as she rushed towards her transformed husband. "I was so worried. Memory said you were dead, consumed by some god-awful devil she called Yajur."

"Stay away from me, Nid. I'm literally too hot to handle." He raised himself into the air in order to avoid her. "Thanks to the Trigregos Sisters," he shouted down to her, "I consumed Thunder and Lightning rather than the other way around. His powers are supposed to make me a Sedon-slayer but there's someone else I have to slay first.

"I've drained the computer-thing of all but its capacity to retain atmospheric controls. All that power's in me now as well. I'm going to put Heliopolis into the grave I thought I'd put him into a dozen years ago. Find cover. Forget about Enan and the others. They're devils now and I exist to kill devils."

"That's Mikelangelo Starrus!" gasped OJ Maxwell from under the table.

"Lord Yajur," Helios corrected him, barely able to contain his excitement, "Lord fucking Future Vajra, that is," he qualified. "The comparatively early on Unity of Order."

He whirled on his Ereba-possessed mate beside him. "You've been playing me false, milady." All aglow, he grabbed her by the throat. "Have to admit I've suspected it ever since the Cosmic Express was blown through the Cathonic Dome and into the Sedon Sphere instead of outer space."

She gagged, programmed powerless to harm him. He ranted on: "There was no black hole for this one. You sent him back through the SAG Gap. To the Triplet Sisters is my guess. Hell's Slippery Slope, it's no guess. You're playing head games not just with the Head. You're playing your own version of the Goddess Gambit.

"But Strife pissed you off. Sent Dame Darkness – Erebe, Lilith, whomever it was – through an actual one. Seriously got rid of her. So you had to take on her template." He infused her with the brightness and the heat of a miniature sun. She shrieked, her body lost consciousness, began to burn. Her face was back in the computer wall but it was smoking – the whole area of the citadel was starting to smoke.

"I'll thank you properly later."

Ignoring both her face and the incinerating mandroid corpse at his feet, his attention went to the devil-possessed cosmicompanions, particularly their captain.

"Been a while, at least a lifetime, since I slaughtered any devils. And you've given me seven, including the one I hate most in the cosmos, old Order himself. All due respects to your Boddhi, Max, but taking them out, starting with this fuckhead, is going to be barf-bags more entertaining than fragmenting your pet 'Void."

Romaine Kinesis had followed his friend's lead under the table. "I thought Memory told Nidaba that Starrus was no longer an issue, Max."

"Computers are only as good as their programmers," Maxwell reminded him, not realizing she programmed herself, albeit under Helios's guidance. "And hers is crazy; has to be given how many different sides she has. Better keep your wits about you, pro. Things are getting nasty and about to get way nastier."

"Then I hope that guardian angel of yours shows up soon. Somehow or other Memory took out my Gypsium; probably into herself. I'm powerless but it looks like Starrus isn't; far from it. In fact, it looks like he's the same powers as Kadmon. They can't be possessed of the same devil, can they?"

"Helios said he wasn't possessed. I assumed that meant he generates his abilities out of the lion pendant he wears. Like the Elemental Twins got theirs from their talismans. Could as easily be he developed them himself over all his lifetimes. Either that or Gypsium gave them to him. Who knows? Guess I should have asked."

"Bit late for that!"

Helios glared at the three-eyed cosmicompanions. Glared then they flared. Nidaba had a devic eye again. Night cloaked her suddenly-on-fire friends. Acheron may have sucked in their flames but, obscured as they were, it was impossible for Max and the professor to be sure.

They did see Helios blaze into Starrus. Saw them repel each other. Mik Starrus faltered but didn't fall to the ground. He only had two eyes. Helios righted himself quickly. He shook violently. Then he had the third eye. Shook again. Wasn't Helios any longer. Was Lord Yajur! Or was he?

A circlet of Gypsium energy formed around the Nidaba-protectively, night-shrouded cosmicompanions. Aristotle Zeross was briefly on the moon. Then he was gone, taking them with him. Mnemosyne's face was in the computer wall but it was dimming. Yajur-Helios was too stunned to realize his danger.

Starrus had just enough of the energy he had sucked out of the computerized mandroid thing left to cause a stellar sword to extend out of his being. It sliced off the Unity's head at the neck then he toppled to the floor, barely conscious. OJ Maxwell scooted out from underneath the table and grabbed Starrus by the collar of his uniform. Yajur's body clawed towards his head.

Kinesis wasn't as fast as Maxwell but he was quick enough to kick the head down the room then race after it. "Put it back," commanded Memory's computer self out of the wall. She wasn't trying to be comical. It just sounded funny. "I warned you what happens when Helios dies."

"Better to die a man than live as a devil!" Kinesis shouted back at her.

"Even if he takes you with him?"

"I'm not done yet."

The one sport he'd enjoyed while growing up – mostly on Aegean Trigon, certainly not its lunar namesake – was football. Called soccer in North America, he'd heard the Celts, with their fondness for beheading their fallen foes, started it in order to wind down after a particularly gruesome battle; started it with severed heads, not balls. He kicked Evidently Yajur's farther ahead of him.

"Then drop your socks and hold onto your cocks, boys, because we are. Just remember you brought it on yourselves."

There was an eruption of pure light. Did it come from Helios-Yajur's decapitated body, a final exhaustion of its ineffable brilliancy? No, it had a shape, a humanoid shape. Was it too late for Kinesis to become a True Believer? Probably not; just not right now. So was that, could it have been ...?

Whatever. It was gone. Mnemosyne was too; her digitized visage vanished from the computer wall.

Lunar Trigon – that's what the Entities' called their tri-towered citadel – began to collapse in on itself. Only what could be some sort of invisible force field or, vaguely possibly, a remnant atmospheric bubble prevented its beams from beaning them. Or, as far as that went, them getting sucked out into the planetoid's airless surface. Max, propping up Starrus, struggled to Kinesis's side.

"Did you see that?" the latter shouted at him as he, Kinesis, skilfully flicked the Yajur-head off the floor and into his arms.

"What?"

"God."

"Fuck off with that Whoop Dee Doo crapola, pro," Max snapped. "You want a light at the end of the tunnel you make your own. Blast and damnation, man, with Machine-Memory gone, there's no telling how long life support will keep functioning. Got anything left, Mik? In the way of powers, I mean."

"I don't think so. What happened?"

"Best guess, you and Helios controlled the same or similar devils. Put in the same space, the devil brought himself together again. That's what's left of him." Max pointed to the decapitated body. Even in the absence of the God-Light, it was still inching painstakingly towards them. "What about you, pro? This whole citadel was full of Gypsium. Any chance you can suck enough in to get us back to the Liberty?"

"Even if I could, I never did learn how to teleport myself, let alone anyone else. Is there another way? Your Boddhi?"

"Had enough of him. Had enough of supras, period. It's every man for Man himself now. How about it, Mik? Any suggestions?"

"The devil's body's still coming for us. Don't know what it is about these things but they seem damn near indestructible. I can try to repossess him. Then again, there's a chance he might repossess me. Wait a minute! If Nidaba and the rest were here, then our cosmicar must be as well."

"Of course," snapped Maxwell. "That was our way out. And Helios showed us where it was. Think you're up to flying it, Mik?"

"You better believe it."

"Let's go. Keep the head, pro."

"What for?"

"Call it a whim." Maxwell changed his mind; grabbed the Yajur-head away from Kinesis and held it like a football. "Never mind. I'll do it myself." He did offer an explanation, however. "Nearly forty years ago, I assassinated a real sick prick named Donar Lancz. His codename was Baphomet, after the talking head the real Knights Templar supposedly worshipped during the crusades. I cut off his head and carted it back to England. Lancz never did talk. I've a feeling this one might.

"Come on. Run! This place isn't going to hold together much longer."

========

The marines finally arrived on the Outer Earth's Centauri Island that afternoon.

========

Were it not for the mystery of where the Nag Gap was hidden, Loxus Abraham Ryne would have turned the largely artificial island over to them for target practice at once. It was Shelter who convinced him to leave it as is; did so without an argument from the marines' commander. He wasn't paid to argue with a guy, or gal, who wore a House Head helmet. He'd leave that to the psych squad.

"Don't worry, sir," said Spherus just before he got on the Signallers' airplane in order to return to System HQ in California.

(Under his Silver armour, Ryne knew Spherus was the Bubble Boy, Cecil Mayhew, nominal son of his onetime factotum, Theodore Mayhew. He may or may not have known what else he was: a clone of his nephew, Jesus Mandam, the King Conqueror. Rather, he may or may not have remembered it. There was a Queen Conqueror, too, and she was a real witch.)

"After we hit Vancouver and deal with the Emperor Mammalian you so reckless had re-engendered – re-engineered? – Signal System will move here full force. Better you concentrate on whatever's on the Moon in the meantime. When that's taken care of, kindly contact Strategos. I'm sure he'd be delighted to let you and your Alliance take over from us if that's what you want."

"We'll have to see about that, won't we?"

What Ryne wants, Ryne gets. Unless, figured Spherus, we get to you first.

========

Jordan Tethys brought the Fatman, wheelchair and all, back to Aka Godbad City that evening.

========

The living side of Alpha's in-town, ancillary headquarters for Centauri Enterprises was wrecked, the rest of the building evacuated. Emergency response crews were still busy mopping up the mess. The balance of the city seemed undamaged; as though All hadn't touched it. Which she wouldn't have.

Her raid was scrupulously focused; in that respect it was akin to Blind Sundown and Raven's Head's while on their Vengeance Quest twenty-seven years earlier, and on the other side of the Dome. A couple of drawings later Tethys found Yataghan raised Montressor, Janna nee St Peche, Connie Lindquist and George Hannibal, a bit bloodied yet not that much the worse for wear, in a boardroom they'd hastily booked at a nearby hotel. Young Life was with them; Nihila wasn't.

"Didn't think Yati, Goldenrod, APM, and the rest would have had that much difficulty with Sharkczar and All," said Centauri, once he settled in with the others.

For someone who'd spent most of a day irresponsibly enjoying the exemplary *'services'* provided by the Dinq, Doinq, Danq Cavern Tavern in the company of an expert, he sounded remarkably coherent; even upbeat. So much so that Hush felt obliged to damper his exuberance.

"Don't say it like they won, Daddy Do the Danq. They didn't. Though, to his credit, Yati the non-Yeti did put paid to Sharkczar. But that just fattened him up for All."

"I see," said Centauri. "And you know this because?"

"She burped, smelled of brimstone." Hush smiled coyly, then switched from elliptical to explanatory. "I told you Sharky was no ordinary mandroid monstrosity and All's definitely no ordinary monster maker. In the wrong mood she's the biggest abomination of them all, no ha, ha. She was out for revenge big time this time."

"For what I ordered Necator and Godbad's air force do to her Prison Beach."

"Just so, Daddy No Brains. I'm afraid Byronics without their father around were – but aren't anymore – particularly run of the millipede."

"Aren't anymore run of the mill," provided Connie, doubling as an interpreter, "On account of all that exercise just made her all the hungrier."

"All didn't stop with Yati and the rest of the Byronics.," said Hannibal. "As soon as she was done here she took herself off between-space and went visiting. From what we heard while you were off attending to your hours of delinquency at the Danq, she just got bolder and bolder.

"Burnt off a lot more than all that energy she got from eating Elephantine and his Byronic sibs." (Elephantine Ganesh had been Hannibal's occupant while he was an Outer Earth Untouchable. He'd been the other one besides APM – the Babar to Connie's All-Eyes – to try to take out OJ Maxwell after Hiyati Samarand quickened the countdown for the launching of the Cosmic Express a week and half ago.)

"Godbadian successes in Hadd and New Valhalla pale in comparison to our failures on the home front."

"How so?"

"She did a number on CE's HQ in Godbad City as well as chewed up runaways there, here, and down in Djerridam-Goatwood. Had most of our air force for dessert."

"President Lemon resigned within an hour of her attacks," Janna informed him matter-of-factly. "God-afraid Bloody Kenton's taken over; says the military wants to send us the bill."

(Both Lemon and Kenton were the Fatman's men. However, there had been that peculiar episode with the latter on the Devauray after the rat-attack in the newly opened Headworld Museum. For some reason the closed circuit television cameras in the HQ's business side canteen blipped off while Kenton was speaking to Jordan Tethys; this while the then vice-president was actually in Goatwood.)

"Mr Hannibal here will deal with them," said Centauri. "That's what he's paid for. How'd you lot get away Scot-free?"

"APM's got lots of eyeballs," said Connie, tapping her forehead nevertheless third-eyelessly. "And she knows how much I like George here."

"And I like Yati the Yeti," added Janna, also third-eyelessly. "Even if he is a little green around not just the gills."

"I don't have gills," said Yataghan.

"Glands then," said Janna, grabbing a quick hug.

"APM's a one-woman power focus," said Hannibal. "Got an extra eye into each of us. They got us away before All ate the rest of her so she's still sort of around."

"I'll see about getting all of her out of All," Hush promised them. "The She-Sphinx saw me with her mom so she might let her go as a favour."

"Mom?"

"Nihila, Dandy Handy Balls," she told Hannibal.

"Oh, no!" groaned the 30-Year Man, intentionally derailing the conversation. Until then, like the good reporter he was, he'd been diligently taking in everything they were saying without comment. "Don't tell me you rented a boardroom without a bar, let alone a fridge?"

Evidently a fellow like him found listening thirsty work; all the more so when it got sidetracked onto Harmony and, inevitably thereafter, how he too-long-distance discovered Helios was on the Moon. Still hadn't figured that out to his own satisfaction; would eventually, he was sure. (Historically, going back to Thrygragon, one devil was as good with Rumour's Brainrock quill as he was and it wasn't anyone who commonly humanized Miracle Memory; was Thrygragos Everyman.)

"Told you, you should have ordered buckets of pills to go," said Centauri.

"You've forgotten my shelter." Hush materialized a cooler stocked with bottles full of the DDD's prized pilsner.

She even drank one herself.

========

The Damnation Brigade came to Sedon's Head eight members strong on Lazam the 5th of Tantalar. One rejoined them that night in Temporis. That made it nine. Seven were now in the Weirdom of Cabalarkon. One was in a tub of Cathonic Fluid; may never get out of it either, except perhaps to be buried.

That left two missing and unaccounted for, albeit presumably still somewhere on the Hidden Headworld. The tenth, they trusted, was safe on the Outer Earth.

It wasn't just tricksters you should never trust.

========

"They will sleep now," promised the God-King of Lathakra. "All of them. Probably for a long time. My family is finally back together again. Go home to yours, Ringleader."

"I can't forgive you for this, Thanatos."

"The mortal thinks we care about forgiveness. Can we forgive his effrontery?"

"Families are families, husband," sympathized the Scarlet Empress, back to wearing a crimson mask again, but nevertheless deigning to speak to a mere mortal. "Be they devils or human, they are still families. Do as King Cold says, Dr Zeross. To judge from the looks of you, it may be the last thing you do."

She wasn't Judge Druj but chances were she wasn't far wrong.

========

Hush had been right about All.

========

Not that the She-Sphinx was necessarily having digestive difficulties by the time she got back to Incain. She was right that mandroids, at least this specific, machine master moulding mandroid, had to obey their mothers. (Weir's ultimately baleful Mother Machine, upon which the Mnemosyne Machine was partially based, wouldn't have designed the first mandroids otherwise.)

Nihila had been as well, in that All was back to sporting the face she was built with again. It wasn't that of a gorgon like Mater Matare or, if she wasn't a Twelfth Born, either of her brood sisters: the Cockatrice and the Basilisk (Euryale and Stheno, unless it was vice versa). It was hers, Memory's, Harmony's, Nihila's, and they had had a long term relationship for multiple centuries because of just that.

All considered her, if not her mother per se, then her mother perforce.

Hush and Nihila had spent most of a dreary day waiting for her to come back to the Prison Beach. Happily, for one of them, she still wasn't altogether full.

========

Once devoured; once she stepped out of the Egyptian Sphinx at the ass end of All's interspatial intestinal tract; once she sliced herself from the Giza plateau to the part of the moon's surface where Jordy, thanks to whomever, drew the Lunar Citadel; she quickly found the decapitated body of Helios only recently – and perhaps for the only time – called Sophos the Wise.

It was buried in a big old hole full of moondust covered by rubble from the Trigon built by the miraculous Mnemosyne Machine and her do-it-yourself minions. It was ruined but the headless remains of her reverted, once again red-robed lover from nearly thirty-five hundred years earlier weren't. They were still warm.

The gods, devils that they were, that she was and continued to be, had celebrated their wedding. They had celebrated his death as well, years later.

Now though, they were nowhere in evidence.

"Why didn't you truly die then?" Freespirit Nihila cried to the stars.

They gave no answer but someone else did. The voice came from a dark, ectoplasmic shape in humanoid form. More, in a devic shape. Hers!

========

The UNES Liberty left the general vicinity of the moon that night. A few days later it reached Near-Earth Orbit, mission ratified accomplished.

========

After the crew put it in mothballs, they came down on the three remaining shuttle crafts. They were interrogated individually, first by Abe Ryne, Dr Angus Skullian and Ryne's SPACE men, next by their own governments' Intelligence Agencies, then, at the collective insistence of the United Nations' distrustful Security Council, by Signal System with its Silver Signallers using Speaking Sticks.

By then without exception, the Liberators – as they proudly proclaimed themselves – to a one stated it had been a very good experience. Added dutifully they would like to go back into space one day. Agreed they had blown hell out of a big old hole full of moondust, thereby disabling the thought-beam transmitters Lunar Assault Crews One and Two found there.

Could not say who planted them, though, and this troubled more than a few of them. Therefore out of necessity, the Great Man, Abe Ryne himself, had a few words with those in the need-to-know. It had been Dr Aristotle Zeross, he told them confidentially but no less confidently.

Harry, the Last of the Supranormals, had been working for the Worldwide Order, the same folks who'd destroyed the Cosmic Express on the Thirtieth. Not only that, he'd run WORLD, the super-secretive criminal association responsible for his wife, newly wed Belificent's murder twenty years ago — and the reason Ryne set up AMERICA in the first place, in order to abolish it. He and his henchmen had been afraid it or one of its cosmicars would stop off on the Moon and get to the transmitters.

Don't worry. SPACE got him, Harry, Ringleader, killer of his own sister, the patriarch's fourth and final wife. Blew up the cargo plane he'd hijacked the previous Thursday, as they all damn well knew. Want to talk to Salvatore Dis L'Orca, the Order's Head of Operations after Harry's finish? He'll verify everything.

Thank God it hadn't been aliens. No such thing – at least there hadn't been any on the Moon, he quickly qualified. And Helios? Everyone on the planet heard him claim responsibility for the beams and riots. No such a being. Dis L'Orca could explain that, too. Helios on the Moon just sounded good. The Lunar Citadel? A bored flight technician's idea of a joke.

Amazing what you can do with computer graphics these days. Holograms are almost tangible; Star Trek a bare decade or two away from reality.

The only casualty among the Liberty's men was Sean Smythe. He had just been too old. Heart wasn't up to it. Flight Commander James Aremar was severely reprimanded for letting him pilot the shuttle craft that went to collect O'Ryan James Maxwell and Professor Romaine Kinesis from the USA's Fancy Dan Columbia.

Their bodies? Don't know, Aremar regretted, chastened by the whole experience. Whole shuttle was lost in space; the Liberty's shuttle, not the Columbia.

Not one said they had spaced the body of Johann Schmidt along with that of Sean Smythe. Nor should they have since the last of the Psychic Siblings had passed away on Centauri Island along with Alfredo Sentalli and his Untouchables, the lot of them poisoned by Prince Translav and his Glomen, working for WORLD. Yes, the Little Prince got rid of his own daughter, the evil maniac.

Not one of the Liberators said they had blown up Cosmicar Two as it left the Moon that Wednesday and requested permission to dock with the Liberty. Not one, that is, after they spoke with Loxus Ryne and Dr Angus Skullian gave them their shots. Annaesthetics worked much better than even the Great Man's fabled voice.

As for what happened to the rest of the cosmicars and the Express's hub craft, well, officially WORLD got it all. Unofficially, that remained to be determined.

========

Did anyone care about what happened to Primeval Lilith, partial mother of all the Sed-sons? Was she even on the Moon humanizing the Memory Entity instead of some hypothetical Erebe Thanatos from a future no one else would ever experience? Did anyone care about the wall of solid darkness Irisiel Mercherm ran into on Lathakra; it with its pink face and unwavering grin? Did anyone even remember the Smiling Fiend?

There might have been answers to suchlike questions — but only if the Mighty Eye-Mouth in the Sky ever questioned himself.

Which he didn't!

========

That Lazam (Friday on the Outer Earth) Demios Sarpedon finally convinced Quentin Anvil to take him to Desecrated Dustmound. In place of his wife's body, they discovered a statue of her. It had to be a bizarre joke. The woman who'd been described as a walking statue on the Outer Earth had been replaced by an actual statue of non-ambulant alabaster.

How it got there was a puzzlement wrapped in nonexistent newspaper like an English takeout of fantasy fish and chips. Demios vowed that before he died it would be erected in the central square of Cabalarkon, in front of those two splendid piles, the Citadel of the Sleepers and the Cathedral of the Thinkers, as well as withing sight of brother Saladin Devason's abhorrent Skyrise.

Of course that likely couldn't happen until he was Master of Weir. He figured that wouldn't take much more than a year. Why shouldn't the most modern civilization on the Head add the most ancient one to its list of satellite states? No reason, Godbadian general Quentin Anvil, anticipating his next big assignment, agreed.

As the statue was being winched onto a carrier copter a couple of days later, Sarpedon spotted a woman on the largest hump of ground in the near-area. Because it was just a pimple of its former self, the Sraddhites no longer dubbed it Diminished Dustmound. Now they called it Desecrated Dustmound. (They couldn't very well call it Desiccated Dustmound because it rained there now, a lot.)

She was dressed like a widow, veiled and all in black. Even though it wasn't raining, for a change, it couldn't be a Haddit Zombie since they'd mostly dug themselves underground, apparently to await a new master or mistress. (Possibly the Molech Xibalba or his father, Night Owl; the former, not so jokingly aka Reilly Haddeus, may have been reborn – hence the rat-attack in the Headworld Museum on the 28th – whereas the latter was something of an anomaly, an Irache vampire.)

Neither he nor the Godbadians he was with reckoned it any other kind of Dead Thing, nor even an Indescribable. Having lost Hadd, those riding vultures or Vultyrie had fled back westward, into the Forbidden Forest of Kala Tal, Vetala's brood sister. Those still on foot were doing a ditto, heading west in perhaps forlorn hope of finding refuge within the arachnid devil's still inviolable protectorate, the southernmost of any Mithradite Master Deva.

Finally, this time because it was broad daylight with nary a cloud in the sky, they reckoned she couldn't be a vampire. She was bending over, seemed to be sifting through the dirt looking for something. So, was she Nergal Vetala, somehow reverted to her devic self and suppressing her third eye, looking for her moon-sickle?

Once again armed with his pre-Earth eye-stave, the oldest on the planet, what still manufactured its own eyeorbs, Demios went over to speak to her. When he came back he said she'd broken a mirror and was trying to find all its pieces so she didn't have any more bad luck. They'd talked for a few minutes and, since she seemed friendly enough, he offered to help. She'd declined, said it kept her busy. That she had all eternity.

Thereafter, since she was often seen again, once Diminished then Desecrated Dustmound became known as Haunted Dustmound.

Should have called it Demon Mound!

========

Some weeks later the Untouchable Diver – Yama Nergal, King Harvest, the devic Grim Reaper, beside him – led the Glorious Dead against the Weirdom of Cabalarkon. Yehudi Cohen was wearing the Crimson Corona, had the Amateramirror strapped to one arm like a shield and was brandishing the Susasword with the other.

Turned out it was just the Master's dream becoming something everyone could see. What Wilderwitch was experiencing that very moment, in that very bed, was real.

'YES, YOU'LL DO JUST FINE!'

She began to scream.

****

Next:

"DAMNATION -- YEAR ONE -- AFTER LIMBO"

JimMcPherson
Decimation
Damnation
The PHANTACEA Mythos continues with
'Year One - After Limbo, Part 1'

DECIMATION DAMNATION

Damn One: **Panharmonium Ends**

========

If you die in your dreams you die in your life.

She wasn't dying. She appreciated that. She was, however, dreaming. Hoped she was anyhow.

September 19, 1981

Greater Vancouver had been washed out to sea in the Second Great Flood, that of late November 1980.

========

So had much of the Fraser Valley. What was now called New Vancouver had once been a small town called Hope. The Fraser River emptied itself here, just as it had on the southern border of Old Vancouver before the Deluge. The Liberation Brigade's celebratory reunion, which was being filmed for everyone with a television on the reunited planet to see, was taking place in the gardens of old Hope's now reconverted city hall. It too was called Hope, though *'Haven'* had been added to give it a better ring.

Outside it Wilderwitch – the only name she acknowledged with any regular-ity – was sitting on a stone bench away from the gathering crowd, of whom an ever increasingly many were uninvited. Even in the wondrous new reality of a whole-again Earth, celebrity retained its magnetic field and the surviving members of the supranormal Liberation Brigade, the Witch being one of the most comparatively ordinary, were well up there in the pantheon of Panharmonium.

Looking the fit, albeit very baby-belly-heavy, off-white, gypsy-type she was, she had been counting down the days, weeks and months ever since she became pregnant; was now counting down the hours. Figured it'd take a few more of them before she could start kicking back. Fifty-three might seem a bit old to be pregnant, but it helped when you were a witch. Helped even more when you were a supranormal witch. Besides, kicking back was one of the things she did really well.

Spotting her sitting alone, Athena Zeross, age 7, decked out in her finest frills, blues and yellows for the most part, detached herself from a group of similarly attired children, and came rushing up to her.

Blonde, though not quite as much so as her mother, whose hair was akin to Christmas tree tinsel, Tina was the youngest of three hybrid daughters of the new Master of Weir, Melina born Sarpedon, 60, Mel-Illuminatus as the Witch still sometimes thought of her.

Before Mel's promotion – mostly due to a dearth of challengers in the wake of an anything except a dearth of death amongst her potential rivals for the title – she was the High Illuminary of the Weirdom of Cabalarkon. She was also, even before that, an Althean witch-healer and a degree-granted, medically certified physician; had only reluctantly traded in her caduceus for the Master's Mace.

Her heroic, indubitably tragic and definitely late husband Harry – Aristotle, Ringleader, Tina's Greco-Cretan father, also a Dr Zeross – was one of the main reasons there was a Panharmonium. Not to mention the remnants of a Liberation Brigade left to publish their memoirs and reap enriching rewards.

Not far behind Tina was her middle sister, Helen, whose thirteenth birthday was coming up on the approaching Autumnal Equinox. Although some of Mel's apprentice Illuminaries were in the vicinity, Helen and their eldest sister, Persephone, 16, who was probably indoors attending their mother, were Tina's designated shadows for the day.

Were most days, but today was special. Once the ceremonies started, their mother, a full-blooded, white-as-light Utopian woman – in contrast to full-blooded Utopian men, who were black as midnight on a starless night – would be in Mastery mode. And before that there were the announcements and formal greetings to be made and endured.

Obadiah Melvin Power, the patriarch of the once strictly Outer Earth based, Illuminated Faith of Xuthros Hor, was the nominal host for Hope Haven's dedication and the festivities to follow. Since he was the father of her unborn child, as well as the father of her first and to date only other child, albeit thirty-five years ago, the Witch would have to be on her feet for most of the formal fluff as well.

Too bad she didn't have a designated baby-belly supporter the same as Tina had sisterly shadows. Maybe what Tina had in that shoebox she was carrying would jump start the smile muscles.

"Look what slimy Auntie Fish caught for us, fat Auntie Wildie," enthused the youngster, all but thrusting the box in her face.

While not much of a supranormal compared to some of the others, whose abilities approached godlike, Wilderwitch did have an affinity for animals; could communicate with them on a empathetic level, as she sometimes described that aspect of her abilities, and indeed, should she be sufficiently persuasive, even get them to do what she wanted them to do.

Consequently, she already knew what was in the box: "My hair look that bad?"

"What's your hair got to do with anything?"

"When I forget to comb it out people call it a rat's nest. And you've brought me a rat to nest in it."

The Witch was right about that. Her dark hair was so thick and long a lot more than a rat could hang out in it. She'd gone to a sweat house this morning, though, and, in addition to having herself scrubbed nearly raw, made sure it was washed and brushed down as straight as it ever got. As a result she was confident nothing besides her and her unborn baby were living in or about her body beautiful.

"It isn't a rat," Tina protested, opening the shoebox. Inside it was a rat-like creature but Tina was correct; strictly speaking it wasn't a rat. "It's a tee-tee."

Wilderwitch deigned to peer into the box. The rodent was no more native to the former Outer Earth than mermen and mermaids, Simian Sapiens, sentient Saurs, Lemurian frogwomen or anthropomorphic ant-men, though Myrmidons did figure in ancient mythologies, as of course did mermen and mermaids. Like all of the above it could talk, if you pulled its tail, and what it talked about was usually some story or another it traded for its life; hence the term tee-tee tales.

"So it is. Did you pull its tail?"

"Sure we did and it told us some stupid story about you getting almost killed by one of the Mother Murder Medusa's Quadrang Nucleoids in Subcranial Temporis. Flying Doltaur, it called her. But that isn't what happened at all. Daddy killed Mother Murder on the Moon, right?"

"Sometimes tee-tees just make things up, Tina. But every tee-tee's got two tales to tell, so maybe its other one's better."

"Read it for me then."

Virtually every creature on both sides of the Cathonic Zone – when there was a Cathonic Zone, or Dome, separating the Inner from the Outer Earth – had individual markings. Tee-tees were no different in that regard, but their differences were more easily discernible than most animals.

Besides the fact they could talk, and that each had a unique tale it could recount vocally, their most notable distinctions were their tails. Not only were they colourful, as if made up of dozens of multicoloured beads or nodes, they could be read as if Celtic knot-writing.

"I'm not very good at that, Tina. You know Jordan Tethys, the Legendarian, the fellow who almost got boiled alive while your masterly Mama Mel was giving you birth on Shenon? He's over there, at the beer pavilion, and he's really good at reading tee-tee tails."

"He's creepy. He bites off their tails and sticks them onto his head. Besides, he always stinks of beer."

"That he does. But tee-tee tails grow back, with a different tale to tell, and who knows, maybe he'll let you keep it."

"And maybe he'll teach me how to read its new tail. Good idea, fat Auntie Wildie. Let's go get gay, Paree."

"I wish you'd stop saying that, Tinny," said Helen, whose nickname was indeed Paree (after Paris, among other things the lover of Helen of Troy in Homer's Iliad). "That was daddy's joke."

"So? Someone around here has to keep having fun. Come on."

As Tina ran off toward the beer pavilion, yelling for her little friends in their pretty party dresses to join her, Helen, who had opted, instead of a dress, for a traditional, Utopian-style neckerchief, cream-coloured jacket, crewneck and pantsuit, the same as the young Illuminaries, paused before following her. She felt the need, which she never would have done prior to the start of Panharmonium and the end of almost everything else, to apologize for her baby sister's behaviour.

"I'm sorry, Witch. You know how silly Tinny gets when she's excited."

"Better silly than severe, Paree. You're overdue-stopping being such a miserable little Helen-Hellion. You should feel proud wearing one of your daddy's rings."

"They're Percy's now."

"Not all of them, I see."

"It's for protection. Anyone comes at me, up they go. Or out they go. Or down they go. Way up, way out, way down. Too bad they don't work for you, eh?"

"Oh, I don't know. I've lots of other things that do."

=========

And so she did: rings and bangles and glowing things off of which she could materialize whatever she kept in her between-space bottomless bag; among them her metallic marigold, as she called the stunted eye-stave Mel gave her months ago when she was only the High Illuminary.

What she should have said, she reconsidered as Helen went to catch up to Tina, was 'too bad they worked so well for your father'. She could also have said something like 'at least we're both still here'. But today was no more a day for showing off than it was for nastiness. Today was a day for celebrating survival.

And celebrating those like Mel's much younger husband, Harry Zeross, her predecessor as Master of Weir, Saladin Devason, her twin brother, Demios Sarpedon, his wife, Saladin's year younger sister, Morgianna, the White Witch or Morrigan. For celebrating Morg's dead daughters, both of them, Tsishah Twilight and the Zerbranid, Andy, Andrea, Andaemyn. For celebrating those whose actions allowed there to be such a celebration in the first place.

As for those whose actions caused the near Armageddon everyone left had survived, their day was coming. She just hoped she'd be there to contribute to the devils' absolute extermination.

Those she hadn't already, that is.

=========

On Christmas Day 1955, twelve year old Harry Zeross – codenamed Kid Ringo, later to become Ringleader – used his teleportive Gypsium Rings to take himself and ten other supranormals to a tiny atoll in the Aleutian chain of islands in the North Pacific known as Damnation Isle.

Those he took with him were the six still-active members of KOC, the King's Own Crimefighters: Cerebrus David Ryne, Wildman Dervish Furie, Old Man Power, Radiant Rider and her adopted siblings, the Elemental Twins, Airealist and Sea Goddess; they along with their oft-times comrades in supra-doings: the Untouchable Diver, Blind Sundown, Raven's Head and Wilderwitch herself.

He left them there, in the Aleutians, to do what they had to in order to deal, finally, with Saul Ryne, Cerebrus's twin brother, the dangerously erratic supra best known as the Magnificent Psycho. They went at each other so comprehensively their bodies were never found.

For those who knew about the 17-year Secret War of Supranormals, who knew about supranormals or supras period, the prevailing theory at the time was their remains had been washed away when a tsunami rolled over the islet. Kid Ringo returned to the Alliance of Man's get-together then going on in Old Vancouver. He was administered amnaesthetics – memory-redacting drugs long used by the Antediluvian Sisterhood of Flowery Anthea, to which the Witch also belonged – and promptly forgot he was the last of the supranormals.

On New Years Day 1956, Loxus Abraham Ryne, the born-with-the-century father of David-Cerebrus and Saul-Psycho, among others, resigned as chairman of New Century Enterprises. Already far richer than Croesus ever was, he intended to devote more time to the philanthropic Alliance of Man, as the Human League was known in those days, its burgeoning Academies of Man, and the panhumanist cause of Xuthrodism.

Alfredo Sentalli, then not quite thirty, took Ryne's place at NCE and turned it into the most profitable multinational corporation in the world. In late April 1960, Harry Zeross and Belificent D'Angelo, Radiant Rider's decade younger sister, married in Toronto Ontario. Bel was promptly kidnapped and executed by a group calling itself the Worldwide Order with the Right to Life and Death.

In response to WORLD's threat, the Great Man, Loxus Ryne, immediately formed the Alliance of Man for the Extermination of Resisting International Criminal Associations. AMERICA became the vanguard of the anti-terrorist movement of the Sixties and early Seventies. It turned out to be extremely successful. Terrorism was reduced or, in some places, eliminated entirely, at least for the time being.

WORLD lasted until 1970. Before it went down, its leadership, a largely artificial man called Steltsar and a mysteriously faceless woman, a rogue witch known only as Strife, learned the real reason behind AMERICA's success. The Alliance of Man employed supranormals, specifically the King Crimefighters, their four friends, and Magnifico, as Saul-Psycho had begun calling himself.

Their deaths had been a ruse. Instead, with the energetic elder Ryne's full knowledge, they had gone into deep cover. Bel's murder and Harry's subsequent disappearance in 1960 brought them out of retirement. After the destruction of WORLD they resurfaced, though still not as declared supras. Even in 1970 that wouldn't have been acceptable.

Obadiah Melvin Power, then as now a giant of a man with a great grey beard, replaced Ryne Senior as the patriarch of the Illuminated Faith of Xuthros Hor. David Ryne took over from his father as chairman of the Alliance, which he renamed the Human League after the onset of Panharmonium. Saul Ryne assumed his father's role as president of the worldwide Academies of Man.

Thus freed from all other duties, the Great Man redirected his formidable energies toward attaining his lifelong goal, namely to set up a meaningful United Nations in order to oversee the transition to a new, enlightened, war-free New World — the precursor to today's Panharmonium.

Yehudi Cohen, aka the Untouchable Diver, became the Israeli Ambassador to the UN in New York. John Sundown, a blind Cheyenne elder, became the inspirational and very influential spokesperson for the betterment of aboriginal societies throughout the globe. He travelled with his sable-black mare, Raven, and was a frequent guest at universities and on television talk shows. Gloriella D'Angelo Dark, as radiant as ever, resuscitated her career, fifteen years in hiatus, as an occasional actress, model and titular chair of Radiant Rainbows Fashion Emporium.

Despite the thus publicity gained, she maintained her role as the devoted wife of the brilliant, but crippled, British-born astrophysicist, Dr Immanuel Dark, and mother to their famous, often infamous daughter, Estrella, who eventually married Magnifico.

Now well into her late forties Gloriel remained one of the most beautiful women in the world. Often cited as the ideal woman, most folks considered her living proof a devout Roman Catholic could be all things to all people. Except, admittedly, one or two fanatical feminists.

Four of the eleven continued to shun the spotlight. Two, Wilderwitch and Dervish Furie, stayed entirely out of sight; the other two, Aires, Airealist, and Thalassa, Sea Goddess, D'Angelo, went to work for Alfredo Sentalli on Centauri Island, off the coast of Maui, Hawaii. The twins didn't age. Despite being born in late 1920, without witch-glamours they continued to look like they were in their early twenties. That was hardly all of it, though.

It wasn't until the events of late November 1980 that the reasons they were so seldom seen became evident. They, like Furie and the Witch, spent next to none of their time on the Outer Earth. In fact, until they were finally reconciled prior to going to the Moon aboard the Liberty, the twins spent most of their lives on the Inner Earth, the domain of all devils, and a lot of other things, trying to track down and dispose of Furie and the Witch.

In 1977 something was detected on the Moon. Aliens? A revitalized WORLD? Witches gone technologically savvy? Utopians rediscovering how everything kept on working in their Weirdom, then applying said rediscoveries in a renewed effort to destroy the Moloch Sedon and his hundreds of possessive devils? No one knew for sure but one thing was certain. Whatever was up there was bombarding the planet with thought-altering mind-beams.

The effects were quickly apparent. Governments began to topple, at first by revolutions, remarkably none of which were overly long, nor particularly bloody, since police the world over kept embracing revolutionaries, then by democratically being voted out of power. Whole armies started laying down arms, refusing to fight. In the void developed a new and never before seen spirit of global cooperation.

The Soviet Union was the first to voluntarily dismantle its biological, chemical and nuclear weapons development and deployment programs. Public outcry in the States forced the Democratic President to begin doing likewise. The birthrate, especially in the Third World, dropped precipitously in three years but, correspondingly, the standard of living rose dramatically. Fossil fuels were rejected as untenable, as were nuclear power plants.

Tremendous strides were made, some close to overnight, at replacing them with renewable, non-polluting energy sources such as the windmills and obelisks capped with firestones threatening to make the globe resemble a spiny sea urchin.

Lumber and mining companies started switching to agriculture in the theory that anything the planet needed could be grown in a sustainable fashion.

Unemployment skyrocketed initially. Inflation and interest rates plummeted. Banks and leading lending institutions were going out of business on a monthly then weekly basis. There should have been rioting everywhere, and there was, but the authorities did nothing.

Sooth said, many of them joined those already marching in the streets. Riots turned to peaceful protests to love-ins. The planet was in the grip of a collective form of mass hysteria. Or, as it turned out, mass sanity.

A year after detection, the United Nations formed the Space Council and chose Loxus Ryne, then 78 years old, to head it. With his propensity for anagrams the Great Man renamed it the Society for the Prevention of Alien Control of Earth. With the cooperation of all the surviving governments on the planet, SPACE funded, built, and sent into Moon-orbit the United Nations of Earth Spaceship Liberty.

About a week later, on November the Thirtieth 1980, New Century Enterprises launched a multiply manned spacecraft of its own from Centauri Island. The Cosmic Express, as it was known, made an unexpected detour somewhere. A few minutes later it reappeared, intact except for one cosmicar. Blasting through the atmosphere it ignited its Gypsium propellant and rocketed towards the stars.

Wilderwitch knew it was still out there, still on its way to wherever, but it was what it left behind in its wake, the greatest cataclysm Planet Earth had experienced in nearly six millennia, that mattered the most. And the last for all too extraordinarily many.

By the tenth of December, the Earth was whole again; had an eighth continent and a couple of billion less people. The Hidden Continent of Sedon's Head was no longer hidden. With the dissolution of the Cathonic Dome, dimensions were rent and the North Pacific returned to being largely a howsoever fractured landform. Put more colourfully, Thousand Isles was no longer just a salad dressing.

The ocean had to go somewhere and it did. Millenarian fatalists who had bought property in Nevada and Arizona in anticipation of just such an event come the Year 2000 had their waterfront vacation sites twenty years early.

========

The crowd announced the arrival of Blind Sundown and Raven's Head with the usual, all too obligatory nowadays, oohing and awing. Looking up the Witch was tempted to join them. One thing about the two creatures of the cosmos was they knew how to make an entrance.

========

For a change it was a clear day, still warm as well. Summer was hanging on, though here in what most folks still called British Columbia, even if there was no British Columbian government anymore, nor a Canadian one for that matter, it was more commonly referred to as Indian Summer. All too appropriately given who, and what, they were.

The solitary cloud more like racing in than wafting in from the southeast, too low to the trees to be an actual cloud, was a dead giveaway. Lest there be any doubt about it, it lit up and was almost as immediately vapourized, revealing a truly spectacular sight. High above them, seemingly suspended on nothing except his much more impressive, even miraculous, mount, a native North American raised his Solar Spear, its spearhead flaring like a miniature sun, in a salute for all to see. He was riding, well … Raven's Head was aptly named.

Mostly a horse with a raven-black coat that, upon closer inspection, was more feathers than fur, she had indeed a raven's bird-head. Had as well the very much telescoping horn of a unicorn, or monoceros, extending out of her forehead. As for how she flew, the talarial wings of Mercury fluttered furiously off both sides of her four fetlock ankles. As for how they kept something of her size aloft – Raven wasn't just a big bird, she was a big mare, a nightmare to more than a few very much deserving some – categorizing her as a creature of the cosmos covered that.

Raven's rider was not Radiant Rider. That was Gloriella D'Angelo Dark, who was around Hope Haven somewhere and to whom the Witch, even if she was gypsy rather than Italian, bore a vague familial resemblance. It was John Sundown.

His eyeholes were covered in a beadwork blindfold. His headdress, what he called his *'issiwan'*, was a de-skulled but still be-furred buffalo's head with its horns turned upwards. His *'star-cloak'* was also made of buffalo, its hide rather than its head. It being not quite Mid-Harvest Day, the illogically official start of autumn, he had it turned fur-side outwards, the better to reflect heat instead of retain it.

Over his otherwise bare chest he wore a washboard vest. Although made primarily of beads, like his blindfold, it featured dozens of animal teeth and claws strung together. His pants and moccasins were as leathern as the Witch's only Radiant Rainbows' designed robe and shawl. (She'd had to hire someone to stitch her clothes together since Gloriel's Fashion Emporium refused to work with animal skins or by-products.) No war paint though, she was happy to report.

"Come along, my fine foetal friend. Time for me to get off our shared butt-end and start with the matters not a whit shit. But, hey, maybe we still have enough time to get lucky. Even with you belly-baking in the baby-burden-oven, it's best never to miss an opportunity to go for a Raven-ride."

=========

For Wilderwitch, riding Raven's Head was not the biggest highlight of that day, that dream, that nightmare, the end of the Panharmonium. Neither was the lowlight what Johnny did to the Male Entity not so long after she and Raven came back to Earth. Although it was one explanation for the explosion that got her giving birth again, for the second time in her life.

By the time Hellion Helen brought her fellow prisoners, the Zerosses' Utopian mother, Mel-Illuminatus, and Tina's accurately identified slimy Aunt Fish, via her father's rings through between-space to her side, the Witch was screaming bloody murder.

"Where's my baby?" she kept repeating, screeching all the louder every time.

"She's still scum-coming, Witch," kept responding Fisherwoman, Scylla Nereid, Lady Achigan, Wilderwitch's nine years' older sister in more than just Flowery Anthea.

"Not her, Fucking Fish-face," the Witch spat anew, giving birth yet again. "Fucking him!"

"Fucking Hell," muttered Mel-Illuminatus, realizing what had happened. There'd been two after all. And the firstborn, a boy and already missing, was Satan Incarnate.

****

Back from the Dead
- Only to Die Anew -
PHANTACEA Revisted
The Damnation Brigade
Jim McPherson
and various artists
The latest graphic novel from
Phantacea Publications
Internet: www.phantacea.com pHantaBlog: www.phantacea.com/blog

Phantacea Revisited
Cataclysm Catalyst
Phantacea Publications
- Anheroic Fantasy since 1977 -
www.phantacea.com

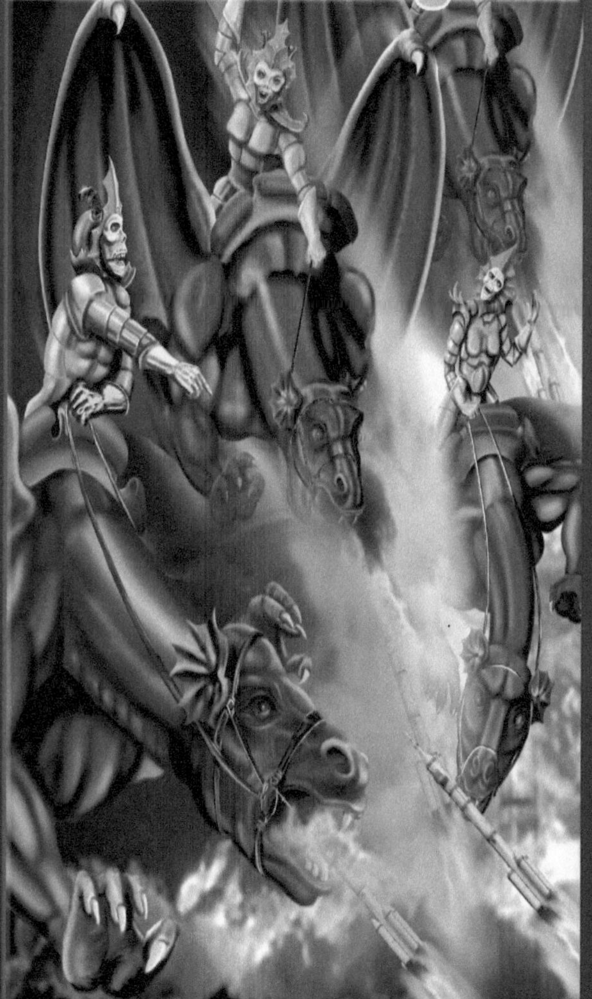

Can anything, let alone anyone, stop ...
- Nuclear Dragons -
The second entry in the 'Launch 1980' epic fantasy
Phantacea Publications
Internet: www.phantacea.com   pHantaBlog: www.phantacea.com/blog

9 781927 844014

Whomsoever touches Gypsium touches both the unknown and the unknowable

The American leader of LAC Squad 1 reckoned it a *'big ole hole full of moondust'*. The Soviet leader of LAC 2 didn't disagree. They were wrong.

=========

"Lunar Assault Crew," Aremar's voice crackled over the radio. "Advance into the crater. At the slightest show of resistance, retreat. We shall concentrate fire from the Liberty. If you locate the transmitter, locate anything of interest, dismantle and preserve it. We shall wish to examine everything you bring back. Good luck, Ned."

"Luck has nothing to do with anything, Jim. Let's go."

Ned Johnson waved his squad into the lunar crater.

A few minutes later, Leonid Kulagin radioed the UNES Liberty. He sounded spooked, if not out and out terrified.

"They just disintegrated."

=========

"Battle Stations! Battle Stations!"

Alarms blared throughout the Liberty. Red lights flashed. James Aremar stood stark still. Projected on the big screen was an amazing sight.

There appeared to be a grey hole in the blackness of space. A huge shape was straining against what might have passed for a membranous seal from the other side of it. Were it not for its proportionate immensity, it looked like a young, humanoid boy.

Two pudgy hands seemed to be struggling to break through the membrane that was holding it back. The cosmicar was comparatively a child's toy between the enormous hands.

On a secondary screen, the stunned deck crew saw a beam of light come out of the cosmicar. It sliced through space, straight into the hole and the godchild. Light, boy, and hole siphoned in on themselves and, like water going down a drain, soon vanished.

Minutes passed then the cosmicar too was gone.

=========

"Hear me, rulers. My all-pervasive thought beams are permeating the Whole Earth. Changing the coherence of sentient beings everywhere. Converting your serfs to my way — the way! The way of totally self-determined freedom.

"Hear me, fascists. Helios is on the Moon. Destroying you!"

HELIOS ON THE MOON

THE *LAUNCH 1980* STORY CYCLE CONCLUDES

Copyright © James H McPherson

A *PHANTACEA* MYTHOS MOSAIC NOVEL

Conceived, written and produced by Jim McPherson
Front and Back Cover artwork by Ricardo Sandoval

Phantacea Publications

(James H McPherson, Publisher)
74689 Kitsilano RPO
2768 West Broadway
Vancouver BC
V6K 4P4 Canada

Library and Archives Canada Cataloguing in Publication

McPherson, Jim, 1951-, author
        Helios on the moon / Jim McPherson.

(Launch 1980 ; bk. 3)
Issued in print and electronic formats.
ISBN 978-1-927844-01-4 (pbk.).--ISBN 978-1-927844-02-1 (html).--
ISBN 978-1-927844-12-0 (pdf)

        I. Title.

PS8625.P535H44 2014   C813'.6   C2014-906569-8
                                          C2014-906570-1